# TIMEDIVER'S DAWN

### From the author of
### *The Magic of Recluce:*

"A splendid fantasy that grips from the first sentence."

—*Interzone*

"Fascinating! A big, exciting novel of the battle between good and evil, and the path between."

—Gordon R. Dickson

### The Forever Hero Trilogy:

"Distinctive andintriguing"

—*Amarillo* (Tex.) *News*

### *The Fires of Paratime:*

"The cosmic concepts are often fascinating, the action fast, and the prose sometimes chilling. . . ."

—*Science Fiction Review*

# *Timediver's Dawn*
## *Heroic science fiction adventure in the classic mold.*

# L.E. MODESITT, JR.

# TIMEDIVER'S DAWN

A TOM DOHERTY ASSOCIATES BOOK
NEW YORK

*For Wendy, Margot, and Mimi:*
*Just because, although*
*each of you knows why.*

TIMEDIVER'S DAWN

Copyright © 1992 by L. E. Modesitt, Jr.

Cover art by Nick Jainschigg

A Tor Book
Published by Tom Doherty Associates, Inc.
175 Fifth Avenue
New York, N. Y. 10010

Tor® is a registered trademark of Tom Doherty Associates, Inc.

ISBN: 0-812-51447-5

First edition: July 1992

Printed in the United States of America

0  9  8  7  6  5  4  3  2  1

# I.

THINK OF A world of witches, of high technology and space travel, of science and superstition. A world on the verge of changing inhabitable planets into green pastures and endless forests, a world so short of energy resources that all fuels are grown or captured from the sun.

You say there is no such world? Or that it is only our world, dressed up for a storyteller's pleasure?

Set aside your doubts . . . this world was as real as any you will know . . . and learn about the timedivers' dawn. Perhaps it began here:

"Meryn." The slight, sandy-haired woman looked as though she carried perhaps a score of years, until she gazed upon one, and the darkness behind her eyes delivered the weight of centuries.

"Yes, Mother." The second woman, also slender and sandy-haired, could have been a twin to the first, except for the lesser depth of her eyes.

"It's time."

"I know."

"There can be no more witches in Eastron. Not now. Not with the Empress of Westron's demands, and the weaknesses in the Duchy."

"But the Bardwalls still stand. . . ."

"And they will, and you may always return to look upon them. You must make a place among the people of

Westron and learn their technologies. Our time has gone and will not come again for centuries. Not until they have stripped the last metals from the ground. Not until they have been hurled from the skies.''

''Mother?''

''Yes.''

''Do you really believe that?''

''Daughter, I know that Eastron is dying, and all the villagers and all the gentry will blame it on the witches. Because of the Duke our faces are too well known. So I will face the Empress with him, come what may, and you will survive.''

''Mother!''

There is no answer, for the older witch has vanished.

The younger woman looked around the retreat, then continued placing her few things in the pack, which will be all that she can carry on her instant yet long journey.

It seems so simple. It is not. It could have begun here as well:

''Witch! Witch!''

*Thud! Crack!*

One rock, then another, struck the whitewashed wall.

Their target, a stocky boy-child with strawberry blond hair, a dazed expression, and shoulders already overbroad, looked down from the low wall where he balanced. Looked down at the whitewashed surface where the rocks had struck near his feet, then back at the gathered handful of women, crippled veterans, and the priest.

''. . . like his mother . . . ''

''. . . dead . . . thank Verlyt . . . !''

*Crack! Whmmmpt!*

''Suffer not a witch, nor a witch's child . . . ''

The boy looked from one face to another, back and forth, as if seeking reassurance.

*Crack!*

One of the rocks struck his shoulder, hard enough to stagger him.

"Witch! Witch! Witch!" The chant began in earnest, echoing between the walls, drowning out the occasional low rumble of dry cloud thunder. Thunder that promised nothing but clouds that delivered no rain, no respite.

"Witch! Witch! Witch . . . !"

*Crack!*

Suddenly, the boy's dazed expression vanished and his face screwed up, as if he were about to cry. In a single motion, he tightened his lips and jumped down on the far side of the wall, away from the crowd, and began to run.

*Pad, pad, pad, pad . . . !* The alleyway remained silent for an instant, the villagers momentarily silenced.

"Witch! Witch! Witch . . . !" The chant took on an even more frantic note.

Some of the veterans dragged themselves over the wall and hobbled or ran, knives in the hands of those who still had hands, after the fleeing child. Others turned back into the main street and dashed around toward the other end of the alley into which the child had fled.

"Witch! Witch! Witch . . . !"

*Thud! Thud, thuuddd, thhuuuddd . . .* The heavy roll of the priests' drums supplemented the chant.

From huts and houses, from the vintners and the villas, the pursuers gathered, pounding down street and alley, tearing through house and hovel.

"There he is!"

". . . witch-child . . . !"

"SUFFER NOT A WITCH TO LIVE, NOR A WITCH'S CHILD!" boomed the amplified voice of the priest.

The boy, backed into a narrow niche between two walls behind the produce market, held a rock in each hand, waiting.

*Crack!* The first rock from a villager slapped against the wall.

*Crack! Thud! Crack! Thud!* The past experience of the rock throwers showed as stone after stone bounced against and around the boy.

He threw one stone back. It missed. He threw the other.

"Devil! Witch-child!"

Overhead, the dry thunder rumbled, and the dry clouds churned.

A rivulet of blood dribbled down the boy's face, no longer expressionless, but filled with rage, even as the tears diluted his blood into pinkish streaks.

*Crack! Thud! Thud!*

"Gone!"

". . . damned witches . . . ! reclaimed their own . . ."

The small niche in the walls was empty, vacant but for rocks and streaks of blood upon the walls.

". . . YOU HAVE RECLAIMED YOUR BIRTH-RIGHT FROM THE WITCHES THIS DAY . . ." bellowed the amplifier.

A third of a world away, two soldiers paused by the roadside to investigate a heap of clothing.

"Kid . . . been beaten . . . "

"Forcer!"

"Frillen, now what? Another discarded sack that has to be an aggrebel?" The heavy-set and silver-haired forcer glared at the two as he spoke.

The trooper points. "Kid. Beaten. He's still breathing."

"He'll live. Put him in the rear freighter with Garchuk. He looks strong. The ConFed home will take him. Now, let's get moving."

The two troopers shrugged. One lifted the boy and marched toward the military freight steamer. The other followed the ConFed forcer.

# II.

". . . AND NOW, IN the presence of the unknowable and the almighty, we wish you the greatest success in your striving to bring us all another world for all people, in peace, for our successors and their successors . . ."

The face of the gray-haired and young-faced Emperor of Westron faded from the solideo link, to be replaced by the coat of arms of the Hrtallen.

"Rather impressive," observed the stocky man, his red hair somehow bushy in spite of its close-cropped nature.

"Isn't that the nature of royalty? To be impressive, I mean?" Her voice held an edge.

"That doesn't make young Hrtallen any less impressive. Besides, getting his formal support for the Mithrada planet-forming can't hurt once the initial enthusiasm dies down."

"Assuming he isn't the politician his mother was."

"Lorinda."

"I know. It had to be done. The Eastron anarchy was a danger to everyone, but did they have to be so damned thorough? All the time that white-haired and sweet-faced old harpy was displaying motherly concern, her peace-makers were rooting out anyone who could pronounce the word anarchy."

The Imperial coat of arms faded from the screen, to be replaced in turn by an official Imperial newscaster in the traditional blue and gold. "That was the sendoff speech of the Emperor, dedicating the unified Queryan mission designed to turn Mithrada into the second habitable planet within our solar system."

The view switched to an ancient circular brownstone tower, flying two banners, one the Westron flag, and the second bearing a sheaf of grain crossed with a single red flower—a ryall.

"But there are those who doubt the practicality and wisdom of tampering with the Mithradan ecosphere, such as it is. One of the doubters, here at the University of Vrecallitt, is Academician Terril Josset . . ."

"Turn it off, Harlon," snapped Lorinda. "One thing worse than a sincere Emperor is an insincere and misguided academic."

The screen returned to a view of the stars before the *Hope*, as it edged inward toward the orbit of the sun's second planet, toward its mission to reform and cool the blistering wastes of Mithrada. To strip the heavy atmosphere and rebuild the planet in the image desired by men and women. To mine the only concentrations of metals within even impractical possibility, now that the thin outer asteroid belts had been stripped of what could be found.

# III.

I was born in Bremarlyn, which no longer exists, like most of the cities and towns of Westron, the great western continent. Then it stood about one hundred kays east of Inequital.

Bremarlyn had little to distinguish it except that it contained the regional revenue office of the Imperial Government. My father was a solicitor in the service of the crown, and he served as the local tax prosecutor of a government and a world that has passed into history.

My thoughts, scattered as they are, will be included in the sealed section of the Archives, while I still retain the power to ensure both their inclusion and the sealing of the records. Some things are best lost, but vanity being what it is, I have settled for censorship over oblivion. Anyone who does unlock the seals will, I trust, also read the factual supplements and data before coming to a final judgment on my follies.

Consecrated to the Temple as Sammis Arloff Olon, I still go by Sammis, although some persist in trying to distinguish me by using my original surname. That too shall pass, at least in another dozen millennia. Time flows more slowly these days, now that Query has left the seasons of the single-night moth and entered the long afternoon of the Immortals.

Why did it happen? How?

No one can answer the first question. As for the second, for me, it began with a dream.

In the dream I stood above four roads. There were no vehicles, no power wagons, no silent steamers, no gliding electrovans, just four roads.

One was gold, cold as the dark between stars.

One was black, and the heat rose from it as from the Grand Highway in summer.

One was red and smelled like memories.

And the last was blue, bright blue like tomorrow's dawn.

Despite the dream of these roads, then I had no special love of travel, nor do I yet. Everything I needed was in Bremarlyn—from the creek where I built dams to see how high I could raise the water behind my assembly of stones and sand to the fields where we played centreslot. No, I cannot say I had close friends, but we all played together most of the time, and, when we did not play, we fought.

In my first dream of the crossroads, I merely stood there paralyzed and unable to set foot on any road. Fear did not prevent me from taking that step. I could not move. Nor could I speak nor sigh. So I watched the four roads, somehow suspended above them, as each disappeared into its colored distance.

The four were not a crossroads exactly, and in the distance that was not distance, each split and splintered into hundreds of different directions, until each created its own horizon—blue, red, black, and gold. Yet all directions were the same, and every road went in all directions.

Wherever I was, watching the roads, it was cold, bone-chilling cold.

Then, abruptly, as I wished to return to my bed and its comfort, I was there, sprawled on cold quilts. Cold quilts, as if I had not been sleeping there during my dream.

Feeling exhausted, though I had done nothing in my dream but watch, I slept . . . deeply. And I did not dream. Not then.

While I seldom remembered most of my dreams, the four roads remained with me, with their promise of anticipation and memory, heat and chill, long after I had roused myself from my quilts, long after I pulled on my Academy uniform and trudged off to classes.

# IV.

"MALFUNCTION ON SENSOR, alpha three, quad four, red." The metallic tone of the speaker reverberated through the module.

The monitoring officer's fingers seemed to meld with the keyboard while she accessed the network controlling the defective sensor. Her eyes widened as the data scripted out on the bluish screen before her. The sensor showed a temperature of $3°$ absolute positive, barely above absolute zero. On Mithrada, less than 120 million kays from the sun, that was patently impossible, not on a planetary surface so hot that water had never occurred in liquid form.

Shaking her head as if to clear her thoughts, she keyed the reset function.

*Bleep.*

The remote readings from the sensor on the planet below remained the same, long after the fractional units it took for the reset command to travel to the remote command network on the high plateau of Mithrada's northern hemisphere.

She took one deep breath, then another, before glancing at the sealed portal that separated the monitoring module from the rest of the planetary reformation station.

"Malfunction on sensor, beta six, quad three, orange. . . .

"Malfunction on sensor, gamma three . . ."

"Malfunction on sensor, omicron eight . . ."

The console before her blazed with maroon malfunction lights, bright points of brilliance that seared at her senses.

"Malfunction on sensor, delta four . . ."

With a sigh, she returned her attention to the original malfunctioning sensor and keyed the reset function again. And waited, ignoring the rising maroon tide that turned the module twilight-colored. And waited.

*Bleep.*

The sensor now registered a reading of 60° AP with a trend rate indicating a return to normal, for Mithrada, of close to 800° AP within one standard unit.

"Malfunction on sensor . . ."

The number of maroon lights continued to increase, even as the temperature on the first sensor continued to rise.

The monitoring officer ignored the more recent failures, finally blanking the row of screens above her on which the lights had flared. Then she returned her attention to the first failure, shaking her head slowly.

"Lorinda? What in Hell is going on planetside?" The intercom speaker carried a male voice.

"Tell you in a demistan. It looks like an impossible planetary cold wave." Her voice was hard, clipped, her eyes still on the sensor data.

"A cold wave? Are you all right?"

"Stop patronizing me, Harlon. This many data points don't lie. We've lost all temperature-sensitive remotes in four dozen subsectors. They all showed near-instantaneous temperature drops of 800 degrees."

"That's impossible."

"Malfunction in sensor, epsilon five . . ."

"Malfunction in sensor . . ."

Lorinda cut off the audio warning system.

"Did you hear those, Harlon? Tell me which is less impossible—identical malfunctions of nearly a hundred randomly located sensors on eight different remote nets . . . simultaneously? Or one hundred severe temperature anomalies?"

"The whole system must be shot to hell . . ." came his reply.

"That could be, but there's an easy enough way to check. Have meteorology check the changes in surface winds. If it's not the sensors, there will be severe local changes."

"You think so?"

"I know so . . . if it's climate-caused. Check it out."

She shifted her monitoring to another early malfunction, which showed the same pattern of abrupt heat loss, followed by a gradual return toward normal Mithradan levels.

Her fingers began a series of calculations, based on the proximity of the apparent temperature drops to each other. With each input, and the resultant analysis, the frown on her face became more severe.

She removed the damper from the bank of display screens, and the module turned twilight-purple again. The light was so depressing that she immediately reblanked the screens. Lorinda hesitated a moment when the last screen analysis scripted out in front of her. Then she touched the intercom.

"Control central, this is monitoring. Analysis of sensor

malfunction patterns indicates event is planet-based and not created from system failure.''

''How do you know, monitoring?''

''Analysis of temperature gradients between malfunctions. Something . . . somethings . . . are acting like an absolute heat sink.''

''Infraheat scan supports that, control central. So does preliminary met data . . .''

''Great . . . so rather than an understandable catastrophic equipment malfunction, we now have an impossible natural occurrence.''

Lorinda shook her head in the privacy of the monitoring module. Not impossible—it had happened. And certainly not natural. Of that, she was all too sure.

# V.

THE SCIENTIST IN the pale blue tunic ran her left hand through her short-cut sandy hair, then tapped the light stylus on the console.

Looking up for a moment around the small windowless room, she pursed her lips. The gesture gave her face an elfin cast, which vanished as she concentrated and touched the keyboard.

On the screen before her, a title appeared in the formal script of Westra: ''Project Vanish—Case III.''

Her fingers played the keyboard again, and the angled script disappeared, replaced by a full-length view of a tall woman standing on a raised platform, surrounded by monitoring equipment. The subject wore a wide belt clustered with sensors over a plain singlesuit.

Abruptly, the woman on the screen vanished, leaving the platform empty.

The sandy-haired woman viewing the screen froze the

image and studied it. Then she backtracked the visual, instant by instant. In one scan, the subject was present. In the next she was not.

Finally, the scientist touched the keyboard to remove the visual and replace it with the data from the monitoring equipment. The data readouts showed the same pattern. The subject's disappearance was instantaneous. No faded signals, no attenuation, only an absolute cut-off simultaneous on all equipment through the entire monitoring range.

The woman in blue pursed her lips again, ignoring the notation at the bottom of the arrayed data.

"Subject A-102-Green failed to return. No body found. No explosions noted simultaneously with disappearance. No other coordinated energy phenomena. Chronological analysis inconclusive."

Her fingers touched the console, almost as if independently of her thoughts, and the index returned to the screen. For a time, she regarded the first page of the lengthy index.

Evidence—that there was plenty of—but verifiable, measurable results indicating success? None to date—except her own personal observations, and they would not be considered objective, not to mention the questions they would raise.

At last, she blanked the index and stood, a woman with an almost elfin face, wearing the pale blue of a scientist. The severity of her hair and clothing hinted at the age she might have been. The smoothness of her complexion and the pale fairness of her skin indicated an age far younger than the expression in her eyes or the position which she held in the scientific hierarchy.

She sighed so softly that the expression was nearly soundless as she pressed the stud which put the computer system on standby. Just as soundlessly, she rose and stood before the darkened console, her eyes sweeping over the equipment for a last time, as if such a search could uncover the key she continued to seek.

Her steps were light, but slow, as they whispered her departure from the small modest office on an afternoon when most others had celebrated the holiday proclaimed by the Emperor.

# VI.

"ALL THE ANOMALIES center here." The technician pointed to a circled area on the screen. "The general direction of movement is toward the planetary southwest— right along that line."

The officer frowned and gestured toward a series of triangles farther along in the direction outlined by the technician. "I assume those represent our planetary stocks."

"Just what we have there, sir."

"How much metal and support gear there?"

"About six months' worth. That's an estimate."

"And if whatever these things are freeze that, we lose six months of production equipment?"

"More than that. Don't forget we had to soft-land all of that, and we lost two of the landers doing it."

"Verlyt!" For a time, the slender man studied the screen and the gradual motions, and the abrupt temperature drops. Then he pointed again. "What's here, if anything?"

"That's the break between the two networks."

"Could we direct the equatorial laser and the microwave collector to focus on that point when the sensors indicate that's where these . . . these . . ."

"Frost Giants is what the recon types call them."

". . . things . . . these things are centered?"

"You want to fry them when they hit that point?"

"That's the idea. We can get plenty of energy from the orbital stations. What we don't have is more equipment, and for some reason that's exactly what your Frost Giants are interested in freezing."

"Do we know what will happen, sir?"

"No. But it can't be much worse than losing the entire planet-forming project, can it?"

The technician frowned. "I guess not, sir. I guess not. But what if the Frost Giants object?"

"It's their planet. If they kick us off, they kick us off, but there can't be more than a few. We may have to re-think, and maybe we can't complete the project, but we need to keep them away from the soft-landed equipment.

"That's my first objective. Then we'll see what happens."

# VII.

FIRST, THERE WERE the rumors. The Academy was always a place for rumors.

"Sammis, did you hear about the problems on Mithrada? Parts of the planet are freezing . . ."

I didn't even bother to answer. Astronomy had taught me enough about Mithrada to show how ridiculous that was. Hot enough to boil water, not to mention the higher atmospheric pressure there.

". . . serious . . . they called my brother off leave . . ."

". . . they're lifting the banned weapons, the big nuclear ones . . ."

At that point, Old Windlass walked in. We didn't have to stand, but were supposed to become silent, immediately.

". . . rebels from Eastron . . . do you think?"

". . . none of them left . . ."

"Master Olon, our lesson is *Carnelia*. I would appreciate it if you would turn your attention to whether *Carnelia* is a tragedy in the true sense of the word. You, too, Master Kryrel." Old Windlass—that was what we all called him, although his real name was Dr. Wendengless—would have discussed literature if the world had been crumbling and the schedule said it was time for literature.

"uhhh . . ."

"Come now. Is *Carnelia* a tragedy? Yes or no? Surely, you must have *some* opinion."

"No, sir. *Carnelia* is a comedy disguised as a tragedy." My idea was not setting well, and all my plans for stringing along with Windlass's fondness for classifying everything as a tragedy had vanished because I had been listening to Jeen Kryrel and thinking why the rumors about Mithrada couldn't be correct.

"A comedy? Pardon the pun, gentlemen, but surely you jest? A comedy?"

"Yes, sir. I mean no, sir. If you take away the trappings of a court, and all the formalities, the situation is really a farce. Just because she had a single romp with the wrong nobleman, she's threatening to commit suicide? By throwing herself into a lily pond? And she drowns in waist-deep water? How can you take that seriously?"

"Master Sammis!" There was a pause. "How do you know the water is waist-deep in the Major Royal?"

"I checked in the Archives when I was in Inequital last week with my mother. The original plans say the pond was built to a quarter rod depth. It was later bricked up to a handspan, but at the time of *Carnelia*, I assume that it was the deeper level." Actually, I really hadn't done all that much research. I'd been discussing it with my mother, and she had mentioned the depths. But she was always right, and Old Windlass wouldn't know the difference.

"And where in the Archives did you find this wonderful information?"

"In the background information on the history of the Palace Major."

Windlass really looked confused, then. Started mumbling to himself, something about the material not being in the public domain. Finally, he looked up. "All right, Master Sammis . . . even if the Major Royal were only a quarter rod deep, you are missing the point through a technicality—"

Jeen was trying to keep from laughing, and Trien was grinning, and if Windlass saw them I was going to be in big trouble.

"—that Carnelia, indeed all the early Western royalty, placed an inordinate emphasis on sexual purity, perhaps because of the lower-class stigma attached to sexually transmitted diseases before the availability of modern medical techniques, and partly because of the need to ensure a clear line of royal descent in order to avoid a repetition of the chaos created by the Fylarian Fragmentation . . ."

I had to hand it to Windlass. He could talk his way out of anything.

". . . so you are correct in saying that in the modern context Carnelia's actions seem farcical. But that is not the question, Master Sammis. Are her actions farcical for the time and the society in which she existed? Are they? Come now?"

"It still seems like she overreacted, but it's hard to say, sir." I could have argued it either way.

"Master Sammis, last week you were disciplined for your reaction to criticism by a comrade of your performance during the centreslot title game. In fact, upon one occasion you failed to place an inflated rubber bladder inside a loose section of netting in the middle of a grassy field. This failure did not affect your survival, your future, or your status. It should not have affected your self-esteem, given your overall athletic reputation, despite your size.

Yet you were so threatened by a mere verbal criticism that you employed bodily violence.

"Carnelia's whole value system and life may be threatened by her thoughtless action. Yet you, who react violently to a meaningless criticism of a generally meaningless game, are going to tell me that context is not important?"

Jeen was still grinning, but now he was laughing *at* me.

"No, sir."

"So you might consider accepting that context is vital in evaluating value systems?"

"Yes, sir."

"Master Kryrel . . ."

For some reason, freezing on Mithrada didn't seem quite so impossible after Old Windlass finished with me.

# VIII.

SOME DREAMS NEVER quite go away. So it was with my dream of the crossroads with its blue and red and gold and black directions that were all the same and all different.

Some nights that dream would flash before me, and then I would dream no more. Other nights, I would find myself moved from the crossroads in one direction or another, buffeted on invisible currents that were no less strong for not being felt or seen, until I was carried almost through a black chill wall into some place or time. Almost, but not quite, carried through that barrier, as though I stood behind a curtain where I could see most of what went on.

One dream was especially vivid. Or perhaps I recalled it because it so closely paralleled what actually occurred.

I had been carried into those black chill curtains that looked into another world, or so it seemed, and stood within a tower that glittered, inside and out. The tower was suffused with an energy that made it a beacon of sorts on both sides of the black curtain. No matter how I tried to look at the walls, they refused to stay in focus, even less than the other objects and people I could see from my obscured perspective.

Yet one thing was clear. The tower did not exist. Yet it was concretely there in my night/dream vision. I could see people walking through that tower. Some few looked ordinary. Ordinary as they looked, they were suffused with the same sort of energy as the tower itself, on a lesser scale.

Far less frequently, I could see others, dressed in tight black uniforms, who radiated a far greater sense of energy. In the most vivid of these dreams, the one that stuck with me, I could see one of the men in black more clearly than the others. He was below average in height, and far smaller than the colorful and uniformed giant who stood beside him. Yet the power which suffused him left the taller figure a mere shadow beside him.

The smaller man seemed graceful, with a narrow face and sandy hair. The strange part was that he stopped talking to the giant and looked straight at me, though I was certain no one could see me, ghost shadow that I was behind the black curtains of time or space or whatever.

I could feel his green eyes burning as he fixed them on me. And then he nodded and made a sign in the air that seemed like a benediction. The giant swung his head toward the smaller man, who answered before turning away from me and leaving me in that no-time place where reality and dreams seemed to almost meet.

The man seemed familiar, too familiar. Why had I seen him? What did the energy levels mean?

Before I could ponder the question, I stumbled from the blackness.

And was in trouble—serious trouble.

I did not wake in merely cold covers, or standing by my bed, as had happened once or twice when I had dreamed about the crossroads. I found myself standing in a winter rain, still wearing but a long nightshirt, and barefoot, at the foot of the stone walkway leading to the front door.

*Whhhsssssttt . . . click, click, click, . . .*

The half-frozen rain pelted down in sheets, as it always did in the Ninis storms, each sheet sweeping across the road and down the valley, followed by a break in the wind, cold ice drizzle, and then another pounding sheet of ice droplets striking hard enough to raise tiny welts on unprotected skin.

Most of my skin was either barely protected or totally uncovered.

Part of my mind was protesting. It was too early in the year for such a violent and chill storm. The afternoon before I had been picking chysts from the trees along the stone fence that separated our grounds from the Davniads, and I had taken my tunic off. That's how warm it had been.

The changed weather wasn't paying any attention to my mental protests, but continued to raise welts on my skin and drench my nightshirt.

So I hurried gingerly toward the overhang of the front doorway, each bare foot planted as carefully as possible on the slick stones.

Not carefully enough, I discovered, as my bare feet slipped from beneath me and my posterior and flailing hands slapped down on the cold stones.

Scrabbling and edging along across stones that were slick as glass and cold as deep winter, I finally managed to reach the overhang and dry stones underfoot. From there getting inside was easy. I opened the heavy door and took three steps until I stood on the polished slate of the entry hall in an instant pool of water, with a few icicles hanging from the edge of my nightshirt.

Only after I was inside the house did I begin to shiver, either from relief or the accumulated impact of cold.

In those days no one in Bremarlyn locked or bolted doors. Why would we? Westron was prosperous; what little crime there might be was punished severely; and few of the lower classes traveled.

The hall was chill, chill enough that normally I would have worn a robe, but that cold was like a warm hearth compared to what I had left outside. What chilled me most was my soaking nightshirt. I wasted little time in stripping it off and carrying it to the kitchen where I wrung it out. Still naked, I took some rags and went back into the entry hall and wiped up the puddle I had left.

According to the big clock at the foot of the formal stairs, dawn was still some time away.

During the whole episode, I heard nothing from the maid down below, or from my parents above, but that may have been because any slight noise I made had been drowned out by the wind and the sound of the ice rain on windows and walls.

Then I put the rags in the empty wash bucket, hoping that Shaera would either think she had overlooked them or not want to mention the problem when she discovered them on the morrow.

Taking my damp nightshirt with me, I tiptoed up the back stairs to my room. I opened the window briefly, got pelted by the rain again, and closed it. After laying the wet nightshirt on the stone sill, I rummaged through my closet and found my other nightshirt, which, as a proper scholar in training, I was not to wear for another day. I yanked it on and climbed under the cold quilts, and began to shiver in earnest.

How had I gotten outside? Had I been sleepwalking? Did the dream have anything to do with it? What?

Surely I would have fallen on the ice going down the walk, and I swore that the chill of the ice underfoot and the rain had been too sudden for an awakening from a nightmare. Had I been sleepwalking, wouldn't I have wakened as soon as the cold and rain struck me, not all the way down the walk?

The questions seemed endless, but, surprisingly, shivers or not, I fell asleep before I could figure out answers that made sense.

When I woke the next morning, it was to a blaze of light. My first thought was that I had been transported to the tower of my night dream vision.

I heard nothing for a moment, but I could smell the odor of burnt sausage, which meant that Shaera was attempting breakfast. While she kept the large house spotless, she attacked cooking as if, like cleaning, it were to receive the full force of her ability and vigor. Full vigor meant high heat and overcooked meats and scorched breads.

The blaze of light came not from some dream tower, but from the sun flaring through and reflecting off the ice that coated the trees, the ground, and even the stones of the roadway.

I struggled from under my quilts, seeing that my breath did not quite turn to steam in the air of my bedroom, and went to the window. The nightshirt was semi-frozen, and I lifted my hands.

The hall light was on, and that told me that the solar power units on the roof had begun to operate. They had been expensive, my father said, but he had always worried about relying totally on the electric current delivered through the semi-ceramic cables from the Imperial power authority. The power authority, of course, received its electricity from the satellite links, which had been the primary reason for the Westron space effort.

By pressing my nose close against the glass, I could see most of the front walk from the window. I pressed and looked. The walk was coated in ice, although it was beginning to steam as the solar cells warmed the coils beneath. There were darker patches where the ice was thinner that could have been footprints. But there was really no way to tell.

I turned and leaned against the wall, wondering which uniform I should wear to school, and realized my posterior was sore, very sore. From what I could see, lifting the nightshirt and craning over my own shoulder at the reflection of my backside, I had the beginning of a nasty bruise.

So I had not been dreaming. Now I was going crazy. First, out-of-season freezing rain, and now dreams about strange towers that left me rods from where I went to sleep.

"Sammis!"

My father's call halted any further speculation, since I had only a few minutes before I would be expected at the table, and fewer minutes after that if I wanted a ride in the steamer that would halve the walk to the Academy. My father did not believe in making things easier, nor did he believe in making things artificially harder. If he were going my way on part of his drive to work at the Imperial offices in Bremarlyn, I could ride as far as our paths converged . . . if I were ready, and if he had no other plans.

I raced for the washroom, mine alone, and certainly one of the few advantages of being an only child.

As I completed washing my face, I looked into the mirror. The face of my dream, the face of the man who had looked at me through the curtains of blackness, had been my face—older, more experienced, and unlined, but my face.

That made the whole mystery less real. How could I ever see myself anywhere? It had to have been a dream.

Since the sun promised to warm the ice, I chose a mid-weight uniform, the same blue and silver tunic over dark blue trousers, with the black boots we all had to wear.

"Sammis!"

"Coming!" I grabbed my pack and cloak and tumbled down the front stairs, taking a quick look at the spot on the floor behind the front door. No sign of water or water damage.

Both of them were at the table. Mother was dressed to go to the city—Inequital, not Bremarlyn—with leather dress boots, wide trousers and matching jacket. Of course, she would be wearing the flynyx coat father had given her for their anniversary and driving the gold steamer. An independent woman, my mother, despite my father's importance as the preeminent regional solicitor of taxes and commerce. That he could also claim to be a descendent of the old Dukes of Ronwic did not disturb her either. Nor did it seem to impress her. Little of pomp seemed to faze her.

I could tell she had been up early and had completed her morning workout, although she had probably not taken a run, as she usually did. Once or twice I had tried to follow her regimen and decided against it. She was only a shade taller than I was; but underneath her careful tailoring were muscles it would take years before I could match. Yet she never made an issue about it. She just got up and did it, without fail, every morning.

She had taken a degree herself, in economic theory and practice, and had published one or two monographs, claiming that it had been "just to keep her hand in," whatever that meant. She also was far more physical than my father, both with her own exercise room in the cellars and her ongoing classes in Delkaiba—that was the old Westron martial art. All the same, I was never quite sure what she did while I was in school or on her infrequent but long and solitary "vacations." Neither she nor my father ever mentioned it. And, somehow, my innumerable questions never quite got answered.

"Have some sausage, Sammis. Need some protein, not just starch."

I reached for the least burned sausage on the platter.

"What do you think about this business on Mithrada?"

"What business?" I was looking for an unburned roll, preferably to avoid having to take another sausage.

"The strange reports about the project problems. You don't discuss it in school?"

My mouth was full. So I nodded. I hadn't paid that much attention. So the Emperor wanted another planet. There was still plenty of room in Westron, and more than that in Eastron.

"Waste of money. Terrible waste of tax revenues . . ." mumbled my father.

My mother frowned, which was also strange. Usually she wore an exercise singlesuit to breakfast and never showed other than a pleasant disposition. Again, she changed the subject quickly. "Are you sure that uniform is warm enough?"

"Ice storm was a freak," I mouthed. "Melting off already."

"Don't talk with your mouth full." That was father.

"All too many freak occurrences," murmured mother, so softly that father, with his bad ear that he refused to have examined, heard nothing.

I looked at her, and she shook her head minutely, as if to tell me not to ask. I didn't. Instead, I grabbed the last roll, taking bites first from an almost ripe chyst and then from the roll.

Father pursed his lips and took a last sip from his cup.

"Coming?"

I swallowed the last mouthful, wiped my face, and nodded.

"Meet you at the steamer."

# IX.

"WHAT HAPPENED . . . ?"

"Get the lights!" That was Jeen Kryrel. He'd been trapped in his uncle's silo as a youngster, still didn't like darkness, even dim corners.

The buzz of the overhead lamps had disappeared with the lights themselves.

"Silence!" Dr. Yellertond's voice cut right through the gloom of the laboratory.

Since I hadn't been looking forward to the lab anyway, the power loss was almost welcome. The heavy slate-topped tables and the aged wood cabinets reeked of sulfur and flame . . . and of age. My father had gone to the Academy, and his father.

"You may remain at your stations while I check with the magister. You may talk *quietly*. Anyone whose voice I can hear will draw holiday duties."

The groan at that was clear. Dr. Yellertond loved to assign holiday duties.

"First power failure I've been in . . ."

"Do you suppose it was the satellite relay?"

"Probably just an interrupter here."

I didn't say anything. There had already been too many coincidences, and the power loss had something to do with the Mithrada situation. For some reason, I thought about my mother. She had not been planning to go to Inequital the night before. Yet she had been up and dressed, and very preoccupied.

She had friends in the capital—that was why she spent so much time there, she said, but that would not have explained her worried expression. She never looked worried. And the ice storm—that was unusual.

"What do you think, Sammis?"

"Yes, what's the runt think?"

What I thought about was giving Reylin a broken leg. My mother had instructed me in Delkaiba, just enough to make me cautious about trying to use it. But Reylin was always asking for a lesson of sorts.

"I think that the lights are going to stay out—for a long time." The words popped out before I could draw them back.

"Now the runt's a prophet . . ."

Already the lab was getting chilly, or it seemed that way to me, and the sulfur smell was more pungent than usual. The bruise I had gotten in falling on the icy front walk in my nightmare, or whatever, hurt if I sat on the lab stool wrong.

"Silence!" Dr. Yellertond was standing in the laboratory doorway.

The murmurs and whispers vanished into the gloom of the big classroom.

"The power outage is not local, but stems from a failure in the satellite relay systems. You are all dismissed. Anyone who does not live within walking distance of the Academy may wait in the library or the main anteroom of the administration building."

The tall, thin professor watched as we gathered books and notes together, and as we trooped out into the corridor, boots scuffling on the polished stone floors.

Like everything else in Westron the Academy was constructed mostly of stone, with slate roofing on heavy timbers. Interior walls were either paneled or plastered and replastered.

That was because most of the petroleum and iron had been exhausted by the First Civilization, or so Dr. Editris had said. He claimed the failure of the few Eastron oil reserves had led to the fall of the Eastron Republic . . . but that was history. I wondered if my father would be home when I got there, or if I would have to avoid Shaera by myself. Certainly, if the power link had failed for the Academy, there would be no power for the small Imperial complex at Bremarlyn, or for the Revenue Court.

". . . could be serious . . ."

". . . first time we've been dismissed in mid-day . . ."

Dr. Yellertond kept swinging around to find someone to glare at, but every time he started to turn the whispers disappeared. Allyson once had told me that the whispers at the girls' academy—it was called Tyrnelle House—were far worse.

Were they sending the girls home from Tyrnelle? If so, I could go over to the Davniads. That would be better than staying at home with Shaera, who, for all her well-intentioned energy, would try to find something for me to do that I was really supposed to do. Allyson was interesting to talk to, even if she did look down on me.

"Silence!" The word had always been Dr. Yellertond's favorite, and he was not opposed to overusing it.

By then, we had all straggled into the central robing hall, where our lockers lined the walls. More than half the upper classes were already there, and Dr. Yellertond winced as the whispers washed over and around him. The man should have been a mystic or a retreat academic, not a teacher of young adults.

Finally, he shrugged, as if to wash his hands of us, and made a vague gesture, muttering something I could not hear.

"Are we officially dismissed?" I asked Loiren, who was grabbing a heavy winter cloak from his locker, right next to mine.

"That's what the assistant magister announced, just before old quiet-ass brought you guys in."

I grabbed my own cloak. I'd tried to take the lightweight one that morning, but Shaera and my mother had forced the heavier one on me, and it was hard to argue against

both of them successfully. Since I'd wanted to catch the
steamer ride with Dad—it did save me nearly a kay in
walking—I'd taken the heavy black one.

Once I had the cloak, I took the pack, but I left all the
books.

"You aren't taking your studies?" asked Loiren in surprise as he closed his locker.

"Why bother? It should be a few days before we get
power back, and they'll have to review anyway."

"It's your head, Sammis."

I ignored Loiren. He meant well, but there were too
many coincidences, and I wanted to get to the Davniads.

Outside, it was still cold and sunny, and the wind coming up the hill from the west chilled my ears immediately.
A good forty others were already marching down toward
the road where most, I suspected, would find steamers to
take them home. The bells in the Academy's temple were
ringing to announce dismissal.

From the east, I could hear the lighter tones from Tyrnelle House, occasionally disappearing in the whistle of
the wind. Clutching my cloak around me tighter, I was
glad that I had not been successful in arguing for the
lighter-weight overwear. Trudging down the paving stones
toward the highway, I hunched up inside the heavy wool.

Clouds were piling up on the horizon, and it looked like
another storm was pelting Inequital. While the capital
wasn't visible from the low hills of Bremarlyn, I'd been
there enough to imagine what it must be like, with sheets
of heavy rain pouring through kay after kay of three, four,
and even five story buildings—and the Grand Tower. Some
of the anarchists claimed that the Emperor and, before her
death, his mother the Grand Empress, had used their power
to keep other towers from being built.

Hoping my mother had left before the storm had hit, I
whistled one or two notes of the Marching Song, but the
wind was too bitter to keep whistling. So I put my head

down and lengthened my steps. Despite my size, I could walk, or run, faster than anyone at the Academy. Not that I was about to in the cold.

By the time I started along the walking trail by the highway, uphill most of the way, my nose was running from the cold. The clouds from the west had begun to shut off the sunlight, and the wind was building up into a gale, bringing with it an acrid odor.

Half a kay further, and I was looking for the occasional steamer that might be headed my way, but most people lived on the eastern side of Bremarlyn. We lived on the more isolated side, closer to Inequital and to the Revenue Court where my father practiced.

Another half a kay, and I had reached the side road that wound gently toward our land. My ears were numb, and my breath made me look like a malfunctioning steamer myself. The ground crackled underfoot, and whatever the storm brought it wouldn't be rain, but snow or ice. Overhead, the clouds were thickening into an ugly gray.

*Wheeep! Wheep!*

Waving from the window of the Davniads' slate gray steamer was Allyson. I stumbled over the half-frozen turf and into the rear seat. Allyson and her mother were in the front.

"You look frozen, Sammis. What on earth are you doing out in this?"

"Mother's in Inequital, and father is at work. At least he was. It was sunny when I left the Academy."

"I do hope your mother is all right, Sammis. All the communications links with the capital are out, just like the power." Germania Davniads was a big woman with a tiny voice. Allyson had her father's booming voice and both parent's build, but she wasn't overweight like her mother. She had a nice figure and a nice smile. She was a good head taller than me, not to mention a year or so older.

As the steamer hummed up the road, I readjusted my

cloak. There was no heat, though, and while I could feel the circulation returning to my fingers and toes, the absence of wind alone was not enough to immediately thaw me out.

"I do hope Jerz managed to leave Jillriko early. He took the runabout." Germania kept her eyes on the winding road as her small voice continued. "It's such a long trip back, especially if the rain gets heavy, and that can easily happen at this time of year . . ."

Allyson half-turned and ran her eyes over my cloak. "It's too cold to rain, Mother. Don't you think so, Sammis?"

"Ice or snow, I suppose."

"I do hope that it isn't ice. The runabout is so light, and the hill to our place is so steep . . . Sammis, would you like me to run you all the way up to your doorway?"

"What . . . ?"

"Mother wanted to know if you wanted to come over and have hot cider, or if you had to get home immediately," added Allyson quickly.

"Cider sounds good . . ."

"Then we'll just take you to our place. All right, Mother?"

"If you think that is all right, dear. But won't your father and mother worry? Especially in this weather . . . and if it gets icy . . ."

By then, the steamer was nearing the turnoff for our drive. I looked up. A pair of soldiers stood by the drive, each carrying some sort of weapon.

"Just keep going, Mother." Allyson's voice was commanding.

"If you say so . . . dear . . . but . . . what are those men doing there? Doesn't your father work for the government, Sammis? Is there something wrong?"

Germania kept driving toward the Davniads, and the soldiers watched us go without even turning their heads.

I felt cold again—very cold. Why would soldiers be stationed at our house? Did it have something to do with all the coincidences, or with the power losses?

Allyson was looking at me. She raised her eyebrows.

I shrugged, and shook my head. "Don't know." My words were barely more than mouthed.

She nodded.

Although I continued to study the lower part of our grounds until we started up the wide drive to the Davniads, nothing seemed changed—except for the soldiers.

"Here we are . . . I do believe that I will put the steamer in the locker. The weather will not do it any good, and we certainly don't plan to go anywhere . . ."

"Sammis?"

"No. When it's time to go home, I'll just take the back path. It's sheltered most of the way, and it's quicker than driving." More important, I could take it and not be seen. Perhaps someone in a case my father had been prosecuting had made a threat against him. That had happened once several years ago, and we had soldiers guarding the area for weeks. But nothing had ever happened.

The steamer hummed to a stop inside the locker building.

"Mother, if you would see to the cider, Sammis and I will drain the tank and close up . . ."

"If you wouldn't mind . . ."

"It's certainly no problem, " I volunteered.

"Would you like your cider straight . . . or with chyst?"

I opened the door and scrambled out, carefully checking the hinges before closing it. "With chyst, please."

The drainage hose was in about the same place as in our locker, and I unrolled it, attaching the funnel clip to the end. The gray steamer—the name plate said Altera—had one of the new side pipe drains, which made it easy.

Unless it was going to be cold enough to freeze, steam-

ers didn't need to have their water drained, but mother—
she was the mechanical one—always insisted that both of
ours be drained whenever they were not in use. Allyson
didn't object when I began to drain the water. It was almost clear, the sign of a well-maintained vehicle.

Allyson was topping off the etheline, presumably so that
she did not have to do it in the morning. But etheline never
froze, not in Bremarlyn, anyway, although in places like
Southpoint all the steamers had to have heating systems
built into the water and fuel bunkers and even into the
steamers themselves.

I finished draining off the water and closed the steamer's
drain valve, then began coiling the hose. My hands were
getting numb again, from the chill and the water I had
spilled on them. Even inside the locker I could see the
steam from my breath.

"How are we going to have hot cider?" I asked.
"There's no power and no sunlight."

"There's a small etheline burner in the kitchen. Mother
insisted on it, and it does come in handy." Allyson was
wiping her hands on the towel by the pump handle.

Straight black hair, but twisted up at her neck, dark blue
eyes, and a warm smile—Allyson was nice-looking, and I
enjoyed being around her, but more as if she were an older
sister. She was just so much taller, and older, in so many
ways, than I was.

"Do you really know what's going on at your house?"

"No. It could be like two years ago, when that oil mer-
chant was caught cheating on his revenue payments and
threatened to have us all boiled in flynyx oil. We had some
soldiers then."

Allyson touched my shoulder. I jumped.

"Sorry. You looked upset."

"I am. My mother left for Inequital this morning, and
she was worried. Very worried, and she's *never* worried."

"What does she do? Nobody knows, for all the years

you Olons have lived here. That house was, what, your grandfather's?''

"Right. It was grandfather's, but I never met him.''

Allyson motioned toward the locker door. She was wearing some kind of scent, like flowers, and it smelled good on her. "The cider should be ready, and you could use some. What about your mother, though?''

That was another thing I liked about Allyson. She didn't play the verbal games so many girls did. Not with me, at least. She just said what she had in mind.

"I really don't know. She travels a lot, and she's published some monographs. She doesn't talk about it.'' Even in the courtyard between the locker and the main house it was cold. I stopped and let Allyson handle the door latch. It was her door, and she was wearing gloves. I'd left mine at home.

The courtyard was cold, but because the Davniads had left more of the woods around their place, the wind was less. Except for the drive, you would scarcely have known a house was there.

"You don't know what your own mother does?''

"I've asked. She's never answered, and when she doesn't want to answer, she doesn't. Period. Besides, you know that.''

Allyson shook her head, as she made sure the latch was secure. "I know, but I was hoping . . .''

We walked quickly up the dozen steps to the rear door that led to the kitchen. The warmth of the house felt good, but I wondered how long the stored energy would last. That was the problem with solar heat, especially when it was cloudy for days on end. Thank Verlyt that Bremarlyn had lots of sun.

"Allyson? Sammis? The cider is set up in the side room, and there's a fire in the grate. I'm resting up here, but I'll be down later.''

So we hung up our cloaks in the back closet, and I

followed Allyson up to the side room, where I found the
explanation for at least some of the warmth. The Davniads
had a small wood-burning stove grate instead of a solar
storage drum or a fireplace. A small table was set with
two cups and two plates. In the center was a serving platter
with cheeses, three or four crumb rolls, and several slices
of chyst, into addition to the wedge set by one cup.

"Wood-burning?"

"Father insisted on some room that could be heated
during storms if we lost the electric power link. There's
one upstairs as well. Mother is probably having her cider
there."

I took the chair by the chyst cider, and Allyson sat down
across from me. For the first time in hours, my ears felt
comfortable. I unbuttoned the collar of my tunic, sipping
the warm cider slowly and realizing just how cold it had
been outside.

"That's snow." Her voice was softer. Her hands cra-
dled the cup as she looked out through the double glass of
the two wide windows.

Outside, the snow drove by the window, almost like
white rain, it was so heavy.

"Verlyt! I'd better get home. No one knows where I
am!"

"Sammis. Wait a bit. You said yourself that no one's
likely to be home. And a few minutes more won't make
that much difference. You need to warm up and have
something else to eat."

Still on the edge of my chair, I reached for one of the
crumb rolls, forcing myself to eat it slowly, with an occasional sip of cider. Nothing seemed to make sense—not
the snow, for we seldom had snow in Bremarlyn; nor the
cold, which was more like Southpoint; nor the soldiers.
Especially not the soldiers.

"The soldiers again?"

I nodded, since my mouth was full.

"It doesn't make much sense." Allyson paused. "Could your mother be one of the Hands?"

". . . ouughchchouupphh . . ." I had all I could do to keep from choking on the spot. My mother, my well-educated and scholarly mother, an Imperial Hand? One of the Emperor's unknown but highly trusted agents?

"Well . . . it does make sense, Sammis. She travels, and no one, not even her family, knows where. She is brilliant and well-educated. She is in fantastic shape, and no one in Inequital or anywhere else would know anything about her."

All of what Allyson said was true, but the whole idea was ridiculous. My well-tailored and devoted mother? With her flynyx coat?

"No, that's ridiculous . . ."

"Then why the soldiers?"

"You might as well ask 'why the snow?', Allyson." I shrugged. "It's got to be tied up with the Mithradan mess . . . but without power we can't even hear the news."

"You don't have batteries?"

"Do you?"

"No . . . father says they're too expensive."

I grinned. "Sounds like mine." I knew I needed something to eat. The mid-day meal at the Academy had been yellow fish stew, which tasted worse than it sounded. But I wanted to gulp the rolls and cheese down and start home. My guts were tightening just thinking about Allyson's suggestion, which made far too much sense. And I was afraid that the soldiers around my home meant nothing good. Nothing at all good.

"Now I've got you worried, don't I?"

"Just a little . . ."

Her hand touched mine, covered it, and I sat there, enjoying her touch and still worrying.

"Let me come with you."

I shook my head. "No. If there's no problem, then

there's no reason for you to freeze. If there is a problem, I wouldn't want you involved."

She nodded, understanding what I meant. The roundups after the Eastron cleanup had been thorough, very thorough.

I slowly chewed a second slice of cheese, not tasting it. I swallowed and felt it settle like ice in my stomach. Even a sip of cider didn't seem to warm the cold weight there. So I stood up.

Allyson did also. "Please be careful."

"I'll try." I tried to grin, but it was forced.

"Before you go . . . let me show you something."

Show me something? Allyson displayed concern, but not the almost romantic implications of her statement.

She blushed as I considered her words.

"That sounds . . . different . . . from what I meant . . . just follow me . . ." She went from the side room into the kitchen and then opened a narrow doorway leading downward into a lower level of the house, toward the old servant's quarters, not that very many of the gentry had servants any longer, as we had Shaera. But the stairway was clean, as was the hallway. At the end was a heavy door to the outside, which opened onto the rear hillside underneath the veranda.

I'd seen the door from the lawn before, and wondered where it went. Now I was seeing it from the inside. Although the lower level was not heated, it wasn't that cold, and I could feel the residual warmth from above and from the main solar tap.

Allyson stepped back from the outside doorway and eased open one of the hallway doors into a small room with a single bed—one covered mattress on a simple wooden frame—and a lamp. The room had no window, and the walls were a clean but old cream plaster.

"There are quilts on the foot of the bed . . . here . . .

and I'll leave the door unbolted. There is still a lock, but the key will be under the rock on the right.''

"Why?" I whispered, knowing I didn't have to, but figuring that this invitation did not exactly have familial approval.

"If no one knows you're here, then they can't say you are, and mother always has to tell everything. This way, if there's something wrong, you can at least have a place where you won't freeze. I'll see if I can find some warmer clothes and some food.''

We both knew what she was saying. If the soldiers were not a protective detail, then anyone who helped me was in danger of losing everything as well. Even in making shelter available in a hidden fashion Allyson was risking a lot.

It would be only a while before her father arrived home, and he certainly, knowing Jerz Davniads, would ask the soldiers what was happening.

"I should be going . . .''

"I know.''

Neither one of us said anything as we climbed back up the old stairs to the kitchen. As I pulled on my cloak, Allyson handed me a pair of faded leather gloves.

"You'll need them. Bring them back when you can.''

I nodded, still having to look up at her.

*Creaakkkk . . . whssllllsss . . .*

The wind nearly tore the kitchen door from my hands as I stepped out into the chill. The afternoon looked more like twilight. The tiny white flakes fell as thick as a summer thundershower.

Not looking back, I plunged into the storm and down the back lawn, where the snow was almost ankle deep, nearly falling several times before I reached the trees and the narrow path that wound along the hillsides toward our house.

*Chhichiii . . .*

A grossjay jabbered from the evergreen branches, his call the only sound above the hissing of the snow and the whining of the wind.

By the time I was five rods into the woods, I could not even tell, looking over my shoulder, that there was a house uphill from where I walked. The path seemed longer than usual; my ears were numb; and my toes tingled by the time I reached the gate in the old stone wall. The wooden gate itself had been removed when my father was a boy. Only a gap in the stonework remained. The wall marked the boundary between our lands and the Davniads', and on the other side were the remnants of grandfather's orchards, mostly chyst, but some pearapple.

A hint of an acrid odor in the air tugged at my nose, and I stopped short of the gate, knowing that to return through the wall led to more than I really wanted to handle. Edging up the gap, I studied the path, but there were no prints in the snow, no sign of anyone this far down in the orchards.

The house was still a good hundred rods or more uphill, and the straggling remnants of the old orchards ran to within twenty rods of the back terrace.

After I went through the wall, my steps were even more deliberate, and I left the path, walking instead from tree to tree, pausing and looking uphill. The acrid odor got stronger and stronger, but I could see nothing through the trees—not until I was almost to the top end of the orchard.

The light from the fire lit up the entire house, and the row of soldiers formed a cordon around it. None of them were looking out into the storm, but at the burning house. All of them had weapons leveled.

I scuttled up into the lower branches of a pearapple, trying to sort it out, trying to keep my guts from turning inside out.

Why were they burning the house? And who were they? I watched for a time, conscious of the cold creeping through me, as the flames continued to leap into the storm. Despite the fire and the cold, none of the soldiers relaxed in their scrutiny of the house.

One figure, presumably an officer, walked the outer perimeter. The second time he passed within a few rods of the tree where I was huddled on the back side of the trunk, peering around at the destruction. That was when I saw the shoulder patch, saw and recognized the emblem of the ConFed Marines, the same Marines who were the shock troops in the Eastron occupation. The same Marines whose intelligence service had handled rounding up the Eastron sympathizers.

Why were they burning my house? Why did they keep studying it as if something were hidden inside?

*CCCRRRUMMMPPPP!*

I had to hang on to the tree as it shook with the force of the explosion.

All of the marines were flattened on the snow. Some moved, as the fire burned even higher, sending billows of black smoke up into evening. Others looked as though they would never move.

Although I did not know what had caused the explosion—certainly it had not been expected by the marines— none of those who survived were likely to be favorably inclined toward anyone or anything associated with the house. Slipping down from the tree, I managed to stagger on unsteady feet through the still-heavy snow toward the path to the Davniads'.

By now, the powdery stuff reached well over my ankles and showed no signs of stopping. Between the oncoming night and the clouds, the darkness made each step uncertain.

I kept looking back, but by the time I reached the wall I could see only a dim glow through the branches and the snow. The wind had not died down, but increased and whipped the edges of my cloak.

When I finally reached the Davniads' lawn, it was a sea of white, churned by the wind. Only a few lights were on, probably etheline lamps or candles. Although the wind might have covered my tracks, I circled the lawn and edged up partly from the side, staying far enough from the veranda wall so that the drifting snow would cover my steps, concealing any sign that would show I knew in advance where I was going.

Probably a vain precaution, one way or another, but that was what I did.

The key was where Allyson had said it would be, although it took me some time to find it in the dark, and even more time to brush snow back in place. Neither the door nor the lock creaked, for which I was thankful.

Closing the door and latching it was more difficult because it was hard to see in the near-total darkness, and I had neither flash nor glow rod. Then, because I wanted to make no noise at all, my progress to the servant's room was even slower. As I opened that door, I discovered I could see, barely. A dim glow rod lay on the single small waist-high wardrobe, next to a small package.

First, I shook out my cloak in the corner away from the door and wardrobe, and brushed the loose snow off my Academy uniform. Then I unlaced my boots and took them off. My toes began to sting as feeling returned. I spread out the cloak, hoping it would dry somewhat, and put the boots next to them.

There was no note by the rod or the package, which contained some dried meat and fruit, several slices of bread, and other wrapped items I could not determine, as well as a small tool kit.

My uniform was damp and clammy. Off it came, and I draped it over the wardrobe and began to shiver even more violently. The two quilts helped, and I curled into a ball on the old bed, trying to sort things out.

Nothing was very clear, nothing at all. The marines had

orders to burn the house, and that was a punishment only sanctioned by the Emperor for traitors and their families. I knew we weren't traitors.

How long I lay there, I don't know, but finally the shivers stopped and my eyes closed, and I could appreciate not being caught in the fire or the cold of the storm. I think I slept.

# X.

THE BLOND WOMAN appeared in a recess off the Fountain Court, shadowed in darkness. Her hair was bound tightly, and she wore a dark single-piece military coverall and formfitting dull black boots. Around her waist was a military-style equipment belt bearing a number of items, including a projectile pistol.

The Fountain Court was deserted, except for a single Imperial guard who stood at the closed bronze doors to the Inner Palace.

The woman slipped an insignia onto each collar and a glistening badge into the holder on her chest as she walked toward the guard. Her breathing was deep, but even, as if she were recovering from heavy exertion.

Making no attempt to conceal her steps, she marched toward the guard.

"Halt. Who goes there?"

"Major Erlynn."

"Advance and be recognized." The guard raised the wide-angle shredder and turned it toward the Major.

The woman vanished. The guard squinted, leaning forward . . .

*Crack!* He slumped to the floor with a broken neck from the single blow delivered by the Major who had appeared next to him.

The Major surveyed the ConFed Marine uniform, and shook her head slowly.

Even through the heavy and ancient walls, she could hear the crowd noise rising as the mobs roared in their surge toward the palace. She had checked the main gate, but those guards had either left or been removed. The gate mechanism had been disabled as well. The broadsides scattered throughout Inequital were slickly printed, far too slickly for revolutionaries in a world that had neither seen nor tolerated revolt for decades.

Another military coup attempt, using the unrest created by the aliens on Mithrada?

A single guard. That was almost planned treason, and now nothing she could do would stop the fall of the Emperor. All she could do to complete her duty was to ensure the usurpers would not profit either. She turned and vanished.

A flash of light blistered from down the court, momentarily illuminating the fallen figure.

"Damned witch."

"She won't save him this time."

Within moments, the mob had begun to pour through the Fountain Court toward the Imperial apartments.

A quarter of a continent away, a woman still wearing the insignia of a Major appeared behind the operator of a lighted full-wall console.

*Crack!*

The operator slumped dead in the seat.

Without moving the body, the Major leaned over and touched the control room locks before she began entering a new set of coordinates.

*Brinnnggg!*

Ignoring the alarm that she had known her actions would trigger, she entered the override codes she was not supposed to have. She touched the launch controls, one after the other, until the signals had been sent to the remaining orbital satellite, the one without personnel, the one untouched by the Enemy. As she waited for the return signal, the one which she must answer with a second confirmation, she could hear the cutting lasers being wheeled to the heavy doors.

*Hsssssttttt . . .*

The sound and smell of molten metal began to permeate the small room.

A single amber light flashed, then another, until five lights were lit. She entered a second set of codes, and triggered them.

*Sssssssssttttt!*

A narrow beam lanced through the hole in the doors, needling through the woman's body.

"Pray I did right . . ." She muttered the words, staggered, then vanished, leaving only several drops of a sticky black substance on the tiles.

Outside the doors, the lasers hissed a moment longer.

Across the solar system, five satellite launch doors opened, waiting for the return signal that would unleash sunfire on the Enemy.

# XI.

AGAIN, THERE WAS the dream of the crossroads, the red and the blue, the black and the gold, and they were even more real, as if I only had to wish to step through the black curtain and stand upon that uncertain intersection.

I held back, almost as if there were something to wait for.

Then—perhaps it was a door opening, a footstep on the staircase, but the faintest of sounds—and I was awake, heart beating quickly and staring at the closed door.

Although the room was dark, except for the dimness of

the glow rod, it could have been morning for all I knew.
I did not think so, not with the tiredness and the soreness
I still felt. Finally warm, I was wrapped in the two old
quilts that Allyson had laid out for me.

Another faint step, and I relaxed slightly. The tread was
too light for Jerz Davniads—he shook the floors when he
moved. Even the stone of the cellar hallway would have
resounded. That meant either Allyson, her much older sister Isolde, or their mother.

*Whsssssppp . . .*

A robed figure slipped inside the doorway, carrying a
second glow rod.

"Sammis?"

I nodded, relieved that it was Allyson, then whispered
as I realized she couldn't see me. "Here. On the bed."

By now I could see a rueful grin. "Where else would
you be?"

"What time is it?"

We were still whispering.

"Close to midnight." She sat down on the very edge
of the bed, her high-necked robe wrapped tightly around
her. "Father stopped by your drive, not long after you
left . . . Sammis, those were ConFed Marines, and they
wouldn't talk to him. They wouldn't even let him go until
they had checked his name and position and searched the
runabout."

"I know. I know. They burned the house . . ." My voice
caught. Despite myself, I had trouble talking. ". . . kept
watching the house, with weapons, ready to shoot anyone
who tried to get out . . ."

"Sammis . . . why? What were you doing?"

"Nothing . . . you know Dad . . . all the trouble he
took for the court . . . all the years . . . and his father . . ."
I shook my head. In the darkness it seemed only half real,
yet I was hiding in the Davniads' servant's quarters.

"Your mother?" She extended a hand, and I took it.

"I just don't know . . . never . . . never would have believed it . . ."

"We're leaving in the morning, father says. That means midday."

"Leaving . . . ?"

"Sammis, things are much worse than we thought. Father says that the whole Mithradan expedition was wiped out, including the space stations there. The power link was destroyed. There were riots in Inequital, and the broadcast video channels are off the air. There are some audio channels broadcasting, but from the east. Nothing from the capital."

I was tired, and sore, and my back was still bruised from the dream fall I had taken—had it only been a day earlier? None of it made sense.

All I could do was shake my head. I couldn't even say anything. I think my cheeks were wet, because even with the glow rods I had trouble focusing.

"Are you all right? No, that's a stupid question . . ." Allyson put an arm around my shoulders, and until she steadied me, I hadn't realized that I was shaking all over. "You can hold on to me. Just hold on to me."

I did. As if she were the only thing solid in a dissolving world, as if she were the only warmth in winter.

One of her hands, cool and warm at the same time, brushed my hair out of my face, kneaded the back of my neck to ease some of the hurt, some of the stiffness.

"Move over a little," she suggested. "My feet are cold."

And I did that too, as she lay down next to me, holding me almost as tightly as I held her.

When I could see again, clearly, Allyson was staring at the ceiling, even though she still had one arm around me, and I had both of mine around her.

"Worried?" My voice was unsteady.

"Me?" She kept looking at the ceiling.

"You."

For a while, neither one of us said anything. I thought I could hear the whistle of the wind outside. Otherwise, the house was silent.

"Yes. Father says that we'll be safer at the summer place in Olviad. It was originally a family refuge from the Ronwic times. The gray steamer . . . is special . . . too. Father used to race, you know."

"Your father wants to wait out the storm?"

Allyson nodded. "He wasn't happy about that, but he said there wasn't any choice. The marines upset him. He didn't say much, but I could tell he was worried. Mother doesn't understand anything. And Isolde—she was in Inequital, but father says there's nothing to be done . . . nothing to be done . . ."

By then, Allyson was shaking. So I told her, "Hold me. Just hold me. I'm right here."

And she did, and I think we both shook, hanging on to each other, knowing that a familiar world was coming apart, and not knowing why.

Outside, the wind whistled softly, on and off, as if the storm might be dying down.

Inside, behind the timber and stone and plaster, Allyson and I held each other, trying to hold off the storm, or what it had so suddenly come to represent, our feelings jumbled together between us and the quilts.

"I need to get back upstairs . . ."

"I know . . ."

"Father will be checking here in the morning, and . . ."

"I know that, too." Jerz Davniads was a friendly man, but he would certainly not hesitate to turn me in to the marines if he thought it would improve the chances of his family's survival. He might not think so, and wouldn't turn me over unless it would help. But there was no sense in risking it.

"Sammis . . . ?" Allyson turned her face toward me, her long hair brushing my cheek.

"Ummm."

"I wish it had turned out differently."

"So do I."

She leaned toward me, letting her lips touch, then warm, mine.

I held Allyson more tightly, feeling for the first time, really, how soft she felt against me, and how sweet she smelled.

"I have to go . . ."

"I know . . ." I knew, but I didn't have to like it. If her father woke up and went searching for his daughter, or couldn't sleep and wanted to prepare for the trip, I didn't want him making his way to the cellar. Neither did I want to let go of Allyson.

"I don't want to go, Sammis."

"I know."

"But I have to." She kissed me again, and then pushed away from me and swung her feet to the floor, reclaiming her slippers. "I have to . . ."

"I know." I felt stupid and helpless repeating the same words time after time, and all I wanted then was to keep holding on to Allyson.

She took her glow rod and slipped to the door. "I've left everything I could get for you . . ." Her voice was a whisper.

"If you hadn't . . . I don't know what . . ."

Her shoulders trembled as she took the three or four steps from the sagging old bed to the door. She was gone before I could even finish my sentence, and I was staring at a softly closed door. A closed door on what might have been. A door closed on . . . but there was no point in dwelling on that.

Queryan memories are long, and the round-ups and the burnings of the Eastron sympathizers, and of the witch-

wraiths before that, had been pounded into my head by
my own father.

For a long time, I lay in the jumbled quilts as the room
cooled, thinking about nothing, then trying to decide what
I could do, or where I could go. For everyone in Bremarlyn would know me, and in this time of chaos, no one
would stand up for me—no one but Allyson, and she had
done what she could. That was more than enough to get
her burned should anyone discover it.

I got up and smoothed out the bed, folding the quilts as
I recalled they had been folded. I checked my own uniform, which remained slightly damp, and put it on.
Strangely, my cloak was dry, and my boots had never been
damp inside.

After dressing as quietly as possible, I looked through
what Allyson had brought—and thanked her mentally
again. Not only was there the food and the tool kit, but
also a small hatchet and a folding knife with several blades,
and a folded square of waterproof ground cloth. All the
non-food items were dusty, which probably meant that they
wouldn't be missed, but all looked serviceable.

I took my nearly empty pack and placed everything in
it, except for the knife, which went into my pocket, and
the gloves Allyson had given me earlier. Then I pulled
on the cloak and the gloves and swung the pack into place.

The door from the room opened easily. I stopped to
listen. Not a sound from upstairs—although I had not expected any, since it had to be well before dawn. Still, my
steps were light, if not noiseless, as I slipped to the big
latched door.

*Hsssst . . . click.* Despite my best efforts, the latch
rasped.

I held my breath and listened. No sounds, except for
the moaning of the wind outside.

Holding the door against the wind so it would not swing

inside and hit the wall, I stepped into the night—or the predawn darkness.

Overhead, I could see some stars between the swirls of fast-moving clouds. The wind was light and skitterish, with gusts of warm air, then cooler air. From what I could see in the dim light, most of my tracks had been covered by snow and wind.

Since there wasn't much I could do about hiding my tracks, I walked to the far end of the wall, where the double stone steps came down to the lawn. The higher ones were clear of snow. Glancing up at the windows and seeing no light, I walked up two steps in the snow, and then turned and retraced my path to the lower door. From there I walked backwards along the wall until I neared the point where the other set of steps went up toward the courtyard and the kitchen. They were clear in the center, and my prints did not show.

The courtyard was dusted with snow, but only in the west corner had it drifted more than a finger deep. By scuffing my boots side to side, I obscured my prints enough that they did not look recent, and with the hint of warmth in the wind, after sunrise they might not be visible at all.

Like our drive, the Davniads' was raised a handspan or so above the lawn, and the center part had been wind-swept. I checked the house, but there were no lights. Going down the drive was a risk, but Jerz Davniads wasn't the sort to chase me without considering the conse-quences—assuming he saw me at all. And taking the drive left fewer tracks.

It might be days before snow left parts of the woods path. Besides, anyone could be coming or going down the drive. Only Sammis Olon would be using the woodlands path.

At the curve in the drive, just before it entered the woods

on its slope down to the road, I looked back at the house. In a way, I had hoped to see a single candle, or something. But the windowpanes were dark, and the hot-cold wind whistled across my cloak. I watched for another moment, then waved to Allyson, or no one, and began the hike downhill.

# XII.

"THE WITCHES OF Eastron? What a strange conceit, coming as it did from the only non-monarchial culture in Queryan history. Yet the thread of the so-called 'witches' appears in folklore, literature, and even in diaries for a period of close to a millennium.

"The references span four phases of government, including the Fylarian Fragmentation, and demonstrate remarkable consistency . . .

". . . women (or men) who did not age, who were seen in places too far apart for them to have travelled the distance, who displayed remarkable skill and dexterity, who avoided war and violence, even for the best causes . . .

"None of the attributes of the so-called 'witches', except for the rapid travel, and that could have been mere coincidence, are that remarkable, especially given the extraordinarily hatred that devolved, either in Eastron or Westron, upon those accused of being witches. Yet even into modern times, the witchcraft charge has been used . . .

"All in all, the remarkableness of the conceit has been its continuation, given the mildness of the evils attributed to such witches—they lived a long life, possibly an endless one, and they could travel far distances in the blink of an eye. Yet such charges destroyed whole families in the early

days of Eastron and even into the founding of the Westron
Chartered Monarchy . . .''

Archival Text Fragment
Temporal Guard Archives
Quest, Query
1200 N.G.E.

# XIII.

I KEPT TO the side of the Davniads' drive, and to the edge
of the road after that. There was nowhere else to go—not
by the road.

Father said that there had been talk of extending the
road until it reached the Wayland Highway on the other
side of the hills, but the Engineers had never started the
work. My choices were clear—blunder through the still
snowy hills or risk the road in the darkness before dawn,
accompanied by wind and chill, before the marines started
their usual canvass of the area and all the residents.

Like the Davniads' drive, the crown of the road was
clear.

*Click . . . click . . . crunch . . .*

My steps sounded louder in my ears than they probably
did in fact, but the sound spurred me to set my feet more
carefully on the downgrade.

Once I reached the sweeping ninety-degree turn above
our driveway, I stopped and listened. Silence, but that
didn't mean anything. Not where the ConFed Marines were
concerned. I edged off the road and into the snow-covered
grassy depression that was almost a ditch—on the opposite
side of the road. Stepping through the snow, I kept my
head low. Before long, I reached the point across the road
from the low stone pillars that marked our drive.

*Whhhsttt . . . whssssss . . .*

Only the whisper of the wind broke the stillness—that and the sound of my breath.

Was there still a guard by the pillars? A Marine detachment watching the smoldering ruins of the house built by my great-great-grandfather?

I glanced toward the pillars, but could see nothing but two smudges of gray against the shadows of the evergreen hedge and the overhanging trees. As I strained to make out whether there was a guard posted, the dream impression of the red-blue, gold-black intersection returned, somehow right behind my eyes, even closer than in my dreams.

*Crack.*

The sound had come from behind me. I could feel eyes on my back, and I grasped in some way for the dark intersection, knowing that only that could save me, if anything could.

Without understanding how, I was on the other side of the black curtain, seeing through a veil the snow-drifted depression where the three marines looked down on a set of footprints that came from nowhere and went nowhere.

From that no-time place, I could hear nothing, but one of the ConFeds made the ward gesture from the Verlyt rites. Another had a shredder aimed at where I would have been, where I had been instants before.

Suspended there, I dared not move, not that I could. So I watched as the three marines stomped through and around where I had been. Finally, one followed my tracks backward until they reached the hard stones of the road and disappeared.

My unplanned disappearance in plain sight might lift suspicion from Allyson and her family, since I hoped that the marines would not walk hundreds of rods back uphill and through the Davniads' courtyard to compare footsteps in the snow. At least, I hoped I had left no tracks in the snow between the two places.

As I hung out of time, waiting, a marine reappeared with an officer, a tall and burly man. The marine pointed to my footprints, gesturing, then shaking his head. The burly man seemed to be exasperated, doing some pointing himself, jabbing a finger toward the marine, who kept backing up.

Even though I could feel nothing where I was suspended, I could tell that I was getting tired. The veil, or curtain, seemed to flicker in front of my eyes. What could I do?

My thoughts jumped back to the ConFed Marines guarding the house, and as they did, the scene through the black curtain wavered, then refocused, and I was standing in the orchard, still behind the curtain of time or place. But this time I knew that as soon as I willed it, I could be in the orchard.

With the marine tents, and the row of coffins laid out, some drifted over with snow, I did not want to reappear there. Not at all.

The Academy? No . . .

Finally, I concentrated on a place where I used to hike with mother—the Long Wall trail above the town, on the far side of Bremarlyn. I knew I could not go very far, but I *had* to go somewhere.

I thought, hard, and tried to visualize the trail and the way station, especially the way station, the one-windowed old log cabin.

*Crrshhh . . . thud . . .*

Sprawled on the trail, perhaps fifty rods from the way station, I looked around quickly. By now, the dim light of predawn lent everything a ghostly aura.

*Chiichiii . . . chchiichii . . .* An enormous grossjay stared down from the overhead branch at the interloper stretched out on the trail.

On this side of Bremarlyn, the snow did not seem to have been quite so heavy, and the temperature was markedly warmer. Not enough that I could do without cloak and gloves, but enough that I was comfortable in what I wore.

Sitting up slowly, I continued to look around. I did not stand. My knees felt like water, and I had a splitting headache.

Even the idea of trying to call up that contradictory mental intersection made me wince. Right now, that was for emergency travel.

*Chichiii . . . chchiiichi . . .*

No other recent footprints marked the mix of loose dirt and drifted snow, and the grossjay's scolding seemed more of a greeting.

The Long Wall trail was more of a summer path, anyway.

Finally, I gathered my feet under me and lurched upright in the dawn. And, after a time, I managed to stagger to the way station.

The latch was rusty, but functional. I scrambled until I found an old wooden bar and slid it into place. Then I looked around in the dimness.

Some little light filtered in from the cracks in the wooden shutters that covered the unglassed window. My feet left tracks in the thin layer of dust that blanketed everything.

Inside were two benches and a table, all of rough wood polished only by time and summer usage. But the bench was as welcome as any soft chair anywhere. Off came the pack, and out came the food. I was so hungry I was drooling. A growl from my guts reminded me not to gulp it down whole. Beginning with a dried chyst, I chewed each bit thoroughly.

With the first mouthful, my shakes began to abate. After I finished the chyst and a chunk of tough but welcome jerky, interspersed with several sips from the small water bottle Allyson had packed, the headache began to lift.

Clearly, my out-of-time or out-of-place travel took energy, lots of it, and I had started out with an empty stomach.

Sitting there in the way station, I tried to call up the black curtain and the contradictory intersection. While I could bring them into mental focus, the effort set off another headache. The warning was sufficient, and I relaxed and started in on a dried pearapple.

After that, I studied the way station. Four log walls, one with a shuttered window, and one with a heavy door. The roof was not raised, but angled. The log wall which had the door was lower than the back wall, and three timbers, each a handspan wide, ran from front to back. The angle also provided the overhang for the unrailed front porch I had ignored during my staggering entrance.

Just the summer before, mother and I had sat there, watching the rain come down.

"Not many people come here any more, Sammis," she had said. "We're not the physical people I . . . we once were."

She had always looked younger than she was, just as I did. On the way up the trail, someone had noted that it was nice to see a brother and sister on such friendly terms. I was too embarrassed to make the correction, and she had just smiled an amused smile.

Yet I knew she was older than my father. That's what the marriage book had shown.

In the early winter dawn, I dropped back from that memory, cut as if by a knife at the thought that I might never see either my mother or father again.

I carefully rewrapped the food, leaving out one last piece of jerky, and replaced the remainder in my pack. As I chewed, I tried to sort out everything that had happened in the last few days.

First, someone or something had attacked the Con-Federation forces on Mithrada and apparently destroyed the planet-forming stations and most of the spacecraft—if the rumors were correct. At least some of the orbital power stations were damaged or destroyed. Nothing was being broadcast from Inequital and from the west. A detachment of ConFed Marines had burned my family's ancestral home. Strange storms and weather had struck Bremarlyn and perhaps much of Westra. Yet there were no strange aircraft, no battles nearby, and no other military forces.

Last of all, somehow, I was learning to travel, or slide out of places and into places, and that travel took as much effort as playing a whole centreslot game, maybe more.

What was I going to do? I had some theoretical knowledge, a little skill with woodworking tools. Small for my age, if stronger than many a head taller, and looking even younger than my size—I couldn't pass as a casual laborer. Not with my gentry talk and uncalloused hands. Or as an orphan of sorts. The gentry didn't abandon children—ever. There were too few.

I didn't have an answer, but I couldn't stay in the woods for too long. And I had no idea how I would be able to find my parents—or what had happened to them without having the same thing happen to me.

For the moment, the problems had to subside with the waves of exhaustion that swept over me. I staggered to my feet and pushed one of the two benches around the table and got both of them side by side. With the pack as a pillow and my cloak as a blanket, I went to sleep. Without a single dream, for the first time in days.

# XIV.

ON THE CONSOLE screen in the laboratory a map appeared, one illustrating the outline of a continent in relief. In addition to the greens and browns depicting different elevations were traceries of red dashed lines. All the dashed lines either began or terminated at the same point near the center of the continent.

The researcher in blue sitting before the screen tapped in a series of commands, and the map vanished, replaced by a chart resembling a star map. She touched the controls, and a three-dimensional version of the star chart appeared. In the center was a red dot, and a handful of red dashed lines curved outward from the red dot. Most ended with a circled black star.

With a frown, the researcher touched the keyboard again. The star map vanished, replaced in turn by a chart listing names, with four columns of entries after each name.

A black star preceded the majority of the names, and those the researcher ignored as she studied in turn the entries following each unstarred name.

Occasionally, she sighed, and the noise echoed in the dimness.

Once the console flickered, as did the power panel lights on the monitoring equipment arrayed around a bare raised platform to her right. The platform stood in roughly the middle of the laboratory, surrounded at equidistant points by four consoles with screens.

Only the console occupied by the lone researcher was functioning.

The researcher glanced at the screen before her, then at the series of inked designs she had added on one side of the hard copy of the report beside the keyboard.

Again, the lights flickered, then failed, plunging the room into darkness and wiping the screen blank.

Sighing once more, the researcher waited, as if to see whether the power would return.

*Wheep.*

With the return of the lights, the screen relit, but displayed only a featureless blue.

The woman touched several keys, and the screen went

black. She took a deep breath, then lifted the thin report that lay on the flat space to the right of the screen and slid it into the drawer in the console under the screen, shaking her head as she did so. Her sandy blond hair flared slightly with the movement, then bounced as she rose fluidly from the chair, and walked toward the bare platform in the middle of the laboratory.

*Click.* Her fingers turned off the monitoring equipment on the right hand side of the platform.

When all the power light panels were dark, she stepped upon the platform and looked around, taking another deep breath, as if attempting a plunge into icy cold water.

With a sad smile, she vanished.

The room remained unpowered, but waiting.

Outside, the emergency etheline generator coughed, and the single set of lights illuminating the console where she had been seated flickered.

The researcher reappeared on the platform, smiling but shaking her head.

Droplets of water cascaded from her onto the platform. Her blue tunic and trousers were soaked, and the thin fabric clung to her like a second skin, outlining a slightly curved and youthful figure.

The lights flickered one last time and went out, leaving the windowless laboratory in near-total darkness, as the emergency generator coughed on the last drops of etheline.

The researcher walked surefootedly toward the doorway, leaving behind a trail of damp footprints that had already begun to fade as she slipped from the laboratory.

# XV.

THE LONG WALL Trail ended nearly five kays from the outskirts of Herfidian, itself a good twenty kays east of Bremarlyn by the Eastern Highway. None of the way stations had offered anything but shelter.

While shelter was indeed welcome amid the continuing strange alternation of snow and ice rain and sunlight and crisp fall afternoons, food was my biggest problem. Water was available from the cascades and the brooks, for the temperature never dropped far enough to freeze more than skim ice over running water. The abrupt changes in temperature had spoiled most of the wild fruits and berries. I had found one blue chyst in a copse of trees near the second way station. The blues are terribly bitter, but nearly a dozen were clear and edible.

I ate one on the spot and put the others in my pack, hoping to save what dried food was left as long as possible.

Rabbits were plentiful, and curious. But I had no way to kill them at a distance, and didn't seem to be able to stalk them. More important, I still didn't like the thought of killing them. Even at home, I'd never been a big mcateater. Neither had mother, and my father had teased her about it, saying that it was the secret to her youthfulness.

From the ridge line part of the trail, I had noticed some other strange changes. In places, huge circles appeared to have been cut out of the forest, and nothing remained but a fine dust. Those places seemed to be near the Eastern Highway, some distance from the trail, and the only things that were left standing were natural hills or the heavy foundation stones of barns or buildings.

It looked like the work of an enemy, because the destruction appeared to be just in or around the inhabited places. But who was this unseen enemy?

While I wasn't about to find out in the hills, trudging along the Long Wall Trail toward the east, I also wasn't in a hurry to make myself visible. What I could have used was a bath or a shower. Despite the earlier snows and sleet, the air was still dusty, so much so that I often found myself sneezing as I made my way eastward.

When I finally stood by the stone marker—the one that said "Long Wall Trail, in memory of Kenth, last Duke of Ronwic"—that signified the end or the beginning of the trail, depending on which way you were going, I still had no real idea what I would do. I couldn't live in the woods, and I had no living relatives—except a second cousin of my father's that I had met exactly once who lived somewhere in Inequital.

The sky was overcast, and the strange dark cloud pillars continued to dominate the western sky, in the general area of Inequital, although the capital itself was farther than I could have seen. A light mist was falling. The air was mostly warm, although the occasional strange cold gusts still accompanied the warmer mist. The dirt of the trail below me was unmarked, sheltered by a double row of overhanging firs. Behind the firs were the usual mix of Westron trees, most of the leafy ones well toward losing their summer foliage and having but scraggly winter leaves.

The marker sat about a hundred rods above the Eastern Highway. Why the trail ended near no town was a mystery to me, but I had never asked. All I knew was that I had another five kays to walk, and that I was getting hungry, and that I wanted a bath.

The last seemed most unlikely. Food was probable, one way or another, and walking was certain for now. I didn't dare waste the energy on place-sliding, not unless I was faced with an emergency, or worse.

Before I headed toward the highway, I unstrapped my

pack and set it on top of the flat stone marker, unfastened it, and removed the last blue chyst. After three days, even the blue ones didn't taste too bad. I needed some energy, and otherwise there were only a few sticks of jerky and two small chunks of cheese left. Those I wanted to save.

Allyson had done well, but like all good things her provisions were about to end. When I finished the chyst, nibbled all the way down to the hard seed, I tossed it into the deep brush to my right.

*Swwiiissshh.*

A grossjay swooped after it, almost catching the seed before it struck the ground. Times had apparently been hard for the birds as well. Grossjays were not known for their fondness for chyst seeds.

I pulled the pack back on, shrugging my shoulders to try to relieve the stiffness that seemed permanent. Then I started down the trail, staying on the short grass on the side, avoiding the slippery combination of dirt and mud in the middle.

The line of firs ended halfway to the highway, and I pulled up short, staying in their shade, as I could hear the rumble of a vehicle in the distance. Instead of walking along the road, stupid in any case, I kept under the overhang of the trees, where I stumbled every so often. While most of the trees were light-leaved for winter, between the mist and the evergreens, I wasn't as exposed as I would be closer to the road, and I could hide quickly. The idea of hiding and skulking around bothered me, but being picked up by the ConFeds would have bothered me a lot more—especially since I didn't know why they were after my family . . . and presumably me.

After about a kay, the rumbling increased in pitch, and I dropped behind a pine, waiting.

Over the hill from the west they came, clear even from a distance. First came a steamer, black, with a flag on the front bumper. The flag was the ConFed banner. Then there were two open steam freighters, carrying full loads covered with tarps. Last came an armored steamer, the kind with the composite ceramic plates and a turret gun. The armored steamer was wreathed in vapor as it rattled along.

In my whole life, I had never seen such a detachment on the Eastern Highway, not near Bremarlyn, so far from Eastron, even father from the Northern Isles—although that conflict had been over even before my father was born.

So I crouched in a hollow behind the pine and waited for them to pass out of sight. The wait wasn't all loss, though. In looking around, I saw what might have been a stunted pearapple, behind the firs to my left, toward Herfidian. As I waited, watching, I marked the pearapple location and studied the steamer as it hum-hissed past my pine tree, less than five rods away. Double-tired and totally enclosed, that black steamer was easily twice the size of my father's official steamer. The black finish was wearing thin and beginning to show the reddish ceramic beneath, and the faded purple stripe along the side, across both doors, was also heavily scratched.

I could feel the ground vibrate as the rest of the road convoy neared. The dull gray freighters looked newer, but still battered. Unlike the steamer, their cabs were open, and one had the windscreen folded down. Both were heavy-laden, with what appeared to be machines under the tarps. An armed ConFed stood in the guard booth at each corner of the cargo bay of each freighter. Eight armed ConFeds—in the center of Westron, thousands of kays from the old borders. And they weren't looking bored. I shrank down further behind the pine as the freighters neared. The guards had weapons out and kept scanning the roadside.

How anyone would catch them I couldn't imagine. All four were travelling nearly as fast as a normal runabout.

But someone had, clearly, because one of the armored guard booths on the first freighter had projectile holes in it and a dull reddish smear on the shattered composite underneath.

I decided not to move as the freighters passed, waiting for the laboring armored steamer to come into my now-restricted view.

The gray double plates were scratched, some of the scratches almost bleeding with red as the ceramic composite beneath showed through. The turret had a steel shield around the gun port. An armored steamer with some steel—that was something else. Steel wasn't that easy to come by any more.

The acrid odor of old steam, old oil, and hot rubber permeated the area as the armed steamer rumbled past. It was the three-axle type, with shields over the double tires, and the gun in the top turret kept swiveling from point to point, although thankfully not in my direction.

I stayed in the hollow behind the pine until the ConFed vehicles had disappeared over another low hill, and until the sound and vibration were gone as well. The bitter smell of abused machinery remained.

I recalled the pearapple. Before I checked out the possibility of fruit, I made my way deeper into the brush, and relieved myself. Seeing the ConFed convoy had created a sudden urge for such relief.

Then I pushed through the thickets of dead summer brush to the tree. Although the birds and weather had taken a toll, I found two partly good fruits. Using the old knife Allyson had left me, I cut away the rotten parts and ate the rest right there.

After wiping the knife clean on some dried grass, and then on the hem edge of my cloak, and doing the same with sticky fingers, I made my way back to the edge of the highway and resumed hiking toward Herfidian.

As I neared the top of a low hill, perhaps the third after the place where I had encountered the convoy, something seemed wrong. My steps slowed, ears alert, eyes looking for a wisp of steam in the air. Sniff . . . sniff—even trying to detect a hint of the scent of oil and steam.

Only the sound of a grossjay broke the stillness as I edged forward.

I shook my head as I saw the emptiness that began just below the crest of the hill. Nothing but a few huge boulders rose out of the circular expanse of dust. It was though a giant lumberman had taken an axe and swung it at ground level in a circle, and then burned everything to dust— except the dust was a fine brownish powder, not gray or black like ashes, and there was no smell of burning. I thought I remembered the place . . . before . . . a water station with the old inn maintained more out of sentiment than anything else. My father had claimed the inn still served one of the better evening meals in the Bremarlyn area.

Where the inn and its outbuildings had stood were only buried lumps, foundation stones covered with shifting dust. The old high firs were gone, as was the steep-pitched barn that dated back to the time of wagons and beasts.

*". . . cccuh . . . cuhh . . . CHEW . . ."* Once the fine dust got into my nose, I couldn't stop sneezing until my eyes were thoroughly running and my shoulders hurt from the violence of the sneezes. Had anyone been around, I would have been helpless.

Finally, I gathered myself together, just short of the dusty wasteland that seemed to stretch nearly a kay before me. Only the tracks of ConFed convoy through the thinner cover over the road itself marred the dust, so light that it seemed to shift with even the slightest breath of air.

How the steamers had made it through I wasn't certain, but there was no way I was going to survive the sneezes and convulsions that each step would generate. Going around the edge would add another kay to the distance to Herfidian—assuming Herfidian was still there and not a dusty wasteland. Assuming I did not run into the ConFed Marines.

I sat down on a fallen log for a moment to think, to think and to recover from my sneezing attack.

Something had destroyed the inn, something that had left only dust, and that something seemed to strike populated areas. I had seen the circular spaces from the trail, though none were actually out in the woods. But the presence of the ConFeds meant that some outposts had survived.

Shrugging, I got up. There wasn't that much choice. So I began to struggle along the edge of the destruction. The trees and brush closest to the actual destruction looked more as if they had been winter-killed than burned, but would extreme cold have the same effect as fire and create an ash-like dust?

By the time I regained the road, or the sheltered edge under the firs that bordered the highway, indeed had bordered all the highways, the afternoon was nearly gone. And I had no handy way-stations in which to shelter myself. So I kept putting one foot in front of the other.

Twice more the rumble of freighters pushed me out of sight—once into the ditch and once behind a thicket. These freighters were also guarded by ConFed Marines bearing nasty looks and nastier weapons.

As the day waned into twilight, and as I neared the top of each hill, I edged over carefully, afraid of what I might find.

Herfidian was in more of a valley, cut by the Oligar River, as I recalled, and the trade section was the part closest to Bremarlyn.

*Had* been the closest to Bremarlyn. The same circle of destruction was evident on the western side of the river. The eastern side looked untouched by that destruction, but I could see the shanties and tents and smell the open fires from more than a kay away.

Some order prevailed. The road had been swept clear of dust, or used enough to keep it mostly clear. That, and there was some sort of gate guarding the old stone bridge that crossed the Oligar. In the early evening light, I could see someone lighting a set of torches there. A soldier of some sort, for the outline of the weapon on his back was clear.

Soldiers and more soldiers!

If I walked down the road, the soldiers would have me, and some might know who I was. But with the river to the south and the swamps to the north . . .

So I retreated into the bushes and relieved myself again. After that, I found a grassy spot behind a tree, out of sight of the road. Once my pack was off, out came the last chunk of cheese and several fractured pieces of jerky. I chewed them slowly, savoring the last taste of each.

I curled up, just to rest—and woke to another set of rumbling wheels. Not that it could have been long, but the lights of the steamers against the thicket and trunks made me squirm even flatter to the ground until all three were past and rumbling down to the guarded bridge.

I thought about the place-sliding. Could I use it to at least get past the bridge?

That wouldn't be a problem, but I'd have to be careful where I ended up. The old Herfidian had been a worn-out trade town, dying bit by bit, and the enemy's destruction of the western part had probably just hastened the inevitable. Off in the older eastern part had been the metalworks where the smiths had built the land steamers and freighters, using the river mills for power.

Supposedly, Jerz Davniads' grandfather had made his fortune by developing a strain of oilseed plants from which etheline was distilled. Idly, I first wondered what had happened to the great oilseed plantations of the north, then briefly wished I had an etheline heater. But wishing was

not about to deliver me a heater, and the soldiers below
would spot the light anyway.

I sighed and put on my pack. Then, sitting in the hollow
behind a fir trunk, partly sheltered from the evening wind
that still bore the bitter cold-burnt odor of enemy destruction, I tried to call up the red-blue-gold-black crossroads
of my mind. This time, surprisingly, I could summon the
image easily, and with almost no effort I dropped behind
the black curtain of no-time.

East Herfidian was no longer just metalworking, but an
armed camp. Combat-ready ConFeds patrolled the streets.
The metalworkers were busy now, apparently repairing
military equipment. Seeing from behind the curtain was a
strain, and East Herfidian did not appeal to me.

What about further east, toward Jillriko, or Halfprince?

I let my mind carry my seemingly disembodied self
farther east, farther from Bremarlyn, farther from Inequital. The Eastern Highway itself seemed more permanent,
as if it stretched through time, than the trees or buildings.

Half of Jillriko was gone, and the town looked nearly
deserted.

Halfprince also looked empty.

Beyond Halfprince were the marshes, the damps, where
the Faiyren River emerged from several creeks and the
marshes before twisting downward and back to Jillriko.

Hot springs intertwined with the creeks, and a mist often covered the small valleys, especially in winter.

My view from behind the black curtain began to flicker,
and I could tell that I was running out of time. The damps
looked more hospitable than two deserted towns and one
ConFed camp. So I looked for a clearing . . . or something . . .

—and dropped heavily into mushy grass anchored in
mud.

With the darkness spinning around me, I took a deep
breath. My eyes cleared, although the bushes were dark

shapes against the darker shadows of the trees. The mud and grass underfoot comprised a shadow carpet whose different elements could be felt, but not seen.

*Chhhiccciiii.*

The sound of the grossjay reassured me as I squished toward drier ground, just looking for a place to sit down.

The odors of mud, swamp, rotting wood and plants filled my head, almost with a jolt compared to the cold no-sense feeling that accompanied my undertime travel.

My boots were holding up well to the mud, tramping, and wet, but the clothing looked more like a shapeless working outfit than the sharp-creased dress uniform that I had worn to the Academy on a morning not that long ago.

As I eased my way from the muddy grass up onto a hillock, the stillness made me edgy. Silence meant people, and the kind of people that went to the damps were not the kind I wanted to meet in the dark. As if I had any choice about it.

My vision began to spin again, and I sat down on the ground, next to a spindly fir. My attempt to rest was too late, and I could feel the darkness sweep over me, even darker than the oncoming night.

# XVI.

"WHERE'D HE COME from?"

"Steps start in the middle of the grass . . ."

"Must be the Enemy."

At first I thought the voices were from a dream, but I could feel my back and shoulders aching, and I wanted to shiver in the cold. Besides, it was clearly light. Had I slept through the night?

Where was I? Then I remembered my attempt to avoid the ConFeds at Herfidian . . . the damps. I was lying somewhere in the damps, recovering from an excess of my mental sliding from place to place. My head was splitting. Even the faint light of dawn was hard on my closed eyes.

"Too young for them, and he's human. One of the spacers said They had four arms and were like giants. That's what Lyron said."

"Damned witch, then."

"Pretty young for that."

"Witches always look young."

"Ever seen a witch?"

Slitting my eyes, I tried to see who was discussing me so coldly, as if I were not even there.

"He's waking up!"

"Open your eyes, boy—slow-like, and keep your hands in the clear."

I did exactly as I was told.

Two bearded men and a woman stood there. They all had long hair. One of the men had crossbow aimed at my midsection. A crossbow—for Verlyt's sake.

"Looks old, but it works, faster than you could blink your eyes and disappear." That was the woman. Her hair was dirtier than the shapeless man's jumpsuit she wore, and it looked like it had been dragged through most of the mud of the damps.

The stench that came from the three made the odor of rotting vegetation smell clean.

"Why you here?" Neither man was more than a shade taller that I was, but the one with the dirty white beard had shoulders like an ancient smith's, and his voice rumbled.

"Trying to avoid the ConFeds."

"The ConFeds? Near here?" The two men exchanged glances.

"Not that near. They've taken over Herfidian, and they're sending armed steamers along all the roads."

"Why would they do that?" Her voice was sharp, almost shrill, and I could see that her teeth were rotten. That proved she was not just lower class, but maybe criminal as well.

I stretched, slowly, still watching the man with the crossbow, and eased into a more comfortable sitting position. My head throbbed with each movement, and my stomach heaved.

"You sick?" asked the woman.

"No. Hungry. Tired. Damned little sleep, and less food."

"Where's your family, boy? Those clothes cost some."

"Gone. Dead . . . I think . . . Enemy . . . while I was coming home from school . . ."

"No other kin?" This came from the younger man, the first time he had spoken.

"A cousin in Inequital."

"Why'd you leave home? What town?"

"The Marines were burning and looting . . ."

Again, the three exchanged worried looks.

"What town?" snapped the woman.

"Bremarlyn . . ." I didn't know about the burning and looting, but they shouldn't have, either.

"Far way to come on foot . . ."

"He didn't come on foot! Damned witch." That was the older man, who kept the crossbow steady on me.

I just sat there, head throbbing, without enough energy to move, trying to keep from puking my empty guts out.

"He's no witch," concluded the woman, "or not much of one. Good witch could have disappeared twice by now."

"What?"

"How?"

"You took your eyes off him twice. That's all it takes, just an eye-blink." She stared at me. "So do you help us, or does Vran kill you, and we turn you into a couple of days' rations?"

I shrugged, knowing that the sweat was beading up on my forehead. "Rather help you, given the choice."

"For now, boy, you got the choice. Hold out on us, and you won't wake some fine morning. My name's Sylvie. That's Vran. And that's Weasel. It's not his name, but he hasn't told us his real name, and we don't ask."

"Sammis," I volunteered.

"Sam will do."

I hated Sam, but now wasn't the time to be choosy. "Fine. Can I stand up?"

"No. You stand up that green, and you'll rip your guts out." From beneath her shapeless garments, she pulled a brown shape and extended it. "It's tough, but your teeth are young."

Tough wasn't the word for the morsel of travel bread, and it had flecks of mold which I brushed away. But after the second bite, my headache lost its edge, and my stomach began to quiet.

"Slower . . ." commanded Sylvie. "You want to lose that, too?"

I obliged her, even though Vran had lowered the crossbow. The small piece of bread would make me feel better, but it wasn't about to provide enough energy for me to leave the company of the three, one way or another. Feeling the looseness of my trousers, I was beginning to realize that my unusual travel took energy, a lot of energy. And I didn't have any. So I chewed, very slowly and very carefully.

My headache subsided to a dull ache, and my guts postponed any further protests.

"Up," grunted Vran.

I eased myself to my feet, still feeling weak.

"What's in the pack?"

"Not much."

"Good to carry forage, boy," said Sylvie.

I didn't like the way she looked at me, or the way she

said "boy," as if there were something more implied. I shrugged. "Where to?"

"That way." Vran gestured with the crossbow toward a gradual slope up from where we stood, not that anything in the damps was particularly far above the marshlands.

With one slow step after another, my guts and head still filled with a dull ache, my feet found their way up a narrow path that was all but invisible.

In time, I stood beside a lean-to sheltered by an ancient boulder and an interwoven black thorn thicket. The limbs composing the frame of the lean-to were a mixture of smoothed, dark and ancient wood, and greener partly leaved branches clearly added later to something that had been abandoned until recently.

"Not much, but hard to find. Out of the winds, even the big ones, boy. Not that I wouldn't mind a bit more warmth on a cold night."

I shivered.

"Sylvie . . . the kid's hungry and cold, and you're treating him like raw meat." The man called Weasel spoke for the first time, and his tone was more cultured than that of the other two. His voice was harder, though.

"Jealous now, Weasel?"

Weasel snorted.

"Then take him with you, and find us something to eat."

I sat down on a fallen and half-rotten log and waited to see what they would say. While the hunger pangs in my stomach had lessened, the light-headedness persisted.

"He's in no shape to go far . . ."

"You won't either," rumbled Vran through his tangled and dirty white beard. He lifted the crossbow, then let it drop.

The man called Weasel looked calmly at Vran. "You rely on weapons too much." Then, without waiting for a reaction, his eyes fixed on me. "And you, young man, have clearly never been exposed to real danger. Not until recently. Can you stand?"

"I think so."

"Then stand, and let us see what forage we can find."

I took a deep breath, letting it out slowly, and eased to my feet. The light-headedness was replaced with a subdued headache, and my stomach growled.

"Let's go."

I let my steps follow Weasel's. Before we had edged our way back along the narrow path and through the swamp firs, I could see the reason for his name. Athletic as I had been at school, I felt like an ox trundling after him. His footsteps were silent, while each step of mine sounded with hisses and crackles.

We wound down toward the marsh itself. There the swamp grasses surrounded an expanse of open water.

Weasel looked back, studied me, and motioned for us to stop. "Verlyt-damned idea for you to be on your feet."

I agreed, but saying so wasn't going to do me much good. So I didn't.

Weasel rummaged through his shapeless jacket. "Catch."

It was a battered but almost ripe and unspoiled chyst.

"Just eat it slowly. Little bites. Real little bites."

I nodded and took one bite. Weasel watched. Almost as soon as I had swallowed the first bite, I could feel the headache lifting. My stomach growled.

Weasel nodded. "Hypoglycemic."

"What?"

"Blood sugar. Too low, and you don't function. Probably runs in . . . your family." He grinned a nasty grin. "But that will be our little secret, won't it, young man?"

"If you say so. I don't think I have much choice at this point." So far as I could see, I had no skills, not like a tradesman or apprentice. I couldn't use my place-diving ability without regular meals, and I had no way to leave the damps without food.

"You don't. Vran would like to use that crossbow on you."

I couldn't help shivering.

"It's not that bad. Vran . . . he just wants to show who's boss."

I took another small bite of the chyst.

"You look like you could take another step or two. Watch how I put my feet down, and try to do the same. You're not as noisy as Vran, but anyone could still hear you coming, and you don't carry a crossbow like him. Try to keep your head down more."

Attempting to emulate his footsteps, I followed as we skirted the highest swamp grass in a round-about trip toward the northern end of the marsh. Every once in a while, I took another small bite of the chyst.

Weasel had to wait for me more than once, but he never said anything, just turned and went on once I caught up. Finally we came to a spot where the barely perceptible trail vanished. He nodded at me, then walked straight toward the marsh.

I shrugged and followed, trying to find the firm footing Weasel used. I was successful in gnawing the chyst right down to the seeds, but not in always finding firm footing.

*Squuuushhh.*

Weasel turned and glared.

I held up my hands apologetically.

He shook his head sadly and turned, brushing through the shoulder-high grass so quietly that he sounded like the faintest of breezes. I sounded like a winter storm.

He was easing a woven basket-like structure from the waters of an inlet off the main part of the small lake in the center of the marsh. Inside were several objects.

Up came a second basket box, also with several creatures inside.

Weasel pulled a worn sack from his belt and emptied each basket in turn.

Both baskets went back into the water.

"There's actually enough for all of us tonight."

"Enough what?" I kept my voice low.

"Crayfish."

"Crayfish?"

"Sort of like freshwater lobsters."

I knew about both lobsters and crayfish. I just wasn't certain how hungry I was. Then my stomach growled, and I remembered that I had eaten the chyst, bite by bite, down to the seeds.

"Still hungry, Sam?"

I nodded reluctantly.

Weasel looked around, then started back along a different route.

I couldn't see the new route either, and I was beginning to sweat under the heavy cloak as even the damps warmed up in the midday.

Abruptly, Weasel stopped. At first, nothing caught my eye, but in the midst of the swamp grass was a greenish cactuslike plant. I watched as he bared a bulbous greenish-brown root and sliced a chunk out of it, splitting the chunk in two. The inside was whitish.

"Here."

"What is it?" I took the slimy chunk of root.

"Kind of swamp lily, but the root's mostly starch. Tastes like sawdust, but it's good for you." He used his knife to cut a small chunk and put it in his mouth. Even his lips puckered a bit. "Didn't say it tasted good, Sam. I said it was good for you."

I used my knife to cut a small chunk of the waxy white root. I looked at it. My stomach growled. I looked at it again, and my stomach growled again. So I ate it.

The swamp lily tasted like waxy sawdust, except I would have preferred the sawdust. And each piece seemed to swell as I chewed it. I had to make a special effort to swallow each bit. But it all stayed down, and my stomach stopped growling.

"Enough. Let's get back before Vran gets upset and starts looking for a reason to use that crossbow."

I had almost—almost—forgotten the broad-shouldered old man with the ancient weapon.

We were nearly halfway back to the hidden campsite before I realized that my headache was gone and that my stomach had stopped growling, but I still wasn't about to recommend swamp lily root except in dire circumstances.

# XVII.

*Chirrriiitt . . . chirrriittt!*

I jumped, almost throwing my cloak aside. The tree toad had seemed to be calling from inside my ear. The sudden movement reminded me how stiff I was from sleeping on the ground. Not quite the ground itself— Weasel had shown me how to put fan leaves over fir branches to keep the worst of the dampness from me, but I still felt cold and wet as I slowly eased into a sitting position, pulling the cloak around me, trying to get ready for the morning routine.

Get up; follow Weasel, either through the swamp or along the ravines, and forage anything that was edible. Then bring it back, rest, and repeat the process in the afternoon. How long had it gone on? It seemed like forever, but probably the ordeal had lasted less than an eight-day.

I glanced over at the lean-to. That was where Sylvie lay. She had caught the damp fever first. Huddled into a ball in a corner of the lean-to, her shakes rustled the branches.

*Hsst . . . hsst, hsst, hsst . . . hsst . . . hsst, hsst, hsst . . .*

The pattern was nearly regular, almost like rain, except that it rarely rained in the damps. Instead there was an almost continual ground fog and mist that kept everything damp, all the time. That's why every damper's hutch, lean-to, or cave, for the few who had staked out the bouldered area at the southern end of the marshes, had a fire pit—as much to ward off the damp as for cooking or heat itself. Not that there was a lot to cook over those fires, especially not with the heavy unseasonable rains and the cold winds that had rotted and stripped even the winter fruits and those that were usually edible for months after harvest, like the chysts.

Weasel was nowhere in sight, but had clearly been up earlier, since a wisp of smoke rose from the fire pit.

Whatever else the Enemy had done, they had ruined the weather and the crops, even the fruit trees.

As on so many days, the wind whistled though the swamp firs, and the mists and clouds were so heavy that not even the outline of the sun was visible. I shivered, either from the chill, although my cloak, bedraggled as it had become, was certainly warm enough, or from watching Sylvie suffer.

*Thwapppp.* The slap caught me unaware and dropped me into the muddy grass.

"Damned witch . . . you did it to her . . ."

Vran was waving his crossbow. Luckily for me, it was not cocked. But that wouldn't take him long, not with his muscles, especially fueled by anger.

Although I gathered my feet under me, I remained on the ground, wondering if I would have to dive away from him in plain sight and reveal that I was in fact one of those damned witches.

"More than likely, she got it from cleaning one of those swamp rats." Weasel's voice was matter-of-fact. The long knife he normally carried in his belt was out, and he was testing the edge with his thumb.

"Sticking up for the witch again?"

"Hardly. Witches don't ever get sick. So if she caught it from him, he's not a witch."

While I was seldom sick, I'd had my share of illnesses growing up. All I could figure was that since I had not been ill in the damps, where everyone seemed to suffer, that Weasel thought I never was sick.

"Hunnnh?" Vran missed Weasel's subtleties. "Swamp rats?"

"Never mind. We'll get some of that marsh rice. Boil it, and maybe Sylvie can eat that."

Vran looked at the huddled heap that was Sylvie.

The cold morning wind whistled again, and I stifled a shiver, looking from Vran to Weasel and back again.

Weasel turned without saying another word. Vran kept looking at Sylvie. I scrambled to my feet, grabbed my pack, and followed Weasel.

Once past the swamp firs shielding the camp, he did not head north for the marsh, but instead southward toward the main branch of the creek that eventually became the Faiyren River. Before long we were nearing the cut the river had worn through the low hills that bordered the swamps.

I could hear the low rushing roar of the river where it billowed from the damps into the small canyon that turned into Faiyren Gorge. We were nearing the pond above the rapids where, sometimes, Weasel had been able to catch migrating wetbill ducks with his snares.

He stopped and turned to face me. "What are you going to do, Sam?"

I knew what he meant. Sylvie was going to die. Vran would blame me, and nothing would stop him from using the crossbow. Nothing.

I shrugged, aware somehow in that post-dawn chill that

another change was coming. "Have to leave, I guess. Unless you have some other ideas."

"If you really had to, you could have left days ago."

I didn't answer that question. I shrugged again. "Nowhere to go. Can't do much of anything, except read and write and do some math. That doesn't count for much right now."

For the first time, Weasel looked puzzled. "What do you mean? There are always jobs for clerks, or bookkeepers."

"Not now. Stores are all looted, those that are left. ConFed Marines control the roads. They've burned out most of the gentry, at least between Bremarlyn and here."

Weasel's mouth dropped open. "Why didn't you say anything about that?"

"I thought you knew."

"Sam, nobody in the damps knows *anything*. We knew there was an Enemy, and some damage to the capital, and a few soldiers on the road. Other than that . . ." He spat on the ground. "This is the place where you go when there's no place else to go, when even the back alleys of Horesard and West Inequital won't take you in."

"Between the Enemy and the looters, most of the towns are gone," I added. "Not much food, either."

Weasel wasn't looking at me at all. He just kept shaking his head. Finally, he grinned. "The main road is downhill and about two kays southwest. If you head east, you should reach Esterly in about a day. You'd better get moving."

I shook my head.

"Long story, Sam. Vran will be after both of us before too long. One way or another, there's a chance I'm clear. You say Bremarlyn's gone?"

I nodded.

"You know the prosecutor there?"

I did, but I wasn't about to admit that he was my father. "No."

"You don't lie well, Sam. Is he still alive?"

I shrugged. "I don't think so, but I really don't know." That was the truth. I had no idea whether my father had died in the blaze. Somehow, I doubted that my mother had, but I felt I'd never know that for sure.

"That's good enough for me." He began to move, even more quickly, down the trail. Then he stopped, and turned, his voice low. "And you'd better keep moving or Vran will catch up to you."

Within moments, Weasel was out of sight.

I kept moving, until I was a good half kay downhill from the top of the rapids. The rumbling *swush* of the water at the top had subsided to a continuous rush. I slowed at the sight of a patch of wild onions and a flowering thorn. The thorn seed pods weren't bad, and the onions actually tasted pretty good. You couldn't eat too many at once, though.

I eased some onions out of the damp soil, wiped off one and ate it, forcing myself to chew it slowly and in small bites. I stashed a handful in my pack, and then began to pick some thorn seed pods. Maybe a half dozen were edible. They went into the pack. Nearby was a blue chyst tree, but it had been stripped clean, either by the squirrel rats or the weather or by some other damper.

Weasel, even in the days I had followed him, had shown me a few more things to put into my stomach, besides the obvious fruits. I'd even gained back some little bit of the weight I'd lost. My mother would have laughed, I knew, at my coming to eat whatever was generally edible. My father would have nodded sagely.

As I thought of them, I had trouble focusing on the tree or on narrow path, partly because I was shaking, and partly because the tears got in the way. But I couldn't stop any longer, not with Vran and his crossbow lurking behind me. So I straightened up and lurched down the path Weasel had started on—the one that led to Esterly.

Every once in a while I looked back over my shoulder, but I could see no one behind me.

"Freeze, damp rat!" The harsh voice had the ring of authority.

I froze, then slowly let my still-watering eyes turn toward the voice.

The Confed Marine uniform caught my eye first, then the shredder, which was aimed at my midsection.

From the noises on the other side of the trail, I could tell at least two others were in hiding. The grin on the marine's face dared me to run, as if he were just itching to turn the shredder on me.

Except for my eyes, I stayed frozen. If I had to, I could probably dive under the now and escape. But what good would that do—except deplete my fragile energy reserves?

"That's a very good swamp rat. Because you're so good at taking orders, we just might have a use for you, damper."

I didn't say a word.

"Don't you want to know, damper?" He paused, and his voice turned nastier. "Answer me!"

"Yes, sir."

"A polite damper. That I can hardly believe. Not too old, either. Might even be some hope for you, boy. Why are you here?"

"Looters . . . got my family, relatives . . . Enemy got the rest . . ."

"Well, you're in real luck today, boy." He stepped back, still keeping the shredder aimed at my midsection. "Just head straight down that trail to our camp. I'll be right behind you; so don't get any ideas."

I followed his instructions to the letter.

Another half kay further, at the base of the slope, were several tents and a portable stockade. Two ConFeds with shredders guarded the fence. Inside were three other men, two youngsters like me, and a bearded man who was about the same age as the forcer who had caught me.

"Just keep moving, swamp rat. Stop right by the gate there. And don't move."

A faint sickly odor drifted toward me, but it disappeared before I could place it. It was clear they wanted me alive, for whatever purpose, and that it would be easier to escape from the stockade later than attempt anything immediately.

"Got another one for you."

"Did you check him?"

"No. Thought you could do it."

One of the guards set his shredder aside, while the other two continued to keep theirs leveled at me.

"Let's see the pack."

I handed it over.

"Ugghhh . . ." He didn't even bother to empty out the onions and seed pods, or the partly moldy chyst in the bottom. Half of it was good. He dropped the pack by the gate. "We'll take the hatchet and the knife. Set them on the ground."

I did that as well, wondering why they bothered with the knife. A knife wasn't much against a shredder.

"You can keep the pack. Now get in there, and don't cause any trouble. Or you end up like that." He gestured toward what I thought was a stump, before I saw the flies and coagulated blood around the shredded flesh and bone.

". . . uuuggghh . . ." Somehow, I managed not to lose what little was in my stomach, but the remaining bitterness burned my throat.

"That's what happens if you don't follow orders, swamp rat."

*Click.*

He had opened the gate while I was trying not to retch my guts out. None of the other three men even looked toward the gate, although all three stared momentarily at me.

Three steps, and I was inside, clutching my tattered pack.

*Clunk.*

"No talking. Any of you."

I sat down and ate the good half of the chyst and another onion. After one look at what I was eating, the three others lost interest. Had I still been at the Academy, I probably would have lost interest too. If not all my appetite and then some. But I needed to keep up what strength I had left, and enough energy for one emergency escape.

After finishing off the onion, I stretched out and used the pack to cushion my head. Besides food, I needed sleep. My days in the damps had been short on both. The ConFeds weren't out catching people for an execution, which meant they had something in mind. At the worst it was probably slave labor—I hoped.

# XVIII.

"NONE OF YOU are good enough to be ConFed Marines! You're not even good enough to be second-rate Secos! You aren't even . . ."

Too tired to ignore the thin man with the hard eyes, I listened to him. Standing at attention with me were the others that the ConFeds had rounded up, perhaps a score in all. Hard bread and water—that was all we had been given, but with my onions, it hadn't been too bad. The hard-eyed man and the others had rousted us from the stockade at dawn and marched us into town. Esterly, I think, though I had never been that far east of Bremarlyn before.

". . . but you're all we've got left, and it's my job to

turn you into an imitation of the real thing. If you live long enough, you just might make second-rate Marines, and that's twice as good as anything else!''

Why we needed more military personnel after the unseen enemy had turned so much of Westron into dust was still unclear to me. The forcer in front of the ranks kept screaming about the need for discipline and the need for order, but most of the others would have scuttled back into the damps right then—except for the five ConFeds with their shredders and hard eyes ranging up and down our ranks.

So we listened and hoped for some bread, perhaps a ground apple.

''We can beat the Enemy—if we work at it! But looters, scroungers and drifters don't work. You aren't looters, scroungers, and drifters anymore. You're the property of the ConFed Marines, and you're going back to work, and you're going to like it.''

Somehow I still couldn't see how more ConFeds in uniform, toting shredders, taking food at weapon-point, and screaming at people, were going to defeat the Enemy. Hell, the Enemy thought we were ants—if the Enemy bothered to think about us at all.

''Any questions?''

I had plenty. All they'd get me was trouble. So my mouth stayed shut.

''No brains here? Any questions? Last chance for questions, you dullards.''

''Why . . . why us?'' stammered a thin youngster. ''What good will more soldiers do?''

''Step forward, boy!'' screamed the ConFed Forcer. His olive-colored singlesuit was dusty. So was his blotchy face, where it wasn't dirt-streaked with sweat.

The kid who asked the question didn't move.

''Bring him forward!''

One guard handed his shredder to another and walked

up to the pale-faced youth. Yanked him right out of line and threw him into the mud in the middle of the road. The dust that seemed everywhere and the intermittent and unpredictable rains left mud puddles everywhere, even on the once-spotless Imperial highways.

The youngster, not even as old as I was, lay there for a second, then scrambled up and started to run.

*Scrut . . . scrut . . . scrut . . . scrut . . .*

The shredders were as terrible as they sounded. He didn't even look like chopped meat—more like blood pudding sprayed on the ground. If I'd had anything in my stomach, it couldn't have stayed there.

"That's the first rule, you worthless bodies. *No* questions. Not ever."

At least three of my companions were retching their guts out, but the forcer let them without even commenting. He just waited for them to finish. My stomach stayed knotted tight.

"Now line up. Double file. Double file, two abreast. Move it, and make an effort to keep in step. An effort, damn you! Move it! Move it!"

I held my guts together, somehow, and I marched westward, toward the ConFed complex at Herfidian, back toward Bremarlyn, toward Inequital.

We all marched, and kept marching. We marched past the way-station that had been Halfprince. We marched through the ford at Jillriko—the bridge and half the town, the western half, had been an enemy target—and through the empty eastern half of Jillriko, trying not to inhale too much of the ever-present dust, trying to breathe through cloth scarves that the ConFeds handed out.

The Faiyren River ran brown, like the creeks, and you could see an occasional trout floating belly up. The carp survived, I guess. They survived everything.

# XIX.

COMPARED TO THE days I had spent in the damps, the physical side of learning how to be a ConFed Marine wasn't bad.

A subforcer rousted us out before dawn, into the near-freezing cold, and put us through calisthenics. Then we went through hand-to-hand combat instruction and drills. After that came a field breakfast, generally hard bread, some sort of meat, dried fruit, and, if you were really hungry, grain porridge.

After breakfast, another group took us to a makeshift rifle range. Obviously, the rifle range part bothered the forcers. They had at least four subforcers behind us with shredders, and we were given single shot projectile rifles.

The bullets were little more than case-hardened clay, not real penetrating ceramic. But they made sure we expended all the ammunition on the range. Then we took the rifles back to some equally makeshift workshops, where we practiced cleaning the weapons. After we finished cleaning, we were led out on a five-to-ten kay quickstep march with full packs.

Halfway through the march came a quick midday ration, which we each had carried in our packs. The second half of the march always had some sort of obstacle—usually difficult, sometimes impossible. But we all tried. The forcers did nothing if you gave everything. One or two slackers didn't. We never saw them again.

After we returned to the camp—or temporary base, as it was called by the head marine, a burly man a good two heads taller than me who titled himself the Colonel-General Odin Thor—we listened to lectures. Some were on weapons. Some were on the situation in Westra, and how the Marines were rebuilding the government structure after the wide-scale destruction by the Enemy.

Unlike many of the other unwilling recruits, I listened, trying to sort out fact and propaganda. You could even ask a question, provided the questions were factual and not questioning the ConFeds.

After the first few days, I could have left at any time, since I knew where the stores were kept and since I had regained the weight I had lost. But the same problem remained. Although some ConFeds had clearly fired my house, and probably killed my father, where would I go?

So I stayed, getting into better physical shape than I had even for athletics at the Academy, learning whatever I could, and keeping my mouth shut. I lost track of the days, blurring as they did into the onset of spring, but kept working, especially at the hand-to-hand. When I left the Marines, I'd need it.

At night, sometimes when I wasn't totally exhausted, I practiced my sliding from place to place. No longer did the dives under the ''now'' leave me exhausted, but my appetite remained enormous.

"Never saw a small man pack away so much," observed Selioman. Probably in his late twenties, old style, he had been in the converted stables that served as barracks when we had arrived.

"I guess I'm just nervous."

"Nervous? Ha! You never get upset, Sammis. You look like you're waiting for something to happen."

I shrugged.

"Look. The forcers all see it. Don't you wonder why one is always watching you?"

"I hadn't thought about it."

"They have. If you weren't so young, Carlis would have made an example out of you early."

"Carlis?"

"The mean one, with the scar. He looks like he's ready to kill you when he sees you practicing out in the yard."

"Do you think I should give it up?" I had discovered that one of the younger subforcers, Henriod, had been a martial arts master, and I had asked him for some pointers in my limited free time. That had grown into a series of pre-dinner workouts. He could still best me, most times, but I was beginning to be able to use my undertime sight to anticipate most of his actions, and before long, I sus- pected, I would be able to beat him. Not that I could afford to let him, or Carlis, know that, especially if what Selio- man had said was true.

"I wouldn't. Everyone, including the Colonel-General, has heard how hard you work. Quitting would give Carlis an advantage and a way to say you were slacking off."

"Hmmmm."

But I thought about it, and took another tack, easing up on the martial arts and getting another subforcer named Weldin to instruct me on some of the marines' gear other than weapons. In practice, that meant the steamers and their accessory equipment. It also meant I spent most of my free time helping him and the maintenance crew clean the big beasts. Every few days, it seemed another one arrived from somewhere, often with a different paint scheme, sometimes even bearing the name of a hauling organization. Weldin and his crew, all men, cleaned them, repaired the ceramic and glass fiber panels where neces- sary, and repainted each with the ConFed logo and colors. I generally got the grubbiest work available for the limited time I was free.

Still . . . what else was I going to do?

For one thing, I started eavesdropping, dropping out of sight for a few moments, from the few places where I wouldn't be bothered, like the outhouse the recruits had to use, to duck under the now and watch.

If I got the right angle, though I couldn't hear from the undertime, I could see, and I was beginning to read lips.

The most interesting place to watch was the room where the Colonel-General had his maps of Westron. Often he and the experienced squads were gone for days at a time. The maps told some of the stories, because when he returned the one that showed the areas controlled by the ConFeds was usually changed, showing an ever-expanding wave of blue moving back toward Inequital.

About the time it was clear that winter would indeed end, they split us up and put us in with the regular squads—scouts, troopers, or maintenance. Because of my work with Weldin and the fact that I clearly had some mechanical ability, I was one of two who went to maintenance. Selioman was the other.

Henriod told me he was sorry I hadn't been selected for scouts, but both Carlis and Weldin had overruled him. I knew why.

Another batch of involuntary recruits arrived, and, then, Weldin called us together in the big barn that housed our dozen or so steamers.

"Now that we have recovered the capital area from the Enemy, the Colonel-General and the scouts have retaken the ConFed base near Mount Persnol, the closest Imperial installation remaining to the capital." Weldin cleared his throat, then smiled. "We will begin transferring our operations there to reinforce a special project which offers us a chance to take the fight to the Enemy."

I kept my face blank. A special project to take the fight to the Enemy? An enemy that apparently could appear at will in much the same way as I could? The strategy maps and my limited undertime lip-reading had shown me nothing of that, but with a shade more free time in the evening, and the ability to walk the grounds behind the outlying wired fences, I had more opportunity to duck undertime. I resolved to use it as soon as possible.

# XX.

THE CONVOY—THREE freighters, the lead steamer, and the repaired armored steamer—waited, chuffing, on the stones of the Eastern Highway bridge at Herfidian, to head through the bridge gates toward the muddied and lifeless hillside. I was on the first freighter, lined up directly behind the lead steamer. Even in the winter-weight uniform, I wanted to shiver.

Watery gray light from a barely risen sun spilled through high and hazy clouds. In the chill morning air, both breath and the exhausts from the steamers cast thin white plumes from the bridge out across the marshes and the knee-deep water of the river.

In addition to the head gate guard, two squads of Marines were turned out, weapons unlimbered, behind the stone ramps flanking the bridge gate—one squad on each side, both squads facing the muddy slope where the highway angled until it reached the brush and trees beyond the enemy's circle of destruction.

"Still clear, sir."

The subforcer received the report without a word and nodded to the gate guard, who in turn began cranking the heavy bridge gate open. That gate had been something else in the time before destruction. Once mother had driven me, in that superb golden steamer of hers, to Jillriko, and the Herfidian bridge had been without gates then. The part of Herfidian west of the river had also existed then. Now there were marines and gates, and only half of the central town remained.

As we lurched forward through the gate, with one hand I clung to the support rail. The other clutched the telescope that came with the lookout's perch where I teetered.

My eyes strayed to the projectile rifle stowed in the holder next to me, ready for use. I hoped I wouldn't have to, but I recalled the holes and blood that had decorated the freighter I had seen from the roadside so many weeks before.

*Whufff . . . chufff . . . whufff . . .* With the slight coating of slippery mud dust on the highway stones, all the steamers began to strain once they reached the beginning of the incline.

*Ccccrrrruuunnnch . . .* Even with the freighter partway up the lower section of the hill, I could hear the sound of the bridge gate finally closing behind the armored steamer.

"Lookouts! Number one and four, rifles on standby. Two and three, cover the brush out there under the trees, out to the side."

Using my ability to slide out of the here and now to check the area from behind the non-time black curtain would have been safer scouting. It would also have revealed my secret and had me killed as one of the witches of Eastron. So I focused the scope out to my right, trying to see who or what might be hiding. One grossjay, patches of winter leaves on closed branches, and browned grasses flashed through the lens at me. We weren't supposed to use the scopes until *after* we spotted something. The restricted vision told me why.

*Wuhhufff . . . chufff . . . skreee . . .* The freighter lurched again as the driver overcorrected on one wheel.

*Clunk!* My head connected with the hard wooden railing of the sentry box.

"Verlyt!"

"Quiet!" snapped Carlis from beneath.

As I swallowed the blood from my just-bitten tongue, I steadied myself with my left hand and stowed the telescope.

*Whuuuufff . . . chuuufff . . . whuff . . .* In approaching the crest of the hill, the freighter lurched forward, pon-

derously, swaying side-to-side with each lurch. And with
each lurch and each sway, my stomach lurched also.

*Whhuuufff . . . skreee . . . whufff . . . chufff . . .*

By now I could smell old oil and bitter steam. Had I
eaten that morning, that food would already have found
its way elsewhere.

"Don't eat if you've got freighter lookout," Selioman
had told me. "If you puke on the freighter, Carliss'll make
you clean all the puke out of the belts and gears—after you
get there. It took Marin a week."

So I had stuffed some hard bread and an unripe but
squishy pearapple into my pack for later. The cooks had
just nodded.

*Whhhuuufff . . . whufff . . . whuff.* The lurching died
down, and the engine sound steadied as we crested the hill
and reached the flatter part of the road heading to and
through Bremarlyn.

Swallowing hard, twice, I leaned out into the breeze,
trying to take in some fresh air. What I inhaled had no oil
scent, no steam, but the bitter odor of mold and dust, of
death and destruction.

"Bandit at quarter one!"

I swiveled to the left to track Rarden's call, but the tarp-
covered supplies blocked my view. Belatedly, I swung back
to scan the quarter three area, trying to see if we were
heading into an ambush.

Nothing moved except one gray bird on a a limb without
even winter leaves and a dark ground dog hole.

"Fire at will!" shouted Carlis.

I unstrapped the rifle, lifted it into the swivel, and released the bolt lock.

*Crump! Crump!* Rarden let fire. One of the ceramic
shells plowed up the ground not a dozen rods from the
freighter.

"Hold your fire!" Carlis sounded disgusted. "Did you
hit that ground dog, number one?"

"No, sir."

"Next time . . . never mind." Carlis waved the green flag from the cab to the freighters behind and to the bewildered lead steamer.

None of it made sense. Scattered bandits wouldn't attack an armed convoy with even one or two lookouts. And nothing, including spaceships and lasers, had been effective in stopping the enemy.

"Stow arms!"

After replacing the rifle, I studied trees, grass, holes in the ground, and occasional birds—usually grossjays.

By mid-morning, we were passing the site of the old inn, just flat mud and plastered dust, not quite covering the blackened and split foundation stones.

The one time I had eaten there on my birthday after leaving first childhood, father had ordered me a blue chyst tart as a special treat. So splendid—I had looked at it and looked at it, not really wanting to eat it.

"Go ahead," he had said.

Mother had smiled her mysterious smile.

So I had eaten it bite by bite, forcing the last bites into an unwilling stomach. While the tart had been tasty, I still wished I hadn't eaten it, and mother knew that.

"Magnificent, isn't it?" Father had mumbled with his mouth full of his own tart.

I swallowed as the freighter continued its lurching past another memory and another place destroyed, past the two stones that were all that remained of the best meal in the region, and past the inn that led back toward Bremarlyn itself.

Two tumbled piles of black sand and stone sat on a bare hillside, bare except for rock and mud, so bare I did not recognize the East Hill entry to Bremarlyn at first. Then, it may have been the angle, since I had never looked down on the gates to Bremarlyn—or what remained of them.

While the steamers were not the quietest of machines,

their hissings and chuffings were low enough and intermittent enough for me to hear the lack of other sounds.
The smell of ash, not dust, clogged the air, and the clouds
overhead seemed to thicken as the freighters whuffed up
and past the ruined stonework.

Peering from the lookout, I strained to see what had
befallen Bremarlyn. Blackened trunks and gray ashes dot-
ted the west side of East Hill, little enough remaining of
the town forest park.

The old Customs Port Building, dating from the early
days of the Compact, which had served as the local library
since the time of my great-grandfather, stood blackened,
roofless, its windows glaring blindly into the gray-hazed
noon. Of the two burned-out steamers in the side parking
area, little remained except the shattered ceramic tubing
trapped in charred and melted glass fiber panels.

Strangely, Bremarlyn had been spared total destruction
by the enemy weapons. Instead, it appeared as though
every dwelling had been torched . . . the more impressive
the building, the greater the damage.

As the freighters hissed downhill, storing energy in their
flywheels, my eyes searched for familiar places. Marshall
Getana's villa—flattened as if by an explosion. Salmarn
Hooste's estate—burned so thoroughly that the walls of the
old stables had collapsed inward.

While few non-gentry had lived in Bremarlyn, even the
more modest homes had not escaped the burnings. Havvy
Sarston's home had been levelled—all four rooms. The
same for Kryn Naerlta's cottage. And under the odor of
fire and ashes was a sickly stench that reflected the rest of
the corruption.

With a still-empty stomach, I managed to spit the bile
welling into my mouth clear of the steamer, half-choking,
half-retching the nothingness within.

Carlis ignored the lookouts, wearing as he did a strange
half-smile I feared I understood. By the time he looked

back up I had wrenched my guts back into semi-obedience and merely looked greenish.

At that moment, I wanted to choke him. I knew I could kill him at leisure—if I felt that way later. But I was sick, sick especially of pointless killing, and, scared as I was, sick of violence because of fear.

On the right as the convoy entered the central square was the meeting hall, now just four toppled walls and charred timbers. At least five steamers were buried under the rubble of the side wall, and the odds were that their owners were buried on the other side of the same wall.

So far as I could tell from my lookout's perch, swaying in the noontime haze and chill, not a structure in Bremarlyn had been left intact. Every one had suffered either fire or explosive damage, or both. Not a single wall stood above shoulder height.

The two big community power receptors stood untouched. But the beamed power receptor grids had been removed. Removed, not destroyed. The antenna bases stood untouched, but the grids themselves had been unbolted. Why? It didn't seem to make much sense, because the power satellites themselves had not functioned since the day I had left the Academy.

In the windless depression beyond the square where the Eastern Highway turned to run arrow-straight toward Inequital, the sick stench of death even turned the ranker sitting by Carlis greenish. Carlis kept smiling. I kept trying to keep from gagging, if only to avoid cleaning the steamer.

After a time, when all the steam vehicles had chuffed through the ashes, and the smells, and the memories, the convoy reached cleaner air and the emptiness and open meadows of the Great Valley that separated Bremarlyn from the capital.

My guts stopped trying to turn inside out, and Carlis stopped smiling and started barking commands again.

# XXI.

*Whufff . . . chufff . . . whuff, chufff, chufff . . .*

I kept looking toward the west, trying to see when I might be able to pick out the famed towers of Inequital.

No steam freighter guaranteed a smooth ride. Each crack in the stone pavement, each joint, translated into a jolt high above the road.

The closer the convoy tracked the Eastern Highway toward Inequital, the more destruction and the less life there were. Bremarlyn had been bad enough, with the Academy a still-smoking ruin and the western half where Kryrel and Hargin and Solbar and so many classmates had lived yet another welter of arson and explosive devastation.

As the afternoon began to fade, the steamers reached two low stone gates, heavily weathered and each standing in a pile of sand. The wind picked up, whistling slightly and coming from the west. I nearly gagged again, cold as the air was across my face, from the odor of destruction and mold.

Belatedly, I recognized where we were as the highway widened. The gates marked the edge of the Imperial Preserve, but there were no trees, no bushes, no flowers. Even beyond them, where the towers should have stood, there was only dust and ash and destruction.

My stomach had taken too many shocks. This time, as the scale of the destruction hit me, it only turned over once or twice in protest. At the same time, the total absurdity of the Colonel-General's plans seemed even more apparent. *We* were going to take the fight to an enemy that had leveled the largest city in our planet's history? An enemy that had done so without a casualty? An enemy we had no way of even finding?

"We'll be taking the road on the left at the crest of the next hill . . ." Carlis was telling the rating at the steamer's controls. ". . . leads toward Mount Persnol . . ."

I looked back toward the flattened low hills, still not believing that nothing remained of Inequital, nothing of the capital where my mother had disappeared.

The steamer lurched, jamming me into the side of the sentry box as it turned onto the narrower stone road that headed directly south toward the mountains. My mother had called them hills, comparing them most unfavorably to the Bardwalls of Eastron.

"The Bardwalls are mountains, Sammis," she had said. "Compared to them, most of the mountains of Westra are mere hills." Strangely, in retrospect, I had never asked how she knew. She knew so much, often revealed merely in passing, that it had never occurred to me to ask until I no longer could.

The wind began to pick up, colder than in the valley. By the time we reached the crest of the second hill, I had refastened all the clips on my parka, and there were traces of rime ice along the depressions beside the road.

The road, not quite wide enough for two big freighters to pass comfortably, looked older than the Eastern Highway, with actual ruts worn in the stone. How long that had taken I could not guess, but it meant that the road probably predated the Westron Monarchy and might have even been built when some Eastron Duke ruled the area.

Ahead, to the right, on my side, I could see a lump or pile of something near the crest of the third hill. Each hill was a little higher than the one before. The fences were still in good repair, untouched by the fires that had gutted the plantation houses and the freeholder's houses.

I focused the telescope on a lump off the shoulder of the road—a burned-out steamer, reduced to a heap of ceramic parts and tubing, and ashes from the now-burned frame. A non-military vehicle, without the metal framing of a ConFed or Security steamer.

When we were within a dozen rods, I saw the gaping holes in the tubing, holes that could only have come from military weapons. The rust was not as heavy as on the wrecks at Bremarlyn, and the ashes were still nearly black.

I glanced down at Carlis, who watched the way ahead as intently as the lookouts, and wondered if the steamer had been merely trying to escape the ConFeds. Since Carlis was not smiling, he hadn't had anything to do with it.

Not one of the ConFeds, including the other troopers, gave the wrecked steamer more than a passing glance. I saw a glint of metal, like a buckle or pin, in the ashes. Then we were past the wreck and heading downhill again.

The road was quiet, except for the sounds of the convoy. Not even a single grossjay appeared on the wooden fences or by the scattered evergreens. Nor did any ground squirrels poke their snouts from burrows. I didn't see any burrows, either.

With each hill came fewer fences, fields, and meadows—and more trees. Older and taller trees. With each hill, Carlis's lips clinched tighter. And the shadows got longer, and the wind colder.

And I got hungrier, my stomach tightening into a dull aching knot.

As the convoy neared the top of a particularly long hill, with the steamer protesting more than usual, I caught sight of some life. Short piles of logs were laid out in stacks beside the road. Tree stumps lined both sides of the old highway, as did piles of ashes, whipped by the gusty wind like snow, where the brush had been burned.

"Camp coming up!" Carlis half-bellowed.

I curled my feet in my boots, trying to keep them from getting too numb. With my luck, and because my guts had rebelled so much, I was facing an even longer wait, if Selioman had been correct. Even if I hadn't puked my guts all over the freighter, at least twice Carlis had seen me losing control.

That probably meant cleanup detail.

*Twheet! Twheet, twheet, twheet!* I jumped, banging my sore thigh against the sentry box from the piercing whistle.

"Slow down. Watch for the flag on the right. The entry road is narrow. Take it easy." Carlis was squinting into the twilight, leaning forward.

I saw the flag before he did. "Flag on the right, sir! About twenty rods up, sir!"

"Slow it down." Carlis ordered the rating.

The steamer slowed and lurched, and I banged up against the sentry box again.

The wind gusts had subsided to a steady moaning, and my breath was beginning to form frost clouds. Even with the extra space provided by the felling of the trees nearest the old highway, I felt hemmed in by the height of those remaining, many of which towered close to fifteen rods above the plateau. Most of the stumps were broader than I was tall.

Black oaks grow slowly. I remembered one which had stood in front of our house, less than two handspans thick. My father told me that he had planted it himself when he had been about my age.

After the turn the convoy was headed west again, along the narrower stones of the side road toward the almost totally faded orange glow of a sun that had set behind the mountain hills. Another kay before brought us to a stone wall. The stones were gray-black, and the old-fashioned parapets by the gate looked down on me a lot more than I looked down to the ground.

Just the area in front of the closed and timbered gate was illuminated by the yellow of the etheline lights. The guard stations and the walls were dark.

The freighter sounded its whistle again, and I jumped.

The big freighter lurched to a stop.

Outside the gate, a single sentry appeared. Several lights flashed along the parapets to indicate that there were more guards waiting. Still, I thought the whole exercise was stupid. A raiding party would try any place but the front gate.

The walls dated back before the Resurgence, probably to before the time of the Eastron occupation. I figured they were that old because of the thickness. While the secrets of powder and guncotton had survived the ups and downs of Queryan history, with each fall more metal had been lost, and the struggling Westron baronies could not afford to use iron or lead shells, not if they wanted other more pressing tools, like lathes and pumps and steam engines. Stone balls were fired from the few bombards that could be sledged from siege to siege. Thick walls tended to defeat the use of the bombards.

"Identify yourself!" demanded the guard wearing the purple uniform of a Security officer.

"ConFed detachment two, sent by Colonel-General Odin Thor. The password is 'Vanish.' " Carlis's voice was merely a half-bellow.

One of the lights on the wall played over Carlis and the rating at the freighter controls, then dropped down to illuminate the stone pavement leading to the gate.

*Creakkkk . . . urrummmbbblle . . .* The gate began to open. The seco vanished back into the wall.

"Follow the line of torches to the barracks," called another voice. "Someone will meet you there to guide you to the unloading docks and the maintenance facilities."

Carlis nodded and grunted. The rating began torquing up the engine pressure, and, by the time the gates were fully open, we were rolling toward the darkness on the other side.

Whatever the installation had been before, it was big. In the early evening darkness, I could not see where the walls ended, only that they continued north-south without reaching a corner or turning point within light or shadow distance.

"Keep it slow . . ." added Carlis.

The line of torches curved to the right. To the left ran another road or street. Both seemed to be lined with foundations of a series of buildings long since taken down. Buildings that had been substantial—if the stone foundations were any indication.

Once the freighter came to the bottom of the incline, the road and the line of torches ran straight to a long two-story stone building able to hold hundreds of troopers. A steamer runabout, with functioning headlamps, waited before the building.

"Welcome to the project." The voice came from the steamer, clear, penetrating, ironic, and distinctly feminine. A woman stood on the running board of the steamer next to the empty driver's seat.

Even in the dim light from the torches and the freighter controls I could see Carlis' surprise. The forcer said nothing.

"Follow me," added the woman, swinging into the steamer in a single fluid motion.

"Go ahead. Follow her," snapped Carlis.

The last glimpses of twilight had completely faded by the time we traversed another half kay of old stone roads and right angle turns.

The convoy finally chuffed to a halt behind another ancient stone structure.

"Download team!"

I winced, wondering if Carlis would add me to the unloading and cleanup party for my failures to keep my stomach totally in line, but he glanced at me, than glanced away. "Road sentries—dismissed! Report to Subforcer Henriod for quarters and grub assignments. Engineers! Report to Subforcer Weldin . . ."

Carlis's instructions went on and on, but I put the sentry

box in order, shouldered the projectile gun and climbed
down. My legs were shaky, and I was very careful with
the handholds and footholds. By the time my feet touched
the hard pavement stones, Carlis was barking more orders
to move the freighters to the unloading docks.

I retrieved my pack from the locker under the sentry
box. It felt like a load of stones.

"Road sentries. Answer up." Henroid's voice was loud,
but tired. "Rarden?"

"Here, sir!"

"Eltar?"

"Here, sir!"

"Sammis?"

"Here, sir!"

Henriod ran through a dozen names, then stopped, and
cleared his throat. "We have quarters in the barracks
building. On the second floor. Take any bunk you want in
the open area. The rooms with double or single bunks are
for officers, forcers, or subforcers.

"You'll have to walk back there. Stay in groups of three,
at least. Keep your weapons until Janth and I get there
with the locks for the armory. Late mess after unloading."
He looked over the sorry appearance we presented. "Dismissed."

Eltar, Farren, and I walked back together, following the
line of torches. The torches were attached to wooden piles
that had once held broadcast light bulbs. The bulbs and
their metal holders had been removed. After less than
twenty rods, my shoulders began to ache from the weight
of the light pack.

"Sammis?"

"Unnh?"

"You came from Bremarlyn . . . ?"

I didn't want to answer that one, but not answering
would have been worse. Just from Carlis' comments, I had
picked up on how little the ConFeds cared for the gentry.

"Um-hummm," I answered.

"Funny, you don't act that way," mused Eltar.

I shrugged. What could I say, really?

"You really gentry, Sammis?" asked Farren. He had a nose that made night-eagles look snub-nosed.

"It depends on how you figure it. My father was. My mother wasn't. I hope I got her common sense along with his name."

That got a chuckle from Farren.

"What's it like, being gentry?" asked Eltar.

*Terwittt, terwittt.* Some night bird punctuated Eltar's question.

I stumbled on a rough paving stone, although, between torches and stars, there was certainly enough light for me.

"I never thought of it that way," I finally answered. "I knew we had more than other people, but at . . . school there were sons of farmers, tradesmen, and mechanics. We lived in a large house, but many were larger. My father was from a long line of gentry, but my mother wasn't. She used to say that she didn't even know her own grandparents. Until everything fell apart, I never gave it much thought . . ." I cleared my throat. That was difficult because it was dry. "Why?"

"Why what?"

"Why did you ask?"

Eltar shrugged. "Always wanted to know. Mother died. Dad ran the store, and he always bowed to the gentry, and they dressed better, but they didn't look any smarter, and they didn't act any smarter. We were poor, and they barely seemed to notice us, except when the taxes were due or when the highway levies were demanded . . ."

". . . and when some young gentry lad showed up in a flashy steamer and made off with the pretty girls and dumped them back pregnant," added Farren.

I was tired, and there wasn't much else I could say. They were talking about things I'd never done or seen.

But, from what I'd overheard, they were the sort of things that had happened. I hadn't been old enough for that, and, besides, neither of my parents would have approved.

"You ever have a steamer?" asked Farren.

"No. Nor a girl," I admitted ruefully.

They both laughed, and by then we were walking up the last few rods to the barracks. Even Eltar, with all his size, kept shrugging his shoulders to keep the weight of his pack from stiffening his muscles.

# XXII.

THE LOW-SLUNG STEAMER runabout was back by the main entrance to the barracks, with a Seco guarding the purple machine. He carried a weapon I'd never seen before, a short-barreled gun not long enough to be a true projectile rifle nor short enough to be a handgun.

"Riot gun," observed Eltar quietly.

I must have looked puzzled.

"That's what the Secos used on the crowds at Wavertown."

"Wavertown?"

The three of us had stopped on the far side of the half-circle stone drive as we surveyed the Seco and the runabout. The security officer turned toward us, casually letting the weapon move in our direction.

"You didn't learn about Wavertown in school?" Farren's voice rose.

"No. What was Wavertown?"

"Wavertown was where the Secos killed 200 miners for refusing to work the deep seams."

"The deep seams?"

"You're hopeless, Sammis," sighed Farren. "Look. All the easy metal is gone. At Wavertown, there were deep seams of iron ore. You know, the stuff they make steel from? The seams were so deep that a lot of miners got sick from the heat and the fumes. Some of them died. The government said they died from drinking too much etheline. The Secos took over the mines. The miners refused to go back to the deep seams. The miners held a public meeting, and the Secos surrounded them and ordered them to the mines. The miners refused. The Secos shot them. Two hundred died, and close to a thousand were wounded.''

I shook my head. The Eastron Sympathy Revolt had been nothing like that. The southern miners had refused to support the war effort against Eastron and had sabotaged the mines so badly that they were never reopened. When the Secos had tried to stop the sabotage, the miners rose and tried to keep the troops from the mines until the destruction was complete.

''Look, Sammis. You're gentry. Or you were. Do you think your folks were going to tell you that they beat down freemen and miners? And what about Nepranza?''

''What about it?'' I asked softly. I'd never heard about it. ''That was a long time ago.''

''Nepranza was three-four years ago. What world were you in? Just because some minor lord got uppity when a few youngsters got too friendly with his daughters, the Secos murdered a dozen. Then they did have riots. The lord's girls were fine, they said, but a lot of the town's daughters weren't. They were dead, or wished they were.''

I just kept shaking my head. Did they think that the newspapers would have hushed up the kind of massacre that Farren said had taken place? Or the supposed events in Nepranza? My pack felt like it weighed as much as the steamer that waited by the barracks.

''Do you really believe that drek about natural choice of the gentry?'' Farren's voice was almost a shout.

The Seco was sneering openly as Eltar grabbed Farren's arm.

"Chill it, Farren. Sammis doesn't honestly know. Can't you see that?"

I wanted to slug them both—Eltar for being so damned condescending, and Farren for believing that all gentry had forked tongues and fangs. I didn't do either. I just walked away from them.

"Still gentry at heart . . ."

". . . just chill it . . . lost both parents . . . made it through ConFeds . . ."

Just as I drew up to the runabout, careful even in my rage to keep a good distance from the dark-haired Seco with the riot gun, he swung to back to face the barracks door, and stiffened.

"Valtar? Have any of the ConFeds arrived back here?" The woman who had greeted Carlis so efficiently stood full in the torch lights, glancing past the Seco toward Eltar and Farren, who were still mumbling about me. "Are those the first?"

I tried to keep my mouth shut as I studied the woman. She had sandy-blond hair that glinted in the light, and a figure that might almost have seemed boyish, with broad shoulders and narrow hips, until I saw her even narrower waist. Despite shoulders nearly as broad as mine and short hair cut square across the back of her neck, she was clearly feminine. Her face was almost elfin, except for the set of her jaw. I liked what I saw of her figure.

She reminded me of someone, but I was in no shape to remember who.

"Trooper." The words were directed at me.

"Yes, Colonel." I had no idea what she might be, but she radiated authority.

At my response, she smiled, a professional smile. Even so, the smile softened her expression momentarily, made her look years younger, close to my own age, before she wiped it away. She was attractive in a familiar sort of way, but that could have been because it had been so long since I had been around any real women. "We're a military project, Trooper, but not military. I'm Dr. Relorn." She studied me again. "How long before the rest of the troops arrive here?"

Her scrutiny left me feeling uneasy, as if she saw right through me.

"The other road scouts, about twelve in all, are on the way back. The unloading crews will be a while yet."

"You are?" she asked, the smile clearly gone.

"Sammis, ConFed maintenance, Doctor."

She frowned, then let the expression drop. "The barracks are yours. There's no power right now, but we should be able, now that you have some mechanics here, to get the standby steam generators on line within a day or two."

I would have liked to talk more, but Farren and Eltar were sauntering up the drive, and the Seco was positively scowling. So I inclined my head. "Thank you, Doctor. We appreciate it."

She nodded in return. "Good night." Again, her eyes seemed to look right through me. She smiled briefly, and it seemed for a moment as she and I were alone in front of the ancient stone barracks.

Then the smile was gone, and a doctor who acted like a Colonel stood there. Probably twice my age for all that she looked young when she smiled. She turned, and I shook my head.

"Did you see *that*?" Farren's voice grated on my nerves. "She talked to you?"

Eltar was shaking his head slowly, whether at me or Farren I couldn't tell.

"Just to say that the barracks were ours and that we'd have power once we could get the standby steam generators working."

"Must be an old Imperial staging base," mused Eltar.

"Not used for military, either," I added.

"Trying to change the subject, Sammis? Hunh?"

"From what?"

"That lady you were giving the eye."

I sighed. Farren was obnoxious. "She acted just like a ConFed Colonel, except she has her professional smile down better. And she acts like this is her base, not ours."

"Probably was . . ."

At that point, I didn't really care. Looking at the Colonel-doctor or whatever she was had been nice, but I didn't see much future in it. Besides, I was tired. My stomach hurt, and my head was close to spinning away on its own. "Let's find some bunks and then look for the mess."

"Good idea."

The doctor had been right. The barracks were ours. Completely. There wasn't a soul in the building. So we took three of the better bunks, ones with lockers built in underneath them.

The cold water was cold, and the hot water was luke-warm, indicating that something worked. I used liberal amounts of both to remove as much road dust, grime, and soot as possible. Even good steamers emitted some soot, and the ones that we had been using were in less than perfect condition.

By the time we had washed up, the rest of the road scouts had found their way into the barracks, followed by Janth and his locks for the armory.

"Let's have those weapons, now . . ."

I was more than glad to get rid of the projectile rifle, just wishing that he would hurry up and finish so that we could get something to eat. I felt as white as the ancient canvas mattress cover on my bunk.

"Field mess in being set up in the dining hall below. That's the big empty room at the back . . ." Janth went on, but I tuned it out, just waiting until we were dismissed to go eat.

After all, lack of food had landed me in the ConFeds, so to speak, and the ConFed organization's single greatest benefit to me had been the halfway square meals that allowed me to rebuild and maintain my strength.

"Sammis . . . just waiting to eat. Again . . ."

I tried to keep from smiling at the comments about my appetite, but I probably looked wolflike thinking about food. That was the way I felt.

"Dismissed."

I was second in line heading down the wide stone stairs toward the dining hall. Eltar liked to eat as much as I did. He was first. That was fine with me. Being first called too much attention to you, just like being gentry, or being an officer. Or a witch.

"Line up on the right! On the right!" Carlis' voice was unmistakable.

There was only one place to line up—on the right. So we did, with Eltar leading us on.

"Lukewarm field slop . . ."

"Boiled rat guts . . ."

". . . tasty rodent brains . . ."

The cooks were used to the comments, and the one who glared at us looked no different than usual as our boots echoed on the stone flooring.

Four long dusty tables had been dragged away from a stack on one side of the hall that must have held two dozen of the massive wooden trestles. The rest loomed there in the shadows cast by the field torches used in place of broadcast power globes or hard-wired lights.

The flickering light made the old building seem ancient, but its age wasn't my predominant concern as I shovelled a double helping onto the field tray.

. . . *grrrrr* . . . Both the light-headedness and my stomach were letting me know of my low energy state.

"You can eat that?" Farren sounded amused.

"He's a damper, Farren."

". . . cannibal type, you know, swamp rat eating swamp rat . . ."

I ignored Rarden's low-voiced comments and took two more slices of hard bread and one of the shriveled chysts that Eltar had spurned. Food was food, and, besides, the stuff we were getting was quite edible, if not exactly a gourmet's delight. My father had been the gourmet, not me. My mother had regarded food only as a necessity, not an end in itself.

I took the tray and sat down on one of the long benches across from Eltar. My light-headedness begin to disappear with the first bite, as did the tightness in my stomach, and I forced myself to eat slowly, methodically chewing each bite.

"That good, hunnnh?"

Again, I ignored Rarden.

"That good, swamp rat?"

"Rarden!" Even I looked up at Carlis' bellow. The subforcer was standing almost at the end of the trestle table.

Rarden blanched. "Yes, sir!"

"Show some brains. That swamp rat is twice as tough and four times as poisonous as you. He has a hide thicker than a rhinopod. But he isn't going to let you insult him forever, and there wouldn't be enough of you left to stuff into a mess kit. So do us both a favor and shut your trap."

Carlis' tone showed he didn't think much of either one of us—except as raw troop fodder. Still, it got Rarden off my back—temporarily.

I returned near-full attention to the field rations and broke the second slab of stale bread in two, taking one bite of the rehydrated and undefined meat and one bite of the heavy bread, one bite of the meat and one bite of the bread, alternating until I finished it all. I saved the chyst until last.

Everyone was gone—except Carlis—when I stood to take the field tray back.

"Swamp rat . . ."

"Yes, sir?"

"Still so very polite. Swamp rat . . . just stay polite and listen to orders, and everything will be just fine."

"Yes, sir."

"You're so polite, swamp rat. You never do anything wrong that you can help. Why don't I trust you?" Carlis was sitting by himself at the very end of the trestle.

"Sir?"

"I don't trust you, swamp rat. I never will. And don't forget it."

"I won't, sir."

"I know you won't, swamp rat." Carlis shook his head, and looked back at his own partly eaten rations. "I know you won't."

Since I appeared to be dismissed, I left to go back to the corner of the barracks I had staked out for some sleep. The next morning would be the typically early ConFed dawn.

# XXIII.

LIFE AT THE new base was an improvement over the temporary encampment at Herfidian, especially once Weldin had managed to get the steam generators going. He claimed that they hadn't really been used in over a century.

I pretty much kept my mouth shut and tried to learn all that I could. While I didn't know much about the systems, at least I could understand the manuals. By reading them and watching what was going on, I learned some practical engineering of sorts.

In walking around the old base—we were never told its name, and maybe that had been lost along with all the other destruction—I realized something else. Less than a handful of Secos had held the base against the riots and raids. Aside from the Secos there were the technicians and some scientists, and the most powerful, it seemed, was the woman who had greeted us—Dr. Relorn.

No one told me that, but it was clear enough. She had the only personal guard and steamer.

While I had my own ways of finding out what was going on, I didn't start sliding under the now and snooping until we'd been at the base for several days and I was both rested and well fed. By then a second group of ConFeds had arrived, and the cooks were actually preparing food a cut above field rations. Not much, since it was still another season until the harvest, assuming enough farmers had planted for there to be a harvest.

After dinner that night, I lingered and cadged thirds, watching Carlis shake his head sadly, and ate everything methodically. Then I walked back outside, heading away from the gate and along one of the old worn stone roads lined with foundations.

By the time I was half a kay from the barracks, twilight was fading into early evening. I knelt down by one of the stone steps leading upward to nothing and slipped under the now, sliding toward the technicians' buildings.

As I headed toward the "reserved" section of the base, a faint spray of lines appeared before me. "Before" isn't the right word, since you really see with your mind and not your eyes in the undertime, and the lines were more like a faint series of afterimages. But all of them radiated from a single point near the center of a large single-story building.

The timbered building was newer than the two stone

structures that flanked it. Age is easy enough to tell from the undertime. Older things seem solid. Newly built structures lack depth, and living things waver—just a bit for trees to quicksilver for birds and other fast-moving, fast-living creatures.

Following the lines backward, I found myself hovering undertime before a single operating console and an empty platform surrounded by other inactive equipment. At the console sat the doctor.

For reasons I could not explain, I slipped from the undertime behind her and watched, with her, silently, as the screen displayed its images.

A man wearing a bulky atmospheric or water diving suit clambered onto the platform, closed the suit's faceplate and vanished. The screen blanked, then displayed a woman, wearing a less extensive version of a self-contained breathing system, who also vanished.

The console shed the only light in the shadowed laboratory, a room the size of a small equipment bunker that smelled of ozone and electronics.

"So you were in charge of the project?" I asked into the stillness.

She turned slowly in the swivel chair, as if she had known all along that I had been there. "So far as I know, I still am."

"You knew I was watching."

She nodded, but remained in the swivel, apparently relaxed, even though a stranger had appeared from nowhere.

"You can dive yourself. Otherwise you would have been more surprised."

For a moment, neither one of us moved.

All the heavy equipment dated from before the time the monarchy had limited the use of metals to bare essentials. That it had not been removed indicated either how important the project had been, how well-connected the doctor had been—or both.

Dr. Relorn continued to look at me, evenly, as though she were cataloguing my every feature.

I looked back—seeing a slender, sandy-haired woman with a narrow, elfin face and eyes that penetrated even through the gloom of the room. Her physical condition had to be good, just from her posture and aura.

"So why aren't you on the screen tapes?"

"I don't dive."

The words were matter-of-fact, but I could hear an edge to her voice.

"Why not?" I was surprised that I had the nerve to ask her.

"Do you know what you are?" Her reply came back to me almost as I finished challenging her.

"Me? I'm just a ConFed trooper, trying to get by."

"That's just not true, and you know it. You're gentry, and an heir of Eastron, if not—"

"No!" The last thing I needed was some idiot doctor blabbing about witches of Eastron. "Look, Doctor. I don't know where you've spent the last year or so, but every freeman and woman in Westron would be just as happy to cut the throat of any stray gentry youth they happened to run across—assuming there are any left outside of your fortress retreat here."

She didn't look convinced, but the anger was gone as quickly as it had appeared, and she looked younger, more relaxed. That her hair was as light as mine, if not lighter, was clear even in the dim light around us.

A muted roll of evening thunder punctuated the momentary silence.

"Why do they call you the swamp rat?"

I wondered how she had discovered that, but she was changing the subject all too successfully. "You never answered my question. Why didn't you try diving under the now?"

"Diving under the now?" Her eyebrows furrowed for a moment.

I could smell my own sweat, that and the odor of metal and oil and machinery. I shrugged. "That's what I call it."

"Why are you with the ConFeds?"

"Don't you understand yet?" I forced myself to be calm. She could probably fry me if she chose. That or put me on the run again. I sighed.

She smiled, and I found myself smiling in return. Her warmth was contagious, and the smile was genuine. Don't ask me how I knew. I knew.

"Why don't you sit down and explain?"

Looking around, I didn't really see anywhere to sit.

"My quarters are down the hall. It's convenient." She gestured vaguely behind her and to my left. "Was convenient," she added absently.

"Might not be convenient to me. If I'm not back in the barracks by last call, it's going to be difficult to explain."

"That's a while, isn't it?" Her voice was businesslike, as the smile faded.

"Enough for a short explanation, I guess."

After touching the console and blanking the screen, she stood in the near darkness, turned, and walked toward the door. The doctor walked the distance without a light. So did I.

*Click.*

A single lamp lit a low table and not much else. It flickered briefly, the way all the electric appliances did every now and again, the result of the imperfect system cobbled together with the backup generators. On each side of the table was a comfortable armchair.

"Would you like something to drink?"

"Water, please."

"Just water?"

"Just water." I sat down in the left-hand chair and

waited. I could smell the faintest of fragrances in the air, just the hint of trilia.

"Here you are."

I took the narrow crystal goblet from her. "No servants?"

"No servants."

"Now, Dr. Relorn, you owe me an answer, and I owe you an explanation." I took a sip from the goblet, an antique similar to my father's Dyleraan, that probably dated back to the establishment of Westron.

"An answer." She leaned forward on the edge of the chair, somehow perched there, yet relaxed. "The question was why I did not attempt to dive, as you put it, 'under the now,' when I am the one running the project." She sat back slightly, as if waiting even as she spoke. "The simple answer is that mental travel—"

"Call it diving," I interrupted. I took another sip of the cold spring water that tasted as fresh as the water I had once scooped from the streams along the Long Wall trail.

"—mental travel, or diving, is blind. You don't know where you're going, and I never liked traveling blind."

"But it's not. Besides, anywhere on Query—"

"We weren't looking on Query—"

My mouth dropped open for two reasons. First, I realized that other witches or divers might not really be able to see their destination. And second, Dr. Relorn was telling me that I could have travelled to other planets.

"—and the diving ability can take you forward or backward in time, but not in our solar system."

"But didn't you know you could travel from point to point on Query?"

"What for? You know the strength of the witch legends. Besides, what's the point of getting hurt in traveling a few thousand rods? If there's danger, the reward ought to worth something. That's why we worked on it as an alternative to mechanical means of stellar travel—"

"Stellar? To other stars?"

"What do you think I've been talking about, Trooper Sammis?"

I shook my head slowly. The stars? I'd never thought about the stars. How much energy would that take?

"But the physical energy?" I couldn't help asking.

She nodded. "That's another reason. Mental travel takes less energy away from Query and even less outside our solar system. It takes more energy to travel from Westron to Eastron than to travel back centuries in the Serianese systems—even wearing one of those pressure suits you saw."

"Pressure suit?" Everything she said raised more questions.

"Other planets don't necessarily have breathable atmospheres."

I knew that. I just hadn't put the pieces together. After sipping, or gulping, from the goblet, I remembered she still hadn't answered my original question.

"But why didn't you dive?"

"I tried several short . . . dives . . . but I . . ." She shook her head. "I told you. I don't like doing things blind."

I could sense the fear. Her fear, and I knew. So I stood up and grasped her hands, trying not to think too much myself. Her fingertips were warm and ice-cold at the same time. "Now. Just let your mind relax. We're going to . . . Bremarlyn." I tried not to think about how supple and warm her hands were in mine.

"Bremarlyn . . . ?"

"No questions."

Diving under the now with the doctor was hard, especially at first, like dragging an anvil with my fingertips, afraid that I would drop her any instant. Once under the now, her fear washed over me like a black tide, almost blinding me and blotting my directional senses.

Fear—that was her blinder. I tried to push a sense of reassurance at her, a feeling of warmth. Her fear receded from me, but I could still detect it cloaking her, blinding her to our position in the undertime. For all that, she *burned* in the undertime, swirling with those sparks I had noted earlier.

Even in forcing myself to ignore both her blackness and her brightness, I carried us to Bremarlyn, to an orchard I had known well. From the undertime, the area where I wanted to emerge appeared empty. In the starlight, the blackened walls of the old house gaped. Around us, the chyst tree leaves whispered in the summer night's breeze.

"Look," I said softly, remembering that I held the doctor's hands, before releasing them abruptly. "You did it. You know I couldn't have carried you. *You* did it."

"Are you always this direct?" Her voice was husky, yet amused.

"No . . . I've never dared. But . . ." I shrugged. With the scent of suddenly ripening chyst around me, I didn't feel like explaining. The last time I had stood in the orchard had been to see the fires which had been the beginning of the end for the old way of life on Query.

The doctor didn't say anything as she studied the ruined home, the overgrown grounds, and the neglected orchard.

"You could see," I added to break the silence, "and you will see . . ."

"Was that you?"

I knew what she meant. "Yes. Your fear blocks your sight from the undertime. You were so afraid to begin with that I had trouble seeing."

"You can see out from the undertime?"

I nodded. "Most of the time. You should be able to."

"Was this your home?"

"My family's. My father's, really. The ConFeds fired it at the beginning of the looting and burnings. All of Bremarlyn looks like this—or worse."

The breeze ruffled my hair and brought the bitterish scent of unripe chyst to us.

"We need to get back." I still worried about Carlis and the ConFeds.

"You're worried about your superiors? When you could leave the ConFeds any time?" Her tone was puzzled.

"You still don't understand, do you? Diving takes energy, plenty of it. And rest. When can you get either, when every freeman, every ConFed, is chasing you?"

The doctor raised her eyebrows. Despite the dimness of the starlight, the gesture was clear.

"Look. The ConFeds fired my house, killed my father. Every gentry house from Inequital to beyond the damps has been destroyed, either by the Enemy or by the ConFeds or someone else. The Enemy and the looters destroyed most of the crops." I could tell she still didn't understand.

"What would you have done? A student, one set of clothes, no money, no valuables, no food, no friends . . . you know that a single word is enough to show you're gentry. No skills to speak of and no family.

"I needed someplace to learn, to be fed, and to stop running." I shook my head in exasperation. "Let's go . . ."

"Where?"

"Back to your quarters."

*Chicchichhii* . . .

I smiled at the grossjay, then grabbed her hands, and dived. Grossjays never called at night.

"The woman . . ."

For an instant I had all I could do to force us under the now, but then the doctor relaxed just enough. Shadows converged on where we had stood, but not quickly enough. The troopers, ConFeds not under Colonel-General Odin Thor's command, for I would have known their postings, were after either me or the doctor . . . the woman. But why?

With the blurriness of the view and my own lightheadedness. I had all I could do to concentrate on getting us back to the doctor's quarters at the base.

On breakout, I released her hands, sat down, and took a long gulp of water from the goblet I had set on the table just minutes before.

"You are rather amazing, Sammis."

I ignored the comment. I was still thinking about the strange ConFeds.

"Would you like something to eat, or do you have time?"

"Yes. There's still a little time before I should go."

As she turned, I studied her. Certainly her figure was youthful, far more youthful than her age—like my mother. Her face was unlined, also like my mother. Was that for whom the troops had been waiting? But why? Was she still alive, or did someone just think so?

I took the last mouthful of water from the heavy goblet, tilting it back to get the last drops. The incipient headache began to fade.

"Will these help?" She offered a tray of biscuits.

"Perfect." I ate two at a single bite while she refilled the goblet. Another gulp, and another pair of biscuits, and another slow mouthful of water, and I began to feel normal.

"You ought to practice diving," I told her.

She reseated herself on the edge of the other chair, after setting the tray on the front center of the table. "I still can't see."

"Can you tell red and blue, black and gold?"

"Yes, but nothing outside the undertime."

"I couldn't at first, either. It takes practice."

"Yes. Perhaps we'll have time to discuss that. Later."

Her voice bore a faint huskiness, a trace of an accent or strangeness that seemed to come and go.

I still didn't know what she had been doing—except that her project had something to do with using the diving ability to visit other planets—even planets in other stellar systems. Why was Odin Thor interested? And what were the other ConFeds doing?

"You've been hiding your ability." Her tone was back to businesslike.

"Wouldn't you?"

"Under the circumstances, it's understandable. But I may be able to help you."

"Oh?"

"What if I tested for the ability? The Colonel-General wants to use mental travel to rebuild Westron."

"How?" To say I was skeptical would have been an understatement. "It's hard enough to carry yourself from point to point."

"He doesn't know, but he's the type to grab for a useful tool even when he doesn't know how it could be helpful."

"Would you test all the ConFeds?"

"Why not? It might help remove some of the stigma. And I might find a few others."

That was a thought worth pursuing . . . if diving could be sanctified by science . . .

"Oh . . . time for me to go."

"Good-bye." That was all she said, as if someone dropping by from nowhere and disappearing back into nowhere were the most commonplace of occurrences.

Good-bye. All my questions—almost all of them—remained unanswered.

# XXIV.

"SAMMIS?"

At the time, I was trying to persuade an antique lathe to shave the tiniest edge of metal from one side of an unused generator casing in order to use it as a replacement for the original, which had shattered because Rarden had knocked a sledge into it. Some of the old metal was so brittle that it took scarcely more than a sharp blow to fragment it.

So much of the equipment Weldin had retrieved from the sealed underground bunkers was in that state. Some of it had to have been pre-disaster—perhaps two millennia old.

"Sammis!"

"Just a moment." I finally got the guide set the way I wanted and edged the casing into place. For someone who knew how to handle machinery, the adjustments would have been simple. I didn't, and they weren't.

One more pass, and the casing would fit the larger rotor shaft with adequate clearance, probably more than adequate clearance.

*Rrrrrrrr. . . .*

I cut the power to the lathe and turned. Weldin was standing there.

"Yes, sir."

"After you get that fitted, get washed up, put on a clean uniform, and report to Janth."

"Janth?" Nothing I did had anything to do with the assistant armorer.

"All of you rankers are being tested by that doctor who used to run the base. The Colonel-General has ordered it."

"Yes, sir."

I must not have looked too happy.

Weldin added, "Don't worry. If the doctor selects you, it will probably mean easier duty."

"Yes, sir."

"Just finish up, and do it, Sammis. Colonel-General's orders."

There I was, being rescued from the ConFeds, and acting as though I were being thrown to the Secos.

The modified generator casing fit, not that I had had any doubt. All that remained was for me to drill out another hole where it joined the base plate. Then I fastened the new casing over the rotors and windings and all the other parts I didn't understand and fastened it in place. That gave us a functioning partial backup generator for the existing backup unit.

Next, I told Selioman before I left, to let him start out the testing.

"Why?"

"To be tested by that doctor . . . for something . . ."

Selioman shook his head. "Good luck. Whatever that is. I couldn't tell what she was testing for."

I shrugged.

Janth was pacing by the time I got to the armory. With him were Eltar and two men I'd seen, but didn't know.

"Let's go." Janth didn't even look at me as he paced out and down the corridor.

"Why so late?" Eltar's voice was pleasant, not probing.

"Caught me in the middle of repairing a generator."

Eltar nodded. He knew I was one of the few younger ConFeds who had any understanding of things mechanical or technical in nature. I didn't, of course. I just understood plans and prints and could read manuals.

Outside the barracks waited an antique open-benched steamer. The driver was a junior Seco.

A breeze ruffled the tattered pennant on the front quarter panel, and a dull rumble of thunder echoed from the direction of Mount Persnol. The overhead clouds promised rain, but not for a while.

Janth sat beside the driver on the padded bench seat. He took off his beret after a gust of wind threatened to blow it off. Eltar and I took the third bench, the last one in the back, without any upholstery.

*Wheeep . . . Thud!*

The steamer lurched forward.

Eltar cracked his elbow on the sideboard. I merely put splinters into my palm by grabbing the top of the sideboard on my side.

"Damned Secos. . . ." muttered the man in front of me.

Eltar muttered something less polite . . . and less audible.

"Shut it down," grumbled Janth. "All of you."

The junior Seco's shoulders slumped momentarily, as with a sigh. No Seco could have possibly have wanted to be isolated with a group of ConFeds. Although, as I thought about it, I had not seen any Secos except those attached to Dr. Relorn since the enemy attacks had destroyed Westron.

Had they all been in Inequital when the enemy had flattened it?

Some of the hills to the south were lit by a patch of sunlight pouring through an opening in the mostly cloudy sky. That one open space almost glittered, bright blue-green. The clouds around it seethed, white and fluffy at the top and dirty dark gray at the bottom. Even as I watched, the clouds closed in and the distant sunlight began to fade.

The steam-wagon lurched uphill toward the laboratory complex.

"What's this all about?"

"You'll find out soon enough," grumbled Janth.

The steamer continued to whistle and lurch its way up the gentle incline, scarcely any faster than we could have marched.

In front of the main entry, off another stone-paved and circular drive, waited a pair of Secos, each armed with a riot gun. They stepped back as we scrambled out, adjusting their grasp on their weapons.

"Line up." Janth's voice was calm.

Without another word, we marched in through the entry door, Janth leading the way. He'd obviously been through the drill.

We marched down the center corridor, all the way to the back of the laboratory, then turned left, along the corridor I had walked myself with the doctor, until we reached the laboratory.

There were no guards outside the open door, and Janth barely hesitated before leading us inside and toward the platform in the center of the room.

Directional lights suspended from the ceiling outlined the platform. Where we lined up waiting to go up the wooden steps to the platform was half-lit by the scattering of the platform lights.

Dr. Relorn, wearing some sort of golden-brown tunic, sat before that screen, her sandy hair glinting in the reflected light. From where I stood, she looked much younger than the subforcer behind her, and almost like a girl compared to the height of the burly head ConFed.

Colonel-General Odin Thor stood beside her with a bored look, his face mostly in shadows. I was standing behind Eltar, wondering how the doctor would use the array of equipment to determine who might be a time diver.

"Next."

Janth nodded to Eltar, who stepped up on the platform.

*Hmmmmmmm* . . .

*Bzzzzzz* . . .

More from force of habit than for any other reason, I glanced at Eltar, first with my eyes, then with my thoughts, the way I did to dive under the now. None of the energy that surrounded me, or even Dr. Relorn, swirled around Eltar. He was just a quiet goldish blob.

Then I looked at the doctor—and the light swirls of gold and black eddied around her.

Another set of currents tugged at my mind, and I tried to scan the laboratory as well as I could without seeming too obvious.

Colonel-General Odin Thor! The head ConFed Marine himself was throwing off black and gold sparks in an undertime display that mirrored the doctor's.

I managed to catch my dropping jaw and turn the movement into a yawn.

Only the doctor saw it, and she frowned but briefly while ostensibly studying her instruments.

We had never talked about undertime sight, and I wondered if the doctor saw what I did, or whether I was some sort of freak in being able to see the time energies.

But I needed to tell her about the Colonel-General—or was that how he had found her to begin with? What was their relationship? In our brief discussion, we hadn't talked about that either.

Right now, they were ignoring each other, but that didn't necessarily mean anything. Were they lovers? Or had the whole thing been coincidence?

Why did it matter? The doctor's private life was hers. So was the head ConFed's, and they both moved in orbits far above my present status.

"Next . . . next!"

"Sammis." Janth's bored voice turned exasperated. "Where's your mind, trooper? Step up there."

Everyone in the laboratory turned to look at me.

"Sorry, sir." I stepped onto the platform.

*Hmmmmmmmmmmmmm . . . cling, cling, cling!*

Now, everyone was really looking at me. My nose itched, although the room couldn't possibly have been dusty.

"Some potential here, Colonel-General."

Odin Thor nodded calmly. "Doesn't surprise me. Always looked like witch-spawn. Do you want him?"

"We'll need some more tests . . ."

"He's yours, on loan, as long as you need him."

I tried to look puzzled, glancing from the Colonel-General to Janth and back again. I opened my mouth, then closed it.

"Report to the doctor with your gear as soon as possible," Odin Thor ordered me, before turning to Janth. "Armorer, list him as support services to the Far Travel Lab."

"Off the platform, Trooper. Wait outside with the others who are done."

I shook my head slowly, as I took the three steps down to the stone floor of the laboratory. I wanted to tell Dr. Relorn about Odin Thor, if only to get her reaction. But I couldn't blurt out my discovery in front of everyone.

"Next . . ."

Outside, Eltar shook his head. "You going to be some sort of experimental type?"

"I don't know. Odin Thor looked happy enough to be rid of me. Rarden will certainly be pleased."

"What about you?"

"I don't know."

Janth came out of the laboratory.

"Sammis. Head back and clean out your gear. Be ready to go when the rest unload."

That was it. Period. I was detailed to the Far Travel Lab and Dr. Relorn.

# XXV.

WORKING FOR THE Far Travel Laboratory had some definite advantages—like a room of my own in the building next to the Lab. The immediate disadvantage? I had to go back to school . . . or learning.

I had not even put the kit bag that held all my worldly possessions on the graystone floor of the room before a thin and dark-haired man appeared.

"Sammis?"

"Yes?" I turned from the comfortable single bunk, complete with linens and a thick blanket.

"My name is Deric Ron Norften." He looked down on me, a good head taller even as he gave me a half bow of greetings.

"Sammis." I waited.

"Dr. Relorn asked me to look in on you, and to bring you these." He extended several thick bound notebooks, along with what appeared to be a stack of datacubes. "Do you know how to operate a console?"

"I used to be able to handle an Omega Vee, but that was a while ago."

"Our Gammas are trickier, I fear, but not impossible. Do you know where the briefing rooms are?"

I shrugged. "No. I know where this room is, where Dr. Relorn's laboratory is, and that's about it."

His soft chuckle erased his formality. "She can ignore a few details."

I nodded, trying to inventory the rest of the room as I did, taking in the two wooden armchairs, the narrow closet, the desk built into the wall, and the single window. A good three-quarters of a rod square, the room qualified as a ConFed officer's quarters. No wonder the Colonel-

General wanted to keep the technicians away from the troops.

"Do I get the tour?"

"Why don't you unpack? Then I'll be back, and you can see how we're laid out. After a quick tour, it will almost be time for dinner."

"And then?" I asked straight-faced.

"Why then . . . you get to work studying all this material."

"What's the point?"

"I thought . . ." He paused and his thin face screwed up slightly. ". . . at the proper time, Dr. Relorn will explain your assignment. I can say that you will need to know all this material before you can actually start your investigations." About three long steps, and Deric was depositing the notebooks on the otherwise bare desktop. He kept the datacubes. "I'll be back shortly. Feel free to look around, but knock before you enter any of the rooms with closed doors. A number are occupied."

He half-bowed again and was gone.

Much classier than the Colonel-General's minions, Deric was, but the bottom line was still the same. The good doctor wanted something from my scrawny carcass.

Unpacking into the closet and built-in drawers did not take long. Three sets of working uniforms and a single-dress uniform don't take up much space, even with underwear, belts, and a few toiletries. The biggest item was the foul-weather parka.

One thing I appreciated immediately. The room, the entire building, smelled clean. The sliding window had been left ajar, and a slight breeze brought the fresh smell of early summer inside. My nose itched slightly, probably from grass pollen, but I'd take pollen over filth any day.

The walls were plain goldenwood panels, with the faint cracks and scratches of age that matched the indentations in the graystone underfoot. The door itself was of the black oak that was tougher than ironwood, but the latch was simple. The lock was a simple bolt.

Since I didn't feel like exploring at that moment, I folded the empty kit bag and put it on the top closet shelf. The notebooks beckoned, despite my lingering irritation with the doctor's cavalier assumption that I would automatically assume whatever duties she had in mind.

So I picked up the one on top. No title on the flexible cover. The page inside read, *Notes on Perceptual Thresholds in the Non-Time Interstice.*

Instead of standing around and waiting for Deric, I sat down in one of the wooden chairs and began to read . . . very slowly. Some phrases made sense and squared with what I had already experienced—

". . . travelling into the red represents apparent temporal regression . . . although whether such regression places the traveler into a backtime setting purely subjective in nature, a setting representing one of a series of alternative universes, or a flexible 'real' backtime position will require further observation . . ."

". . . gold (cold) orientation is non-mass/non-energy oriented . . . black (hot) represents mass/energy concentrations . . . in a quasi-logarithmic representation . . .

". . . intensity of subjective color perception appears related to the apparent temporal velocity . . ."

—while others seemed so much gibberish . . .

". . . autonomous unwilled determinism . . . as a manifestation of free will . . ."

". . . difficult if not impossible to ascertain the validity of the ancestral suicide theorem . . ."

". . . mass-cubed energy progressions inapplicable . . . or apparently so . . ."

"Are you ready?" The thin-faced blond man was standing by the half-open door I'd never bothered to close. "The doctor would be impressed . . ."

"Nothing else to do, and I might as well learn what I'm supposed to learn. It might even come in useful."

He frowned, but I really didn't care. "This way, then." His voice wasn't quite as cheerful.

"Who lives here—on this level?"

"Several technicians and three travelers, at the moment, I believe, and you, of course."

I looked down the long straight corridor. On one side ran a line of windows, beginning at waist height and extending nearly to the inside roofline. On the other side were nearly a score of the heavy black oak doors.

Deric followed my eyes. "Only about half are occupied, now. A number of those associated with the project . . . left . . . with the disruptions."

I nodded, not wanting to say more.

"Doctor Relorn anticipates we will be adding several more from your contingent."

I shrugged. I didn't know all the ConFeds personally, especially some of the senior forcers or the newer recruits.

Deric wiped a stray wisp of his thin blond hair back off his high forehead and began to walk down the corridor in uneven long strides.

"The Security Forces are billeted on the level below, while the senior project members are either in the few quarters in the main laboratory or in the family quarters."

Deric only gestured at the first level corridor as we left the building. "Security quarters. On the first level on the other wing are the messing facilities."

"And the second level?"

"Empty quarters, for now."

His tone was so matter-of-fact that I didn't bother probing. I used my undertime sight to study Deric while we crossed the old stone-paved road to the main laboratory. Trying to walk and look undertime, I stumbled and almost crashed into the side of the graystone archway leading up the wide front steps of the laboratory.

Deric cast a few sparks into the undertime. Not many, but enough that he could probably travel short distances.

"Are you all right?"

I nodded. "Just looking and not watching where I was going."

". . . *aaaccuuughhh . . .*" My guide cleared his throat. "We'll take the right-hand corridor. The first few offices are for administration, although we have little of that now. Beyond the double doors is our mathematical section . . ."

"Mathematical section?"

Deric raised his eyebrows again, this time further. "Someone has to calculate at least general directional vectors."

"Oh . . ." I'd never needed vectors, but since I hadn't tried stellar travel, perhaps I just hadn't gone far enough to need them.

"Now that the main power net is gone, and we no longer have access to the mainframe at the university, we've had to simplify things somewhat."

I really didn't comprehend the complexity of the calculations he was describing. Still, I got the message. Mental travel or time-diving—whatever you called it—was a lot more complicated than I had realized. Either that, or I was more talented than the others. Or both.

We passed two open doors. The first held a young man sitting behind a desk, apparently waiting for something to happen or someone to enter. The second held an empty desk and chair, and several antique filing cabinets.

Next, we passed a closed door, with a wooden plate in the middle of the upper panel which proclaimed in gilded letters, "Mathematical Section."

Farther down the corridor, Deric opened an unmarked door and stepped inside. The room was larger than the plain black oak door would have indicated, long and narrow, with nearly a score of black and white consoles lined up against each wall. Several blocked doorways, and two lighter colored sections of wall paneling—each about a handspan wide—testified as to where interior walls had been removed.

Two men and three women were scattered along the rows, their backs to the aisle in the middle of the room. I wondered at the placement, since, for engineering hookup, it would have been easier to have placed the consoles back-to-back down the center. That arrangement would have allowed more privacy as well.

"Your console is number fourteen, over there."

I followed his gesture and walked as quietly as I could past a small dark-haired woman, who did not even glance up as I passed behind her. Sure enough, on the console with the number fourteen was a brand new nameplate— "Sammis."

A notebook, similar to the others I had already received, lay on the flat surface beside the screen, while several datacubes were racked next to the input slot.

I nodded. Dr. Relorn definitely did not waste time. I wondered how she would do in a showdown with the Colonel-General.

"We'll come back later," Deric added, moving up beside me.

I sniffed back an itch in my nose, refraining from scratching it. The room smelled both of dust and of long use.

The tall, thin man shambled back out through the same doorway, then down past the two doorways blocked on the inside by consoles. He turned right down another corridor, which narrowed into a covered walkway leading to the west wing of the laboratory building.

"Here's the main travel laboratory."

As Deric opened the door, I recognized the big enclosed space again, and mentally located the doctor's quarters—down the corridor we had not taken.

"I've been here. That's where I was tested."

"Have you actually done any mental travel?" Deric's tone was bland.

"From what you indicate is possible, nothing at all."

"Well, learning it should be an interesting experience for you, then."

I stared around the empty laboratory from the half-open doorway, wondering where the good doctor was. "You don't operate this late?"

"We're working back up to a full schedule, but our operations were curtailed by the lack of power."

"I'm not sure I understand." How did the lack of electrical power have anything to do with time-diving?

"Without power, we couldn't run the gammas, or the necessary time-vectors for the travelers . . ."

It sounded like all their divers were as blind as the good doctor. That or they couldn't recognize what they saw. Trying to use charts in the undertime sounded difficult. Or were they trying to memorize them before diving? I shivered at the thought of all that memorization.

"What next?"

"Down below are the electronics shop and the equipment rooms . . ."

"Good. I'd like to see them." I said that because Deric clearly didn't want to show them to me.

With a shrug, he turned and waited for me to back away from the door before closing it.

As I looked down the hallway, I could see that the late afternoon shadows were fading under the clouds that gathered from the north.

"This way." Deric turned to head back the way we had come.

"What's down that way?" I pointed to the direction we had not gone.

"Just some guest quarters for visiting dignitaries." His steps were hurried as he led me through another hallway door into a staircase leading down. At the bottom, a second doorway opened onto a hall identical to the one above, except that it had no windows, not surprisingly, since it had to be below ground level.

We walked silently to the left, away from the side of the building holding the "visiting dignitaries' " quarters. After another ten steps or so, Deric halted. On the door of the equipment room was a square metal panel with numbered buttons. Deric punched several in quick succession.

Looking through the undertime, I caught the numbers—six, thirteen, twenty-seven—noted the pattern, and then nearly laughed. So long as the room was big enough to stand in, I could enter it whether it happened to be locked or not.

The doorway's modest size gave no clue to the size of the space—which sloped downward and into dim shadows beyond the range of an unaided eye. The doorway was nothing more than an interior building entrance to an equipment bunker that probably included the space under the parklike square across the stone-paved street from the laboratory.

I caught a glimpse of the pressure suits, interspersed with racks and racks of equipment I failed to recognize. In the gloom beyond the equipment racks, one object's general shape caught my attention, as much for its massiveness as for its purpose. A laser-cannon, or as near to it as possible. Supposedly, only a handful had ever been built because of the immense power demands. Now, it had to be useless without the broadcast power satellites.

Deric just stood there, not exactly barring my entry, but clearly indicating that I was not going to be allowed to wander through the entire equipment bunker.

So I just gazed around, and nodded. "Very impressive. Very impressive." Then I stepped back. "Anything else down here I should know about?"

"No. Not really. Down the other corridor are the disciplinary cells that were used before the Westron Monarchy. They were never removed when the structure was converted.''

"Back for dinner, then?"

"I'll show you the dining area on the way back to your quarters. You'll have a little time to wash up. Evening meal is around 1800 for us."

"Fine." The ConFeds ate earlier, and my stomach was growling already.

The way back to my quarters was almost the same as the way we had come.

"You can take the walkway across, and those stairs . . ."

"If I take them now, and cross there . . . that will lead back to my room?"

"Exactly."

"And the facilities—showers?"

"Oh . . . I forgot. Just at the end of the hallway from your room."

"Do I just walk into dinner?"

"Yes. I'm afraid we don't have much ceremony. Your name has been posted, and the cook will expect you." Deric straightened, cleared his throat. "I do have one or two things to do . . ."

"I understand, and I can find my way back without any problem. Thank you very much."

"It was my pleasure."

He didn't sound convinced, and I'd just have to find out why.

# XXVI.

THE DINING SECTION of the quarters building appeared more like a restaurant than a military establishment—light wooden shutters on the inside of the windows and cloths on the dozen or so tables.

When I stepped through the double doors, I could see only five people—Deric and four others, three women and one man—all standing by a circular table.

"Sammis." Deric called.

"Deric." Nodding my head, I stepped toward the five. Except for Deric, I had met none of them. As I crossed the ten steps that separated us, the aroma of peffin filled my nostrils.

"Sammis, I'd like you to meet several of your fellow-travelers." Deric nodded toward a muscular red-headed woman. "This is Mellorie."

Mellorie's smile was instantaneous, and genuine, especially compared to Deric's. "It's nice to meet you, Sammis."

"It's nice to be here."

"This is Arlean, who runs the math and information section . . . and Gerloc, who found Sertis . . . and Amenda, who was our last brand-new traveler until the doctor found you."

Arlean looked like a librarian, with a narrow face and sharp eyes that missed nothing. Her smile was pleasant and showed even white teeth.

"Pleased . . ." Gerloc was about the same height as me, but rail thin, almost frail. His voice was deep, and contrasted with his sparse and wispy blond hair.

Amenda, slender and dark-haired, and half a head taller than me, nodded politely, but said nothing.

"The uniform . . . ?" asked Arlean, the mathematical librarian.

"Recruited straight from the ConFeds, lady, with nothing to my name but uniforms."

"Looks like he's in shape, Arlean." Gerloc's tone was not quite mocking. "Arlean's always complaining that none of the male divers have enough muscle to carry all the monitoring equipment necessary."

I tried not to frown.

"Arlean is the one who coordinates the out-system data. Her library science background comes in handy," explained Deric.

Again, I had trouble understanding the continued obsession with data. Some of it made sense—like a general catalogue of the habitable or visitable plants and whether the air was breathable and the level of gravity. But collecting mountains of data when our entire civilization was falling in shards around us . . . ? When an unseen Enemy had leveled most of the cities? When every freeman's hand was set against education and knowledge and the gentry whom they held responsible for the disaster?

"You look rather doubtful . . . is it . . . Sammis?" Mellorie's voice was low, husky, and warm, far more sultry in a friendly way than I would have expected.

"I suspect I am."

"You're no farm boy ConFed, either."

"Mellorie, please introduce yourself to Sammis slowly," Deric suggested, with an edge to his tone. The edge bordered on a whine.

"I'm sorry, Deric." She curtsied to him and returned her glance to me. "Would you care to join us—Gerloc and Amenda and me—for dinner tonight?"

"I'd be honored."

"Enjoy your dinner, Sammis," added Deric. "I trust you will not mind if I occasionally introduce you to someone else."

"Not at all, Deric. Thank you again for the tour."

"Tour? Deric actually took the time to show you around?" Amenda's voice was low, though not as husky or low as Mellorie's.

"It was brief," I explained. "Just these two buildings, really."

"Still . . . ?"

"We should pick a table and sit down, even if we are

to be saddled with peffin after all.'' Gerloc's tone was resigned.

Peffin stew or casserole sounded wonderful after ConFed slop. ''Is it that bad?''

''No,'' answered Mellorie with a low laugh. ''But Greffin serves it so often. But we've been eating it once every five days for more than a year.''

That was a bit frequent for something as spicy as peffin stew. On the other hand, it was my first meal prepared with any care in nearly a year—or more.

Amenda pulled out one of the chairs at a circular table set for four.

I offered the chair across from her to Mellorie.

''Like I said, no ConFed farm boy.''

I ignored the implication and sat on her left, facing the main doors, with Amenda on my left.

Gerloc took the last chair and sat, brushing his wispy blond hair off his high forehead after he edged his chair into place. ''You're not obligated to tell us anything, Sammis, but we are curious . . .''

I took a sip of the water in the glass before me. ''There's really not much to say. Born and raised in Bremarlyn, went to the Academy, escaped from the ConFeds who fired my family's house, escaped from the looters, and ended up being impressed by another group of ConFeds. When Dr. Relorn decided to test for . . . mental travel talent . . . I showed up as having it.''

Mellorie nodded. ''I thought so.''

''Thought what, Mellorie?'' asked Amenda.

''What I thought . . . that Sammis came from a good family and a solid background. Besides, he looks like a traveler.''

''Old-style . . .'' added Gerloc in a softer voice.

''I have been called witch-spawn, or worse.'' I had the feeling Mellorie had more to say, but had held her tongue.

Amenda shivered, as if the term were all too familiar.

Mellorie nodded.

Over her shoulder, I saw another threesome enter the dining area, none of whom I recognized, since neither of the two women happened to be Dr. Relorn.

"How would I put this . . . ?" Gerloc's voice was softer, pitched not to carry beyond the table. "Your . . . shall we say . . . experience level . . . ?"

"I don't know. No basis for comparison." Gerloc might be friendly, but I was reluctant to blurt out anything. "I can travel from point to point on Query. Too much travel burns a lot of energy, though."

Gerloc opened his mouth.

"I certainly have no experience in travelling to the stars or other planets. You discovered someplace called Sertis? Could you tell me about it?"

Gerloc closed his mouth, then took a sip of water.

Mellorie chuckled. "Guess what, Gerloc? He listens."

With a sheepish grin, Gerloc looked at Mellorie, then back at me. "I gather I don't have much choice."

"You're right. You don't," said Amenda pleasantly.

"I'll skip the details of how I stumbled onto Sertis, because they're in the notebooks you'll be reading. I'm pretty limited in terms of how far back or forward I can travel—seems to be in the neighborhood of fifteen hundred to two thousand years back and about half that forward. The forward side is always shady. That's because of the uncertainty factors, I gather . . ."

"You might try getting to the point . . ." Mellorie's voice was friendly.

"I will. I am simply not as direct as you are, Mellorie." Gerloc took another swallow and cleared his throat. "The point to which dear Mellorie refers is that Sertis doesn't change. The buildings are occasionally modified, but the population and technology are always the same, at least as far as any of us have been able to tell."

I frowned. "Does that mean we're different? Or they are?"

"They are." That was Mellorie. "We've found half a dozen other cultures out there, and they change. Dramatically, sometimes within local decades."

I was still frowning. So what difference did it make whether one culture on another planet in another solar system was stable?

"You look even more displeased, Sammis." Amenda's voice was softer, less persistent than Mellorie, yet removed.

"I'm new here." I swallowed, then spit out what I shouldn't have said. "Everything I hear still sounds like a research project. All very interesting, but so what? We've been destroyed by an unseen enemy, and our entire civilization is crashing around us, and we're gathering data?"

Now Amenda and Gerloc were the ones frowning.

I found myself wiping my forehead with the cloth napkin, a true social blunder, but sweat was oozing from my forehead, despite the room's coolness.

"Salads here." With that a waitress set a bowl before each of us.

"Thank you." My response was automatic.

The silence around the table lengthened as the waitress departed with a nod to me. No one else said anything. So I took a bite of the salad. Even with bitter reddish leaves interspersed with some mushrooms and wild onions, it was refreshing.

"What would you do, then?" Mellorie asked.

"I'm scarcely in charge," I mumbled with a mouth half-full of leaves and crunchy mushrooms that tasted of nutbark.

"That's begging the question. You raised it."

Gerloc and Amenda looked from Mellorie to me, and back, as if they were watching a contest.

"Something useful."

Mellorie looked ready to snap back, when she smiled over my shoulder.

"May I interrupt?" Deric's question was only half-whine.

"Of course," Mellorie's voice dripped syrup.

I turned, caught a glimpse of a woman and found myself standing and bowing. The old traditions don't die.

"Sammis, I believe you know Dr. Relorn. I just wanted to reassure her that you had in fact arrived and were enjoying our hospitality."

"Everyone has been most hospitable, Deric. Most hospitable." I inclined my head toward my tablemates.

The doctor nodded politely under the makeup designed to make her look like an older woman trying to look young. "I'm glad to see you have been so well received, Sammis. Although I have interrupted an animated conversations, I do not intend to take much of your time."

"It's good to see you, Doctor, outside the testing laboratory, and I appreciate your efforts. Very much." I bowed slightly, again.

"He's quite the gentry, Doctor, isn't he?" observed Deric.

"I believe he is, Deric. But he also survived the ConFeds." She turned back to face me. "I hope you will enjoy working with us."

"I'm certain I will, Doctor, especially under your direction." I could have bitten my tongue for the last, particularly with Mellorie hanging on every word, but old habits die hard.

"Enjoy your dinner." With that, she and Deric turned and headed toward a table set for two.

I sat down.

"Can you doubt he's gentry born after that?" Amenda said to Gerloc.

"It was quite a performance, Sammis." The corners of Mellorie's mouth were twisted in a wry gesture.

I took the last mouthful of salad.

"Do you wish to honor us with your suggestions for what the laboratory should do amidst our crumbling culture?"

I set down my glass. "Pure knowledge isn't much help when you're facing someone armed with a riot gun or a crossbow. Within seasons, unless things change, we'll be out of both ammunition, arms, and food, with no way to resupply ourselves."

"So what do you want us to do?"

"I've been here one day, and I'm supposed to supply an answer?"

"That's good enough for now, I think." Mellorie's voice had turned much softer. "You're right. We see it too, but we don't have an answer either."

Amenda was suddenly looking at her nearly untouched salad.

Gerloc shrugged.

"You see, Sammis," continued Mellorie, "we don't have many action-oriented travelers left. Most of them left when the riots started."

I understood. All too well. Those who had remained were the cautious ones, the scared ones, or those with no place to go. I understood all right. I was just like them. "I understand."

"As a ConFed?" Amenda's tone was gentle.

"There are ConFeds, and there are ConFeds," noted Mellorie in a voice so low as to be little more than a whisper.

I ignored her observation. I didn't want to distinguish between Odin Thor's ConFeds and the ones that fired my home. "I understand—even as a ConFed. I didn't have much choice, you know. No family, no friends, and every time I opened my mouth I was tagged as gentry."

"You survived, though. That means you're not exactly as helpless—"

"Here is the famous peffin casserole," announced the waitress.

I still couldn't believe that the Far Travel Laboratory had cooks and serving personnel. The waitress wasn't young, probably in her early fifth decade, but she carried the casserole dish with authority and placed it in the center of the table, laying two serving utensils beside it.

"I'll serve," announced Amenda. "Sammis?"

I handed over my platter, glad to have escaped, even momentarily, the questions that Mellorie kept throwing at me.

"Gerloc?"

*Thuddd* . . .

"LAZY BOORNIKS. MISERABLE GENLOVERS! MOTHERSWILLS!"

The shouts would have roused the damps, let alone the modest dining area. I found myself turning and on my feet, recognizing the voice.

Rarden was standing alone inside the doors bellowing. Looking through the undertime, I could see two other figures outside, but not who they were.

Because everyone seemed in shock, I was there even before the Seco who shadowed the doctor.

"Oh, it's the brave little swamp rat, is it? Ready to defend the genlovers . . . but you're one, too, aren't you?"

I just looked up at him.

"So now they've bought themselves a real ConFed . . . cause the Secos aren't enough."

I ignored the Seco coming up behind me and took another step toward Rarden, stopping just short of easy reach.

"Rarden. Get the hell away from here." I didn't even raise my voice.

"Threaten me, swamp rat . . . go ahead, threaten me."

"I don't make threats."

For some reason, he turned pale.

"You . . . always you . . ." He stumbled backwards and out the door.

I waited until he staggered back, and Selioman steered him down the corridor toward the outside entrance. Then I closed both double doors.

The Seco stood there holding the useless riot gun.

"Put that away. It won't scare any of the ConFeds, just make them kill you quicker." I walked around him.

Both Deric and the doctor were looking in my direction. I ignored them.

"No, he's not exactly helpless," muttered Mellorie. She flushed as she realized I had heard her comment to Gerloc and Amenda.

"I never said I was. I said I understood." I was tired of trying to justify anything. So I didn't. I just enjoyed the peffin casserole.

Neither of the other three said anything, either to each other, or to me, until the ubiquitous waitress collected the serving dish and our platters.

"Greffin is good with desserts," volunteered Amenda.

Since I hadn't had a dessert since before I had left the Academy, the idea sounded intriguing. "Such as?"

"Tonight is berrycream tort."

I hadn't cared much for desserts even when they had been available, and two bites were enough. I finished the tort on general principles. Desserts did contain an ample supply of calories.

Except for Mellorie's comment, everyone ignored my actions in running Rarden off, as if they were in bad taste. Yet Rarden would have destroyed the entire dining room to get attention. In terms of my father's background, though, my actions probably were in bad taste. My mother might have approved.

After dessert, Gerloc and Amenda rose together.

"Good night, Sammis, Mellorie."

I half rose. "Good night."

Mellorie nodded.

I reseated myself.

"You made quite an impression, Sammis."

"An unfortunate impression."

"You're a rare one," she mused, almost as if I were not there. "Your understanding is greater than your knowledge. You're not afraid to act."

"That's not quite true, Mellorie."

She just smiled.

She wasn't listening, exactly, and I was tired of explaining.

"Would you care to walk me back to my quarters?" She extended her hand as she rose from the straight-backed dining chair.

"I'd be honored, dear lady."

So I walked her to her doorway, which was less than half a corridor from mine. That was all I did.

# XXVII.

AFTER PULLING OFF my boots, I stretched out on the bed, leaving the window open and listening to the breeze. I intended to enjoy the rustle of black oak leaves and the touch of crispness to the evening that would disappear over the days ahead.

The mattress was firm, but not rock-hard like a ConFed pallet. The pillows emphasized the non-military nature of the Far Travel Lab.

For all the apparent friendliness of the dinner, and for all of the interest of Mellorie, including her almost-invitation into her quarters, things were just not what they seemed. None of them, except perhaps the doctor, appeared to understand that we had been attacked by an enemy we couldn't even find, and that Query was collapsing around them. They just seemed to be going through the motions.

Mellorie seemed to be the only one actually thinking, and I wondered how much that was from contrariness. Her on and off invitations left me confused.

Then there was the doctor, clearly made up to be as old as she claimed, rather than as old as she looked. I knew how old she could be, but I didn't believe it. The woman had to be decades older than me, for all that she looked like a young woman, for all that she wore severe and dowdy clothes to project an image older than she was. The silver streaks in her hair were probably dyed, since they didn't go all the way to the roots.

Outside, the twilight slowly faded into gloom, leaving my room, with its single wide window, even darker.

*Chhhiritt, chhirritt* . . . The sound of some night bird drifted through the open window.

Why had Dr. Wryan Relorn even listened to me on that night I had invaded her laboratory, let alone gone out of her way to have me transferred out of the ConFeds? If Deric were any example, her own senior staffers weren't exactly thrilled about my presence.

Nothing quite added up. The laboratory had been and still was gathering essentially useless data while it could have been performing a function vital to the Westron Monarchy. Except there wasn't a monarchy. There wasn't even a capital city. The nominal second-in-command verged on incompetent. Unless the doctor were keeping it to herself, no one had thought about redirecting the role of the divers to fit the current situation.

I shook my head, then stared into the darkness. Not that darkness was a barrier to someone who could look through the undertime. That raised another question—why couldn't the other divers see? Even Dr. Relorn seemed only to be able to see *from* the undertime, not through it.

Shrugging again, I sat up on the edge of the bed and

pulled my boots back on. Waiting wouldn't provide me with any more answers.

As I slipped under the now for the short dive across to the other building, I wondered if anyone could track me in the same way I had found the doctor.

She was alone, sitting in one of the comfortable armchairs, leafing through a thick notebook.

"Greetings."

"Greeting, Sammis."

"You were expecting me."

"I thought you might show up . . . although I wasn't certain exactly when." She had removed the heavy makeup and looked years, if not decades younger. "You have some questions? Good. So do I."

I took the other chair without waiting for it to be offered. "Why don't your travelers do anything?"

She smiled faintly. "What would you have them do?"

"Everything is crumbling around us . . . couldn't they bring back some technology . . . something . . . ?"

"Such as?"

I felt like I were back in school. "What have I missed?"

She grinned. "Very bright . . ." After shifting her weight and crossing one trousered leg over another, she added, "You know none of my travelers can carry very much. That means we can't bring back metals—which we need—not in any meaningful quantity. We can't bring back equipment that we cannot understand, or that requires different power inputs. When you think about it, that doesn't leave much."

"What about knowledge?"

"How can you translate it into usable equipment?"

This time the silence stretched out as I thought and she silently waited.

"I'm not educated, Doctor . . ."

"Just call me Wryan. You're far more educated than

most people left around here, including the ones with degrees and honors.''

Both her comments left me open-mouthed, at least momentarily. "I have to disagree, Doc—"

"Wryan." Her tone was no-nonsense.

"Are you called Wryan by the other divers?"

"No."

I shook my head, knowing from her tone that she wasn't about to explain. As she set down the notebook and leaned forward to place it on the low table, I watched, somehow taking in the grace of her movements.

Finally, I spoke again. "It still seems to me that we could benefit from what other cultures have to offer."

"We could—if we could find it, understand it, and copy it."

"Finding it . . ." I shut my mouth. What an idiot I had been! No wonder they had problems. None of them had learned how to see into real time from the undertime, and searching a culture by having to break out every time you went someplace would prove too exhausting for much productive effort. "I see . . ." But there was one item . . . and I saw that, too. "Weapons . . . is that why the Colonel-General. . . ?

She nodded.

I realized there was something else I had not told her. "He's also a diver."

"The Colonel-General? How do you know?"

I took a deep breath, wondering whether I could trust this doctor I scarcely knew, deciding I could, and thinking I was a fool for it. "The energies play around him the way they do around all the divers."

"In the undertime?"

"Yes."

"That was how you found me?"

It was my turn to nod.

"Who else knows?"

"About the Colonel-General? No one I know of. I'm not sure he knows."

"That would make sense." She frowned, and I could see the darkness behind her eyes that was the only indication of her age. Otherwise, seated less than two paces from me, she could have been nearly a contemporary. "Does anyone else know how you found out."

"No. Probably shouldn't have told you . . ."

She smiled, and I couldn't help but feel better. The smile wasn't the professional one she had presented at dinner, but more impish . . . more personal.

I found myself smiling back.

"Would you like some cider? Hot?"

Hot cider? That last one who had offered me hot cider had been Allyson . . . had it been years ago?

"Are you all right?"

Her concern just made it worse, and at first I could barely keep from shaking. Then I couldn't, and I couldn't see, either. I could feel her hands on my shoulders, but she didn't say anything, and neither did I.

After a while, she handed me a small soft towel, and I wiped my face.

"I'm sorry . . ." She was kneeling next to my chair with one hand covering mine.

I just shook my head again, not really wanting to speak.

How long she stayed by me I didn't know, but when I looked at the small antique clock on the wall, the hands registered past midnight.

"Sorry . . ."

"Don't be . . . I'm glad I was here."

I just nodded.

"I meant it, Sammis."

"Talk to me . . . about you . . ."

"All right . . ." She shifted her position on the floor, and I let go of her hand. "Do you mind if I move? I think my legs are mostly asleep . . ."

"Oh . . . I didn't—"

"Don't worry about it." She reseated herself in the other chair and rubbed her calves with one hand. "There's not that much to say . . ."

But she did talk, about growing up as an orphan in the cold of Southpoint, having to sneak off when she realized she was not changing in looks, except to look more and more like her mother, the lady lost at sea and termed the "witch-captain." In posing as a wanton gentry daughter, she managed to accrue a degree or two from some of the lesser southern Westron universities, which she had used to get into the civil science bureaucracy . . .

". . . but it's getting late, and you're exhausted . . ."

I jerked upright, realizing I had not heard what she had been saying. "Not that tired . . ."

"You snored through my last three sentences." Her tone was gentle.

"You could be a princess, lady."

"Wryan," she corrected.

"You could be a princess, Wryan. Even when you chastise, you make people feel good."

"A princess? All little girls want to be princesses." She paused. "Some of them get to be. Some decide it isn't worth the bother, but most of them never give up. There just aren't enough princes, and most of them are bastards."

That didn't make any sense at all. Finally, I asked, "What . . . I mean . . . princes?"

"You're tired, and we'll talk about it later. Was she nice?" Wryan stood up.

"Nice?" I had to think.

"The girl you remembered when I asked about the hot cider."

"Oh . . . it wasn't like that. She was very nice, and I never saw her again. I don't think she and her parents made it. No one else from Bremarlyn did, so far as I know."

She was next to me, and the faintest hint of trilia touched me. "Good night, Sammis."

"Good night." I still couldn't call her Wryan. "Good night."

Somehow, I made it under the now and back to my room. I got my boots off, but that was all, before collapsing onto the bed.

# XXVIII.

A WISP OF condensing water vapor floated from the steamer like a momentary banner in the cool of the early morning. The subforcer seated next to the technician at the controls checked the map, noting the steamer's position. While the topography and the road remained, most of the towns were no longer even recognizable.

"Should make Bremarlyn before long," observed the officer.

"Yes, sir. Nice day."

"Really wish we could get power at Herfidian, the way they do at the base camp on the plateau . . ."

The driver ignored the officer's comments and concentrated on the controls to guide the top-heavy steamer along the old stone-paved highway where it curved through a low point between two hillocks.

*Crump!*

"Verlyt!"

*Crump!*

"Power. Full power to the drive wheels! Down below—skirmish squad out! Skirmish squad out!

"Sir? They're firing from in front of us!"

"Full power!"

*Clang!*
"Skirmish squad is clear, sir."
"Hunt down those bastards, Froman!"
"Yes, sir. Good luck."
*Crump! Thud!*
The steamer lurched.
"Full power!"
*Crump! Crump!*

# XXIX.

". . . IN THEORY, INTENSE gravitational relativistic pres-
sures exerted by collapsed stellar masses should narrow
the perception of 'black' pathways . . ."

I yawned. Just as I thought I might read three straight
paragraphs of interest, the material lapsed into speculations. I had enough personal speculations not to have to
worry about theoretical abstractions on the reconciliation
of space-time theory with time-diving observations. And
the personal speculations kept nagging at me, unlike the
dry words on the screen.

Why did the doctor want me to call her Wryan? Why
had a few kind words, well meant, dissolved me? Why
did she seem to trust me? Or why, for Verlyt's sake, was
I trusting her?

Without answers, I stifled another yawn and pushed
onward through the theoretical material on time-diving,
trying to ignore the questions at the back of my mind.

". . . even in the absence of empirical or validated experimental data, several facts are clear. . . ."

Clear as swamp water, I reflected, stretching and taking
a quick look around the console room. Only Amenda and
two other women I had not met were in the long room.
None of them glanced up from their consoles.

My nose twitched from the faint odor of ozone. I rubbed it and shrugged my shoulders to release the tightness. Then I looked back at the screen.

". . . that the so-called time-paths are tied to the intensity of gravitational forces, or more precisely, to the proximity and concentration of mass and energy . . ."

I took a deep breath and forced myself to keep going through the text.

"Sammis?"

I looked up to see a tall figure standing just inside the doorway. Since Deric had caught me studying the material on my console, boring stuff if ever there was, I was more receptive to the interruption than I might have been. I waited. I didn't bother standing.

He ambled over. "Dr. Relorn would appreciate it if you would meet her in the main travel laboratory."

"Just a moment." I flipped to the front of the notebook to find the log-off code and used it. "Is that the big laboratory around the corner and across . . . ?"

"Right . . . but I'll go with you to make sure."

I didn't shrug, but felt like it. "All right." After stacking the notebooks on the shelf, I stood up. "Lead on."

Deric said nothing until we were in the corridor, where he took a half dozen steps, then stopped. "You were rather . . . effective . . . the other night at dinner . . . With your size . . . I mean . . . one wouldn't normally assume . . ."

"Rarden's always been after me. I felt it was my problem to solve."

"Do the others . . . ConFeds . . . feel the same way about you?"

"Deric, I wouldn't have the faintest idea. No one bothers me."

"Oh."

"How do your Secos feel? Like the one who reacted too late?"

"Karsnish?" Deric looked at the floor, then toward the end of the corridor.

I waited.

"Karsnish . . . understands why we need the ConFeds on our side . . . now . . ."

With a shake of my head, I turned and started toward the laboratory. Deric caught up quickly, but only to match steps with me.

He stopped outside the doorway. "Your Colonel-General is there also."

The Colonel-General? Why? Another setup? Had my trust in Dr. Wryan Relorn been misplaced after all?

I stepped inside, leaving Deric, who showed no intention of following me, outside.

She was standing by the same master console where I had first found her. She wore pale ice-green trousers and a matching short-sleeved tunic. Her eyes seemed to sparkle, though her mouth was stern, and she still wore the old lady makeup.

The head ConFed wore his usual off-purple fatigues, sharply creased, and his eyes followed me all the way from the doorway.

"The Colonel-General has a request, Sammis." Her voice was neutral. I bowed slightly to them both, denying Odin-Thor the salute he would have liked.

"Trooper Sammis . . . you're still a trooper . . . on detail."

"Yes, Colonel-General . . . you wanted something . . ."

Odin-Thor cleared his throat, and his eyes centered on me.

I met his glare.

He cleared his throat again. Then, he blinked. His jaw tightened, and he pursed his lips. "Yes. You were from Bremarlyn. We have lost two supply steamers in the area. Both without any trace. I was hoping that someone from the Travel Laboratory would be able to find some sign of what happened.''

He nodded at the doctor. ''Dr. Relorn has informed me that none of her other travelers has the capability of . . . traveling . . . here on Query. With your background and training, I was hoping that you might be able to find out what happened.''

I didn't like it at all. I glanced from the Colonel-General to the doctor. Not only was she wearing the heavy makeup again, but there were dark circles under her eyes, almost too dark to be real. Her lips stayed tight after her statement.

''That might not be a simple as it sounds, Colonel-General. It takes a great deal of energy to use mental travel here on Query. I *might* be able to find out something if I knew what I was looking for and where it was supposed to be. There's no way that I can search the entire Bremarlyn area. I can get to specific points instantly, but it takes as much energy as though I'd spent half day on a steamer getting there.''

The ConFed leader nodded. ''So you could check several points quickly, but not sweep an area?''

''I can sometimes tell if there's anyone nearby, but not always.''

''Here's what happened. A regular convoy steamer from Herfidian to here disappeared. We sent a light armed steamer with a skirmish squad. It vanished as well. They both went by the highway—the Eastern Highway from Inequital toward Herfidian.'' The Colonel-General glanced at Dr. Relorn, then back to me. ''If you could even discover what happened—a wreck or attack, or if there's a large group of bandits . . . that would be most helpful.''

''I'll do what I can, assuming that meets with your approval and the doctor's approval.''

His frown was momentary as he turned toward her. ''If you could—''

"If Sammis can help you, it would benefit all of us." The clarity and professionalism with which she spoke reminded me again that, despite her youthful looks under the makeup, Dr. Relorn probably had more experience than the Colonel-General might ever have.

"Thank you, Doctor." He bowed.

"Not at all. You and your men have already done so much. We would only be repaying a portion of that debt." Her tone remained matter-of-fact.

He nodded again, and I tried to keep from shaking my head.

"Here is the general area where we think both groups disappeared." He extended a map, basically a reproduction of an Imperial road map, and pointed to an area highlighted in yellow, slightly east of Bremarlyn.

After studying the general topography, I straightened. "May I keep this for a while, sir?"

"Of course . . . ah . . . how long . . . ?"

"I'll try now. Trying isn't the problem, you understand. I just can't make many trips."

"Oh . . . I see . . ."

He didn't, and I looked at Dr. Relorn. "While I'm searching, Doctor, perhaps you could explain the energy deficits associated with diving. And . . ."

"I'll have something waiting for you, Sammis."

I thought I heard a trace more than professionalism there, but I wasn't sure.

#

So I HAD lied to the great Colonel-General? Was that so great a moral fault?

Dropping under the now, sliding away toward Bremarlyn and the apparently missing ConFeds, I still worried

whether Odin Thor would find out about my ability to look
at events from the undertime, whether Dr. Wryan Relorn
would tell him what she knew, and how long it would take
for Odin Thor to find out that I could do more than I said
I could. Or would he find out at all?

I pushed the doubts and questions away, focusing instead on the hazy black path that carried me closer to
Bremarlyn. Although I tried to follow the road, it didn't
really work that way. What sliding under the now or diving
through time really follows is the patterns of mass and
energy concentrations, and you skip from concentration to
concentration—in a way. It was hard to parallel a real road
from the undertime, and after a few attempts I didn't even
try.

Then I tried to locate a steamer by backtiming. Backtime was what the red direction represented. But a steamer
doesn't have that much energy, and I tried to latch onto
the point source that I thought was a laser rifle.

Except that it disappeared. But energy just doesn't disappear. It dissipates when the rifle is fired. That was how
I located one attack where I could see ConFeds firing shells
from a short-tubed cannon that lofted shells over a hill and
down around the steamer. Finally a shell blew the boilers
and steam-cooked the subforcer and the driver.

Then the strange ConFeds just waited for the steam to
clear, picked off the handful of survivors with projectile
rifles, and appeared with a tug to cart off the wrecked
steamer. All very dispassionately.

I could follow them, but nothing more. That squared
with what I had read in the notebooks and with my own
past experience. On Query, you can only enter and leave
the undertime in your own subjective present. Period. No
exceptions. Because the ambush took place in my past, I
could only watch. And I could tell from my growing light-
headedness that the watching alone took some effort.

Before I was totally exhausted, I tracked the strange

ConFeds back to a concealed tunnel less than five kays from the ruins of a house I knew well. While I was too exhausted to follow further, what I could see showed an elaborate underground installation, and an old one at that, with lots of metal and energy concentrations.

By then, black spots were interspersed with the light-headedness.

Still, breaking out in the laboratory was not particularly difficult. Standing up after I did was a real problem.

"Sammis . . . are you all right?" Dr. Relorn reached out to steady me.

With no strength and no ability to maintain my balance, I practically collapsed on her.

Her strength was far greater than I would have expected, and she eased me into one of the padded armchairs. The faint scent of trilia surrounded her, like a mist from my past.

While the Colonel-General looked as though I had crawled from the sewer, his sour expression didn't stop his questions. "Did you find anything? What happened? Who did it?"

My head was pounding, and each question sounded like a thunderbolt.

"Just wait a moment, Colonel, and let him take a sip of this."

What she shoved under my nose was pungent, though not unpleasant. After just a sip or two, the headache began to subside.

"The whole steamer crew was ambushed . . . by a group of ConFeds . . . same kind of uniforms . . . tracked them to a hidden underground base near Bremarlyn . . ." Talking was a slight effort. So I stopped and took a full gulp from the narrow beaker that the doctor had handed me.

She was staring intently at me, but I couldn't understand the expression.

"So . . . they found it . . ." The Colonel-General pulled at his chin. Then he looked at me. "Could you locate it on a map?"

"Why bother? I'll take you there . . . once I recover . . . in a day or so . . ."

If looks could have buried people, the doctor would have had me at the bottom of an ancient graveyard. But she said nothing.

I ignored her. Odin Thor, Colonel-General or not, had to understand what he was playing with.

"What do you mean?"

"You're a latent diver, Colonel-General. So I'll take you there through the undertime, and you can mount your own assault from inside, if you want, while your troops hit the outside." I finished the beaker. "Do you have a map?"

He thrust it at me.

I ignored it, too. Instead, I closed my eyes and rested, almost in a trance.

"Trooper . . ."

"Colonel . . . don't push him—"

Even in my dazed state, I could recognize the steel in the doctor's words.

"—he did what you asked. You'll have answers as soon as he's able to give them. Mental travel is extremely fatiguing."

I was feeling better, but decided to keep my eyes closed.

"But he was only gone a few instants . . ."

"Wasn't Sammis one of your better trainees? Physically?"

"That's what they told me."

"That should tell you something about the physical effort required."

I could hear the doctor's soft steps moving away.

"He only went a handful of kays. You say that you have

mapped the stars.'' The Colonel-General's voice was more like a rumble.

''If you will recall your earlier briefings, Colonel Odin Thor, it takes more energy to cross a room here on Query than to reach the nearest star.''

''Then what good are your travelers?''

I wanted to open my eyes and enter the discussion, but even more to hear what the doctor might say. So I kept them closed a while longer and listened, listened to the soft footsteps and a gentle strong woman's voice.

''Could any dozen of your scouts found out what Sammis just did? Those are some of the immediate benefits. Over the longer term, once we find other civilizations, we should provide knowledge, better ways to generate or use energy—the possibilities are considerable.''

''But for now, Doctor, I have defend this base with rather limited resources. Not only against bandits, but against a renegade group of ConFeds.''

''Odin Thor.'' Her voice was cold, and I almost sat up right then. ''We know who the renegades are.''

''Survival is a matter of strength, madam.''

''We add to your strength.''

''Just see that you do.''

I yawned, groaned, and tried to imitate coming awake. It wasn't entirely an act.

Odin Thor still stood there like a tree that had scarcely moved, while the doctor was on the other side of the console. She began to rummage through a small locker and stacked something on a tray.

''Try these. They might help.''

I rubbed the back of my neck where it ached, and the self-massage helped ease some of the remaining headache. Several bites of the crackers that tasted like the pungent liquid helped.

Odin had the map ready, waiting for the moment when I stopped stuffing my face, tapping his booted feet on the

cracked insulating tiles of the laboratory floor. The fingers
of his free left hand clenched and unclenched, clenched
and unclenched, almost in rhythm to my chewing.

After a large pile of crackers, I began to feel better.
"Could I see that map, Colonel-General?"

He glared. I stayed seated, since standing wouldn't have
done me any good.

"Here."

"Here's a stylus, Sammis . . ."

The map had enough landmarks for me to be able to
locate the stronghold of the real ConFeds. The fact that
they were the real ones made it easier for me. A great deal
easier.

"Be difficult to get them out . . ."

I shook my head. "Very easy. Very easy."

"I know the kind of installation they're in. Couldn't
burn your way through with a battle laser . . ."

"They still have to breathe . . ."

The doctor turned whitish-green as she understood what
I had in mind.

Odin Thor looked puzzled.

"Gas. Any kind of gas. Like the monarchy used on the
Eastron installations that refused to surrender."

"But how . . . ?"

"Leave that to me, Colonel-General. My pleasure . . ."

# XXXI.

FROM SOMEWHERE IN the equipment bunkers, Janth came
up with a case of gas grenades. I stared at the black
mushroom-shapes. Each had a brilliant yellow danger
warning, a set of crossed bones, painted on the top. The
stemlike part was a handle.

"Ugly beasts, aren't they?" Janth frowned at the four

on the armorer's table. On the floor remained a case. Two other grenades lay in the top layer of padding. "Should be another eighteen or so left there."

"They just left this lying in the old armory?"

"Verlyt, no. All the chemical stuff was in the sealed vault in the back. This was just the outer case. They had another airtight seal around this."

I leaned over to look at one of the black objects. A heavy metal ring protruded from one side of the mushroom's "cap." "What's this?" I pointed.

"Don't touch it. That's the arming ring. Once you pull that, the valve between the two gas fractions opens, and they combine."

"It just seeps out?"

"Not exactly, trooper. Not exactly." Janth pursed his lips. "Been a long time . . . but . . . There's a lot of heat, which builds up as they combine. Eventually, you get an explosion. Combines the best of a frag grenade with the long-term kill power of the nerve gas."

"Eventually?" I managed to repress a shudder. "Nerve gas?"

"Paralyzes the nerves . . . you know, stops your brain. Stops your heartbeat. There's no cure."

"They used this . . . ?"

"Not since the Eastron revolt."

Since Eastron had been independent, as my mother had pointed out so often, the term "revolt" was inaccurate. "Can I pick one up? I need to know how heavy they are."

"Be careful, Trooper. That plastic should last forever, but that's got to be nearly a century old, and I really don't want it going off."

Neither did I. The grenade was heavier than the killer mushroom it resembled. Carrying more than three or four would be a problem. I put down the grenade and shook my head.

The slick paper of the instruction sheet was yellowed,

and fine cracks ran from the central fold. The print of the instructions was crisp and black. So was the information. The Mark Delta contained enough nerve toxin to cover an area of fifty square rods in a no-wind condition. The toxin worked through contact, surface or inhalation, and one microjot (whatever that was) was sufficient to ensure lethality in ninety percent of the exposures.

There was also a bold-print warning.

DO NOT USE IN UNFAVORABLE WIND CONDITIONS!

The preferred method of delivery for the Mark Delta was with the projectile rifle modified launcher.

"Projectile rifle modified launcher?"

"None in the inventory. There haven't been for years."

I shrugged. The new preferred delivery method was the Sammis Mark One diver. "I'll be back when the time comes, Janth."

"That's what the Colonel-General said, Trooper. Can't say I envy you."

Neither could I.

After walking around the corner, I slipped undertime and back to my room to think about the options again. I was glancing outside at the clouds over the southern peaks, having second thoughts about delivering death.

*Tap, tap. Tap, tap.*

"Yes?"

"Sammis?" The husky feminine voice was familiar.

"Come on in, Mellorie."

Wearing a clinging aqua coverall of some sort of soft material that indicated that she was very feminine, Mellorie eased open the unlatched door and stepped inside. She stopped. "When did you get back?"

"Just now."

"I didn't hear you in the corridor . . ." Her eyebrows were raised, and the corners of her eyes crinkled.

I tried not to grin. "I didn't come in that way."

"Oh . . ."

"I was down in the armory, getting a briefing on some antique weapons." I coughed to clear my throat.

Mellorie slipped into one of the chairs without waiting for the invitation I was reluctant to issue.

I sat on the foot of the bunk, not quite facing her. The wooden armchairs got uncomfortable after a while.

She crossed her ankles and sat up a little straighter. She pursed her lips before leaning forward.

As she did, I realized how deep the cut of her coveralls was, how much narrower her waist was than I had realized, and how shapely her breasts were.

I must have stared where I shouldn't have, because I could see her flush, the color rising from her neck into her lightly freckled and tanned face.

"Sorry . . ." I apologized.

"You are . . . rather direct . . ." Her voice was still throaty.

I looked away, shrugging. "Sorry. Dealing with women was a part of my education that I never reached." Outside the clouds had spread to cover the sun, and a breeze from the half-open sliding window ruffled my hair.

"You didn't have any sisters?"

"No sister. No brother." I continued to watch the clouds pile up over the mountains.

"What about your mother?"

"We didn't get around to talking much about women. I wasn't too interested . . . before the . . . disaster . . ."

"You liked your mother."

"Yes. I respected her, too." I still didn't want to think about her for too long.

"Any women friends?"

"In the ConFeds?"

"I meant before . . . and could you look this way? Please."

I shifted my weight and turned. Mellorie was sitting

back a bit in the chair. The coverall still revealed too much for me to take easily.

"Thank you. I like looking at your face better." She crossed one leg over the other and twisted in the chair.

"They are uncomfortable."

She lifted her eyebrows.

"The chairs, I meant."

"Do you mind if I move?"

"Of course not. I said they were uncomfortable."

She uncrossed her legs and slipped to her feet, then sat down on the bed next to me. She brought with her the sweetness of ryall.

"Sammis . . . ?"

"Yes."

"If you wanted something, and you could have it now, but knew you couldn't keep it, would you take it now? Even if losing it would hurt?"

Mellorie's voice was low, and she wasn't looking at me.

I didn't look at her either, but I could feel myself stiffening, excited, and yet afraid I knew exactly what she meant.

"I suppose I would, if it were offered. I'm not up to just taking."

"I know. I could tell, but are you offering?"

"I . . . hadn't thought about it."

"Look at me . . ."

I did. Her brown eyes were clear, direct, her lips slightly parted.

Her hand touched mine, covered it, and tightened gently. The soft warmth of her touch sent a jolt up my arm.

I turned my hand in hers, returning the pressure.

"I'll take that for an offering."

I scarcely moved as her fingers touched my face, gently suggesting I turn toward her. I did, and found warm and soft lips on mine.

My hands were on her back and shoulders, and I realized she wore nothing under the clinging coverall.

"Gently . . . kiss me again."

Somehow . . . we ended up lying next to each other on the bed. The kisses lasted so long I was short of breath, and what breath I had was filled with the scent of ryall, and Mellorie.

Her hands slipped under my tunic, guiding it off me, and in time, I discovered that she had indeed been wearing nothing under the coverall.

I had been wearing plenty, but her hands were deft, and her warmth more than enough to balance the breeze from the afternoon thunderstorm that played over us.

Too soon was my release, and I felt cheated somehow.

"Just relax."

I couldn't. So I let my hands stroke her smooth skin, her soft hair, exploring the curves and lines I had always imagined, but never before felt.

She shivered. "I'm cold." She had some goose bumps on her back.

The blanket was soft enough, and warm enough, especially as close as we were. I began to kiss her neck, but I kept touching her skin.

The warmth began to return to her skin.

"Roll over," she directed.

So I did, and Mellorie began to massage my back, starting at the base of my neck and working down. She took a long time, and by the time she had reached more sensitive areas, neither one of us was interested in just touching.

The second time took longer, and I didn't feel cheated . . . at all.

I must have fallen asleep, because it was much later when the sound of the thunder and the pelting rain woke me.

Mellorie was still curled next to me, but her eyes were open. One hand rested on my shoulder.

"Did you sleep?" I asked.

"A little."

*Crrasssh* . . .

"Sammis . . ."

"Don't say anything," I told her. "Don't say anything."

In the craziness outside, in the storm, and inside, in me, there wasn't any room for saying the obvious. Tomorrow was a long way off, and while I hadn't known enough to love Allyson when we should have, Mellorie had given me something I didn't want to lose before I had to.

So I put my arms around her and held her while the thunder played outside, and I think I cried, but neither of us said anything.

# XXXII.

ODIN THOR GLARED at the hand-drawn map on the plotting table, then at me. His glance softened slightly, when he turned and looked at Wryan—Dr. Relorn. The three of us stood each on a different side of the table.

"You can't mean that," he repeated.

I sighed. "I do. The tunneled spaces are about ten rods wide and a rod high, and there's about four hundred rods of tunnels all told. That's a lot of cubic rods. To get total coverage of the tunnels would take almost a gross of the gas grenades—without accounting for all the problems caused by walls and ventilation."

I could see Wryan rolling her eyes. "At the *outside*, I can make four or five dives before I can't carry any more. That's if no one gives the alarm. I can carry four or five of those monsters each time. That just isn't enough for a brute force approach.

"What we've suggested will allow you to capture the remainder with minimal casualties for our troops." I couldn't really call Odin Thor's force the ConFeds. What Wryan had suggested was simplicity itself. Don't try to cover the whole redoubt, but plant the grenades in the ventilation systems and in the exit corridors.

"But we'll have to stand off so far that some of them will escape."

"Not many," I asserted.

Wryan shook her head sadly. "There will be a few left to murder."

Odin Thor looked away from her quickly, as though she were a rock snake.

I glared at him.

"And you, Trooper. I could have you shot tomorrow."

"Not if you want this mission carried out."

"True!" He laughed again, as if I had forgotten something important. "We'll see." Then he shook his head, as if our disagreement were of only passing interest. "How about the day after tomorrow?"

"Fine," I answered, just wanting to get the meeting over. "I'll start the drops just before first light."

Odin Thor glanced around the old laboratory, his eyes passing over the instrumented diving stage and taking in the shut-down consoles. "That should do it for now."

I nodded.

"Good day, Doctor. Good day, Trooper." His feet shook the floor as he left.

*Click.*

As the laboratory door shut behind him, we exchanged glances.

"He knows something we don't," I said.

"I'm sure he does, but we know something he doesn't."

Frowning, I looked at the dusty tiles before glancing back at Wryan. She wore a baggy blackish-green tunic over straight-cut gray-blue trousers—an ideal combination to make her cosmetics look garish and her face pale.

"We do? You, maybe. Not me."

"You know it, too, Sammis. You may not wish to recognize it."

A shivery feeling quivered down my back at the matter-of-fact tone.

"Do you want me to spell it out?"

Finally, I nodded.

"What's to keep you from applying a gas grenade to him in his sleep? Or anything else lethal? No guard or wall could stop you. Or me, assuming you teach me what you say you can." Her voice was flat.

I hadn't wanted to face that truth. Now Wryan was deliberately recalling it. Bad enough to think about killing faceless enemies who had tried to kill me and my family, but I owed Odin Thor *something*.

"Are you still willing to murder the ConFeds in their fortress?"

"They murdered my father and a lot of other innocents. They tried to kill me. And you, that one night."

She smiled gently, with a twist to her lips. "Don't make me a part of your decision, Sammis. If you do this, the blood will be on your hands."

"You don't have any on yours, Doctor?"

"It's Wryan, not doctor," she corrected me. "I have my share, more than my share. What you do remains for life, and that may be a *very* long time."

Again, she was acting as though I would be around forever. Even the witches all died. It just took longer; that was all.

"You're acting as if you don't want me to do this. You tell me that the blood will be on my hands, and that I can certainly stop Odin Thor."

She shrugged, and her gesture was like looking in a

mirror. "This is your decision, and not anyone else's. You have to live with it—one way or the other."

"Wonderful. If I don't do something, we'll have a war between two groups of ConFeds who will destroy everything that's left. The other side might even win, and they want to kill me, and probably you. That leaves me a choice?"

She sighed. "It does. Don't you think the old witches of Eastron could have killed more than a few of their persecutors?"

"I thought they had."

"Some did; some didn't. Some left Eastron, took other names, had children, and avoided their heritage." She was looking intently at me.

"So . . . avoiding the problem is only a short-term solution. But the longer-term solutions have higher prices. Is that what you're telling me?"

"I'm just pointing out the alternatives."

"Why don't you decide?"

"Because." Again, there was that ghost of a smile, as she stepped away from the plotting table and the hand-drawn map. "Because it's your choice."

"Why, why, why do you insist on making it all my choice?" I was almost screaming.

"Because that is the way *you* will see it when you are older."

As her eyes caught mine, I could see a deep blackness behind the light piercing green, a glimpse of a darkness deeper than the undertime. I shivered where I stood, at having seen just that sliver of hell.

# XXXIII.

I LINED UP the grenades on the armorer's workbench in five groups of four.

"*Oooaaaah . . .*" yawned Janth, before covering his mouth.

I couldn't say I blamed him. Getting up well before first light is not conducive to alertness.

Even as he yawned, the assistant armorer's eyes never left the grenades, and his hand remained on the holstered butt of the projectile pistol. "How long before you make your first . . . trip . . . ?"

Concentrating on adjusting the equipment belt, I did not answer immediately. A quick release snap kept snagging. Finally, I got it unjammed. "Not very long. . . ."

"And how long between?" He was serious.

"No one briefed you?"

"Just that you'd be done before first muster. The Colonel-General told me not to tell anyone."

I sighed. Secrecy about the mission was fine, but keeping the fundamentals of time-diving secret was just plain stupid. "I don't have time to tell you everything, but the duration between trips will be exactly the amount of time it takes me to place these," and I held up one of the black killer mushroom grenades, "at the other end. Actually diving under time doesn't take any time at all. So . . . if I don't show up back here pretty quickly, you had better tell the Colonel-General that there's trouble."

"How quickly?"

I had to shrug. "Can't tell you that because I don't know how long it will take to place them. Not very long, because I'll be back for the others."

I slipped four of the grenades into the release clips on

my equipment belt. "Looks like it's time, Janth. Wish me luck."

"Luck, Trooper." He even smiled.

The first dive entry was smooth, splitting the now like a needle through a morning-still pond. The exit was almost as slick as I broke out in the middle of one of the four main ventilation ducts heading from the air-recirculating plant. The duct was carved from the rock and was wider than my armspan, though not much higher than the top of my head.

In quick motions that I had practiced with dummies Janth and I had put together, I released the four grenades from the equipment belt and spaced them equidistantly from the walls and each other. Then I pulled the arming pin of the first, then the second, the third, and the last. As I placed and armed the grenades, the forced air smelling of oil and metal whipped through my hair and past the squat and deadly black mushrooms. So heavy were the grenades that the wind that tore at me did not even rock them.

After dropping under the now as quickly as possible, I slid across the undertime from the hills of Bremarlyn back to Mount Persnol where the assistant armorer waited.

My second exit was still smooth.

"Quick there, Trooper."

"Hope we can keep it that way," I reached for the next of the black mushrooms. Janth clipped two of the second batch of grenades to my belt as I did two.

"Good—"

His sendoff was cut short as I dropped under the now, threading my way back along the silvery/gray/black undertime line I had travelled just moments before.

From what I could sense from the undertime, nothing in the underground ConFed base had changed between my departure and return.

Again, breakout was uneventful, and, in the second major ventilation duct, once more fighting the wind and odor of metal and oil, I placed and armed the grenades. This time my nose itched, almost enough to cause me to sneeze before I dropped undertime.

The trip back to Base was unpleasant—annoying, if you will. Imagine being suspended with the terrible itchy feeling and anticipation that comes just before a sneeze.

*Kkkkatchhewww!!!*

I felt like I had bruised every bone in my body, but I wiped my suddenly running nose on my sleeve and grabbed for another grenade.

"Cold there?" asked the assistant armorer as he clipped a second grenade to my equipment belt.

"No. Damned allergy . . . dust . . . oil . . ."

With that, I was gone again, back along the same track toward the real ConFed base to plant four more grenades in the third tunnel.

Again, there were no signs that my entries had been detected, or that the first two sets of grenades had exploded.

This time, fighting the wind and arming the grenades seemed harder. My nose itched and ran from the dusty metallic wind that swirled around me, but I still managed to get back undertime on schedule.

Breakout in the armory was a little rough. I came out above the floor level and staggered.

"Easy, Trooper." Janth steadied me.

I wiped my streaming nose on my sleeve again and grabbed for the next grenade.

"You all right?"

"So far. So far."

The fourth breakout in the ventilation system was even rougher.

Again, I was high, and dropped. It sounded to me like an explosion.

*Clank.*

I knocked over last grenade as I tried to arm it.

*CRRRUMMPPP!*

The sound of the first grenade going off in the other duct sent me undertime, with the fourth grenade rolling free and unarmed. But there was no way I was staying.

The return was the worst yet. My head was beginning to ache. I wanted to tear my nose off because it itched so badly. While I didn't break out high, I did lurch out of the undertime off-balance, almost knocking Janth over.

*KKKAATTCCHEWW!!!*

"You all right?"

"No, but it's all shot if I don't make the last one."

I could tell the fifth dive would be my last for awhile. I could only fasten one grenade in the time Janth did three. But I staggered back undertime and let my mind carry me back to the ConFed Base.

I could still sense no action, but I wasn't looking for action, only for the two main exit locks.

No careful placement of grenades this time. I broke out in the empty center lock, and yanked the grenades off my belt, one after the other, arming them and dropping them on the floor.

The second lock was worse. I fell, bashed my elbow, and rolled over, yanking the first grenade clear.

*BRINNNNGGGG!!!*

Even I could tell that was an alarm.

I sort of flung the second grenade behind me as I dropped under the now.

*Brattttttt. . . .*

Whether the flechettes missed or I had ducked undertime before they reached me, I didn't know, and didn't care. White spots flickered in front of me and my head felt like it would explode.

Literally sliding out of the undertime, I ended up in a heap under the edge of the armorer's work bench, sneezing with the little energy I had left.

"Verlyt! You look like hell, Trooper."

"Thanks," I mumbled, still pretty much in a heap.

*Click.*.

I could see a pair of trousered legs on the other side of the work bench, trousers and booted feet.

"Who are you?" demanded Janth, reaching for the projectile pistol.

"It's all right," I rasped, trying to sit up.

"Dr. Relorn," snapped Wryan, "and if you want Sammis to recover, you'd better let me give this to him."

Janth stood back, hand still on the gun, as Wryan put a beaker of the bitter-tasting stuff she had poured down me once before under my nose. I didn't wait this time. If I did, I wouldn't be in any shape to drink it.

"You push yourself too hard," she said quietly.

"Not much choice," I said, between small sips.

"There's always a choice."

I didn't want to talk about it. "Janth?"

"Yes, Trooper?"

"Might as well stow the rest of the stuff back in the vault for now. It either worked or it didn't."

"How soon will we know?"

"As soon as Odin Thor lets us know, or as soon as I recover enough to check on it. But that won't be for awhile." I managed to struggle into a half-sitting position.

Janth peered down at me. "I can see that."

"Take some more of this," ordered Wryan.

Janth took another look at me before beginning to replace the seals on the grenade storage cases.

*Thump. Creak.* . . .

As the armorer worked, I took a mouthful. The liquid wasn't as bad as swamp water in the damps, but the taste had little to recommend it. The results were better than the taste. The flickering lights before my eyes had disappeared.

"Can you get up?" Wryan asked.

"I'll be fine."

"Not for awhile, you won't," she corrected.

She was right. It took her hand, surprisingly strong for all its softness, to help me to my feet.

"How did you know?" That question had escaped me while I was trying to pull myself together.

"I just did." She shrugged. Her tone and gesture told me that she wasn't about to say more.

I looked over at Janth. "If the Colonel-General is interested, I'll be recovering."

"I think you could use it, Trooper." He shook his head. "There's a lot more to that mental travel business than meets the eye, that's for sure."

Nodding at that, I took a first step toward the doorway. "Janth? The seals?"

For a moment, the assistant armorer looked blank. "But she got in."

"Sorry," I apologized. "I thought you knew. This is Dr. Relorn. She's the head of the entire travel lab."

The armorer inclined his head. "I'm sorry I didn't recognize you, but I hadn't expected you . . ."

"That's all right. I'm not at my best this early in the day."

But she was at her best. Without the makeup, she looked scarcely older than either Mellorie or Amenda. I'd thought she would look years younger without it, but this was the first time I'd seen her naturally in full light.

Her hair was mussed as well, and her tunic and trousers slightly creased, not quite up to the immaculate impression she usually projected.

Janth was still shaking his head as he undid the seals.

From the armory up through the tunnels to the first floor of the barracks had never seemed such a long walk. Outside, however, waited the steamer, the one I had first seen on a cool evening.

Wryan had said nothing since we had left the armory. Nor had I.

"How do you feel?" she asked once I was seated next to her.

"Better. Still shaky."

"I'll have some high-energy food sent to your room. You'll need that, and some sleep. By yourself," she added.

"Do you know everything?"

"No. But I've waited a long time, and seen a great deal. It's not surprising, and it's necessary. Whether I like it or not." While her tone was matter-of-fact, her voice did not ring quite true.

"Necessary? Whether you like what?"

She ignored my question. "You need to recover. I'm sure Odin Thor will want a report on the situation inside the ConFed redoubt, although he knows what it is. And you need to see for yourself. From the undertime."

The steamer was moving faster than I had expected, and Wryan took some of the corners nearly on two wheels.

"You never answered my question. What's necessary?"

"Mellorie, of course."

I decided not to ask any more questions of that nature, knowing I might not like the answers. Before I could have formulated any, the steamer screeched to a halt before the travel lab quarters.

"Are you all right to get up the stairs?"

"I'm fine. Just fine."

"Good. When you scout out the fortress, let me know what you find."

"I will. I certainly will."

"That would be helpful. Now, get some rest." She gave me a fleeting smile before speeding away in the steamer.

She was definitely not happy about my relationship with Mellorie, and didn't care if I knew it. Yet she had been there when I collapsed.

My steps up the stairs were slow. Very slow. I didn't

see Mellorie. A tray of steaming food, including hot chyst cider, was waiting on my desk.

I pulled up one of the wooden armchairs and began to eat. Slowly. Although the amount of food seemed excessive, I plowed through it all. But I barely managed to get out of the uniform before sinking into the bed.

# XXXIV.

I SLEPT FOR most of the day, because it was late afternoon when I finally woke out of some nightmare I could not remember.

"You're finally awake." Mellorie's voice was a welcome relief. "You must have had some strange dreams."

"How long have you been here? Did I say anything?"

"Not long," she laughed softly. "You are suspicious." She paused, then uncrossed her legs, and moved from the chair to the bed next to me, running her fingers over my bare shoulders. "You were groaning, and I was about to wake you."

She wasn't saying something, but her fingers felt good kneading out the stiffness. So I waited.

Mellorie's hands stopped, and she put her arm around me and squeezed before letting go. "Your mind is somewhere else."

I nodded, stifling a yawn. "On food . . ."

"And?"

"I still have to find out how effective . . . my efforts . . . were . . ."

Mellorie stood up, not exactly looking at me or out the window, or anywhere. "Just what were you doing this morning, Sammis?"

"Killing people."

"Be serious."

"I am being serious. I killed some of the people who were killing our troops. I just don't know how many."

"The other ConFeds?" She was wearing a dark blue tunic and trousers, with matching, if scuffed, blue boots.

"You've heard about them?"

"They're the real ConFeds, aren't they?"

"Both groups are real. The others were in Eastron and did all the dirty work, though. At least from what I can tell."

"I hope you killed them all." Her voice wasn't husky. It was hard. "I hope you killed every single one of them."

The coldness of her words gave me a shiver, even as she turned to look directly out the window.

"Do you want to talk about it?" I asked.

"No."

"Are you certain?"

"I'm *very* certain, Sammis. Don't ever ask me again. Not if you care one bit for me." She still kept her face from me.

"That was why I asked . . ."

"I understand. But . . . just don't ask."

"All right. I won't." I slowly swung my feet onto the floor.

"If you don't mind . . . I don't feel well . . ." Her voice was brittle as well as hard. "I'll see you later." She walked to the door and let herself out without looking back.

Whatever had happened to her at the hands of the ConFeds was internal, or long ago, because there weren't any scars on her body. Scars on her soul—that was something else.

The light outside was dimming as another late afternoon storm built up.

The door Mellorie had left ajar blew shut with a gust that also brought the odor of rain into my room.

I was hungry, again. So I looked around. While I had

been sleeping, someone had removed the tray and its dishes and replaced it with some fruits—chyst and pear-apple—and cheese, flanked by a small pile of biscuits. I sat down at the desk, uncomfortable chair and all, and ate every last bit, alternating the biscuits and cheese with the fruit.

A hot shower in the antique tiled stall remedied some of the lingering stiffness. After toweling myself dry, I pulled on another undress uniform. Despite my growing dislike of the uniforms, I had nothing else to wear.

The roll of thunder outside indicated the oncoming storm might drop some needed rain.

I found myself licking my lips, staring at nothing. Should I report to Wryan? Odin Thor? Finally, I slipped under the now and out toward the hills of Bremarlyn. A ghost of a grayish thread was all that marked my morning route, probably invisible in the undertime to any diver who was not looking for it. Not that I was looking, suspended in the motionless chill of that place between worlds, between time, but the more I dived, the more I saw with my mind, rather than my eyes.

As I reached the underground redoubt, the silence struck me—the absolute lack of energy, almost that same lack of energy that had marked those places the enemy had obliterated. Here, near Bremarlyn, the grass waved in the breeze, and the trees gathered the sunlight, and Odin Thor's armored steamers and their crews lounged in the last warmth before twilight.

And beneath?

Nothing. Nothing but chill, silence, and darkness.

I reached out without breaking from under the now, trying to capture a mental image of the underground retreat of the real ConFeds, attempting to find those who had survived.

Nothing. Nothing but motionless machinery, and scattered lumps of flesh that had been men. Even in the sensationless undertime, the odor of death clogged my nostrils.

Knowing my time was limited, my strength not restored, and also aware that I needed to know what had happened, I eased myself backtime, red direction, careful that I should not overlap with my previous visit, even though you cannot contact yourself in the undertime . . . or in the now.

*AAAAAAeeeeeeeeeeeeeeeeeeeeeeeeeeeeeeeeeeeeeeeeeeeeeeeeee-eee. . . . . . .*

*Noooooooooooooooooooooo!!!!!!!!!!!!!!!!!!!!!!!!*

*. . . . . Verlytttt!!! . . . .*

*. . . dying . . . dying . . . dying . . .*

Red lenses slashed across my eyes. Needles lanced my lips, and acid etched my throat. Breathing fire, I tried to rip my guts out, spew my innards across the cold of undertime . . . trying to escape the pyramiding agony . . .

Flares flashed across my visions . . .

. . . a thin man slashing his own throat . . .

. . . a woman grabbing a brain-spattered projectile gun from a dead ConFed's hand, to turn it against her own skull . . .

. . . a man with shaking hands injecting himself, biting his lips raw and trying to keep from screaming . . .

. . . a young soldier, crawling, scrabbling, leaving a pink frothed trail on the stone behind him . . .

. . . a Captain, standing in the doorway of an underground barracks, propped against the casement, bringing up the heavy riot gun while trying to keep from shaking, trying to bring the gun to bear on the men writhing on the floor . . .

*AAEEEIIIIIIIIIIIIIIIIIIIIIIIIIIIIIIIIIIiiiiiiiiiiiiiiiiiiiiiiiii . . .*

The silent screams from the undertime chased me all the way back to the camp.

*Uuuuuthuuuuuupppppp . . . uuuutthhhuuuupppp . . . uuupppthuuuuppp . . .*

Despite the violence of the contractions and eruptions within me, it took a long time to empty my guts, and even longer for the dry retching to subside.

Longer still was it before I could stand and peel off my dishonored and soaked uniform and wad it up and stuff it into the empty rubbish bucket. I had to lean on the tile wall to be able to lather and wash myself clean. Hot as the water was, I shivered, and my teeth chattered. My knees threatened to buckle with each shiver, and each breath felt like it rasped my throat raw.

Would I ever feel clean inside again? I wondered, but not for long, because I needed every jot of strength I had to wend my way stark naked down the hallway to my room.

I did not make it under the quilt. Lifting even the coverlet was beyond me.

When I woke, I was in a strange room. Hanging tubes connected to needles seemed to run ice into my veins.

A cold sweat beaded on my forehead as I shivered under the weight of blankets that did not keep me warm.

I opened one eye.

A woman saw the gesture and scuttled from the light-walled area.

I licked my too-dry lips, swallowed, and waited for the room to stop circling around me.

While waiting, I fell asleep again.

The next time, I drifted into consciousness, feeling a hand that was simultaneously warm and cold upon my forehead.

"Sammis?"

"Ummmmm . . ." I meant to say "yes," but my tongue didn't fully cooperate.

"Just rest. You'll be just fine."

". . . uuuhhmmmm . . ." My mouth was swollen, and my tongue still refused to cooperate.

Why wouldn't I be fine? I'd just overextended myself by

a factor of ten or so, but rest and intravenous replenishment should help.

At some point, I actually woke up clearheaded, and I was hungry—until I thought about food. I decided not to think about food and looked around.

Through the half-shuttered window blinds I could tell it was night. Clearly, more had affected me than simple exhaustion. Because I had not breached the undertime barrier, I could not have been poisoned by the gas grenades. The food left for me?

"Well, our sleeping prince has finally awakened . . ."

The heartiness of the doctor's voice instantly annoyed me. "How long have I been sick?"

"Feisty, he is, too. And that is a good sign . . ."

"How long?" I snapped.

"Let's see . . . about ten days . . ."

"TEN DAYS?" That was impossible.

"You're lucky to be alive, young man. Surviving nerve poison isn't exactly commonplace." She studied my eyes, and flashed a small light around.

"Nerve poison?"

"We don't know how you managed to get a small enough exposure to survive, but once you made it past the first few hours, it was just a matter of treating the symptoms. You're just lucky that your lady friend found you before it was too late." She was taking my pulse or listening to my heart.

"Lady friend?"

"But your signs are good, and I think we can get rid of this last tube and let you have clear liquids. The sooner, the better. You're too thin. All you travelers have too high a metabolic rate."

I wanted to say something.

"Not that any of you will ever get fat, but you'll starve on a diet that would feed a healthy farmer." She prodded my too-tight shoulder muscles. "Well, let's get started."

"Started?"

"Some high-protein, high-energy, clear liquids before you turn into a true shadow of your former self. Don't you feel light-headed when you work too hard for too long?"

I had to nod, feeling wrung out as well as light-headed.

"Tendency to chronically low blood sugars. Runs in the breed, I suspect. Now, let's get you something to drink."

"Water would be fine."

"Not enough. You want to end up with more tubes in you?"

"No."

"Didn't think so. I'll be right back. Or Nerlis will."

Nerlis?

As she swept out and opened the door, my view of the room improved with the increased light from the corridor outside. There wasn't much to see, just the bed, a plastic chair, a hospital-type table, and several thin structures on wheels draped with tubing. And one bouquet of sun daisies, framed by greens, with a card beside it, sitting on the window sill.

The flowers drooped, as if they had been there for some time.

*Click, click, click.*

Then the single overhead light flashed on, and my eyes watered.

"Let's get that out of you. I'm Nerlis, trooper, and I'm glad to see you awake." She had short silvered hair, wrinkles, and a genuine smile.

"So am I. So am I." I coughed to clear my throat. "Where am I?"

"You wouldn't know; would you?" She laughed, a soft hoarse sound. "You're in the base infirmary. That's why you're still alive."

"But . . ."

"Everyone knew you had to go back. But it wasn't your

fault. The armorer committed suicide, you know, after giving you the wrong weapons.''

"Janth . . ."

"His family was killed in the looting after the enemy attacks. They say he's never been quite the same since. The Colonel-General had worried about that, but there never were enough trained armorers.'' She busied herself with the needle attached to the tubing. "Look somewhere else, and relax.''

"Somewhere else . . . ? All right.''

"Aaaah . . . bring your arm up. That's it.'' She maneuvered a dressing into place where the needle had come out. "Now just hold your arm like that for a few minutes while I get the Sustain.''

"Sustain?'' I hated asking stupid questions.

"High-energy clear liquid,'' said Nerlis as she marched out of the room, her boot heels clicking on the tiles.

I licked my lips and tried to swallow. Tried, because my throat was so dry. Outside, the darkness was beginning to lighten, and I could see blurred clouds.

". . . in a little while . . .''

Nerlis's voice echoed down the corridor. She was talking to someone else. Their words were muffled. So I tried to shift my weight one-armed, leaving the dressing in place. How long before I could straighten my arm?

*Click, click, click . . .*

"Here we go.'' She was carrying a beaker of an off-purplish liquid and a cup, both of which she placed on the bedside table. After pouring a small amount into the cup, she held it up. "Take a sip. A *small* sip . . . and you can relax your arm. Any bleeding should have stopped by now.''

My hands shook as I lifted the cup, easing a few drops into a mouth so dry that none even seemed to reach my throat. The second sip lubricated my throat, and a third may have reached my stomach.

"Wait a moment."

I put down the cup, marveling at how much effort three small sips took.

"Shouldn't be too long before some of the light-headedness starts to pass. Might be a minor stomach cramp or two."

"Uh . . ." Minor stomach cramp? I could barely keep from doubling over, and my forehead burst out in another cold sweat.

"Try to relax." Nerlis wiped off my forehead with a dry cloth, before folding it neatly and putting on the bed-table next to the cup. "The reaction should pass quickly."

She was right about that, too.

"Another sip," she commanded.

I just looked at her.

She looked back at me.

I picked up the cup and took another series of small sips. My hands didn't shake the second time.

"The second set of cramps should be less violent."

They were. Instead of wanting to double up and die, I only felt like the three ConFeds had charged into my guts. I fumbled for the cloth and managed to wipe off my own forehead.

"Another sip?" I asked after the sweat and cramps passed.

"One more. Then wait for a while. You should start to feel better. You need to finish the entire beaker by mid-morning." She started to leave, then turned back. "And no matter how good you think you feel, don't try to get out of that bed or sit up with your legs over the side."

"But . . ."

"You're dehydrated enough you don't need to use the facilities immediately, and we don't need you plastered face down on the stone."

"Yes, Nerlis."

"Thank you, Trooper." She left shaking her head.

I waited, then took another series of sips from the cup, and suffered through the entire process of cramps and cold sweats again. By the time I had recovered from the third round of Sustain, I could see a gray, gray morning.

Wryan stood at the foot of the bed—from nowhere.

I gaped. It was one thing to surprise others, another to be surprised.

"Are you feeling better?"

"I thought you didn't dive?"

"I didn't." She smiled wryly. "But someone told me it was possible, and then left me hanging, and I worked on it."

"What really happened to me?" I found myself lowering my voice.

"Did you actually enter the ConFed fort?" The doctor was frowning, but she didn't look as formidable as before.

"No. Stayed strictly under the now. I'm not that stupid . . . but . . ." I shook my head. "Didn't seem to make that much difference . . ."

"It did. You'd be dead otherwise. Your reaction was from the mental feedback, I think, trying to convince your body to replicate the symptoms."

"Replicate?" I shivered. "Do you know . . . really know?"

Wryan just kept watching me, meeting my eyes.

". . . never . . . never . . . again . . ."

"Killing people, you mean?"

"Not that. Torturing them. Do you have any idea . . . ?" I was not just shivering, but shaking all over as the images pounded back at me.

"Try not to remember. Not just yet." Wryan's hands covered mine.

"Try not to remember? How . . . ?" That woman putting a gun to her head . . . or the man slashing his own throat . . . or the whole screaming, pounding pulsation of pain that had buried me . . . how could I not remember?

I could feel her hands tremble. "You felt it, too? You looked?"

"Not so closely as you did." Her face had paled momentarily.

"What happened?" As I freed one hand and used the cloth to wipe my forehead again, I was beginning to get an idea of what had occurred.

"They think you picked up traces of the nerve poison. You showed all the symptoms. The doctors claimed Odin Thor could be tried for murder. The nerve gas was banned throughout Query generations ago."

"Ahhhhh . . . and then the Colonel-General claimed he thought it was only nausea gas to flush them out?"

"Exactly."

"Poor Janth."

"The armorer?"

I nodded.

"He really did suicide, Sammis. Not that I blame him."

"I don't either."

Slowly, as I stopped shaking, she removed her hands from mine and stepped back. I realized she had stopped wearing the makeup to make her look older.

I laughed harshly. "All that equipment's lost, at least for a season."

"Not nearly that long, unfortunately. The nerve gas will decompose within days." Wryan looked around. "You're not supposed to have visitors yet."

After the stimulation of seeing Wryan, and the reaction to those too-vivid memories, I felt drained again. So I reached for the Sustain. This time, the reaction was but a slight jolt and a damp forehead.

"Don't they understand? How horribly they all died? The background sheets said it was quick, not that it was like an eternal agony compressed into a thousand breaths.

Even after. . . . even after . . . my father . . . no one . . .
nobody . . . should die like that . . ."

"No . . . but you didn't know."

"Does that excuse it, Doctor?"

"No." Wryan looked straight back at me, her eyes clear.
I respected her for that lack of evasion. "But it means you
understand."

I had to lean back on the pillows, Sustain or no Sustain.

"You will have to kill again, Sammis. You know that.
Chaos leads to violence, and some violence can only be
halted by removing the causes."

Unfortunately, I knew what she meant. "Not now."

"No." She shook her head. "Not now." Looking
around, she smiled faintly. "Good-bye."

She was gone, just like I had left her on those nights I
had appeared in her quarters.

*Click, click, click* . . .

"Trooper? Who were you talking to?"

"Me?" I forced a grin. "Guess I was talking to myself."

Nerlis didn't believe me, but she just looked around,
shook her head, and pointed to the cup. "Keep drinking."

"Yes, nurse." I reached for the cup again. It was going
to be a long morning, a very long morning.

# XXXV.

ONCE I HAD struggled through the entire beaker of the
Sustain, my recovery was a matter of time, and enough
calories. I was ready to leave. Neither Nerlis nor Dr. Dyrell would agree.

"You have no bodily reserves, Trooper. None at all.
Your immune system is depressed . . ." Dr. Dyrell, al-

though hearty in tone, was less flexible than Odin Thor. ". . . and you probably never ate enough."

"I can't eat any more."

Dr. Dyrell just shook her round face at me. Her dark hair, peppered with gray, was so short and curly that it didn't even move. "You can't take in enough calories with three standard meals. You need a minimum of five full meals. Three or four and an equal number of heavy snacks will do the same thing." She glared at me. "Until you get some weight on that scrawny frame, you can't leave. Trying to do it overnight puts too much strain on your heart. We'll measure it out until we get you up where you belong.

"In the meantime, if you leave here using those mental travel tricks, it's your health. Maybe your death."

She wasn't joking. I had to go for the meals plus snacks routine. Five full meals I just couldn't take. Even after a day or two, I could tell the difference. Not that I looked much different, but I could use my undertime sight—and it was sharper—without feeling an instantaneous physical drain. Hard to believe that I had been operating on the edge of starvation, or that eating the diet of a healthy farmer had been insufficient.

Deric arrived with a stack of notebooks and the suggestion that I could spent my recuperation learning what every good diver should know. Most of the time, studying beat staring out the window, and gave me a welcome break.

Two days later, plowing through some overripe fruit and stale cheese and leafing through the third notebook, I heard footsteps.

"Sammis?"

"Mmmmpphhh . . ." With my mouth full, I just mumbled at Mellorie.

"Is that all you have to say?" She grinned momentarily. In her dark blue tunic and white trousers, she looked professional.

I shrugged, swallowing quickly. "Medical opinion was that I was near starvation. They won't let me out—officially—until I remedy that."

"Poor Sammis . . . you look a sight better than when they carted you out of your room. I'm sorry I didn't come earlier, but . . ." She looked down, then out the window, where high white clouds darkened into afternoon thunderstorms.

Something—more than just something—was bothering Mellorie.

"Do you want to talk about it?"

"No . . . but I should." She kept her back to me, with her hands clasped. "You . . . you thought . . . but I didn't. I couldn't. Not after Nepranza . . ." If she hadn't found me, who had? The doctor had said "woman friend."

"Nepranza?" I temporized. "That bad . . . ?" I didn't know what she was talking about.

"They said it wasn't that bad." Her voice was flat. "They say I must have been imagining things. They say that no one would have touched a child. Not the daughter of a lord. That's what they say. . . ."

Nepranza! The name connected. Farren had mentioned the place—molesting a lord's daughter . . . as if the only bad thing had been the killings of nearly innocent young men.

"They never talked to you?"

"My father wouldn't let them—before. He died in the riots. The ConFeds made sure of that. They made sure of a few other things."

"I see . . ." Not that I did. "Is that why you were attracted to me?"

Mellorie shrugged, still looking out the half-open window.

A roll of distant thunder punctuated her gesture.

"Yes."

I could barely hear her voice.

"Sammis . . ." She finally turned around, but she did not look at me. Her tunic was buttoned all the way to the neck. "Don't you understand? I was afraid. I knew you were sick, but I wouldn't go into your room. I wouldn't come see you until you were well." Mellorie finally looked up and into my eyes, almost glaring at me.

"Why don't you sit down?" I took a deep breath.

"You want me to stay? After I nearly killed you?"

"First," I sighed, "you didn't nearly kill me. I did. Second, there was nothing physically wrong with me. And third . . . we'll get to that. Now sit down. You owe me that."

She didn't owe me anything, but I wanted her to sit down.

"Do you know what happened?" I asked.

"They said you must have tried to check—"

"No. I'm smarter than that. I just wasn't prepared for the feedback. For all the deaths."

Mellorie's face went blank, as if a screen had covered it. "They deserved it. Every instant of it."

"Even the woman who took her lover's gun and blew out her own brains because the pain was so great? Or the boy who kept banging his head against the stone walls . . ."

"Don't talk to me about them . . . please . . . don't talk to me about them . . ."

"Mellorie . . . I damned near died because I picked up their deaths . . . my brain was trying to tell my body it was dying—five hundred times over. Do you know what it was like dying—"

"Stop it! Stop it, stop it, STOP IT!!!!" Mellorie lurched to her feet. She grabbed the railing at the bottom of the bed and shook it enough to make the heavy bed sway. "STOP IT!!!"

*Click, click, click, click!*

Nerlis stood in the doorway. I motioned her back, but she stayed there.

Mellorie didn't seem to notice. "All you can think about is their deaths! What about my sister? What about my father? What about me?"

"What about my father?" I asked quietly. "They burned him alive in his own house."

"Then how can you feel anything for them?" Her voice was lower.

"Because I felt every single one of them die. And nobody should have died like that."

"Would you do it again?"

"Would you do it?" I countered.

"In an instant. Would you?" A thin film of perspiration coated her forehead. "Would you do it again?"

"I don't know." I tried not to shake my head, but the images kept running through my thoughts—the woman grasping for the gun, the soldier with bloody fingers clawing his way along the floor . . .

"Good-by, Sammis." She brushed the red hair back off her damp forehead with her right hand, as if nothing had happened. Her left still held the bed frame. "I hope you're back to normal before too long. Let's have dinner some time when you come back." Her face was almost expressionless. Then she grinned, and the falsity made her face look like a carnival mask. "Just mark it down as the hysteria of a pampered lady gentry. All right?"

Nerlis eased back into the corridor, although Mellorie had never even taken notice of her.

"Whatever you say, Mellorie. Whatever you say."

She let go of the bed frame. "I still like you, Sammis, but you don't understand. So let's just be friends. All right?"

I nodded slowly. "Friends."

"Friends." This time I got a faint smile, but a real one. For a long time, I looked blankly out the window, letting the breeze ruffle my hair, drawing in the air that bore the hint of the on-coming storm, and the ebbing scent of the one just departed.

"Are you all right, Trooper?"

"Call me Sammis, Nerlis."

A gust of wind tugged at my sheets, and Nerlis slid the window almost shut as the rain began to pelt against the pane. She went back into the corridor, presumably to check on other windows.

The rest of the cheese was still waiting, still stale. I could have eaten the chyst I had started, brown as it had become, if I'd been in the damps, but I picked up the pearapple instead and finished it in five bites. Then I took a deep swig of the Sustain, not because I liked the swill, but because I wanted out.

After that, I picked up the notebook, the one with the theories on the Laws of Time in it, and began to read again.

When the thunder and rain had died away, and the room was getting stuffy again, I tossed back the sheet and walked to the window, opening it wide. Then I went to the narrow wardrobe. Not a stitch of clothing.

I laughed. I hadn't been wearing anything when I had collapsed. I didn't get back into the bed, but wrapped the robe around me and sat in the chair.

Hatred. There was so much of it. Westron hated Eastron; the farmers and townies hated the gentry; the Con-Feds hated the Secos; the gentry hated the Temple; and everyone hated the witches—and the Frost Giants. Mellorie was close to hating me because I refused to hate the people I had killed.

The room began to darken, both from the clouds and the twilight, but I wasn't cold. And I was tired of the bed, tired of lying around getting fattened up, tired of studying theories, no matter how valuable they might be.

"Your friend was a little upset." Nerlis carried a tray.

"Can I just eat it here?" I stood up, put the notebooks in a pile on the floor, and wheeled the bed table over.

*Creeakkk.*

"Turn it the other way." Nerlis set the wooden tray on the just-lowered table.

At its lowest setting, the table was higher than I would have preferred. What surprised me was that I was, if not hungry, certainly able to eat the food before me—slices of cold roast, jellied rice, sprouts, greens, and a pair of biscuits with some flambard preserves.

"Watching you eat just amazes me. You eat more than most guardsmen."

"It amazes me, too," I muttered between mouthfuls. I wanted out of the place, and, if it took eating everything in sight, so be it.

As I continued to munch, Nerlis left me with the diminishing pile of food and my thoughts.

The breeze had died as the air cooled, and outside the clouds were breaking up. In the west, the clouds glistened a greenish pink, underlit by the setting sun.

*Terwhit . . . terwhit . . .*

Whatever bird called, the sound was better than the harshness of the grossjays, those scavengers that had fed so well on the looting and burning following the Frost Giant attacks.

*Terwhit . . . terwhit . . .*

After pushing the table back from the straight-backed, two-armed wooden chair I stood and made my way to the window. Studying the dimming southern sky, and trying to pick out stars between the scattered clouds, I wondered if I could go undertime and follow a straight line to each.

The pinkness of the dying sunset faded into purple, then near-black.

One bright point of light emerged from behind a cloud. More properly, the fast-moving cloud left it unobscured in the evening, glittering and untwinkling above the dark and lightless building housing the Far Travel Lab.

Mithrada—the next planet inward from Query; host to the ill-fated planet-forming and metal-mining expedition that had brought on the Frost Giant attacks; evening or morning star to how many generations?

I tried to swallow the lump in my throat. When swallowing didn't help, I tried thinking. Except my thoughts skittered from crazy Mellorie to Allyson, and whether Mellorie could dive or not, I would have traded her for sweet, perceptive and intelligent Allyson without an instant's hesitation.

Those memories didn't help the lump in my throat, either, especially recalling lying in the darkness with Allyson, holding her and being held. In addition to a heavy throat, I was having trouble seeing, and my cheeks were wet. Above it all, Mithrada glittered, like a heartless diamond in the sky.

*Terwhit . . . terwhit . . .*

Hearing the unknown bird helped, and I hoped he or she would call again, as I listened and the darkness deepened. In time, another cloud obscured Mithrada, and I turned back to my bed.

"Oh . . ." I mumbled, barely keeping myself from jumping at the sight of someone in the chair. I glanced through the undertime to avoid the darkness.

The woman in the chair was Wryan, and there were deep circles under her eyes. My food tray had been removed while I had thought and looked and looked and thought. I hadn't even noticed.

"Troubles?" I asked. "I'm sorry. Have you been here long?"

"Not too long, and it was peaceful to sit here and watch you, and listen to the wind." She paused. "There are always troubles, Sammis." She took a breath that verged on a sigh before continuing. "I understand that you had a few of your own this afternoon."

"Did Nerlis call you?" My tone was snappish.

"No. She told me when I came. It works better if I announce my arrival officially." There was a trace of wryness in her tone.

I sat on the edge of the bed. My legs were a little stiff from standing so long. Otherwise, I felt fine.

"Do you want to talk about it?"

I couldn't help grinning as she used the same words I had employed earlier. "Yes . . . and no."

Wryan sat there waiting.

"Either Mellorie's not quite sane, or I'm not quite sane, or maybe we're both crazy." I found that the table had been raised and moved back to its place beside the bed. I took a gulp of Sustain before saying another word. Verlyt, I wanted out.

Wryan sat there, leaning forward, her left arm propped on the chair, her chin resting on her left hand, and her right arm loosely in her lap.

"She came to apologize about not being able to help me. She has this . . . fear . . . about sickness. That didn't bother me—except that I didn't realize I owe you—but when I tried to tell her what happened, she didn't hear me."

Wryan watched, waiting for me to go on.

"It was easier for her to believe I was sick, and that she had let me down, than it was for her to hear how horribly those ConFeds died. All she said was that they deserved it. Every instant of agony. Because they raped her—or worse." I shook my head. "I know she was hurt. I know her father was killed at Nepranza. But she's alive. They're not. Some of them were innocent.

"Like the woman who blew her brains out with her dead lover's gun. She didn't rape Mellorie. Or the young soldier my age . . . or . . ." I slid off the bed and walked back to the open window. For some reason, I didn't want to look at Wryan, perhaps because she was a woman.

"Some of them deserved the gas. But every one of them died. Odin Thor knew they would. I should have, but I was too busy proving that I could do it to think about what it meant. When they were all dying, it was a little too late."

"Would you bring them back?" Wryan's voice was soft.

The clouds had passed clear of Mithrada again, and the planet shone diamondlike just above the horizon.

"I said I didn't know."

"You know."

"You're right. I'd probably do it again, and I wouldn't bring them back. That makes me worse than Mellorie. Doesn't it?" I took my hands from the window frame and slowly turned to face Wryan. "Doesn't it?"

"Not necessarily. What would happen if you hadn't killed them? How many people would die? And who would they be?" She had leaned back in the chair.

"You're saying that it's all right to kill to stop more deaths? Hell! Why does there have to be so much hatred? So much killing?"

Wryan didn't have an answer. Neither did I.

*Terwhit . . . terwhit . . .*

I couldn't help but smile momentarily. The bird had a point. You sing when you can, not when someone wants you to. I glanced out the window, but, even looking into the undertime, couldn't locate the bird.

"Do you understand?" I asked Wryan.

"Understand what? That you killed real people? That some of them were innocent? That you hate yourself for doing it? Or that you know this is just the beginning?"

All of a sudden, with Wryan's last words, the room was cold, as cold as I had ever experienced, even in that dream ice-storm that had launched me into time-diving. "Just the beginning . . . ?"

I knew what she meant. The farmers weren't farming as much. The Frost Giants were out there somewhere. No one except Odin Thor's ConFeds had any way to hold things together. I stepped away from the breeze that ran through my robe and gave me a physical chill.

". . . just the beginning . . ." I sighed. "How bad is it?"

"Worse than that." She shook her head. "Odin Thor has his hands full with what amounts to two provinces of old Westron. Outside of that . . ." she shrugged. "Any place else, no one really farms . . . most of the crafters were killed with the gentry . . ."

The silence and the darkness stretched out between us. *Terwhit . . . terwhit . . . terwhit . . .*

I smiled at the cheerfulness of the call. The bird was definitely right. "So we do what we can."

She was smiling also, though more faintly. "I suppose. What other choice is there?" Her quiet voice was firm.

The sound brought back another memory. "Thank you."

"You're welcome."

"How did you know?"

"I'm not sure. But I did."

Her tone told me not to pursue that question. I didn't. "You kept visiting me when I couldn't even think, when nobody thought I would live?"

"Yes."

"Why?"

"Because."

I grinned. "That's not good enough, Doctor."

"Because you gave me back part of myself."

That wasn't all, but it was enough. "You need some sleep." I took a step toward her, then stopped.

"I know."

"So . . . why don't you go get some? And have pleasant dreams?"

She stood up, looking ghost-like in the light-colored tunic and trousers. "I will."

"Thank you . . ." I wanted to say more, but couldn't say what . . . or why. Besides, she was probably a good century older than me. So I didn't.

"Good night, Sammis."

*Click, click, click.* . . . Her boots sounded lonely as she walked out, and I stood there for a long time. When I looked out the window, before climbing into the hospital bed, Mithrada had dropped below the horizon.

# XXXVI.

NERLIS AND DR. Dyrell officially discharged me two days after Mellorie and I "became friends." They also required all divers to come in for checkups every ten-day.

Gerloc, Amenda, and Arlean were all on the verge of starvation. So were several others I didn't know. One of the newest divers, a recruit ConFed named Jerlyk, was barely above the minimums. That led to a divers' nutrition chart, which ended up posted in the dining area.

In the meantime, between my efforts in the hospital and my efforts while on "light duty," I had finished all the background material on diving. At the end of the next ten-day, I was cleared to dive again.

"I have a loose end or two to follow," I told Wryan, after squeezing in to see her before Odin Thor arrived. He was already pacing down the hallway toward the main lab. "What I find out could be helpful."

"Such as?"

"Even though we can't break out on Query, except in real time, I could see backtime at least several days when I scouted the ConFed fort. I'd like to see what the limits are."

"Take it easy. We'll call it extended reconnaissance research for now." She smiled, almost sadly. "Good luck."

"Good luck to you. Odin Thor's almost here." I ducked out just as the Colonel-General arrived. I avoided saluting him and was around the corner before he reacted.

"Trooper!"

I ignored the call, smiling, since I was out of sight. It was bad enough that circumstances required I do Odin Thor's dirty work without making him into a tin god. Besides, I had more important things to do.

After stopping by the snack table—another innovation of Wryan's—at the dining area and picking up cheese, hard biscuits, and fruit, I headed back to my room—by foot.

I had also gone back into conditioning, running and doing exercises. I didn't like them, but diving was clearly a strenuous business, and I was going to be in top condition. That was why Jerlyk and I met on the grassy square behind the quarters before every breakfast. After a few days, Gerloc and Amenda joined us, though neither could match us.

Grabbing some snack foods, I headed back to my room, which was fine with me. The next few subjective hours would be tough enough without any distractions.

Once inside, I eased the window wide open, trying to coax a breeze inside. For early fall, the weather was warm, almost hot. Entering the undertime too warm would make the entire dive uncomfortable.

After I opened the window and laid out my mid-morning snack, I sat before the desk and forced myself to eat all the elements of the semi-meal slowly, following it with a watered-down and tastier version of Sustain.

Then I stood up and walked around, trying to figure out what route I would take, but merely thinking about it didn't offer much insight.

Where and when I wanted to view was clear, although why was another question I didn't really want to address.

Still . . . I had promised myself that I would try, and a promise was a promise, even to me.

After a last gulp of the Sustain, I stopped pacing and dropped through the now and into the undertime.

Not that I went all that far back, or even that far geographically—less than a year and less than two hundred kays—just back to Bremarlyn. Back to the evening of a freak snowstorm and the morning afterwards.

I could have tried to watch a scared youngster wearing a heavy uniform cloak slip down a snow-filled gully and disappear to avoid being shot. But I didn't.

Slipping further toward the dawn, I fought to see through the hazy barrier between the then and the undertime, as well as to see through the fat swirling flakes of the untimely snow.

As the indirect light of a dawn grayed by clouds waxed on that stately house I had not seen intact since then, I watched, trying to shift my view toward whatever had happened.

Did I really want to know?

I watched from outside the house. I could have drifted inside, looking at the Davniads, watching Allyson, but I would have felt somehow unclean, like a voyeur, or . . . a ConFed. So I watched from outside.

First, a puff of smoke fluffed from the chimney. I let myself drift further foretime, when the snowflakes had stopped and the light was brighter. Not yet mid-morning, but no longer early morning.

A figure—Jerz Davniads—opened the doors to the steamer locker. His breath trailed above him like a smoke plume.

Allyson appeared, moving quickly, with several bags, which she dropped by the steamer. Her father said something, but she did not even turn as she hurried back across the courtyard to the house to return with yet another pair of bags. Jerz waited until she had returned with the second set.

This time Allyson gestured at the bags and motioned toward the steamer. Jerz shook his head and walked back across the courtyard with her. They brought back four more bags, and Germania Davniads followed with two large baskets, which she put in the rear seat of the steamer. Allyson handed her father the bags as he placed five of them in the rear storage trunk.

As he lashed down the remaining bag on the storage rack, Germania slipped into the driver's seat and began the lightoff. Allyson stood by the locker door, but Jerz motioned her into the steamer. Then Allyson's mother backed the steamer out of the locker, set the brakes, and slid into the passenger seat. Jerz closed the locker before climbing stolidly into the driver's seat.

The steamer eased down the long drive, trailing a thin plume of white. At the road, the vehicle lurched slightly on some ice, but Jerz smoothly corrected and turned downhill toward the highway. He slowed as he approached the sweeping ninety degree turn above where our drive joined the road.

A single ConFed stood by the drive as the steamer slipped past. The Marine turned and lifted his projectile gun.

Either Jerz Davniads did not see the weapon, or he ignored it, believing that no ConFed would turn a weapon upon a member of the gentry. The steamer continued on untouched, but the ConFed turned and sprinted up the drive.

I followed the steamer, now almost careening, as if the Davniads had realized the danger.

Undertime, I could only watch, asking whether I wanted to know what had happened, hoping that they would, or had, escaped, and doubting as I watched.

Two military steamers waited at the spot where the road

met the highway, and I could see another civilian steamer had been stopped. Some of the ConFeds were dragging one of the passengers out, a woman, and from the picture I got, I did not watch further, especially since there was nothing I could do.

I slipped time again, to the instant where the heavy Davniads steamer plunged down the road. For an instant, the woman being assaulted by the ConFeds broke free, and tried to run toward the oncoming steamer. Her tunic had been mostly ripped away, and blood streaked across her uncovered shoulder and partly bared breast. Two ConFeds caught her and forced her down.

Jerz Davniads throttled up the steamer and aimed the heavy vehicle at the narrow shoulder of the road that offered the only chance of passage.

I refused to move closer in the undertime or to look at either Allyson or Germania, still hoping that the former steamer racer could bring them through.

The Davniads' steamer edged the outside military vehicle and the bag lashed to the trunk ripped off. But the steamer was clear, skidding around the corner and onto the Eastern Highway, headed east, away from Inequital.

Then, I hoped—until a ConFed slammed a heavy black weapon onto a swivel and rammed it around, levelling it at the back of the steamer.

*NOOOOOOOOO!!!!*

Laws or not, I slammed my mind against the barrier of the now. Once, twice, holding that scene suspended in stasis, trying, somehow, to stop what was going to happen.

*. . . nooooo . . .*

Try as I did, nothing happened. The ConFed stood there, ready to destroy Allyson and her family, and I could alter nothing. All I did was freeze myself in time to avoid seeing what would happen.

Another thrust at the undertime, and nothing changed,

except I began to feel light-headed. Another jab, not nearly as forceful, and little flashing lights began to appear.

But the ConFed stood immobile with his shredder . . .

. . . and I finally watched . . .

I could almost feel the impact of the shredder on the steamer, and even through the undertime, the blast of flame from the ruptured cans of etheline was bright enough not to mistake.

Twisting forward in time, I skipped another blast of death and agony. Cowardly, but more death, more loss, I did not need. I had already lost Allyson twice. A third time, reliving the emotions of her death, I was not strong enough to undergo.

That was it. I watched just enough to see whether anyone else escaped. No one left the flaming mass that had been a heavy steamer.

Trying to swallow both a throat that felt swollen and tears that could not occur in the undertime, I moved forward to avoid watching more. That burned steamer I had seen before, on my trip to Mount Persnol, along with several others. I just hadn't recognized it or realized that had represented my last contact with Allyson. Not that it changed anything.

I had proved that, even if I couldn't emerge in the past, I could see some of it from the undertime. See more than I ever really wanted to see.

Releasing my hold on the undertime past, I let the time-paths carry me back to my room. Back to the sanitary facilities where I lost most of my mid-morning snack.

When the heaves stopped, I rinsed out my mouth with Sustain. The bitter taste served two purposes—restoring some minor measure of strength, and reminding me of— I didn't know what—but it was reminding me of something.

Then I slumped onto the bed. Outside, the breeze had

stopped, and, inside, as I sat stewing, the sweat beaded up on my forehead.

My stomach had gotten too sensitive. What had happened to the youngster who had eaten swamp roots and held them down? Who had seen an innocent student shredded in front of him?

But I might have loved Allyson, given time, given a better world.

I wiped my forehead and took another sip of Sustain, from a new bottle.

Mellorie. She had lost her self-respect, and her family, and she hated the real ConFeds and wanted them all to die horribly. She couldn't accept anyone who didn't share that hatred.

And I didn't. The ConFeds I had murdered died in more agony than Allyson, than my father, or than Mellorie's family. Necessary as those ConFed deaths might have been, I did not have to share hatred. Responsibility . . . but not hatred.

I took another sip of warm Sustain. And another, wondering where the chain of hatred and death would end.

# XXXVII.

THE FIRST SIGN, which I overlooked because I was not that fond of sweets, came the night Greffin announced berrycream tarts would not be available.

"But . . . we've always had berrycreams . . ." protested Arlean.

"Since when? Since you became librarian when Orite left?" Gerloc's voice was calm, as if he were discussing the weather.

Arlean glared at the thin diver.

I went on eating the last of the buffalo stew. While buffalo was usually chewy, Greffin had clearly marinated it in something with the potency of acid, because it fell apart at the touch of a knife.

"Soon we'll be eating ConFed rations," sniffed Arlean.

"That's better than foraging in the damps." I kept my voice level.

"Too bad your taste didn't improve with the cuisine."

I tried not to wince at Mellorie's low-voiced comment.

Gerloc cleared his throat loudly. "We still have wheat-cakes."

So I ate wheatcakes with sweet cream, noting loudly how much better they were than the delicacies of the damps, such as snake eyes and frond hearts.

The second sign came the first night Mellorie appeared on Jerlyk's arm, not long after the fall harvest.

Outside, the wind was whining, and, now that the crops couldn't use the moisture, a cold heavy rain beat against the old leaded glass panes.

Like me, Jerlyk had been a trooper with one of Odin Thor's units—the one operating well beyond Halfprince. Unlike me, he hadn't been cautious, and the armorer had reported his disappearance.

". . . and the Colonel-General suggested I report here immediately," Jerlyk told me. "We lost two guards on the run before mine doing their collecting."

"Collecting? Collecting what?" I asked.

"Food supplies from the farming groups. That's what the outlying units do now—police against the hill bandits and protect the farmers and the towns against the looters. In return, they 'request' a share of the crops." Jerlyk was smallish, wiry, like me, but had jet black hair to go with the fair skin, and blue eyes that seemed to twinkle all the time.

"Is the looting that bad?" Mellorie leaned closer to him.

"It's gotten worse. The harvest wasn't that good . . ." Jerlyk's voice trailed off.

I understood. "The farmers need winter hold-out and seed for planting, and they resent a supply levy?"

"Right."

"But they wouldn't have even that without the ConFed patrols, would they?" asked Amenda.

"No," added Jerlyk between bites, "but they don't think that way."

They didn't, and Jerlyk and I had a chance to find out the details much sooner than I had anticipated.

Four days later, we were in the Far Travel Lab, in uniform, standing before the Colonel-General and Wryan.

"Troopers, we have a problem. Some of the farmers are hoarding far more than they need." Odin Thor paused and cleared his throat.

I looked him straight in the eye. Jerlyk looked at the floor.

"We need the farmers to keep farming, but we need the surplus grain. That means we have to find out who's hoarding."

In no way did I want to dive and spy on the farmers, not so the ConFeds could destroy some poor farmer's harvest and home.

"This isn't the monarchy. We can't just take their food," continued Odin Thor. "If we do, they'll revolt and throw in with the bandits. If we don't let them know who's in charge, and distribute the surplus food, we won't have much of a society left by spring."

Wryan nodded before speaking. "What is your overall strategy? To use the divers to find out the hoarders, and then make them an offer they can't refuse?"

"Ahhhhhmmmmm," coughed the Colonel-General. "What . . . well . . . that is the general idea . . ."

"What do we have to trade?" pursued Wryan. "Technical support, which they don't need . . . replacement parts, which have limited applicability.''

"Etheline . . ." I suggested.

"Etheline?"

"The old ConFed fort has tanks and tanks of it," I noted. "And some of them aren't in the fort itself. It would take some cleaning up, but the farmers are going to need it for planting, even for heating this winter.''

"You'd better get that trading program set up quickly," added Wryan.

Odin Thor looked puzzled, but said nothing.

"They could use old-fashioned stills to turn the grain we need to eat into alcohol, which would work almost as well as etheline.'' She added quietly, "Some people are already close to starvation. Some of those supplies will have to be reallocated if you want to keep local support.''

The head ConFed nodded slowly as the implications sunk in. "Can you work with my staff to set up the details?''

"I would be happy to help there, Colonel. We need to announce that we will be helping the poorest and offering trades—''

"Above the supply levy," insisted the Colonel-General.

I could see that, because all the farmers would claim poverty and lack of grain to hold out for the etheline.

"—before we start officially scouting around.''

"I have to insist, Doctor, that at least my two troopers here start looking now. If we wait until the announcements are made to find out where the hidden stocks are, then we risk setting off looting between the farmers.''

The Colonel-General made sense. I didn't like it, but he made sense.

Even Wryan bowed her head to his logic.

". . . and I would like you two to ride the next steamer out to Llordian. You are not to reveal you are divers.''

I filled in the picture, not that I was particularly thrilled by the landscape. We were going to be tax-collectors. Tax-collectors have always had short life-expectancies in rural Westron.

"Colonel . . ." added Wryan.

"Yes, Doctor." Odin Thor was already glancing toward the door.

"My people will be able to post notices about food distributions for the needy at an instant's notice. I hope the redistribution effort will commence along with the collection and trading program." Wryan's voice was calm.

Odin Thor half-bowed. "I understand your concerns, Doctor. We wouldn't have it any other way."

"I do appreciate that, Colonel."

He started to leave, then twisted back. "The steamers leave tomorrow for Halfprince. The base there will run you out to Llordian."

"Yes, Colonel-General," answered Jerlyk.

I nodded.

Odin Thor fixed me with a stare, but said nothing.

"Good day, Doctor."

"Good day, Colonel."

After he had left, Wryan looked at us both. "Sammis, you need to stay."

Jerlyk glanced at me, then at the stern-faced doctor. "Then I will be leaving, Dr. Relorn."

She nodded curtly.

Jerlyk didn't quite double-time his way out.

I stood there, and she sat in her chair. Finally, she stood and walked toward one of the deserted consoles.

"You're playing with flame," I said.

"So are you. Why do you refuse to salute him? Or address him by title?"

"ME? Every time you call him Colonel, he burns. His Colonel-General rank is five grades above Colonel."

Wryan smiled. "He was never confirmed in a rank above Colonel."

"This business of posting notices . . . that was nearly a threat."

"No. It *was* a threat, and one we can carry out, if necessary. Without more popular support, we won't have anything. Odin Thor knows that."

I almost took a step toward her. Wryan wore the same off-tan tunic and trousers she seemed to wear every other day. The makeup was gone. I hadn't seen it in days. Now she wore her hair too short, but it didn't matter. She still looked not that much older than I did—at least to my unpracticed eye.

"Sammis?"

Her voice was so soft I almost didn't hear it.

"What?"

"Did you find what you were looking for?"

"No. She was dead. You knew that." My words dropped like stones. I hadn't told anyone. Who could I have told?

"Only because you already knew. You went back to confirm what your heart already had told you." Wryan's voice was gentle, almost as if she understood how watching Allyson die had hurt. I hadn't known it would hurt. How stupid can you be?

"I can definitely see some things on Query from the undertime—only for a few years either side of the now. That was enough."

"I can't. I've tried. I can do it on Sertis, but not here. I don't envy you that ability, not now." She pursed her lips, then walked back to the console, still lit. "Are you sure you're up to this spy mission?"

I shrugged. "It's better than the alternatives."

We both nodded simultaneously, and I wanted to laugh as we did so. I didn't, and neither did she, but there was a quirk to her mouth.

"You'd better go."

So I did, wondering why I enjoyed talking to a woman four times my age.

# XXXVIII.

FOUR CONFEDS STOOD in a rough square. Only one had a shredder. Two held handguns, and a fourth only a dress knife.

Rough groupings of bearded men, women, and a few children encircled them. Gaunt face after gaunt face stared at the four, edging forward, backing them up to the statueless pedestal. Since the town was Llordian, the missing statue had probably been the old emperor.

"Killers . . ."

"Hogs! Oink! Oink! Oink!"

". . . genlovers!"

I frowned at the last epithet, but Jerlyk, standing beside me in the shadows, winced. So did the ConFed with the shredder.

The crowd, salted with a few crones and one white-bearded man with a single arm who stood a head taller than anyone else, reacted to the gesture.

"Genlovers! Genlovers! Genlovers . . . !"

Jerlyk whispered, "Means gentry-lover. Today for the gentry."

"But why? Why the anger? We're the ones they should be angry at."

"Let's talk about it later, Sammis."

That made sense, because the tension in the town square was rising. If I appeared from nowhere and disarmed the ConFeds, then the crowd would kill them. I could still escape. The troopers couldn't.

The sun was strangely hot, like midsummer, and the warmth from the white walls of the trade quarter and from the pavement underfoot created heat shadows on the eastern walls of the square. The too-thin people in their drab and faded clothes, mostly unwashed, stood unmoved by the heat.

I wiped my forehead. After a ten-day plus of snooping around, I knew most of the townies were hungry. They had nothing to trade to the farmers. The ConFeds were protecting the farmers not just from the bandits, but from hungry townies.

*Crack!*

A single rock slammed into the pedestal behind the ConFeds. The lead trooper leveled the shredder.

"Go ahead! Throw another rock! Just give him the chance to use that shredder. He's a killer, and he'll kill all your children. So throw another rock!" The screaming voice cracked, but it was loud enough to break the heat-trance that had settled over the crowd.

Unfortunately, the voice was mine. The words were fine, but while I was wearing an unmarked tunic, it still looked too military. Or too gentrified.

"Genlover!" spat a boy who could not have been eight.

"The ConFed tax-collectors! It's them!"

"Bloodsuckers!"

Attention passed from the armed ConFeds in the square to the unarmed pair of ConFed tax-collectors in the alleyway adjoining the square.

"Now what?" hissed Jerlyk.

"I think we run."

So we did.

"Get them . . . bloodsuckers! Bloodsuckers! Genlovers! Genlovers!"

"Genlovers . . . genlovers . . . genlovers . . ." The words turned into a chant as the mob crowded into the alleyway.

We sprinted straight down the alley, then past the near-empty fruit stand and the orange-haired woman who stared as we pounded past.

". . . to the right . . ." I mumbled, trying to angle for the ConFed guard station by the western end of the town nearest the Eastern Highway.

"Look ahead . . ."

Jerlyk had a point. Some of the mob had left the square by the avenue and would reach the next corner before we would.

". . . then left . . ."

"That's a dead end . . ."

". . . climb . . ."

The low wall ahead, not even as high as my shoulder, would be easy enough to climb. Vaulting onto the flat section which turned out to be a covered storm drain, I glanced around. The other side was an empty yard, with empty racks that had once held lumber or timber—or something.

Some of the crowd headed around to cut us off.

"Down and out of sight, and dive. Out to the guard station."

I jumped down by the nearest lumber rack. No one could see us, and the windows in the back of the building were both shuttered and closed. We broke out of the undertime behind in the narrow space between the old town wall and the guard station. I stumbled and scraped an elbow on the wall.

"Verlyt!"

"So what did you scrape?" I asked, in between deep breaths, as I tried to catch my wind and simultaneously navigate my way toward the guard station.

"Forget it!" snapped Jerlyk.

We came around the corner just in time to meet the other four ConFeds racing in from the south end of the avenue.

The lead trooper, still carrying the shredder, opened his

mouth, then shut it, then opened it again before stammering, "What . . . how . . ."

"Just a little misdirection. We almost didn't get clear."

The lead ConFed shut his mouth without saying a word.

The one behind him, a wiry man with copper hair, grinned. "We owe you, and I'm real glad to let you know that. I'm Nylen."

"Sammis."

"Jerlyk."

All the time we were talking, we were trotting toward the compound gate.

"Forcer! Forcer! Riot in the town!" yelled the man with the shredder.

*Clang! Clang! Clang!*

We were inside the compound, and the duty crew was already manning the guard towers and breaking out shredders and handguns. I found a projectile rifle thrust into my hands, and my way being directed toward a sandbagged position below the main guard tower.

To my left, the heavy wooden gate rolled shut. A pair of recruits began shoring it in place with the sandbags piled at each end. The post had been an old mail station, but somewhere along the line, someone had staked it out for military purposes, since it sat on the crest of a gentle hill at the western end of Llordian—the highest point amid the flat fields and sometime marsh grass.

I swallowed, listening to the shouting and muttering as the crowd flowed across the dusty parade ground toward the perimeter stockade. There didn't seem to be so many people once they were out in the open—scarcely a hundred or so, and mostly women and children, with a few disabled troublemakers like the tall one-armed man. Not even a challenge for the twenty or so armed troopers.

"There they are! Hiding behind their walls and guns!" The one-armed man's voice carried to the stockade.

One trooper lifted a projectile rifle. Before he could

bring it to bear, a subforcer knocked it down and hissed something at the man.

"There they are! Protecting the rich hoarders and taking their cut while you go hungry! Look at them! They won't always have guns!"

The crowd milled around, listening to the high-pitched voice of the agitator.

The sweat rolled down my face, turning dust on my skin into mud.

*Buzzzzz . . . buzzzzz . . .* The black flies kept trying to land on my neck and bite, but I used a free hand to wave them away.

"See how they hide behind their guns! Do they look hungry? They aren't hungry. They don't have children who cry themselves to sleep."

"No, they don't have families any more. They already lost them!" That same stupid screaming voice again—mine. "At least you still have your children. At least we're trying to keep you from being killed in your sleep!"

"He's lying! Don't listen. He's lying!"

That was the wrong thing for the one-armed man to say. The crowd muttered, mumbled, and stopped.

"Why'd you say that?" demanded the subforcer who appeared at my elbow.

"Talk is cheaper than guns or bullets. And my family is dead." I turned to look at him.

"You . . ." he snorted. "I might have known."

At that moment, I nearly saw red. Bright red. But I just looked.

Finally, he looked to the side and walked away.

"Verlyt . . ." the oath was soft.

I glanced at the trooper beside me.

"Swashte will hate you for that."

"Probably." I didn't really care. Wryan had been absolutely right. Odin Thor would lose the entire province without a shot if he didn't get some food to those children. And soon.

As it became clear that the crowd had no intention of even halfheartedly storming the station, the senior forcer stood. "Stand down. First squad, hold the stockade. Purtell, deploy your men."

I ambled over to the station to turn in the projectile rifle.

Jerlyk grinned as he followed me. "Big mouth."

"Better than bullets," I repeated.

Swashte, the subforcer I had glared down, was talking to the senior forcer, Gleddell, and gesturing in my direction. Gleddell looked bored and shrugged. Swashte headed toward me.

"Trooper, I don't like your attitude. The senior forcer feels that you and I could use a little extra workout. Just to loosen up the muscles."

I shrugged. "If you think so."

"We could have a good match if you're not afraid of getting messed up."

"You sure that Gleddell doesn't want a disabled subforcer?"

"Verlyt, you really do have a mouth, Trooper. You really do."

I was tired of games. "What rules, Subforcer Swashte?"

"Just a friendly match, Trooper. Don't need rules for that, do we?"

"Not for a friendly match, I suppose. But if you should trip and break anything, I certainly wouldn't continue. What you do is up to you, of course." I stepped back and stripped off my tunic and equipment belt.

Swashte did the same and thrust his tunic and belt at a youngster right out of training.

"Ready, Trooper?"

I nodded, slipping into a balanced posture, half-looking into the undertime to anticipate his attack.

Quicker than he looked, Swashte feinted with a straightened left arm, then threw a half-kick at my back knee.

I could have played with him. Instead, I broke his planted leg and snapped his arm. Henriod had taught me well, and I cheated.

"Verlyt!"

"Did you see that?"

"Hell-fired killer . . ."

Gleddell had turned white, as he saw Swashte writhing on the ground.

I half-bowed to the grimacing subforcer. "I regret our friendly match was so short. Any time you want a rematch, I'd be pleased to oblige you."

Then I walked over to Gleddell. "I strongly suggest that Trooper Jerlyk's and my mission here is complete."

Gleddell shook his lank black hair off his forehead, ran his eyes over me as if he could not quite believe what he saw.

"Who are you?"

"Trooper Sammis, sir."

He glanced at my unmarked uniform, then at the ground. "Two nice bits of work today, Trooper, three if I understand what Nylen told me. I don't like any of them." He paused. "I hope I never see you again."

"Yes, sir."

"That's all."

I saluted him. It made him feel happier.

Everyone besides Jerlyk backed away as I walked back toward the barracks.

# XXXIX.

THE TRIP BACK from Llordian was long and boring. But the new diet must have helped. Neither one of us felt sick when we arrived back at base. Jerlyk hurried off, presumably to find Mellorie.

Somehow, despite that, I hoped Mellorie—or someone—would be waiting. No one was, and the room smelled musty. I opened the windows and let the wind in. The unseasonal warmth of Llordian was fading into normal early winter—wet, cold, and raw—still preferable to the mustiness.

Turning on the single lamp improved the gloomy late afternoon, and, after I had unpacked my few items, closing the window reduced the chill.

After taking care of my laundry, I braved the grimy shower and changed into a clean undress uniform, then headed for dinner—early.

Apparently, I wasn't the only one anxious for company. Gerloc was pacing, and Jerlyk had pulled out a chair from one of the unused tables.

Amenda walked in within minutes of me.

"Sammis, you're back." She was wearing a clean, if rumpled, blue tunic and trousers.

"So is Jerlyk. The ConFeds only like us in small doses. You're looking nice tonight."

She made a face. "How could you say that? The maids all left, and took all the small irons. I'm a rumpled mess."

"Advantage of ConFed uniforms, I guess. What else had been going on here?" I kept my tone light.

"Besides boring meals, a new diving schedule for everyone, and the disappearance of most of the support staff?"

"Greffin?" I hoped the chef at least would stay.

"He was still here at mid-day, but he was complaining to the doctor."

"Things are getting tough all over."

For some reason, Amenda nodded.

Then Mellorie walked in. Unlike Amenda or me, she had on another tailored coverall and a matching jacket which was definitely unrumpled. The scrape of Jerlyk's chair told me he had seen her as well. She looked past the rest of us and favored him with a smile that would have melted ice.

As I shook my head, Amenda cleared her throat. "What are you thinking?"

"Nothing . . . well . . . not nothing . . ."

"Are you jealous?" She seemed disinterested in the question, looking absently at Gerloc.

I had to laugh. "It was nice while it lasted."

"What did you mean about things being tough all over?" She acted as if her mind were in Eastron, or farther away.

Like me, I guess, making small talk. So I told her a bit about the problems at Llordian, just how the farmers didn't care if the townies starved, and how the ConFeds just wanted the supply levies.

"Sammis, don't you see?" Her eyes focused on me.

"See what? The farmers and the townies are going to be at each other's necks. Odin Thor doesn't have enough troops to police every area. Besides, if we take sides . . ."

Amenda nodded. "What will happen if we don't?"

I thought about that. "The townies will attack the farmers, and only the strong ones will survive."

"Will they?"

Amenda's question jolted me.

"Why wouldn't they?"

"The farmers are spread out. If they get together, that leaves their stores unprotected. Aren't there a lot more townspeople than farmers?"

Most of the successful farmers were the larger ones, who had their own equipment shops, even draft animals, and plenty of seed reserves. Some had enough hired hands to use as guards. Against petty bandits, at least. Their success against an enraged mob was another question.

"We're trading etheline for food, though."

"For how long, Sammis?"

I had to shrug. I didn't know.

"That brings up another question." Amenda pursed her lips, then tried to pat down her wrinkled tunic as Arlean walked through the doorway.

Arlean's tunic looked wrinkled, too, if not quite so rumpled as Amenda's.

"How long can the steamers run without parts?" pursued Amenda. "Even if the etheline-food trades and food taxes get us through this winter, what happens next year, or when we run out of etheline to trade?"

I didn't have a good answer, but I didn't have to come up with it right then.

# XL.

THE PORRIDGE WAS cold, and the brown bread was harder than ever. All the other divers had gone, late as I had staggered down.

I ladled the remaining congealed cereal into a large bowl and sprinkled it with a double handful of raisins, covering both raisins and porridge with molasses. A mess, but one with enough calories.

"Sammis?" I looked up from where I was shoveling the cereal in.

Deric's lips were tight, and he squinted, even though the morning skies were cloudy, and the lights in the dining area dim.

"Yes, Deric?" I mumbled. The heavy porridge tasted like glue, even with the handful of dried raisins I had poured over the glop. I missed the buns and the fresh fruit. Funny, how little you need luxuries when you're worrying about survival. Then, when you have them for a while, you miss them more than if you never had them.

"The Colonel-General has requested your presence in his office."

"Does the doctor know?"

"She . . . asked me to convey the message."

I swallowed the last of the gray mess and followed it with a deep pull of water. "I'll head right there."

Deric turned and left without a word.

What did Odin Thor want?

Another ConFed I didn't know sat behind an empty desk outside the Colonel-General's office.

"Sammis," I announced. "The Colonel-General requested my presence."

"I'll tell him." The trooper, an arrogant-looking tough nearly as tall as Odin-Thor, remained seated.

Because I was me, I looked undertime to see what the esteemed Colonel-General was doing. He was doing nothing at all, and doing it alone.

"The Colonel-General is alone, and he's not engaged. So I suggest you tell him I'm here."

"I'll tell him when it's time."

I walked past him and toward the door.

His hand grabbed at my shoulder.

*Thud.*

The arrogant expression was replaced by a puzzled one as he looked up from the floor.

"Don't *ever* lay hands on me."

"The Colonel-General . . ."

". . . will probably do absolutely nothing," added a new voice.

Henriod, the head of the scouts for Odin Thor, stood there. "It's good to see you again, Sammis. You've improved some more."

I shrugged. "I try. Jerlyk and I work out almost every day."

By now, the ConFed orderly had scrambled to his feet.

"Hasslek, this is former trooper Sammis." Henriod

grinned. "Possibly the most dangerous man in either the travelers or the ConFeds." Then he looked at me. "Odin Thor was amused at what you did to Swashte. Told him that unless he got his act together, he'd set up a return match."

That didn't sound like Odin Thor at all. Not at all, not when he had been so adamant about not revealing that some ConFeds were divers.

Hasslek nodded and backed in through the door I had been about to open.

"If he's using me as a threat, things must really be getting tight."

Hasslek was standing in the door again, leaving it open. "The Colonel-General will see you, gentlemen."

While I had been promoted a bit in Hasslek's regard, why Odin Thor wanted to see both Henriod and me was another question.

"Forcer Henriod, Trooper Sammis . . . if you would have a seat . . ." Odin Thor was all smiles.

I trusted him even less than before, but I sat down in the battered wooden chair next to the old and expansive red oak desk. Henriod sat in the chair next to me, leaving a vacant chair beside the closed outside window, which rattled in the morning wind.

"Sammis, how did you find Llordian?"

I shrugged. "Townies are close to starving, with no way to get food. Don't trust the farmers, but they trust us even less."

"Henriod, what is our current strength?"

"All bodies, sir?"

Odin Thor nodded.

"The main maintenance facility in Esterly still has about three hundred. Perhaps almost that many here. Another two hundred or so in places like Halfprince and Llordian. Add to that maybe . . . what? Fifty travelers . . . ? I'd say nine hundred, counting those I don't know."

"How many of the townspeople are able-bodied enough for even light ConFed duty?"

Henriod looked at me. I looked at Henriod. We both looked at Odin Thor.

"Not many," I volunteered. "Probably mostly women."

"The ConFeds don't take women," pointed out Henriod.

"Then you've got damned few . . ."

"So there are very few able-bodied townspeople left, but they threaten present food supplies and future crops. Is that a fair assessment?"

"Not totally, Colonel-General." Henriod had a thin sheen of perspiration on his forehead as he went on. "The townspeople are the only remnant of crafting skills left. Over time, their absence would be felt."

Their absence? What was Odin Thor proposing? Murder? Genocide?

"Anything else?"

"What about the next generation?" I asked.

Odin Thor almost smiled when he looked at me. "What about them, Sammis?"

"Without the townies, you won't have one," I blurted.

"There is that," admitted Odin Thor. "But, based on your observations and those of Forcer Henriod, I do not feel that the ConFeds—or your travelers . . . or timedivers, if you prefer—should continue to impose discipline where we are not wanted."

Odin Thor couldn't be serious.

"It's very simple, really," the Colonel-General continued. "We will remain only where we are wanted. Since Llordian seems to have mixed feelings about our presence and services, we will hold a totally free election. We'll even let them conduct it. If the townspeople and the farmers in the surrounding area want us to leave and vote for us to leave, we will."

"A truly honest election?" I asked.

"Why not? You indicated that it would be difficult to hold the place against a really determined mob without killing a large number of townspeople. We don't need to risk our limited manpower where we aren't wanted."

"But what about supplies?" asked Henriod.

"If we're careful, we have enough to last until early summer without any more levies, but I anticipate that some areas will request our presence."

"If the Llordians get to vote, won't you have let others vote?" I asked.

"Absolutely. Because this is a first case, I would appreciate it if we make no announcements except in Llordian until after the election is completed." Odin Thor shook his head. "No. I'm not planning to use force if they vote us out. I expect the Llordians will. We can't stage elections all over the place at once. They will have to be phased so that we can pull out of areas that don't want us in an orderly fashion."

Henriod looked at me, and I looked at Henriod. Odin Thor was sincere in allowing the elections, but the whole thing still smelled.

"Why are we here?" Henriod's words reflected his puzzlement.

"You, Forcer Henriod, need to develop a withdrawal plan that will ensure we leave Llordian in a way that does not invite any attack or violence against us. That is very important. We must be perceived as impartial and not imposing our will by force in any way. That image could be endangered if any riots or outbreaks occur. That means the instant the vote is in, we must be on the way out, before it becomes known that we are leaving. Likewise, we cannot make advance preparations that can be seen or interpreted as evidence that we have decided to leave before the vote.

"Do you understand?"

Henriod nodded. I could understand why *I* would be concerned about such a withdrawal, but I couldn't see why Odin Thor would be.

"What about me?"

"Yes . . . Sammis. I have two reasons. First, you are in effect the ConFed's liaison with the travelers. Second, I would like you to use your diving ability to monitor and record the process at Llordian. We need to document on viewtape that we allowed full and free elections, that we left the area immediately, and any later follow-up. For rather obvious reasons and for this to be objective, we cannot have our observer visible after the elections."

I nodded. If any observer remained after the ConFeds left, he or she would certainly be a clear target. "Do we have any recording equipment left?"

Odin Thor smiled again. "We have some very good portable equipment which Eltar has restored. You can work with him, I trust."

Eltar? He still talked to me, unlike some of the others. "Yes, Colonel."

Odin Thor almost glared at me for using his real rank. "Will you make the arrangements for recording and let your fellow-travelers know that we will be holding free elections in Llordian, and, later, in other communities?"

I nodded. "Is there anything else?"

"For now that's all. When you're ready, get together with Eltar."

Odin Thor looked at Henriod. "Do you think you could have your plans ready by the day after tomorrow?"

"Shouldn't be a problem, sir."

"Good." Odin Thor stood. "Thank you both."

Since we were clearly dismissed, we left.

Outside in the chill under the gray clouds that promised freezing rain or worse, I stopped and looked at Henriod.

"Does this make sense?"

"In a way," answered the forcer. "We'd lose too many

men if we had to put down wide-scale riots. If we didn't stop them, we'd lose any credibility.''

"So you think Odin Thor is making a graceful withdrawal and using the free election bit to place the blame on the Llordians?''

Henriod shrugged. "That's the way it looks.''

It did look that way, but I still kept remembering Odin Thor's smile.

My next stop was Dr. Relorn's office. She had some explaining to do, and she needed to know about Odin Thor's plans. I just dropped undertime and slid into the laboratory she used as an office.

She was alone, twiddling with one of the consoles.

"Greetings, Sammis.'' She turned in the swivel chair to face me. This time she had on a tan tunic and trousers. The cut was flattering, but not the color, which left her washed-out looking.

"You were expecting me.''

"Who else would you tell about Odin Thor's latest scheme?''

She sounded so matter-of-fact that I felt like leaving. But no one else seemed to understand anything. So instead of leaving, I said nothing.

Neither did she.

I kept my mouth shut.

"Sammis . . . you can either accept the truth and keep growing up. Or you can pout, in which case I won't bother to spend time with you.''

"Both you and Odin Thor are playing some type of game I still don't understand, and both of you are pushing me around.''

Wryan looked at me, almost from head to toe. "Odin Thor is playing a game.'' She paused. "It could look like I am.''

"Are you?''

"No. I try to tell you, but you don't want to hear it.

And sometimes you don't hear what I say the way I meant.''

If her words weren't an evasion, I hadn't ever heard one. ''That's an evasion.''

She grinned and looked like a youngster. ''You're right.''

I was getting tired of people deciding what was best for Sammis to know.

''I can only tell you that I have your best interests at heart.'' She smiled softly. ''Mine, too, I hope.''

Despite my anger, the softness and the near-wistful tone of her voice kept me from lashing out. Whatever she had in mind, it wasn't deadly or malicious, and that would have to do for the present. I shrugged.

''How about my quarters?'' she asked. ''It is warmer than here.''

That was fine with me, and I followed her from the laboratory after she switched off the console and most of the lights. The laboratory seemed dark and ancient with the lights off, like a relic from the past.

Again, she flicked on the single lamp on the table, just like the first time I had visited her, and nodded toward a chair.

''Do you have anything . . . to eat?''

''You,'' she said, ''are always hungry.''

''Curse of the breed.''

Wryan put out a plate with a chyst, a chunk of old yellow cheese, and a row of hard crackers. Before sitting down, she sliced several smaller pieces of cheese, taking one of the crackers and a slice for herself.

''Look who else is hungry,'' I had to mumble because my mouth was full.

She smiled, her mouth full as well.

''Odin Thor's going to offer open elections to the Llordians. Let them vote on whether the ConFeds stay or go.

He thinks they'll vote us out. He wants me to play reporter and get the whole thing on viewtape.''

Frowning, Wryan took another cracker and cut some more cheese. ''After they vote no on the ConFeds, what does he plan?''

''He told Henriod to arrange for pullout, one that would get us out before anything happened. He wants me to tape the pullout and the aftermath.''

Wryan finished chewing the cheese and hard cracker as she went for a pitcher of water and two tumblers—the heavy crystal ones that reminded me of my father's Dyleraan. She poured me a glassful, then one for herself. ''You think he's telling the truth?''

''Yes. That's what bothers me.''

''Did he say what he'll do in the other towns?''

''He said they could have elections, too, but they'd have to be phased. Why go to all that trouble? He didn't spend the last year building up all this power just to let it go.''

''You're right. He didn't.''

The chair was getting uncomfortable, and I shifted my weight. ''So what is he doing? And what happened to his plan to attack the Frost Giants?''

''I don't know . . . for certain. But you had better make sure you do a good job recording what happens at Llordian.''

Wryan had an idea of what the Colonel-General was doing. She also wasn't telling.

''Why aren't you telling me?''

''I might be wrong. You need to figure out why people act the way they do without relying on me or on Odin Thor.''

I swallowed hard on her words. Relying on her? Especially on Odin Thor? She wouldn't relent, and after I finished the cheese and the chyst, I left, diving back to my room before heading out to find Eltar.

# XLI.

CARRYING THE PORTABLE equipment that Eltar had put together wasn't all that difficult, and that alone showed me how much stronger I was getting. The equipment was easily twice the weight of the nerve gas grenades, and I had no trouble with it—provided I didn't try it when I was hungry.

"Sammis," protested Eltar the first time I popped back into the small corner of maintenance that Odin Thor had set aside for him, "I'll never get used to you appearing out of nowhere."

He did, though.

I started out by taking shots of Llordian proper—breaking out on the tops of buildings, odd corners, anywhere to provide an accurate picture. Getting the people was harder, and I finally ended up dressed like a ragged peddler. The pack contained all the gear except the hand-held recorder. Even that was difficult, since several times I had to sit for hours in dusty corners just to get a few minutes of tape when no one was looking. I tried to record from the undertime, but the equipment just didn't work there.

Getting shots of the posters announcing the referendum was easier. Since everyone crowded around each one posted, no one was watching a ragged peddler. Later, I went out at dawn and took some clear shots of the posters.

"You expect me to mix and splice and put together something that looks professional?" Eltar protested.

"No. Just something that looks honest and real."

"Honest and real—from you?" interrupted another voice—Rarden.

When I'd faced him down at the divers' mess, I thought

I'd seen the last of the troublesome ConFed. "Yes, honest and real." I kept my voice cheerful.

Wearing a grease suit, he was carrying a toolbox for heavy maintenance work on the steamers. "This is *honest* work."

"Very honest work. Without the steamers, we'd be in big trouble."

"Not like your sneak thieving."

I shrugged.

"Not like sneak thieves," Rarden repeated.

"Rarden . . ." I answered slowly. "You don't like me, and I don't like you. If I wanted you dead, you would be, and no one could save your ass. So . . . why don't you think instead of opening your mouth without thinking?"

Both Rarden and Eltar turned pale.

When Rarden had carted his toolbox to the steamer at the far end of the bay, Eltar glanced at me, then at the floor. "Did you mean what you said?"

"What?" I replied absently, wondering why Rarden had hated me so much even before he had discovered I was a diver.

"That nothing could save him if you wanted him dead?"

At that point, I wished I hadn't said it. "Yes and no," I hedged. "Do you really want an answer?"

"I think I deserve one, Sammis." Eltar was still pale.

"You do." I sighed. "It's like this. What would happen if I appeared right behind Rarden with a projectile gun? Could he stop me?"

"Of course not."

"And who else could do that?"

"The other divers."

"But whom among them would want to?"

"Oh . . ."

"So . . . I could dispose of Rarden any time. But everyone would know it was me, and what would keep Carlis from keeping his own projectile rifle handy to pot me at a distance when I wasn't even aware of him?''

Eltar nodded slowly. "You need to eat and sleep just like everyone else. But . . .''

I knew where he was headed. "If . . . *if* I wanted to live like a total sneak thief and recluse the rest of my life, never trusting anyone, with every person's hand against me, like they were against the witches of Eastron, then I *might* be able to run around killing people. Except then, all the other divers would eliminate me as a danger. And they could.''

The ConFed who might be my friend looked only slightly relieved.

I tried one more time. "Look, Eltar. I got caught by Odin Thor's men because there was no place else to go. Now it's going to get worse.''

"What?''

"The farmers—those that are left—aren't farming enough to feed everyone. The townies are close to starvation, and everyone hates the ConFeds. There's enough food to go around now. What about next year?''

"Can't you, and the other divers . . .''

I sighed, loudly. "Eltar, this is about as much weight as I can carry, and I'm one of the stronger divers. Second, I'd have to find spare food to carry, and the situation here is the same all over Query.''

"Oh . . .'' Eltar looked pale again. I was doing great violence to his mental well-being.

I shrugged. "That's why I'm still supporting Odin Thor. He seems to be the only chance. Verlyt knows it's a slim one. And who knows if we'll ever get around to the Frost Giant problem?''

Nodding, Eltar turned to the workbench. "Let's see that last tape pack. Are you going out again soon?''

"Not until after noon meal.'' I handed over the tape pack I had extracted from the recorder.

"When are the elections?"

"Two days."

He laughed mirthlessly. "Then we'll see."

I nodded. We would indeed, but what we might see was another question.

# XLII.

ON THE DAY of the referendum in Llordian, the ragged and dirty peddler was back in harness, recording the happy Llordian townies as they cast their ballots.

My site was in the market, behind a pottery stand run by an old woman who never seemed to sell anything. I had set out various small carvings and trinkets in front of me, on the stone ledge next to the empty fountain—it had been empty the first time I saw Llordian and still was.

While I waited, I carved—mostly things like napkin rings and awkward grossjays. Terrible carvings, but sometimes people actually offered me something for them, usually a piece of fruit, a roll, or cast-off clothing. I took the food, but not the clothing.

I never spoke, just shook my head and pointed to my throat. By election day, the pottery woman just told people not to bother the mute peddler.

The townies all crowed as they stuffed paper ballot after paper ballot into the big boxes. A pair of armed ConFeds watched each box, but only to make sure no one walked off with it. They ignored the people stuffing in two or three ballots, all marked with big black crosses in the space indicating the ConFeds should leave.

"That one . . ." grunted a bearded man.

He pointed at a carved wooden ring, a crude copy of a silver napkin ring I had remembered from childhood.

I nodded as he held up a small copper—one of the few

coins I had been offered. Then again, the napkin ring was one of my better efforts.

As he took the ring, the sound of a steamer hissing whispered into the square. Two large farmers, flanked with guards of their own, scanned the ballot box, but did not leave the steamer.

I risked getting caught and trained the recorder hidden in my pack at the disgusted look on the white-haired man's face. The younger farmer, as big as Odin Thor, but with skin like cream toffee, shook his head.

The steamer hissed again and picked up speed.

The bearded man, now walking from the dry fountain toward the steamer, spat on the stones in the direction of the farmers. An urchin—one who had tried to steal one of my wooden grossjays—made an obscene gesture. Two women hurried from the steamer's path, covering their faces with scarves. Another boy picked up a stone, only to have it knocked from his hand by his mother.

Not a single other farmer did I see, and, after I crept away in the late afternoon, I back-checked all of the other polling locations. No farmers to speak of.

Under the cover of darkness, Henriod implemented his pullout, and when the townies arrived the next morning brandishing the polling results, the old postal station that had been the ConFed fort was empty, the gate wide open.

I was hidden behind the low parapet on the roof, recording the faces, the dust, and the townies' indignation.

"Swine . . ."

". . . knew before we finished . . ."

". . . last of them . . ."

*Crack* . . . One desultory stone clacked against the open gate.

". . . anything left?"

A handful of older men, including the ubiquitous one-armed man, entered the main building, rummaged through every room. I could hear crashes and slams and other sounds.

In time, they left, empty-handed, grumbling, swearing, with the old postal station a shambles. So did I, bringing the footage back to Eltar.

Then I had noon meal, by myself, and took a nap.

Something was going to happen at Llordian later. When or what, I didn't know, but I could feel it. Because I couldn't explain it, I didn't even try and talk about it. Besides, Wryan seemed to be avoiding me, and no one else would understand.

So I slept, not well. First, my room was too cold. Then the sun came out and heated everything up, and I woke up sweating.

I wanted to dive out to Llordian and see what was happening, but figured that was unwise, at least on an empty stomach. That reasoning got me down to the snack table in the divers' mess, where I polished off two chysts, a large chunk of cheese and a handful of very hard crackers, all washed down with warm and almost sour citril.

Gerloc wandered in when I was finishing, nodded, picked up a chyst, and wandered out.

Was everybody avoiding me? Or was I giving off some sort of signal?

At the front door I looked south, up toward Mount Persnol, where the clouds were turning cherry pink in the late winter twilight, wondering what, if anything, might be happening in Llordian.

With a sigh, I walked back to my room and pulled on a black foul-weather sweater and the darkest trousers I owned, making a note that we really ought to develop a set of dark uniforms for time diving. Then I added a dark jacket and gloves. If I were going to skulk around in the shadows, I might as well look like the shadows.

Recorder in hand, pack on back, I dropped under the now and slipped out to Llordian, breaking out on a little ledge on the top of the meeting house overlooking the square.

A heavy door shut somewhere.

". . . if you think . . .

". . . too young . . . at that price . . ."

Two figures whispered in the shadows nearly directly underneath my perch.

A bell rang softly in the distance.

Nothing was happening, and I was frowning. Then it struck me. Of course nothing was happening in Llordian.

My first breakout was on the roof of a long wooden porch on the front of a timber and stone farmhouse.

*Scrufff.* I winced at the sound. The roof sloped, and I had skidded on the heavy tiles, trying to keep my balance.

"What's that? Scurrit? Scurrit!"

"There's nothing out there. Ferly would have hissed, or something."

"Keep your voices down," added another voice, hard and female.

I eased myself flat on the tiles, grateful their finish was rough enough to keep me place in spite of the gentle slope.

For a time, everything was silent, except for the whisper of the wind, which, light as it was, wasted no time in chilling me.

"Stop it," whispered the female voice.

"Annya, none of those townies will be around tonight. It'll take a couple of nights before they're convinced the ConFeds are gone."

"Maybe . . . but what did we hear? Ghosts?" The woman's voice was low.

"Could have been a branch scraping on the barn wall."

"Maybe. We'll wait a while. Then you watch until midnight . . ."

I didn't stay any longer.

After checking several other farms I had visited "officially" as a ConFed, I was convinced the farm woman was right. If the townies were going to attack any farms, it wouldn't be that night.

Which night? How long? I didn't know, and I wasn't about to tell Odin Thor. And Wryan wasn't about to do my thinking for me.

So, day by day, I kept checking and recording, watching as the townies whispered and the farmers worked towards spring, weapons always nearby.

# XLIII.

FIVE RAGGED FIGURES —three older men and two women— trudged up the hard dirt road, their feet barely raising the heavy dust under the bright late winter sun. The men wore blanket jackets with patches, the women old shawls, folded and refolded around them. All five had tattered trousers and shapeless shoes.

Two farmers armed with antique projectile rifles stood behind the wooden gate, their shoulders and heads outlined against the green-blue sky. Both wore heavy leather jackets—the kind that were quilted on the inside.

The five stopped a good rod from the gate. From the underbrush uphill, I caught both the townies and the farmers in the recorder.

"Peace," croaked the lead ancient.

"What do you want?" asked the heavier farmer, his brown hair shot with gray, as he leveled the weapon at the townspeople.

"Food . . . our children are hungry. Our gardens are bare, and the convoys have stopped coming."

"We need food . . ." protested a heavy-set woman.

"You don't look like it, woman."

"Our children need food." Her breath was a thin line of white smoke.

"We don't have any, not if we want to plant."

"You're hoarding it . . ." A thin woman at the back whined.

The farmer sighed. "You don't know . . . you know nothing . . ." His face was weathered and lined.

"You won't give us food?"

"There isn't any."

The younger farmer—not much older than I was—frowned.

"See . . . even *he* doesn't believe you." The white-haired whiner jabbed a finger.

"Just go on back to town." The older farmer gestured with the gun. The younger one leveled his own weapon.

"So we can watch our children starve while you hoard?"

"Woman, my seed grains wouldn't feed a handful of people, and then you'd have nothing next year."

"We won't last until next year."

The farmer gestured with the weapon again. "I can't help you."

"You won't . . ."

". . . Verlyt judge you, miserly . . ."

They turned back toward Llordian, their shoulders stooped and their feet scuffing. As the townspeople dwindled into stick figures straggling back along the road to Llordian, the younger farmer caught the older man's eyes.

"They'd just take everything because they're hungry now. If we gave them what we could afford, it wouldn't be enough. Then they'd be back demanding more. And more." The older farmer sighed.

"They will be anyway. At night."

The younger man looked down at the gate, then at the stone wall that ran gently uphill toward the thicket where I lay concealed. Finally, he looked back at the gate. "Think we should have asked those ConFeds for help?"

The older man shrugged. "Which thief do you ask into your home? Now, the ConFeds look better."

The younger man shrugged in turn and looked back up the road to the farmhouse. "Gero will be down in a while. Need to see about those etheline globes. You think tonight?"

The other shook his head. "Be a while yet."

# XLIV.

TORCHES. A LINE of the flickering lights showed the townies snaking through the darkness.

I didn't know how well the scene would record, but I did the best I could from an exposed hilltop overlooking the road. Then I dropped undertime.

Anger was a smoldering mist, compounded with fear, that shrouded the entire mob. It was a mob, carrying staffs, knives, a few dart rifles, and one or two projectile rifles—ConFed issue.

They didn't chant. They weren't marching, but there must have been more than a hundred of them walking up that dark and winter-dusty road.

At the head of the mob was a one-armed man. He gestured; he gesticulated; he exhorted.

They responded, flowing uphill toward the gate and a handful of farmers.

Since Odin Thor would most definitely want a record of the confrontation, I broke out near where I had recorded the first demands of the townies.

"Food . . . we want food . . . food . . . we want food . . ." The cracked voice of the one-armed man ran like an off-key note through the muttering chorus.

"Ready?" asked a voice from the darkness below me.

"Not yet. Wait until they get closer."

A spark flickered on the farm road, momentarily illuminating two men beside a wooden framework.

". . . food . . . we want food . . . food . . . we want food . . ."

The chorus swelled as the mob straggled toward the dark gate, oblivious to the farmers hidden there.

A blaze of yellow flame splashed across the clay of the road a few rods before the leading edge of the mob.

The chorus died into mutters—momentarily.

"Just go home, and no one will get hurt!" boomed a voice from the darkness behind and below me.

". . . food . . . we want food . . . food . . . we want food . . ." The one-armed man began the chant again, and the crowd picked up on his words.

This time the flame splattered nearly at the feet of the one-armed man.

"Just go home!"

". . . food . . . we want food . . . we want food . . ."

"AAEEEEEEeeeeee . . ." The blankets of a woman burst into flames.

"Killers! Killers! Get the killers!" screamed the one-armed man, as he grabbed a youth by the arm and pushed him toward the gate, running for an instant with him. Then he did the same with a young woman . . . and another man, older.

". . . food . . . we want food . . ."

*Crack!* One of the farmers' projectile rifles sounded, but I couldn't see anyone fall as the mob began to lurch toward the farmers.

The one-armed man kept alternating chants, either "get the killers" or "food . . . we want food" as the townies surged forward.

*Crack!* This time an older woman staggered.

By now, the smoldering oil and smoke gave a hellish atmosphere to the road. My own reaction was to slip under the now and take out the one-armed troublemaker, but I wasn't certain if that would make the situation better or worse. Then again, maybe I really didn't feel like either side deserved help.

*Crack! Crack! Crack!* This time the shots came from the mob.

"They got Gero!"

"We can do it!" screamed the one-armed man. "We want food . . . food . . . we want food . . ."

The mob surged toward the wooden gate, and the handful of farmers scrambled back up the road, leaving one lying face down by the wooden framework, and another trying to lift the wounded or dead man.

As he saw the mob pouring over and around the gate, the last farmer released the body, then bent down and lit the top globe on the pile of globes by the wooden framework. He sprinted uphill after the others.

The mob continued toward the down farmer.

*WWWWHHHHHSSSSTTTTTTT!!!!!* The entire pile of etheline missiles burst into flames, spewing fireballs in all directions and turning a good dozen townies into instant torches.

Using the light of the human bonfire, the farmers dropped three more townies. But the killings went almost unnoticed as the mob moved toward the farm buildings near the hill crest.

". . . food . . . we want . . . food . . ."

Somehow, the chant and the smell of burning flesh got to me, even if no one else paid attention. I retched.

"There's one on the hillside!"

I dropped undertime before both sides finished targeting the unmistakable sound of guts being turned inside out.

I could have carried off two or three people, but which ones, and where? And for what purpose? They would have hated me for not taking their part, or feared me for my ability, or both.

Instead, I staggered back to my not very clean quarters, washing off in the grimy facilities down the hall. Once again, no one noticed. Or if they did, they ignored me, smelling as I did of burning and death.

I don't think I slept, just lay there, thinking about bodies burning like torches, and that reminded me of Allyson.

At dawn, after a healthy helping of bland fare— porridge, cheese and hard crackers, I reshouldered my pack and started back to Llordian.

The morning light showed the trail of bodies up the road. I stopped counting after the first twenty. Besides the farmer shot in the first moments, I only found one other farmer's body.

Greasy black smoke wisps, interspersed with puffs of white smoke or steam, still smoldered from heaps along the road and from the blackened stone walls of the farm-house, the silo, and the two barns. The tile roofs had col-lapsed into the buildings when the supporting beams had burned. A trail of corn betrayed someone's success at loot-ing.

A few rods farther on a dark splotch stained the stone fence enclosing the small front yard of the farmhouse. Beside the stone walk, littered with small pieces of charred wood, lay a small hand-carved doll.

Overhead, the gray clouds emphasized the desolation. The wind kept the stench of burned grain and charred flesh from becoming overpowering, and I managed to hold back another round of retching as I recorded it all.

No livestock remained, but whether the farmers had re-covered it or the townies had made off with it I couldn't tell. What I could tell was that the townies had destroyed far more than they obtained.

*Chhichii . . . chichiii*

Two grossjays perched in a bare-limbed tree.

*Chhiichiii . . .*

Another scavenger fluttered down out of sight on the road where most of the townies had died.

After another sweeping pan of the destruction, I dropped undertime, heading back toward Mount Persnol.

# XLV.

OVER THE NEXT tenday, I recorded, after the fact, the results of another three attacks around Llordian. I refused to witness or record another attack in progress, since, short of killing off the townies wholesale, no reasonable solution was possible.

Wryan and I argued over it—one of the first real arguments we had.

"You don't think losing a leader will stop them?" I had asked late one night, since we still did not meet openly. She was sipping hot cider.

"No. It's a structural problem. Removing one person won't solve anything." Wryan set down her heavy mug.

"No one else can lead them so effectively."

"Sammis, that isn't the problem." She gave me an exasperated look, the kind that I hated, perhaps because my mother had done the same. So had Dr. Wendengless.

"They're starving."

Wryan shook her head. "They're hungry. They don't know what starving is. Not yet." The coolness in her voice chilled me.

"Then what is the problem?"

"You tell me."

"Why?"

"Because I can't afford to do your thinking for you."

Sounding like the difficult student I didn't really want to be, I asked again. "Why?"

"That's enough. Sometimes . . ." She gave me an exasperated sigh this time, not just a look.

"All right," I conceded. "They don't understand the entire concept of seed grain."

"They don't care, but that's not the real problem."

I almost sighed. "They hate the farmers, and they hate us."

Wryan shrugged, as if to ask what else was new.

"The farmers don't trust them."

"True."

"So . . . that's the problem."

"That is *a* problem, but it's not the critical one." She yawned. "Now, it's late, and you'll probably have to record more disasters for Odin Thor—"

"You agree with all this recording? With Odor Thor letting Llordian tear itself apart?"

"Yes. It's the only thing. It may not work."

I shook my head. Sometimes she was so warm, and others . . . well, then she was the cool and calculating Dr. Relorn.

I dropped back undertime to my single room and its stack of equipment and viewtapes to think over what she had said. I didn't get to sleep immediately, not with the old memories of smoke and a burned-out steamer and the newer recollections of greasy smoke, blackened empty walls, and the charred heaps that had been people.

Of the three attacks around Llordian, two had resulted in burnouts like the first one I had observed. In the third, the farmers had killed nearly fifty townies—mostly with the etheline firebombs—and someone had picked off the one-armed man.

The morning after our argument, I began another undertime sweep of the Llordian area—only to find another small and burned-out farm. Few if any of the farmers had gotten away.

Most of the grain had been carted off in the farm's own steam truck. I found it stored in an old house in Llordian,

guarded by three townies armed with ConFed-issue projectile guns.

At least one slaughtered hog was being roasted in a pit
contrived in the dry fountain in the town square.

More important, urchins acting as sentries had been
posted on every road leading to Llordian. I dropped in out
of nowhere and told Odin Thor.

"Getting organized, are they?" He just smiled. "Very
interesting. Just keep a close watch, Sammis, if you would.
Let me know what happens."

"Don't you think we should do something?"

"What?" asked the Colonel-General, smiling his false
smile. "They don't like us. They certainly don't want us
around. You think I should risk our forces for people who
would attack us?"

I shrugged. What he said was certainly true. Yet it rang
false.

"Let me know as things develop," he repeated, looking
at the door.

I got the hint. "I will." I dropped undertime.

As I wandered around my room, straightening it up for
lack of anything better to do, and using the sinks in the
facilities to wash uniforms, I wondered if I could look
foretime, to get a hint of what might happen.

According to all the texts and materials Deric had forced
on me, and whose "training" I was ignoring on the pre-
text of the Llordian assignment, other divers could break
out in future times in other planetary systems.

So . . . after I hung up the uniforms and made a desultory effort at cleaning up the sanitary facilities somewhat, I went and stuffed my body. Then I reviewed the
notebooks on future breakouts.

By mid-afternoon, I had pulled back on the heavy black
sweater and dropped under the now, heading for Llordian.
Hanging over the square, undertime, I edged myself to-

ward the blue direction, gently pushing. That was the easy part. I didn't even feel light-headed.

Seeing what would happen in the future was another question.

At first, the outlines of the town flickered and fuzzed, much as they normally looked from the undertime, even in the "now." Then, further uptime the barrier to seeing Query became solid gray. That was what most divers normally saw. I pushed further into the blue, and the gray barrier dissolved into more of a grayish haze.

Through the haze, I could make out one thing clearly. Most of Llordian was gone in whatever future I was watching. I concentrated harder, not moving farther foretime, in trying to make out some hint of what might happen. The haze remained, but I could see two images superimposed on each other.

One view was of unkempt and grass-dotted dunes. The other was of a fountain, the same dry fountain from the Llordian central square, surrounded by a low wall. The hills beyond the wall were covered with grasses and scattered trees.

My head was aching, but the two images shifting back and forth were the best I could do before retreating back to my room. The room was empty and cold. Some days the power wasn't on in the afternoons. That was to provide enough for the maintenance facilities.

I kept the heavy sweater on and sat on the edge of the bed.

No matter what happened, Llordian was dead. In one case, it looked like a lot more than Llordian was dead, but drawing a conclusion from just one part of a continent could be dangerous.

If Llordian was dead for all practical purposes, why did Odin Thor and Wryan both think it was important? And why wouldn't either one tell me?

# XLVI.

MORE ATTACKS AND burnings in Llordian and occurred over the next ten-day.

Then the elders and farmers of another farming town, Felshtar, came to Odin Thor complaining about the ConFed levies. Odin Thor asked for an election. They voted—sixty percent for the ConFed departure—and Henriod pulled out the ConFed troops. Two days later, the Felshtar townies attacked a small farm. The farmers retaliated by burning an outlying house.

About the same time, the Llordian farmers mounted an attack on the once-empty Llordian houses where grains had been taken and stored.

I eased back into Llordian as the ragged peddler, trudging down the road from Halfprince. Even from the edge of town, the stench was nearly unbearable, in spite of the cold south wind. The old postal building had been pressed into service as lodgings, and two women, armed with ancient scatterguns, stood by the nearly closed gate.

The town's wall facings that had been white-washed and flecked with silver were scraped, scarred, and covered with dust and blackish grit. An odor of charred flesh and burned wood lingered in the air. Dark reddish blotches stained the curb stones.

In the square, the pottery lady's stand was a crushed pile of fabric and broken wood, interspersed with colored clay shards. By the still-dry fountain stood the empty spits where the stolen and slaughtered hogs had been roasted, with a heap of days-old bones kicked into a corner. A rat gnawed at one in the gray mid-morning light.

One whole row of dwellings on one side of the square had been fired, and the roofs had collapsed in on themselves. Two bent men glanced at me, then returned to scavenging items and carrying them to the small wagon.

"You!"

I turned slowly, letting the hidden recorder in my pack pan the destruction. A thin man, almost as tall as Odin Thor, silver hair streaked with soot or worse, wearing a farmer's jacket over a mechanic's grease suit, aimed a projectile gun at me. He wasn't a farmer, not with the projectile holes in the jacket, and the prison brand on his forehead.

"What you doing here?"

I looked around wide-eyed, reached slowly for one of the trinkets I had carved, ready to drop undertime instantly. He leveled the gun directly at me as I displayed a badly carved napkin ring.

"Oh, it's you. The mute boy." He shook his head. "Get out of here. No one has anything. The farmers will shoot you just like us, maybe faster."

I looked puzzled, pointed to the pottery stand.

"Merdith? They got her, too. She didn't want to lose her pots." He snorted. "Swine! Starve us . . . hoarders . . ." The man almost forgot me, then stopped and gestured with the gun back toward the Halfprince road. "Go on. Someone might shoot you because they don't know you. Go on!"

I nodded, let my shoulders sag, and plodded back the way I had come, toward the postal building—the ex-ConFed fort—that had become the latest housing in Llordian.

Something seared through my shoulder. I staggered undertime, holding to my concentration like a precious jewel until I fell on breakout right in front of Nerlis, the nurse in the infirmary.

"Sorry . . ." I think I said.

When I woke up again, I was lying on a flat table with

Dr. Dyrell using a long instrument on my chest. The fire redoubled and dropped around me like a prickly red haze.

How long I drifted there, I don't know, except that I was in a room where people seemed to come and go, and look at me, and come and go. Wryan came at least once. So, I think, did Odin Thor. Even in my haze Wryan stood out like a silver star.

When I woke up for real, there were, again, all sorts of tubes attached to me, and a large flexible pad across my left shoulder and chest.

Nerlis arrived within instants.

"Well . . . are you really awake?"

I nodded.

She shook her head slowly, not quite fondly, but not totally disapprovingly. "You get into more trouble . . ."

I just looked at the mass of tubes connected to me.

She followed my eyes. "Those stay there until we're sure you're not starving again."

"When . . . can . . . I . . . eat?" My voice felt rusty, and my throat was dry.

She laughed. "That's a good sign. Let's try liquids, first. There's nothing wrong with your digestive system."

I glanced to the window as she checked me, before bustling out for the liquids she had promised. Outside were high soft white clouds and a bright green-blue sky, almost springlike.

Wryan arrived shortly, dropping from nowhere into the infirmary room. She glanced over the tubing. "I think I've seen you like this before."

"Doctor . . ." acknowledged Nerlis, returning with a beaker. She barely hesitated before bringing it up to my lips.

The first sip was hard, so dry were my lips and mouth. The second was easier. The third hit my stomach like a centreslot ball to the groin. I'd forgotten the impact of

Sustain on an empty stomach, but my body brought back the recollection instantly.

Nerlis wiped the sweat off my forehead, then nodded. "He's all yours, Doctor Relorn. I'll be back in a while to disconnect the tubes."

Wryan pulled the chair closer to the bed. "Sammis . . . who told you that you were invulnerable?"

I didn't want to answer that one.

"Walking into Llordian . . ." she didn't finish her statement.

"All right . . . was stupid." I took another sip of Sustain with a shaking hand. "Should I have dived in and recorded and disappeared?"

"Why not?" Wryan's voice was calm.

"How about the witches of Eastron?"

"It's a different time and a different place." She looked at me critically. "You should be dead, you know?"

I didn't ask why, not wanting to move much.

"Your wounds weren't survivable, according to Dr. Dyrell." She stood up and pointed a finger at me. "But you're still not invulnerable."

I yawned. All of a sudden, I felt tired.

"I'll talk to you later."

As I recovered over the next ten-day, I discovered that the remaining farmers had nearly leveled Llordian, but not before the last remnant of the townies had attacked and leveled a dozen more farms—empty because the farmers had retreated to one they had made into a stronghold.

The townies attacked, and three quarters of them were wiped out—as were nearly half the farmers and most of the stored crops and seed grain.

At Felshtar, nearly the same thing had happened, because the farmers, hearing what had happened at Llordian, waited until the next townie attack. Then they burned the entire town, while the townies were out burning every farmhouse they could reach.

Jerlyk made some tapes of the destruction.

Algern, another town near Esterly, complained about the ConFed levies. Odin Thor showed them the tapes, then sent a handful of townies and farmers by steamer to Llordian. They didn't even ask for an election. They did ask, after talking with Wryan, for a committee of townies and farmers, under ConFed supervision, to verify townie food needs and farmer supplies.

By the time I was well enough to leave the infirmary, I had figured out what had to be done, if we were to avoid self-destruction and get back on the road to dealing with the Frost Giants.

Wryan didn't encourage me or oppose me. What she said was, "If you think so, go ahead and persuade everyone."

I didn't have to persuade everyone, just Odin Thor.

# XLVII.

THE SUNSHINE THAT had promised an early spring vanished as we walked into the Colonel-General's office. My shoulder still twinged when I stretched too far, but the redness of the scars had already begun to fade.

Odin Thor stood behind his desk and peered at me, and I still didn't know whether Wryan was really behind me or not. At least, she'd agreed to come.

"The divers can't stay here any longer."

"Why not, Trooper Sammis?"

"First, because it makes your troopers uneasy. Second, because they need to adjust to the real world. And third, because this base isn't suited to rebuilding the future." My voice almost squeaked, but I got it all out.

Wryan said nothing, just stood there with a faint smile on her face.

Odin Thor smiled even more broadly. "My troopers will do what I say."

"Not necessarily."

"Oh . . . ?"

"Not if I tell them your big secret—that you're a diver yourself."

For once, the Colonel-General looked surprised. He opened his mouth, then shut it. Then he just sat there.

"You, madame." he finally said, "Do you believe such an absurdity?"

"Colonel," she said with a wry twist to her lips, "what I believe is not the issue. Is it?"

Odin Thor glanced toward the closed door, then looked at me. "What could you possibly gain by making such a statement?"

"Look," I said, hoping the words came out the way I had rehearsed them. "What happened at Llordian and Felshtar showed that right now people only respect force. They also try to destroy what they don't want to understand. I'm a diver. I'm not a trooper, and I never will be again."

Odin Thor's hairy eyebrows furrowed.

"Do you really think you could keep me from destroying most of your forces—if I had to?"

"You wouldn't."

"Not unless you forced him," added Wryan.

Odin Thor stepped back. "Let's start this over." He resumed the false jollity. "Why don't you just explain this whole wonderful scheme of yours?"

"It's not wonderful. It's designed for survival." I cleared my throat. "It's simple when you think about it. From the divers' viewpoint, they have to sleep, and get rest. If the ConFeds are three buildings away, some of the divers are always vulnerable. Plus, several of them have had rather unpleasant prior experiences with ConFeds.

"Second, the divers are still living in the past. They

still look at what they're doing as a research project. They need to become more self-reliant, and building their own camp will require that. In addition, the ConFeds are already beginning to resent having to support the divers. If the divers support themselves, then they're not a drain on the ConFeds. And the ConFeds are going to need every man possible to maintain some sort of order in the next year or so." I rubbed my shoulder, recalling Llordian.

"Now . . . you asked about you. If you are known to be a diver, and divers can neutralize people at will, no one is likely to challenge you. But . . . you can't make that known until the divers, who, presumably, would be viewed as your power base, are out of easy physical reach of the ConFeds."

Odin Thor paced back toward me. A good two heads taller than me, he radiated physical power. "Why couldn't I just remove you?"

"Because you can't survive over the long term without divers," interjected Wryan.

"I beg your pardon?" Odin Thor's politeness was strained.

"Look," I almost shouted. "Your damned steamers are your lifelines. They're more than half ceramic, and there's not a ceramics facility left on the planet. Where are the etheline refineries? The Enemy—the Frost Giants—whatever they are, leveled all the factories and took out the solar satellite links. We can reach them. You can't. *Maybe* in time we could repair them. You can't. How long will those standby generators last?"

Odin Thor wasn't stupid. "All of that may be true, but what good are your divers? There's not an engineer among them, you two excepted."

I swallowed. "We can bring small things back from other planetary systems. Weapons, certainly tools, some limited metals. Perhaps technology."

Odin Thor raised his eyebrows.

"We've already proved to be able to provide instant communications."

He looked out the window. "You're telling me I have no choice."

"Not exactly," added Wryan. "Sammis is telling you that over the long term you have no choice."

"Madame, I am not that short-sighted. I have no choice. Will you keep your bargain?"

"We have to," I added. "For the same reason. We have to be viewed as helpful. Otherwise, any time a diver appears, we'll be back in the old witches of Eastron days, having to hide and run."

"I'm not sure I believe that."

"If I bring Weldin copper wire, iron plates or scavenge materials from ruins in Eastron, he can rebuild a generator for power generation. I can't build one."

Odin Thor said nothing, looked out at the clouds.

Wryan nodded faintly.

"All right. What comes first?"

I'd thought about that. First, the divers brought raw materials and goodies for the ConFeds. Then, they decided they wanted their own village, not an armed camp, with some strong hints from Odin Thor that he really couldn't guarantee day-in, day-out security unless the divers were in a less accessible location.

Odin Thor would let his men gradually—bring in women. Only willing ones, and the divers could police that. With the women would come children. That would take care of some resentment against there being female divers and no female ConFeds.

"Sit down, why don't you?" I suggested.

Wryan smiled faintly from behind Odin Thor as she pulled up a chair. Odin Thor turned and retreated behind his desk.

I sat in the chair right before him. It would be a long morning.

# XLVIII.

NONE OF THE divers really liked the whole plan. Mellorie liked getting away from the ConFeds, but protested the idea that *she* would have to help build the new divers' village, with her own hands yet. Arlean liked leaving the ConFeds and the walls, but disliked the isolated location on the other side of Mount Persnol, and hated the idea of leaving the library where it was. But she didn't want to hand-carry it, along with all the equipment, to the village.

Gerloc protested having to be a porter, perhaps because he didn't want to admit he was relatively fragile as a diver. Jerlyk didn't like having to set up defenses for the new village—minor as they were—when the apparent protection of old Camp Persnol had been so great. Amenda said nothing, but looked relieved and sad simultaneously.

Deric protested the loudest.

". . . most absurd . . . idiotic idea . . . throwing away a generation of research . . . going back to nature . . . mind over matter doesn't work without technology . . ."

By the time he had repeated himself three times, even Gerloc and Arlean were looking away.

Then there was me. I protested, too, about the self-centeredness of everyone else, one afternoon as we stood in the far hills comparing on-site progress with the plans Deric had reluctantly developed. "Why do we have to drag everything out of everyone? Why can't they just understand? They're all hanging onto a time that's dead."

"Are you sure you don't see this new community as an easy way to bury the past and avoid facing unpleasant memories?" asked Wryan, turning toward me so that she didn't squint into the setting sun. Though it was late in the afternoon and the sun was about to drop behind Mount Persnol, the spring air was still warm.

"Of course not."

Wryan looked at me.

I shrugged. "A little, maybe."

"You realize we need more divers." Wryan continued as if she had not mentioned unpleasant memories.

"Why do we need more divers?" I kicked a small limb away from the stone foundation.

She gestured around the foundation stones, mortar troughs, and stacked beams that were eventually supposed to be a divers' cottage. A rutted muddy track in front of the foundations showed on the neatly drafted plans as a stone-paved roadway.

"Not enough people," I ventured.

"You just might show signs of brilliance, Sammis."

From her tone, I gathered I had missed more than I had grasped. So I tried again. "If Odim Thor is going to succeed, he needs more than we can get . . ."

That wasn't it. Wryan just kept looking from the plans and to the foundations.

"If Odin Thor doesn't succeed . . ." That wasn't it either. Finally, I rubbed my shoulder—still aching at the end of long days—and thought. "Oh . . . if he *does* succeed . . ."

Wryan nodded. "Correct. Can you take some time tomorrow morning to get this back on track?" She pointed to the plans. "Then you can start searching in the afternoon. Work with the crews in the morning, and search in the afternoon. We can't exactly forget that the Frost Giants are still out there, and we don't have enough divers if they return."

"Damned recipe for exhaustion . . ."

"You're brilliantly correct about that as well." She rolled up the plans. "These aren't getting built the way they should. I'll follow up on your searches in the morning, and work with the crews in the afternoon."

That was what happened. The building part was the easiest, actually less energy-consuming than diving, and gave me a few new muscles, lots of aches and blisters, and more than a few headaches.

"Why do we have to use so much stone . . . ?"

". . . not enough power tools. . . ."

". . . who made you Verlyt . . ."

". . . liked the old quarters better . . ."

Searching for new divers was almost a relief after those mornings. I didn't have to actually make the contacts—Wryan and Amenda handled that. In practice, it turned out to be simple . . . and time-consuming.

I could see the time energy controls through the undertime. That was the easy part. After that, I had to find out exactly who possessed the talent, which wasn't exactly easy when most of them didn't know they had it, didn't want to know, or tried to suppress it.

Then Wryan and Amenda had to decide how to approach the diver, or his or her parents or both.

"Let the parents come here, if they want." That had been Jerlyk's solution.

Not a bad idea, but—like so many good ideas—a little hard to sell. As a compromise, we ended up building two villages, separated by a fairly imposing ridge, and connected by a single narrow road. Originally, one location had been an Imperial forest research station and the other a Seco recreation center. Both were in poor shape.

One village, initially the Seco recreation center and somewhat larger, was for non-divers who wanted to stay with us, for young divers and their families, and for any relations of divers. The other was for divers alone. I hoped the distinctions would blur over time.

Needless to say, the mixed diver/non-diver village got underway much more quickly, once we actually trans-

ported the non-divers on site. It was nearly a day from the
old camp by steamer, up through so many switchbacks on
a narrow road that arrival anywhere would have been a
relief.

One way or another, we struggled through the spring
and early summer, finally finishing three good-sized cottages in the divers' village, with several others nearing
completion. A small water-driven generator supplied some
power, intermittently, although Wryan insisted on complete wiring.

The garden idea went better than the cottages, probably
because by the end of spring, everyone was sick of flour-
cakes, dried chysts, and all the staples. Amenda spent almost every free instant in the sunlight, seemingly happy
for the first time since I had arrived.

Once the first cottages were completed, most of us
moved, except for Deric, who, surprisingly, had taken
charge of quietly teaching Odin Thor how to be a diver.

By midsummer, we had located an additional two dozen
divers, mostly with families. All but a handful lived in the
mixed village.

Also by midsummer, Odin Thor was demanding the
metals, goods, weapons, and technology I had promised.

# XLIX.

ONE THING LEADS to another, and pretty soon everything
gets complicated. After the complications arrive, then
anyone can screw it up. The idea I had proposed to Odin
Thor had seemed simple—use time-diving to skim the surplus off other high-tech cultures in order to help rebuild
Query and to figure out how to deal with the Frost Giants.

Explaining doesn't explain anything.

The day after I could no longer ignore Odin Thor's demands, I fitted myself out with what I considered a diving uniform—tight-fitting black exercise trousers and tunic, with a light pair of black hiking boots, and a old thermal windbreaker from the bunkers under the old fort. I wore an equipment belt, the kind with concealed pouches and pockets, as well as the obvious gear, such as a small-caliber pistol, a knife, and some rope. The windbreaker was also black and long enough to cover the belt, knife, pistol and all. On top of it all I carried a small backpack, empty except for several days' dried foods, mostly fruits with some jerky.

Then there was the thin notebook, based on all the notes from Wryan and the other timedivers, which laid out a sort of map of the nearer stellar systems. My idea was simple enough, just to skim through the backtime to see if any cultures had developed ideas or items we could use— and carry. That was the big problem. Unless a timediver could lift an item, he or she couldn't bring it back. Some divers were barely strong enough to carry themselves, let alone additional loads.

The kitchen was empty when I sat down for a bite of breakfast—cheese and bread, washed down with some citril. Outside the flat and mismatched panes, the purple of early dawn faded toward gray as the sun neared the underside of the horizon. No one else was awake. Wryan would probably be the next one up, but I intended to be gone before she rose.

Saying good-bye to her was getting too hard, and there would be all too many good-byes over the days and seasons ahead.

I sliced off another hunk of cheese, sealed the wedge, and put it back in the cooler. The battery charge was running low, but there wasn't time to fix that right then. We missed the luxury of the broadcast power that had been one of the first casualties of the Frost Giant attack.

Paring the cheese into smaller slices, I put them on the

second slice of rough grain bread and began to eat, finally washing the remnants down with the last of the citril in my mug.

The gray dawn became a grayer morning as I stood, seeing that there would be no sunrise, not with the heavy clouds overhead and the promise of more rain. After I rinsed out the mug and stacked it in the rack, I swung up my backpack.

"Ready to go, I see." Wryan stood by the open archway that led to the room the three women shared. Her sandy hair was tousled, and her small feet were bare, as if she had pulled on the sweater and trousers on the run.

"No sense in wasting time." I looked at her, nearly my size, almost eye to eye, and set the pack on the chair.

She smiled sadly.

I smiled back.

She grinned.

I grinned. "Not much good at good-bye."

"Neither am I."

Somehow, this time I knew what to do. I reached for her and pulled her close. In the end, she was holding me as tightly as I held her. She was shaking, as if she were crying.

I wanted to say something, but couldn't. So I kissed her forehead, and brushed away some tears.

Funny, it took me until then to realize I was shaking too, but Wryan touched my cheek and leaned back to look at me. I kissed her, but, again, she kissed me even as my lips reached for hers.

That was the first time we had held each other, or kissed.

For a long time after that lasting kiss, neither one of us could do anything but hold the other.

"You deserve better . . ." I had to say it. What was I but an undereducated and spoiled gentry brat who could time-dive and survive trouble? ". . . and I'm too young, too shallow for you . . ."

"Let me worry about that, Sammis. The age doesn't matter, not at all, not the way things are looking . . ."

"True . . ." I had to grin ruefully, but lost it when I felt she meant something else. "What do you mean?"

"That's my secret until you come back . . ."

"Working on my curiosity, then, lady?"

Her arms were tighter around me, and I gave in, letting my lips find hers.

How much time passed, I did not know, but it was definitely later when we let go, except for two hands tightly intertwined.

"When you come back, we'll talk about it."

"About it?"

"My secret, as you call it. It's already becoming obvious, but . . ."

I nodded. Whatever she had discovered was not something that should get to Odin Thor, at least not until we had worked out how to handle it. That was becoming more and more our operating style.

She disengaged her hand from mine and straightened her sweater. "Now get out of here while we're still relatively intact."

I knew exactly what she meant. So I leaned toward her and brushed her lips, then leaned back and grabbed my pack. And I was undertime, knowing she was crying again and that I wasn't in much better shape.

That's why the first dive wasn't much of a dive, just enough to get me into the abandoned polar space station. I'd checked earlier, and it still had an atmosphere.

Staggering out of the undertime, I was ready to bolt if the air had disappeared or turned foul, but neither had happened. So there I was, hovering in the old operations center, swaying from side to side, ready to fall, except for the fact that I was weightless.

From the station's size and equipment, it had to have been the base from which the ill-fated Mithradan planet-forming had been launched and supported. While I could have floated as easily as finding a place to light, I felt better with the illusion of sitting and strapped myself into one of the operations' center chairs, in front of a dull black screen.

My hands were still shaking, and that had never happened before. Then again, something like Wryan had never happened before. If I didn't know better, I would have said that, tousled as she had been that morning, she looked more like my age than hers. Yet she had to be more like four times my age—at least.

But then, no one believed I was my own age either. People still thought of me as a school-age brat when they first saw me.

My thoughts were wandering because I did not want to deal with my entanglement with Wryan. So I pulled out the thin notebook and began to study the stellar/time maps I had so carefully tried to integrate.

Too many of the systems were blanks, meaning that they were either uninhabited or we had no information.

We couldn't risk losing any divers, and that was a circular problem too. A good diver could skip undertime without getting frozen stiff or suffocated, but the good divers were those who could transport what we needed.

At that point, I groaned. Once again, I had missed the obvious. Sitting in an orbital space station filled with space suits designed for at least some hostile environments, I had a solution.

I dropped undertime and popped back into the kitchen where Wryan was staring out the window over a cup of something.

"Don't move. I shouldn't be back, but here's an idea for the information we need—"

She looked at me, and from even across the room I could see her eyes were bloodshot.

"—on other systems." I had to plunge on or I'd stop,

and then I'd never leave. "You know the big orbital station? The one involved in the Mithrada fiasco? It's got a bunch of space suits in it—not just one or two like you had in the lab. Put the marginal divers in suits and get them to scout systems. Just present time. If they find traces of civilizations or cultures, then someone else can follow up."

"Like you?"

"Or you," I added.

"Next time, we go together, Sammis Arloff Olon. Or you don't go."

I thought about that. "Let me think that over."

"Please do, and I'll put together a plan for your mapping idea while you follow the leads you have. Now kindly get on your way . . . and be careful."

I nodded and ducked undertime, swallowing as I did. I couldn't finish the swallow until I popped back out in the space station. Then I began looking at the maps.

Sertis was first on the list, a mere two stellar systems away.

# L.

SERTIS—WHAT SHOULD I say about the place?

Crowded, at least in the cities. I picked the largest one, at the intersection of a large river and a wide bay filled with a range of vessels. Some were powered with energy flows I could sense from the undertime. Others were clearly sailing ships.

With each dive I had become more and more sensitive to the flows of energy from the now, perceived from the undertime. None of the other timedivers could sense them, but I suspected some would develop the ability with more experience. That made homing in on large energy concentrations easy; cities particularly.

That was about the only easy part.

First, I'm not a linguist. The gabble of voices was just that—verbal confusion. Second, the signs and written languages were even worse. Third, what I was wearing was clearly enough to attract unwanted attention. The Sertians apparently were strong on flowing robes and hoods. The men were mostly bearded, and the women wore colorful scarves.

The clothing was the easiest to remedy. Slipping under the now, I located and liberated an appropriately-sized cloak, along with an exterior belt and purse. After the Llordian mess, I was more than a little apprehensive about walking alone in places where my disposal would be easy from a distance. So I stayed with the crowds near what seemed to be an open market. The air was like an oven. Only the lack of humidity made either the temperature or the odor bearable. And I had thought the damps were rank!

"Hslop?" A ragged child grinned at me. His face was almost squarish, and his hair was black and tight-curled around an olive face.

Since I didn't know what the urchin meant, I scowled.

"Hslop? Hslop?"

I just turned away, ducking between two substantial matrons, and moving toward a line of stands, each draped in purple.

Despite my hopes, I was still staggered. The first stand had a wide range of steel knives, real steel, laid out. I nodded and passed by.

"Hssilinglop?" asked the woman tending the stand.

I ignored her, wishing I could understand the language.

The second stand was more interesting, with an assortment of hand tools. I watched as the owner and a thin young man bargained over a hatchet. Finally, I drifted on, noting that the urchins still trailed me, at a distance.

A quarter of the way around the market, past the food stands and the fabrics, I found the power tools. Some of them looked like they ran on etheline, or some liquid hydrocarbon. One or two were battery-powered, but they were covered with a film of dust. Several were not familiar, but one looked like a tree saw. I could make out another saw with an assortment of circular blades that looked as though it would cut finished timbers and boards, and a power drill.

"Hssilinglop?" asked the stall tender.

I pointed to the circular saw, thinking that we could try it out. If it worked, someone like Gerloc could get some more.

"Res thorp."

Not knowing what "res thorp" meant, I pawed around in the purse that I had liberated, and offered a small silver coin—far less than an earlier customer had paid for the tree saw.

He held up four fingers, pointing to the silver coin. I didn't have four of them, but I did have a gold piece of some sort. So I held up two fingers. He gave me a sad face. I shrugged.

Finally, he held up three.

I winced, thinking about having to show the gold piece.

He shrugged and gave me two and a crooked finger. I guessed that was a half.

I scrabbled through the purse and came up with two silvers, and a quarter of a silver, it looked like, plus some smaller and lighter coins. I put them all on the wooden counter.

He shrugged, trying not to smile too much, and took them. I think the smaller coins added up to more than half a silver because he dragged out a carrying case and threw in all the blades, plus a wrench and a small can of lubricant.

I walked to the nearest alley and disappeared undertime.

Someone else could certainly handle Sertis, even if I had to write a manual. That would provide goodies for both the divers and Odin Thor.

# LI.

COLLECTING WEAPONS IS hard work for a timediver. A knife I could carry, but it would be useless against a Frost Giant. A projectile rifle presented the same problem.

Nuclear weapons worked effectively on the Frost Giants. But nukes also destroyed large chunks of real estate and possessed too much mass for a timediver to carry. From what Wryan had determined, particle beams also would work, but not lasers. The difference was academic, since any particle beam ever built by Westron with enough force to fragment a Frost Giant wouldn't fit on a steamer, much less on a timediver's back.

Only high-tech worlds can build small and destructive weapons, and high-technology cultures tend to be short-lived because they are complex and require a continuing high level of education. There are always exceptions, but the exceptions presented another problem.

Not that either kind of high-tech system was hard for me to find because their energy use beat through the undertime like a flare.

High-tech meant unstable and short-lived or stable and lasting. The first of the longline high-tech cultures I found was Muria. That's what I called it, but who knows what they called themselves?

Tall and slender people, bipedal, with brains and eyes in their heads, finely scaled green skin and white silk hair. Scales and hair don't go together? On Muria they did.

Three sexes, or maybe four, and they all looked alike. The Murians had created a paradise. Golden-fronded trees lined paths that were permanent, yet cushioned every foot-step and wound between close-linked clusters of hive houses. Each hive house group was separated from other groups by a varying mixture of orchards, forests, and low-effort cultivated fields. All their nourishment seemed to come from vegetation, but some of the fruits or vegetables looked more like meat.

It rained on Muria just enough, and the cloud patterns kept a favorable range of temperature and breezes. Just enough Murians were born, so that while the settlements changed, the total number of them stayed about the same. Murian medicine, or genetics, or culture, provided long lives, and Murian science had reduced power generation to small fusion generators. Too big to carry, but small enough to fit into a large closet. They were fusion pow-ered, that I could tell from the energy flows.

I couldn't believe the planet. So I went backtime for two or three centuries. I couldn't see any differences. Then I went foretime, and there wasn't much change there, ex-cept that the locations of some towns changed.

After that, I started looking for weapons, and I couldn't find any. I could dive into hidden places, but those were very few. I could seize any document or text, but I couldn't read them. I could disassemble any machine, but those I understood I didn't need, and those I didn't understand I couldn't figure out.

Understand, these Murian people were intelligent—and nonviolent. Short of creating a one-person crime wave, there didn't seem to be any way I could persuade them to employ force. Violence was becoming a last resort for me, not that I hadn't employed it effectively.

The Murians had an interstellar drive, and a few ex-plorers who used it. That was where I focused my efforts and where I came up with the duplicator, an accident if ever there was one, since I was looking for weapons.

Their interstellar ships were small, too small to handle

distances without supplies and more spare parts and equipment. But they did well, quite well. So I continued to watch from the undertime until I discovered the strange gadget in the ship that duplicated everything from food to tools, with apparently no input except electrical power.

Then the real work began. I tracked a new ship backtime to its construction until I could watch a team of Murians install the duplicator. That night it was my turn.

The shell of the ship was quiet as I broke out of the undertime. No alarms, no bells, not even any energy flows. With my recently acquired Murian tools, I studied the duplicator up close—an elongated octagonal donut that fit on a cabinet about half the size of the kitchen table in our cottage. The central "hole" was where they put items to be duplicated and at first glance seemed limited to items about two handspans square. Because the Murians built most equipment in modular form, the size limit probably didn't cause that many problems. In any case, it was better than anything we had, because we had nothing to speak of, and less on the way.

The duplicator was in a separate compartment next to what I figured were the fusion generators. A glistening blue wire ran from the octagonal machine into a square junction box. In a few moments I had removed the cover of the junction box and set it out of the way on the green-gray deck.

The Murians liked their planet humid, and inside the ship was no exception. I stopped and wiped the sweat off my forehead and out of my eyes. A deep breath followed, and I ignored the musky smell that was part me, part leftover Murians.

Inside the junction box the glistening blue wire split into three smaller insulated filaments. The uncovered end of each filament was purplish. Each was wound around a metal plug the size of my thumb. With some effort, I carefully unhooked the insulated filament wires from the three plugs and withdrew the wire through the side opening in the junction box.

Now the duplicator was free of the power system, and all I had to do was release it from its mountings. That meant standing nearly on my head to release the bolts anchoring the machine to the built-in counter. There were eight bolts, and I had to rest after twisting each one free. Rested and wiped my forehead and tried to get the sweaty salt out of my eyes.

My tunic was dripping, and the ship definitely smelled like sweating human being by the time I twisted the last bolt free and laid it on the floor next to the seven others.

After wiping my forehead again, I tried to lift the duplicator. I could not break it free of the counter, although it seemed to wobble sideways. I let go and sat on the deck to catch my breath and to think.

One Murian had carried the device, and they weren't that much bigger than I was.

I took a swig from my small water bottle. Not that I really needed it in most circumstances, but it did make me feel more comfortable.

Next I checked under the counter, looking for another bolt or fastening. There weren't any. Then I studied the eight-sided machine itself, to see if there were brackets holding it on the sides. Nothing.

I pulled on it. Again, no result. I pushed it toward the bulkhead, losing my balance because it slid so quickly, then stopped cold just before hitting the bulkhead, apparently locked in place.

After some more experimentation, I discovered that it had been threaded through a series of "lock" positions on the metallic plastic bench top. Once I finally maneuvered it free, still having to stop to wipe the sweat off my forehead, I set it on the deck.

I rested, wondering if it would take this long for everything I attempted to make off with.

Standing up, I checked the counter surface on which the duplicator had rested, running my fingers over the flat metallic plastic or plastic metal. The surface was absolutely smooth to my touch—absolutely.

I ran the Murian screwdriver, which had a triangular blade, over the surface. Again, nothing. Then I had another thought and pulled my own knife from my belt and drew it over the surface. It ran into a faint, barely detectable tackiness.

I frowned. The Murians had forged what amounted to a lock. More important, they had established some sort of directional bonds that weren't magnetic and which only operated in certain positions in certain directions. The duplicator could not have been lifted off that counter without destroying both duplicator and counter. The bolts had been there just to keep it from sliding around accidentally.

Looking down at the eight-sided machine with its short glistening blue wire, I had the feeling my troubles were only beginning. After repacking the Murian tools into my belt pouch, I picked up the duplicator and staggered undertime.

While it had taken me one straight dive to Muria from the Queryan orbital station, it took three subjective days and twenty rest breaks to get back to camp, breaking out in the small work room Wryan shared with me. I carefully eased the duplicator onto a solid bench and turned around to see Wryan coming through the doorway.

"You look like hell," she observed.

"Hell probably feels better."

"What did you bring back?"

"A duplicator. If we can get it to work."

"Duplicator?"

"It copies anything you put in the middle there—fish, fowl, or electronic components."

"How?"

I shrugged. "Don't know. But the only input is ship power."

"How much power? What kind? Alternating, direct, burst?"

I shrugged again. "How would I know? I never even finished the Academy. It does take a lot of power. A whole lot. I could feel that when the Murians used it."

"Murians?"

"Intelligent amphibian descended. Very cultured. *Very* advanced."

Wryan fingered the blue wiring. "Getting it to work could be a real problem. If this is the only power input, and it takes as much power as you say, we could be in trouble. And we'll probably need two anyway."

"Took me everything I had to get *one* of them back here."

"Even if it is a duplicator, how can we duplicate it? We'll need more than one."

My shoulders sagged. I hadn't thought about that, but she was right.

"Don't worry about it now. I'm going to have to study this first, and I'll probably need you to study one in operation to make sure we set this up right."

Since I didn't exactly feel like dragging another one of the duplicators across the galaxy any time soon, and since I would have gone to hell for Wryan, I just nodded. "In a day or so."

She looked at me. "In a week or so. Maybe longer. You need something to eat, and then some rest." Her eyes radiated concern, and, tired as I was, I only wished that they had radiated more than just that.

A thought struck me belatedly. "How did you know I was back?"

"I just knew."

I wanted to pursue that but couldn't figure out how, and besides, the room seemed shaky. I sat down on the bench.

"Are you all right?"

"I'll be fine."

She had an arm around me, helping me up. "You need something to eat. No blood sugar and no rest. Just lean on me."

So I did. Concern was better than nothing, if less than what I really wanted. We made it to the kitchen, and I slumped into a chair.

"What about the duplicator?"

"It can wait," answered Wryan as she began pulling items from the cooler. "It can wait."


# LII.

FINDING THE DAMNED duplicator was just the beginning of my problems.

"Sammis, this wire is superconductive."

I nodded as I munched through a half wedge of cheese. I never seemed to eat enough to keep me from running through my personal energy reserves.

"At room temperature." Wryan sipped something from a mug.

"I'm not sure I understand." As I looked up, I could see one of the new divers, Kerina, peer into the kitchen and withdraw. I could have checked by looking undertime, but didn't bother.

Wryan frowned. "Think about it. The duplicator takes enormous power. It all goes through this wire. That means that the wire and the insulation are both incredibly advanced. It also means that the duplicator is useless unless we can hook it to a power plant."

"We have several . . ."

"Not designed for this. Do the Murians?"

I nodded again, thinking about the ship generators. This time I was working on a chyst.

"Do they come in parts? This duplicator is modular." Wryan stood up and walked to the sink, where she rinsed out her mug and set it on the rack.

After a mouthful of chyst, I answered. "I don't know."

"We still may have some physicists left, Sammis. In a generation we won't, even with . . ."

"Translated loosely, if I don't come up with a miniature fusion plant that we can build, or duplicate, we're pretty much through."

Wryan smiled that sad smile. "That's one way of putting it."

"We do have an operating power plant."

"Yes. I'm not certain it will produce electrical power at the right frequencies for the duplicator. I don't know if we could produce the proper transformers, rectifiers, whatever it might take to convert it."

I sighed and looked at the kitchen floor. Before long I could see myself having to lift most of the Murians' technology, piece by piece, just because nothing matched and we no longer had the scientific expertise to make it match.

"Fine. I'll bring you back a fusion power plant. Except for the fuel. I'm not about to try that."

"My guess is that they use water."

"Water? Plain water?"

"That won't be the problem, Sammis."

"What will be?"

"Getting the power to create the first fields."

At that point, I gave up trying to understand, at least for the moment, and decided to concentrate on the problem at hand.

"Before I kill myself doing all this, Dr. Relorn, I want to strike a deal."

"Deal?" Wryan was clearly puzzled. "A deal?"

"I don't trust our dear Colonel-General. Neither do you.

So I want us to put together our first duplicator and fusion power plant complex someplace unknown to and unfindable by the good Colonel-General. If it works, we'll supply both to the timedivers, without revealing our hidden facility, and we'll set up the second facility as if it were the first.''

Wryan started grinning.

"Why are you grinning like an idiot?"

"You wouldn't believe me if I told you."

"Try me."

"Your deal was my next idea. I can even tell you what kind of location we need."

Wryan's idea was simple. We would find a high mountain location, preferably on the Bardwalls of Eastron, where no one went even before the annexation, near a stream with enough force to power a small hydro turbine. Wryan was confident she could re-engineer, one way or another, the output to generate the mag bottle for a fusion system.

"Only the mag bottle, you understand."

Sounded great.

Reality, as usual, intruded.

Right after we got the duplicator out of sight, I started hunting for a location. It only took us an afternoon to find the right place on the Bardwalls, a sheltered valley inaccessible except by a diver, with a southern exposure and even a set of caves we could, with only a little work, seal off for storage.

I began scavenging doors and frames from the wreckage of Bremarlyn for the largest cave and cobbled together enough to keep any possible animal intruders away.

Wryan began locating the equipment she needed, with what time she could spare from her work in administering, salvaging, and troubleshooting for the timedivers' villages.

Within days, Odin Thor showed up at our official workroom in the divers' village. He and his aide, a ninny called Verlin, who was nothing more than a directional guide for the good Colonel-General, caught me actually working on planning out a phase of Odin Thor's weapons' scouting project, rather than ours. Once Deric had taught Odin Thor how to dive, within ten-days he had been replaced by Verlin.

I was sitting at the cottage table trying to figure out my next series of time sweeps for mid and high-tech cultures along a spiral arm of the galaxy. Wryan had theorized that the high percentage of what she called second generation stars argued for a greater probability of inhabited systems. What second generations stars had to do with anything was beyond me, but if Wryan said so there was a good chance it was so.

"Sammis! You promised us better weapons. Where are they?"

I hadn't really even had a chance to stand, not that I wanted to for Odin Thor, but, giving him the benefit of the doubt, I pushed my chair and waited for him to finish glaring. I was still holding the small ceramic tile I had been fingering as I had pondered where to begin the time-diving sweeps.

"Colonel-General, I have already supplied tools. Gerloc and some of the other divers are providing new equipment. But there are only so many of us. I was to have three timedivers to help map the possible technical systems. All I have is Derika, because you said the equipment was more important."

Odin Thor opened his mouth.

I held up my hand. "Let me explain. A star system lasts for millions of years. Not all systems have habitable planets. Those that are habitable are used for only a fraction of their physical lifespan. An even smaller number of those have high-technology civilizations, and those civilizations do not last long."

"But you can time-dive!"

"Diving takes a fraction of an instant. That's true. But," I lied, "you know you cannot see real time from the undertime, and that means spending real time investigating each possibility. With just two timedivers, you cannot expect great progress in a mere few ten-days."

"You argue too much, Sammis. Former Trooper Sammis."

"Yes, Colonel-General. It is one of my faults, but I also do my best to produce. So let me."

Odin Thor knew that. So he glowered at me again and stomped out of the cottage kitchen. Verlin had not said a word, and he followed Odin Thor. The two of them stood by the vegetable garden that Tyra had planted and continued to cultivate. As they whispered to each other, it looked like a conspiracy, but it was only a discussion of where Odin Thor wanted to go next. He put his hand on Verlin's shoulder, as if congratulating the fellow, and they disappeared into the undertime.

I could sense the vortex. Odin Thor spent energy like water. That might be because he never felt what he was doing.

I decided to see if I could catch Wryan before Odin Thor did. My first thought was our hidden operational center in the Eastron mountains. I was so upset that I dropped undertime still holding on to the small ceramic tile I had been fingering.

When I emerged near the waterfall on the Bardwalls, the tile was flashing with flecks of timelight or energy or something. I set it on the ground and stared at it. A thought at the back of my mind tickled at me, some memory of something, but I could not exactly recall what. I picked the tile back up and studied it. The energy flows were looped into the undertime somehow, and my fingers had a tendency to skitter off the surface.

The tile was linked undertime, not totally either in or

out of the now. Why hadn't anything like that happened before? To me or to anyone else?

*Crack!*

The noise was an impact on the boulder. The tile was unscathed, but there was a dent in the granite.

Plain old fired clay, wrapped into the undertime some way, was tougher than solid granite. If you could do that with stone or metal, what a building material you'd have. I could see it wouldn't work for weapons, even knives, because the time flows had made the tile hard to hold.

"Oh . . ." Then I remembered a long ago dream about a tower built with glittering stone. A real dive made half-asleep?

I picked up a chunk of stone the size of my fist and dropped undertime, then popped back out. There was no change in the stone that I could see or sense.

I sat down on the boulder to think.

Was it the clay? I picked up the tile and went undertime, and popped back out. The glitter was gone, and I could tell the tile was a plain and ordinary tile again.

I thought some more.

"Sammis? What are you doing?" Wryan was standing almost at my shoulder. Like me, she was almost undetectable when she went undertime or emerged. Strange how we seemed able to find each other.

"Thinking."

"Thinking? About Odin Thor?"

"I was. Came here looking for you. Try to tell you about his latest complaint—but I got side-tracked."

"He caught me with Jerlyk, trying to develop a full-time hydro generator for the diver's camp, enough to handle what we had in mind. If we were successful, we could always borrow it . . ."

"We need two . . . just like the duplicators."

"Damn." She shook her head. "You're right."

"What did the great Colonel-General say?"

"We weren't keeping up with the needs of the Marines and the Guard, and you were becoming impossible."

I grinned for a moment. "I'm glad he thinks so highly of me."

"You are impossible." She gave me a smile. "What sidetracked you?"

I told her about the tile and showed her the gouge on the boulder.

"Did you know you had the tile in your hand?"

"Not the first time."

"What about the second?"

As I saw where she was headed, I nodded. "But that won't work. You're implying that this time-protection only works if you aren't conscious of it."

"Time-diving is mind over matter, Sammis. What you can carry with you is a function of your strength of will."

"So you think that if I dive and concentrate on *not* carrying something, I can duplicate the effect?"

This time she was the one who shrugged.

I tried it—and was too successful. The tile fell out of thin air onto a rock outcropping and shattered.

Wryan tried it with one of the fragments and had similar results.

Then I recalled the looping fields around the tile and picked up a fist-sized rock and tried to slide undertime and replicate the fields. Wryan was watching when I dropped back into the now.

"It glitters a bit."

The once-dull stone shimmered, but the looping wasn't strong enough and seemed to unravel as we watched. That effort was a start, another skill to practice, along with everything else we had to do. As for erecting a tower or a building . . . I was not sure how I was going to link two stones together at all, but I knew it could be done, and that I would do it.

In the meantime, I still had find a fusion power plant

and another duplicator—and some weapons for Odin Thor before he got totally out of hand.

"Sammis . . . now what?"

I could feel myself grinning for no good reason at all. "We learn how to build buildings that are indestructible, duplicate the unduplicatable, steal the unstealable, and in general lay the foundation to become the gods of this corner of the galaxy."

Wryan gave me another one of those sad smiles. "Is that where we are headed?"

I stopped grinning. "Is there any choice?"

Neither one of us had much to say about that. So I left the rock fragment glittering on the ground, shot through with looped time energies, and slid undertime back to the cottage workroom, while Wryan went her way.

# LIII.

As USUAL, I ended up spending time on the wrong things. Instead of immediately looking for a way to get the Murian fusion plant or to find Odin Thor some weapons, I began wondering about time looping of materials.

One of my goals was personal. If Wryan and I could build a retreat that was time-warp protected and could be entered only by diving, not even Odin Thor would have much success getting at us.

So I spent most of the afternoon mentally playing with fields, trying to loop them around objects. One thing became clear. The composition of an object had less to do with the ease of time-warping than its mass. With one exception—nothing which contained electrical energy would stay warped out of time.

I carried a small battery under the now, just next to the cottage workbench, and looping the fields went fine. When

I dropped back into the now, the strands of time-loop sprayed away from the ceramic case like water off a hot skillet. Once in the now, they just wouldn't stay looped.

The other thing that became clear was that the fields reinforced each other. I put two time-warped rocks next to each other, and the fields I had created intertwined.

Then I tried it by the brook with some mud. Mud? I didn't have mortar to play with, and I wanted to see whether you could mortar together two time-linked objects.

Yes . . . and no. I could attach the mud to the rock and loop it, or I could loop a bunch of mud and apply it. But I couldn't use unlooped mud between two time-warped objects.

My mud-slinging completed, I washed my hands in the brook and decided that, after I got something to eat, I would have to trudge back to Muria, or someplace, to find Odin Thor something vaguely resembling a destructive toy.

What troubled me was not that I wouldn't find it, but that I probably would. If it weren't for the vague and uneasy understanding that the Frost Giants were still lurking somewhere in the undertime, I would have told Odin Thor where to put his weapons.

The more we got into time-diving, the more likely they would be back, and we still didn't have the faintest idea of how to stop them.

So I dropped undertime for the cottage and some more to eat before heading back to Muria—or whenever.

# LIV.

THE PROBLEM WITH the energy pistol wasn't what it did. It drilled large holes in solid rock, metal and sundry other substances. It also weighed half a stone. Amenda couldn't even point it.

Wryan suggested I look for something lighter. I did. There wasn't.

So . . . what else could I do?

I pulled on my blacks one cloudy fall morning, smiled brightly, and announced I was off to find a lightweight energy weapon.

"Find one?" asked Wryan with a critical look. Even when she was critical and tousled, I wanted to hold her. And a bit more.

Instead I just nodded. "A few angles left to explore."

"Be *very* careful, Sammis." She looked dubious.

If she'd had any idea exactly what I was going to try, she would have been even more dubious. Then again, maybe she knew.

I dropped back to Ydris with the ease of routine. Finding the place had been an accident. Then, again, my whole life resembled an accident.

On one of my too frequent theft-trips to Muria, I noticed another one of those thin energy lines, one that wavered and blasted and screamed for all of its tenuousness. Being inherently curious, I came back. It was clearly a track made by a timediver, yet it was opaque to me. So I followed it—all the way back to Ydris. Back a good long ways, probably halfway to the end of my backtime range.

Ydris—home of rod-tall amphibians with dexterous claws and enormous brains. Ydris, where both brains and claws were employed in supporting a duel-based culture.

Lace towers rose from artificial lakes and held the sunrise, speared the sun, and held its light well into the night. Light and energy—the Ydrisians squandered them like water.

I took a score of dives to scout out Ydris, from the empty and arid poles where ice winds whistled across sea ice sculpted into knife-shaped dunes to the tropical jungles where each instant held battles between beasts so savage that even the Ydrisians avoided their own equator—except for the outcasts.

The cities, built of pale jade nearly as hard as time-warped granite, circled and twisted along narrow peninsulas too regular to be natural. And in those cities, well, Thor would have drooled.

Just in passing, I had liberated the heavy energy pistol for Odin Thor. That stopped his complaints about the wisdom of time-diving. Initially. Before the problems.

Problems? One of the ConFeds, Beran, put the whole pistol in a duplicator. Fuel cell/power source/battery and all. After the blast and flash that momentarily blinded a score of ConFeds drilling nearby, turned Beran into molecules too fine to discover, and sent three others to the infirmary, we discovered, at the cost of one duplicator, that attempting to duplicate stored power produced rather messy results.

Cleaning up required building another duplicator from scratch, stealing another heavy energy pistol, and conducting a few educational lectures for dumb ConFeds.

Everything had more problems and angles than I ever anticipated.

So . . . I was diving back to Ydris, red-flashing into the past, knowing what I had in mind, but not exactly how to do it.

First, I tracked back to where I had found the first energy pistol. Easy enough. Then I traced that back to where it was manufactured—a small black stone building on the end of a peninsula. No real help from that—just a group of machines, each one stamping or forming or drawing little parts that were assembled by another machine. It would have been a good place from which to lift more pistols, but that wasn't the idea.

I lifted one pistol, barely emerging from the undertime, then dropped further backtime, to the point where the factory was being built. In time, I zeroed in on a single Ydrisian who was assembling a much larger version of an energy weapon.

When he, it, she left the room, I deposited the smaller version.

That didn't work. The technician, researcher, whatever, nodded, squawked, and made a few changes. I could scarcely feel a chill in the time currents. So I reclaimed the weapon and looked at geography.

A cooler continent in the southern hemisphere was also a technical center. I never did figure out the local politics or what passed for them, but even from the outside and undertime, it was clear that the southern continent and the northern continent did not exactly get along.

So I went back foretime and retrieved some more energy guns, as well as a few other technical devices, and deposited them in various locales on the southern continent, hoping. . . .

The jolt to the undertime was like a cold wind, shivering the timepaths around Ydris like leaves in a storm, and confirming that I'd done *something*.

I had, all right.

When I returned to the time when I had picked up the pistol, all I could see from the undertime was a shimmering flow of energy and a sea of hot glass fused into strange shapes and emitting a hellish glare quite discernible from the undertime.

That was the bad news. The good news was that a few hundred local years earlier, the ''new'' Ydrisians had developed some much smaller and more highly directed energy weapons, one of which was worn on the foreleg, or whatever they used for manipulation.

It took awhile, but this time, I tracked down all the components, including the miniature power cells just before they were energized. And I brought them back.

Wryan was waiting.

"What did you . . ." she shook her head. "I felt it from here."

"Don't ask," I mumbled. I laid out the band on the work bench. "This should be able to be made into a wrist band, a gauntlet. Fires directed energy beams. Here's an uncharged power source. It holds about the equivalent of one of our fusion plant's energy for—I don't know exactly . . . and here's the key to the charger. I can get the rest later."

I slumped against the bench, feeling the blood drain from my face.

"Sammis . . ."

Wryan's voice was coming from a distance, but I managed to sip from whatever she held in front of me. Then I could stand up—except my legs started to shake.

That wasn't physical.

I had only wanted to spur the Ydrisians into building smaller weapons—not into destroying themselves. They weren't admirable, and they fought all the time, but so did we.

I wondered if the Frost Giants looked at us that way.

"Sammis . . . ?"

Wryan's arm was around me. Her warmth and strength helped, but I wondered, absently, if my eyes were beginning to show the almost hidden blackness I sometimes glimpsed in hers.

# LV.

EVERYTHING APPEARED TO be improving. Between Gerloc and Amenda and the new divers like Kerina and Hadron and the use of the duplicators, we had gathered enough originals from Sertis and were producing enough tools and food to stop the levy on the farmers and to supply them with a few goods.

Wryan even worked out a continuous duplication stream for etheline.

The big hang-up was getting new fusion generators on line, but we had four of them operating officially. That didn't count Wryan's and my private one up in the Bardwalls.

With the batteries from Ydris, we even dispensed with the water turbines for the start-up fields.

Then, on the hills that had been Inequital, Odin Thor turned a work crew loose and leveled an area for a headquarters complex. Wryan and I—mostly me—prevailed upon him to let the divers build a tower/monument in the center, one built with time-warped stone that would stand forever. I badgered Deric to design something that looked like my dream, and then took over as project manager, when I wasn't scouting or doing miscellaneous-type engineering.

It sounds easy, but it wasn't. I started to cart building stones from Bremarlyn and glowstones from Muria before it dawned on me after about two trips—we only needed one perfect stone of each type, plus a duplicator. Of course, it took time to assemble another fusion plant and duplicator, but Odin Thor lent me some discipline cases, not that they remained that way.

And, yes, the gauntlets. Wryan and I made several modifications to them, one of which involved time-warping. Unless a diver could warp time around the gauntlets after donning them, they didn't work. The field didn't have to last, but its creation was the first step in arming them. I insisted on the idea, and Wryan, swearing quietly under her breath, figured out how to do it. One circuit was all we needed, of course, since we could duplicate the rest. Strictly an arming circuit, but that particular feature ensured that they couldn't be removed from a diver and used by anyone else. That also meant some of the divers couldn't use them, but both Wryan and I were adamant about that safeguard.

There's nothing like nearing success in survival to ensure something goes wrong.

"Sammis . . ."

I was studying a cooler from Sertis, trying to discover how we could incorporate something to attach to the cooler to convert the cycle frequency from our handy dandy Murian fusion system into the Sertian equivalent. Then we could just duplicate the coolers and hook them up directly to the community power system. Yes, we had coolers, but they were big, cumbersome and didn't work all that well. They were murder to duplicate because it had to be done piece by piece, and replacing parts entailed standing on your head, sweating profusely, and swearing liberally—when you weren't muttering under your breath.

Along the way, I was trying, and often losing, in my efforts to ensure our tools, equipment, and appliances were roughly compatible and interchangeable. Aside from me and Wryan, who was too busy to do much about it, no one else cared. Why I did, I wasn't certain, but I seemed to get stuck caring about the details no one else bothered with, that and Odin Thor's interminable quest for weapons.

"Sammis . . ." Wryan's voice was cool.

I looked up.

"The Frost Giants are back."

I sat up so suddenly my head crashed into the work bench. "Uuufff . . ." I shook my head. "How do you know?"

"They froze two cottages in the other village."

"The other village? Why there?"

"Targeted the fusion plant, I think. They are energy seekers, as you may recall."

I scrambled to my feet. "Have you alerted any of the others?"

"Most everyone."

"Now what?"

"I was hoping you'd have an idea."

The problem was that I didn't. Except one that I didn't like.

"You're not going . . . ?" asked Wryan with a look at my face.

"Anyone else better suited?"

We both knew the answer to that one.

So I went and pulled on full gauntlets, diving suit, and went hunting for Frost Giants.

Finding the track from the village wasn't hard; it was almost bluish and jagged in the undertime. Nor was dropping backtime to see what had happened earlier in the day difficult, not that I could break out, but I could watch a hazy view.

Even from undertime, I shivered as the blocky figure sucked heat and energy from the fusion plant and the surrounding cottages. Frost Giant—a misnomer in some ways. The figure I saw was oblong, with two legs, and what appeared to be four wide and stubby arms. It wore no apparent clothing, except a bluish energy shimmer, and while it had a "head" of sorts, that was more a protrusion than a head resting upon a neck. It was cold, so cold that I felt it was sucking energy from the undertime as well.

Then it was gone, leaving a bright blue and jagged time-trail that seemed both sideways and backtime simultaneously.

I followed, although the effort was like ricocheting through a rock canyon on a high-speed steamer that bounced off every wall. Each "bounce" gave me a headache.

When the bouncing stopped, I was still undertime in the Queryan solar system. That was easy to figure because I couldn't break out from the undertime. The planet was Thoses, the one out beyond Query. Rumor had it that the First Empire had put a base there.

Someone had. Once. But the Frost Giants had frozen it solid, too.

From the undertime, all I could see was the energy drain and the collapse of empty domes and plastics into dust. Sure, it had happened a millennia or more before I was born, but watching it happen and being unable to do anything about it was unnerving.

As I shivered in the undertime, I worried. I worried a lot. The Frost Giants didn't seem all that bright, but more like some sort of cosmic energy grazer. And the trail from Query to Thoses had been without stops, as if they passed from solar system to solar system and grazed on all the artificial and natural heat and energy they could reach within their time range.

Another bright blue jagged trail, this one foretime, toward Mithrada.

I dropped away and headed back to the divers' village.

The problem was simple, and nearly impossible. Unless we could either find a Frost Giant in real time, or in another time outside the Queryan system, we couldn't even try to attack it. I needed to talk to Wryan, to design some sort of tracking plan or strategy.

Execution I could handle, but not long-range planning. Not well.

# LVI.

"OUT OF MY WAY, Sammis." Even when he was trying to keep it down, Odin Thor's voice boomed. He twisted the bosses on the gauntlets to activate the microcircuitry.

When I looked at Odin Thor, I wished I'd never found

Ydris. The gauntlets were too powerful for his ego. Bad enough for me, and I'd survived his damned ConFed Marines with no illusions of justice.

"They won't work very well in here, Odin Thor." I used both his last names to irritate him. Dangerous, but he lost most rudiments of logic when he was angry. "Or too accurately."

"Don't you ever say anything straight out, runt?" All of Colonel-General Augurt Odin Thor looked ready to assault me. Which would have been fine, except that was the moment Wryan walked into the travel hall, or what there was of it we had built.

"Dr. Relorn . . ." Odin Thor was all charm again, bowing low, almost from the waist. "I was about to depart to see if I could localize the latest manifestations of the Frost Giants. The ones that young Sammis here tracked across the cluster."

"You are so determined, Colonel. Do you think that it is necessary? Especially when we have no effective way of neutralizing individual giants?"

"Madam, we know who the enemy is. That enemy has just destroyed another timediver's innocent family."

"What will you do once you find all the Frost Giants, Odin Thor?" I interjected.

"Keep track of them until we can destroy them. They'll be a threat until we do."

I wanted to know how Odin Thor could keep track of anything when he couldn't find his way across a room under the now. Instead, I asked, "Do you remember what happened the last time?"

Wryan shook her head, but I ignored her. This one wasn't going by logic.

"That was years ago!" snapped Odin Thor.

"Not to the Frost Giants. Barely an instant for them." Wryan looked even more distressed, and I knew why.

"So we're going to cower in our half-built city and our

half-built tower and hope they leave us alone? Hope they don't freeze another poor family with their curiosity? Can I tell my people that the great Doctor Relorn and her intrepid scout, who can avoid the Giants, wish to run and hide and leave them to face the terrible freezings? That you two have no wish even to track the Giants to warn them?''

"What are you going to do, great Odin Thor? Track them all over the galaxy until they get tired and turn on us again?"

Wryan was making motions behind Odin Thor's back for me to shut up, but it wouldn't make much difference. He was going to do what he was going to do, and we'd end up picking up the pieces again.

"Don't you understand?" By now he was bellowing.

Deric had dashed in from supervising the time-warping of the wall stones in the adjoining hall. Another young-looking diver who carried a youngster in a sack upon her back stood frowning in the archway.

"Understand what?" asked Wryan calmly.

"That the giants are our enemy. That they will threaten us as long as they roam free through the galaxy."

By now, half a dozen divers had popped in, and, unfortunately, out. Word would be through the community within the afternoon, if not within instants.

I could see the handwriting on the wall, and it was written in blood. Mine and Wryan's especially.

Sighing loudly, I got their attention. Once again, it was my mess, a mess that I should have seen coming sooner.

The travel hall was silent, too silent.

"Why don't we discuss it at a full meeting of all the timedivers tonight? It affects everyone, and everyone should have a say in it."

"Great idea, Sammis!" boomed Odin Thor. His voice was not quite mocking. "What time?"

"After dinner . . . whenever you want . . ."

"I'll let you know." And the Colonel-General was off, on foot. He couldn't afford the embarrassment of planet-sliding, since he still had little enough directional sense. He was smiling every step of the way.

Wryan looked over at me sadly. "You know what will happen."

"Got any better ideas, Doctor?"

"Do you?"

"Just one."

She did not ask, but continued to look at me sadly.

"Finding something that destroys Frost Giants before they destroy us."

"Ignorance rules again."

"Always has. Probably always will."

"How long will it take you to find something?" Wryan seldom wasted time on formalities or useless commentary.

"That's simple enough. Until I do or until there's nothing left unfrozen on Query."

"And now?"

I took her hand and held it, cool as it was. "You and I go over the possibilities." I leered a little bit.

That got a faint smile. "Not those possibilities . . ." She took her hand back.

"If you say so, but we really need a good physicist to talk with, assuming there's one alive somewhere. Who would know?"

"Jerlyk or Mellorie—they were with the university."

We touched hands and slid undertime, under the clinging black surface of the now, slipping sideways and out toward the half-built settlement on the hilltop below Mount Persnol. Thor was probably trying to calculate the directionality of his planet slide. Sooner or later, he'd come booming in with an energy swathe half a world wide. Not that more than a handful of our timedivers could sense the energy flows. But his dives, like him, were so violent that I winced whenever he broke out near me.

While I could detect Wryan in the undertime, as usual, there was no sense of feeling, no sense of movement, until we lanced back into the now, right in the middle of a cloudburst.

"Should have looked first," I sputtered.

Wryan let go of my hand and dashed through the muddy street and into a half-completed cottage. I followed, since the building did have a roof and the rain was pelting down in big, cold drops.

No one was working there, although several tools had been carefully laid out.

Wryan looked around, studying the footprints in the dust. "They were working earlier."

"Odin Thor?"

"Looks like it."

That was worse than I had thought, because he'd already organized at least some of the divers and was probably holding an informal meeting of his own right now. "Let's try to slide to Jerlyk's. Don't really want to wander through this rain."

Wryan took my hand this time, and we dipped under the now and finally emerged on Jerlyk's front stoop. I was shaking a bit. Even after all my practice, sometimes the little dives, where you're trying to hit a small point in the now, were still more tiring than the long ones in a different system. And, of course, no one had ever been able to backtime or foretime in our own system. That was one of the problems in dealing with the Frost Giants. They could and we couldn't. They had all time, and we had the now.

# LVII.

MY STOMACH JITTERED as I chewed through the marinated buffalo steak. Greffin was still a superb chef, not that we saw him much, but he only had to prepare one meal. The duplicator, and an idea of Mellorie's, made eating his creations possible at any time.

Mellorie—somehow, coming from her it made sense. She had simply asked whether the duplicator could only duplicate what was put in it, or if a duplicated pattern could be retrieved later.

I could have bashed my head on the wall. With that question, the reasons for the settings and the fact that some duplicators on Muria were linked to the lattice crystal memory banks made instant sense.

Jerlyk retrieved—stole, if you will—some blank crystals, and Wryan helped him and Mellorie in setting up a couple of master duplicators. We couldn't steal more than two initially, because of the effort required. While setting up a closet-sized fusion plant wasn't impossible, that was just the first step. You still had to do wiring and all the time-consuming details to put the infrastructure together.

But . . . if Wryan or I wanted to visit Mellorie's cottage, she and Jerlyk were happy to punch a button and provide us with one of Greffin's best meals, hot as the moment it was duplicated.

Wryan had done the honors just before we ate, insisting it was her turn.

So we sat there, at the cottage table, alone, since, with the construction of additional cottages, Kerina and Hadron had moved out and left the place to us. Derika had left even earlier.

"You're worried about the meeting tonight?" Wryan asked.

"Aren't you?"

"Of course. What are you going to say? It's your meeting."

That bothered me, too. I'd come up with the meeting because the divers and the ConFeds had to face reality together, but I had the feeling that Wryan and I were the only ones who cared about reality. So what could I say?

I took another sip of citril and another mouthful of the buffalo steak. Finally, I looked at the cabinets behind and above Wryan's shoulder. "I guess that I'll say what I said to Odin Thor."

"They won't like it." Her tone was not critical, just gentle, reminding me of the facts.

I knew they wouldn't like what I had to say. So we finished eating in silence.

Wryan and I arrived in the travel hall early, waiting to see who would appear. Gerloc and Amenda were already there, along with Mellorie and Jerlyk. In a corner, by himself, was Verlin. As soon as he saw me, Verlin popped out of sight.

"Off to tell everyone," I muttered under my breath.

Sure enough, within moments, divers and even a handful of ConFed forcers and subforcers—probably those living the ConFed quarters near the half-built tower—arrived.

Then Odin Thor marched through the door and straight toward me.

"We're all here, Sammis. What do you plan to do about the Frost Giants?"

Everyone looked at me, and I wanted to dive right out from underneath their sight because almost every eye stared accusingly at me, as if I had created the problem. Then again, maybe that was just the way I felt.

Instead of speaking immediately, I took a long look around the room, trying not to swallow too hard as I did so.

"Well?" demanded the man who towered over me.

"I'll tell you what I'm going to do, Colonel Odin Thor. Then I'll tell you what I recommend we do. And then, all of you can do exactly what you please." You will anyway, I thought, without voicing it.

Odin Thor looked momentarily puzzled, but said nothing.

Nearly a hundred people clustered around Wryan and me in the big empty hall, and it was so silent you could hear every isolated cough, every foot scuffle.

"First," I said. "We have not developed or found a weapon which an individual diver can carry that will destroy a Frost Giant. I have found, as you all know, a number of weapons, and I am continuing to search for one which will do the job. In the meantime, I strongly suggest that we have a group of divers mount a general search of the more likely timepaths to provide a warning if another Giant or group of Giants appear to move our way.

"Right now, all we can do is avoid them. I will continue trying to find the necessary weapons—"

"Is that all?" asked Odin Thor, his voice barely below a bellow. "Is that all?"

I could sense the unrest rippling around the room. They were all looking for a miraculous solution from good young Sammis—the man who had brought them the duplicator, the gauntlets, and some idea of hope. And I didn't have an answer.

"Is that all?" repeated Odin Thor, his voice not quite mocking.

I looked at him, and my eyes were colder than a Frost Giant. "If you want to drag out the last one or two nuclear devices buried under Westron and invite every Frost Giant in the galaxy to come and attack, be my guest. But don't blame me."

There was actually a moment of silence, and I seized it. "I've told you what I can do, and what I will do. You have to decide what you want. You know where to find me."

And I left, diving undertime from where I stood, taking even Wryan by surprise. The damned idiots!

Wryan did not arrive until later.

"Proud of yourself?" she asked, her voice somewhere between dry and bitter.

"No. But we've given them damned-near everything, and we don't have a last miracle in hand. We don't have that many energy sources, and if we don't stir things up, we'll probably have enough time to find an answer. But Odin Thor doesn't want a good answer; he wants an answer now."

Wryan sighed, and her shoulders slumped for a moment. "Do you think your departure did any good?"

"I don't know. I do know that staying would have been worse, because I would have lost my temper."

Wryan looked at me. "That would have been worse, you think?"

"I don't think you can hold people's loyalty through force."

"You . . ." she stopped. "Well, it's done, and we'll have to see."

"What happened after I left?"

"Odin Thor delivered a long sermon on the need to bring the fight to the Frost Giants. He said that your first step was absolutely right, that we couldn't attack an enemy if we didn't know where they were. Then he went on to suggest that the ConFed techs would develop some 'traps' for any Frost Giant who attacked Query.

"Gerloc volunteered to put together the scouting patrols. And Odin Thor reminded everyone that you *might* just find an answer, but that the ConFeds would be ready whether or not you were successful or not." She smiled wryly. "All in all, he did a masterful job of taking control without directly slamming you, and—"

"In making me look like a spoiled brat," I finished.

"I didn't say that."

I sighed. "I have a lot to learn. But the whole thing just . . . I don't know . . . why do people put up with such falseness?"

"Because, unlike you, Sammis Arloff Olon, most people cannot live without certainty and hope, and Odin Thor is good at appealing to their needs."

She was right, and there wasn't much I could say. I just hoped I could find a weapon or a defense before Odin Thor found a nuclear device.

# LVIII.

FOR A WHILE, nothing happened. Gerloc's patrols found tracks and traces of one cluster of Giants, and the ConFeds continued to work on their trap. I was splitting my time trying to find weapons and trying to find a better way to track the Frost Giants.

If the Frost Giants descended upon Inequital from Mithrada, I could sense their undertime tracks, but actually breaking into those tracks or breaking out on Query would be blocked to me. Why?

Because, as Wryan explained it to me, according to the Laws of Time, foretiming and backtiming within your home system are not possible.

Had I, as a descendent of Query, been born on Sertis, would my home system have been Query or Sertis? Or would both be blocked to me? My gut reaction was that both systems would be blocked. Otherwise, a race with both interstellar colonies and time-diving abilities could screw up the entire universe. Then again, maybe I didn't like that idea because it was just the sort of thing that Odin Thor liked to get involved in.

Still, as I pulled on the insulated time-diving uniform— the material represented another theft from some outsystem by Kerina—I knew I had to try the chance of backtracking the Frost Giants, if only to find out where they had come from before Odin Thor did. I knew from my earlier attempts that I could see some scenes, even if I could not act. Seeing and following those tracks might give me some hint of their origin.

Wryan had left early, presumably to talk to Odin Thor and try to keep him from mounting his nuclear attack on the isolated pocket of the Frost Giants that Gerloc had found in the globular cluster out beyond Sertis. I had no love of the Frost Giants or Odin Thor, but I had yet to see anything that a diver could carry that would destroy one of them. Even after my statement at the meeting, no one seemed to understand that. Or they didn't want to, as Wryan suggested.

After what the Frost Giants had done to Inequital, I wasn't interested in stirring them up without any way to neutralize them or destroy them.

If I could discover that the Frost Giants were spread across a good chunk of the galaxy, that *might* provide us some breathing room before Odin Thor started another witch-burning crusade, just like those of the Westron past.

So I pulled on the black uniform, the boots, and the equipment belt, including the heaviest gauntlets around, one of the few technological remnants of Ydris. With just one little push, I had shoved the Ydrisians from violence and fighting into such high-tech disaster that they had destroyed each other. While I might have wished otherwise, it had happened, and it would be difficult if not impossible for me to undo it. Besides, sadly, the divers needed the gauntlets for personal survival, and I wasn't about to go back to the witches of Eastron days, not after my own trials in the damps.

No one else was around in the cottage as I stuffed down a high-energy breakfast. I put some additional food in the thin backpack, mostly hard bread, cheeses and dried fruit and meat. After my first diving experiences, and after my stint in the hospital, I didn't feel comfortable without carrying some food. Then I sighed . . . and dived, letting my mind carry me sideways in time to the hilly plains that had been Inequital. While I could neither break out in the foretime or backtime on Query, nor see more than a few years past or future, there was nothing to prevent me from slipping backwards and watching for the tell-tale paths of the Frost Giants . . . or other timedivers.

As I suspected, near the present there were no traces or tracks, not the slightest "warping" of the time arrows that might indicate the passage of a traveler. Perhaps two or three years in the past the undertime twisted almost violently, so violently that I had to refocus my concentration to remain there. The clutter and distortion were so great, the blue twisting in upon the red and the black and gold interleaving with each other, that I forced myself farther into the red.

Farther backtime meant fewer trails and a chance to find a Frost Giant track discrete enough to trace back to another home planet or base.

That wasn't what I found.

Backtime of the Frost Giants, clear and thin as a razor, I found a time-line edged with crimson and vibrating with pain. Not that it was obvious, or that anyone else would have sensed the pain, because I've had Wryan ask about it. No one else can see more than a blur through the undertime, and no one else can sense strong emotions through the undertime. Wryan always thought it was funny that I have no empathy sense except through the time walls.

In this case, the pain was there. I almost missed it, and I had to have missed it before. But I was getting more sensitive with experience, and I was looking for that sort of thing. It wasn't really a backtime line, but a crosstime line, running from somewhere west of Inequital to Inequital itself, and then further to the east. Toward Esterly—or Bremarlyn. Maybe farther.

My blood was as cold as if a Frost Giant had appeared before me, and, even in the suspension of the undertime

I felt like my heart was racing. Mentally, I took a deep breath. Mentally, because you have no physical abilities in the undertime. Everything is suspended—itches, elation, pain.

That was why my mind wanted to make my body shudder. If that trail represented what I feared . . .

Taking a mental hold of myself, I did my best to mark the timing and place of that crimson line. Then I dived back to the cottage.

No one was there.

I ate a chyst, and paced from the workroom to the kitchen area and back again. I went outside and looked around. The overcast looked like it was building to a storm that matched what was building inside me. I could almost see my breath steaming, and I shivered, but not from the cold.

Serla looked through the shutters from next door, but she must have seen my face, because she disappeared.

I walked back inside and cut some stale brown bread and two slices of yellow cheese. Tough chewing, but it gave me something to do.

Wishing Wryan were back, I paced back down to the workroom and looked at the new duplicator and the original of the Ydrisian handgun, the one that had led to my manipulations of Ydris, and set the change-winds howling down the corridors of time. Most of the butt and the area under the barrel were taken up by energy cells.

A thought occurred to me, and, while I waited, I jotted it down on the tablet by the bench.

"Time-diving energy flows. Diverted to energy cells for weapon power?"

After all, if the power inherent in time flows could be tapped for weapons, the whole problem of energy storage would be minimized. Even if—I dropped the thought. Either it could be done or it couldn't.

I wished Wryan would appear, but I still didn't want to

show my face down at the Marine camp. In Odin Thor's current mood, there was always the chance for some sort of "accident" to happen to me. He thought he still needed Wryan, but he had no use for me, now that he had the duplicator, the gauntlets, and the closet-sized fusion plant.

From the cluttered workroom I walked back to the kitchen and ate a pearapple. I looked out the window again. The thunderheads were building up to the south, and the sky was turning a purpled black.

A single jagged lightning bolt flared in the distance.

Tempted to eat something else, I deferred, mainly because my guts were feeling heavy. I still wanted to bite things, chew them. I kept pacing.

Heavy cold raindrops were striking the roof and the cottage walls and windows.

I could feel the undertime tension and turned to face the open space in the middle of the kitchen where Wryan would appear. She was wearing a black diving suit.

"I don't know which storm's worse—the one outside or the one inside," commented Wryan after taking a quick look at my face.

"Inside, this time. I need your opinion. Hold my hand and dive with me. Inequital, just before the Frost Giant attack."

"It wasn't exactly an attack, Sammis."

"This isn't about the attack . . ."

She looked at my face and asked, "Can I get something to eat? Will it wait that long?"

I didn't want to wait. I'd waited all morning, it seemed, but she looked pale, and, besides, who knew where the dive would lead? I nodded. "Anything special?"

"Just fix me some tea."

So I turned on the burner to heat the water, while she rummaged through the cooler. Then I nibbled another corner of the hard yellow cheese.

"What is it?"

I shook my head. "I'm not sure, but I have a feeling that it's not at all good."

"Is it the Frost Giants or Odin Thor?" She was fitting together a combination of sliced meats, greens, and cheese too thick to be properly called a sandwich.

"Something else. Very different."

"You are upset. Just let me finish. Sit down and stop pacing. I don't need indigestion, too."

Perching on the edge of the chair, I watched her. Even eating that monstrous sandwich, she looked graceful. When she picked up the heavy tea mug, she could have been handling the imperial china. Yet those slender hands were as strong as mine and a lot more skilled. She'd been a medical doctor before she'd gone into the time-diving research and probably had several careers before that, although I had never had the nerve to ask her about them. She made me feel so young, so hell-fired inexperienced, at times.

I reached for the cheese.

"Are you really that hungry?" Her eyes were smiling, but caring, too, at the same time.

"No. Nervous."

"I know. I'll be ready in a minute, but I haven't had anything to eat since dawn. Trying to explain Frost Giant migration patterns takes a lot of effort when Odin Thor doesn't really want to hear. But he finally got the point."

"Which was?"

"Migration patterns, by themselves, mean that there are probably many more Frost Giants lurking around and that it isn't wise to act until you know exactly how many. That's because they react to temporal and energy disruptions. Destroying Frost Giants will create both." She took a last bite of the sandwich, chewing it thoroughly, unlike me.

"How long will he wait?"

"Maybe ten days . . . unless we can find several other clusters of Giants."

"You know—"

"I know. You can't find weapons and track Frost Giants simultaneously. And you're the only one who can see clearly enough from the undertime."

"You can . . ."

"Not quite as well, and, besides, we agreed not to let him know that."

I shook my head. Concealing things from Odin Thor was always a two-edged sword.

"I'm about ready. Will I need anything special?"

"A medical kit . . . maybe . . . But I think it's too late . . . was too late a long time ago."

"Is this an off-system, back-time injury case?"

"I'm not sure."

"Just a moment." She left the kitchen.

I waited, but before I had a chance to grab another chunk of cheese she was back, strapping a small case to her equipment belt.

"And stay away from the cheese."

I shrugged, flushing slightly in spite of myself. "Then let's go." I extended my hand.

"Wait." Both her arms went around me, and she pulled us together, holding me tight, and somehow warming part of the chill inside me. "I know . . . I know . . ."

She knew me all right, too well, but she was also right, and I stood there and hung onto her, while her fingers crept up my back and kneaded away some of the tightness in my shoulders. After a time, she lifted her head from my shoulder and brushed my lips with hers. "All right?"

"Yes. Much better." I tried to smile, but took a deep breath instead.

Then we held hands and slipped undertime, crosstime toward Inequital. The thin crimson dive-line was still there, like a slash of blood at right angles to the Frost Giant tracks.

Perhaps Wryan tensed as I guided us along that line. I

felt she did, but since our physical condition remained exactly the same as when we entered the undertime, any tension had to be strictly mental.

What I did not understand about the crosstime track was its intensity. All tracks faded over subjective time. At least all those I had run across did. Time-diving is a subjective mental feat. Only entry and breakout actually have an objective reality.

So why was this track so unfaded? I thought I knew, and I was scared.

All I could do was try to match our dive with that of the crimson track, trying to trace it to the end.

Reaching the end of the track was not that difficult, except that the diver had never broken out back into the now. The crosstime slide ran from somewhere west of Inequital through Bremarlyn and into Eastron . . . and stopped, as if the diver were suspended.

In peering into that backtime view of Query, I could only see a hazy view of the "then," a view of a cave of some sort, high in the Bardwalls, a cave filled with old-fashioned cabinetry and wardrobes and other objects I could not make out. Certainly, more than a cave.

Investigating the cave would not solve the problem of the suspended diver, and the screaming of the crosstime track that tore at both heart and soul.

With a mental shrug, I tried to look through the barrier that separated me from the endlessly fading energy that had to be another timediver. All I could gather was a end-less scream, a mindless feeling of agony, that blotted out any sense of description.

I could sense the shakiness coming on for me, and, looking for a breakout point, chose the closest one—the current time position of the equipment cave.

Legs trembling, I glanced around the room, lit through a pair of diffused and hidden skylights, and took a deep breath. That was a mistake.

I knew . . . and my legs would not hold me, not while I shuddered and wept in the darkness. Not while Wryan held me and said nothing, though I could feel her tears mingle with mine.

Less than the thinnest of barriers separated us from that endlessly dying diver I knew too well, and that barrier might have been the length of eternity, for all that I could not cross it.

Nothing . . . nothing had I suffered, nor would I ever suffer, in comparison, even should I find some way to break that endless dive of agony.

In time—how long I did not know—I finally managed to gather myself together, shaking from more than one cause, and to sit up in the dim light. I could not look at anything too closely, especially not at the wardrobe with the one open door, as I grasped for my pack and a small chunk of hard bread. Offering Wryan a piece silently, I broke off a small chunk and chewed it slowly, thoroughly.

"How . . . terrible . . ."

I nodded. Banal as the word "terrible" was, what other word was there?

"To be trapped in an endless death . . . without the strength or consciousness to break out . . . even to die . . ."

". . . dying forever . . ."

"Sammis . . . I'm . . . sorry . . ." Her voice said more than the words. So did her hand as she squeezed mine. "You knew?"

"No . . . felt it . . . guessed it . . . I think . . ." I took another bite of the hard bread, trying to get enough energy back into my system to stop the shakes, to allow me to think.

One way or another, thought was all I had. Thought was all I had.

Wryan and I eventually chewed through the entire loaf, the cheese, the dried fruits and meats, although most of the bites were mine. By then the sun was dropping over the Bardwalls and the cave was lit only by some sort of emergency lamp that functioned still.

Wryan looked like hell, which was better than I felt.

"You knew your mother hadn't died in the fire, didn't you?"

"Yes. I couldn't explain why."

"You were close to her."

"Not exactly. We never spoke much. We just did things together. My father did all the talking."

"Could you tell when she was around? Could she tell when you were near?"

I had to think about that. In some ways, that had been another lifetime. "I think so."

She snorted. "You think so? How did you know she was here? And why did you insist I come, with a medical kit?"

Wryan definitely had me there.

"All right. I knew."

"That's important. There might be one way . . ."

"How? We can't touch her. We can't merge, and we're from two separate times."

"Whose mind controls the dive?"

"Hers . . ."

"So all you have to do is reach her thoughts . . . that's all."

"That's all? That sounds like reaching across eternity."

"Sammis."

I knew what she meant. I just wasn't sure about meshing with that agony again. Especially meshing and keeping my own sanity. The whole idea was insane. The thought of leaving anyone—let alone who that forever-dying diver was—in such endless agony was even worse.

"I'll be with you," Wryan added, taking my hand.

"Let's go." I closed my pack.

"What are you going to do . . . exactly?"

That was a good question, and one for which I had no ready answer. So I sat down on the floor. I didn't really want to touch anything. "I'm not sure. But I have to push as close as I can, try and force the barrier . . ."

". . . and . . . ?"

". . . don't know. Do I send reassurance? Or encouragement? Or strength?" I sighed. "Hell! I don't even know if this will work. How can I make her feel anything?"

"I don't know. It may not work."

"I know. But I have to try."

"*We* have to try."

I scrambled around in that dawn-lit retreat until I could hug her again. Then I pulled on my pack and checked my equipment.

"Ready?"

Wryan just nodded, and we took each other's hands, and eased under the now toward that endless scream.

The second time was worse.

In that undertime, drawn by the crimson line like an iron filing to a lodestone, the thin black curtain seemed to fade into dark translucence.

They say you can't smell in the undertime, but the odor of burning cloth and flesh seared my nose, throat, and lungs.

Somehow my thoughts reached for my mother, who had left to do her duty and never made it back, and—

. . . *find the darkness . . . the shelter . . . no leads . . . must not . . . cannot . . . lead them back . . . not to Sammis . . . burns . . . Verlyt! Just hold on . . . just another instant . . .*

Images flew at me and through me.

. . . Standing on the point of a narrow rock jutting out over a canyon, where a blue ribbon wound through dust-crimson rocks below, watching a night-eagle launch itself into the first flight of twilight, listening to another woman . . .

"You have a responsibility, Meryn. It will last longer than you can possibly conceive, past the fall of Eastron, perhaps beyond the fall of Westron. And should you let anyone know what you are, you will be called 'witch', and worse, and every man, every woman, and every child will rise against you. You will see most of your children die of old age . . ."

. . . Appearing from the shadows, slipping across the hard-packed dirt path to the stacked barrels and placing one flare, then another, then lighting them, both and dropping into the no-time place, feeling the explosions in the Westron camp from undertime, and knowing that the delays would be futile . . .

. . . Looking down at the inlaid casket of the Duke, remembering the unlined face of years past, the blond hair before it silvered, the capable hands—before the onslaught of the Confederation Marines of Westron, ignoring the whispers of the three women at the other side of the chapel . . . "How could she? After all the years, and looking like that. She has to be a witch . . . why he never remarried . . ."

. . . Running the wooded path, feet set quickly and silently in place, breathing easily and leaving the flat-footed soldiers of the Empress gasping far behind, taking the trails where the steamers could not follow, enjoying the pure physical effort, the ability to leave the Empress's best with their mouths gaping . . .

. . . Nodding at the round-faced solicitor, whose decency could not be disguised by his profession and position, wondering whether it would be a kindness or a mistake to accept his proposition, wondering if, this time, there would be a child, and hoping, again, that there would . . . "On my terms, Aldus? That is more than generous . . ."

. . . Looking down at the blond-haired boy infant, with the elfin face even so soon after birth, wanting to cry after so long, yet not daring to, and knowing that the long toll of years would be ending. ". . . forever may a she-witch live, until she is with child and mortal . . ."

. . . Seeing the fire, the flames, the shells from the ConFeds, and the crumpled body of a round-faced solicitor; knowing that Aldus wore the same puzzled expression in death that he had in life; seeing the houses of the Westron gentry fall, fired and shelled; seeing the empire crumple with each shell . . .

. . . Walking through the Fountain Court toward a single sentry; seeing the lone guard as a sacrifice against the mob howling toward the Palace walls; wondering what sacrifice would be called for; asking whether she could; knowing that her son would understand . . .

*"No!"* Though I could not utter the word, I screamed it in that undertime prison, and the barriers between the three of us shivered—but did not shatter nor break.

. . . *break out . . . now . . . somehow . . . Sammis . . .*

One fragmentary thought—that was all—and the crimson thread I had held on to, locked my soul to, was gone, nothing more than a fast-fading memory.

*You did it.* That second thought was warmer, closer.

*But . . . how . . . ?*

*I don't know. Isn't it better than diving in silence?*

It was. Much better.

*Shall we check the retreat?*

*No. Leave her there. One death is enough.*

Wryan knew what I meant. There was no way to save her, and to find her dust and bones where they lay somehow was wrong. Wrong for me, anyway. I had my goodbye. Years late, but that's usually the way the ones that hurt come to you.

# LIX.

I was shaking again when I staggered into the kitchen of the cottage.

Wryan may have been, also, but I wasn't in the best of conditions to determine that as I slumped into one of the heavy wooden chairs.

*Thump.* Wryan hit the other chair harder than I had landed.

I put my head on the table, trying to sort it all out, from the memories of Eastron that were not mine to the views of me seen through my mother's eyes. I knew I had never been female, but I shivered at the memories of having been so, at the recollection of joy at my own birth, and the desperation . . .

". . . Verlyt . . ." The exclamation stumbled from numb lips. Too much was happening—again—all too quickly. I lifted my head to look at Wryan.

Her face was pale. Mine probably was, too. Looking at her features was like looking at mine. Same elfin face. Same green eyes. Same not-quite-blond but sandy hair. Same wiry muscles.

"How long . . . ?" I asked. My mouth was dry.

"How terrible . . ."

I realized Wryan had not even heard my question, and I could see the darkness in her eyes. "The memories . . . ?"

"Just through you . . . mainly feelings, and that was more than enough."

It was hard just keeping my head up, splitting as it was with memories that were not mine, and yet that would always belong to me. I shivered again.

"How long?" I asked again, not wanting to deal with

the memories or the still-raw remembrance of pain, and
stench of burning flesh that clung to my nostrils.

"How long for what?"

"Look at me. What do you see?"

"I see you." Despite the pain in her voice, the wry
warmth was still there.

"I look at you, and I see me. Just like my mother saw
me."

"I know. I knew that from the day you arrived with
Odin Thor. But you had to see for yourself. We're probably related, but how I couldn't tell you."

"How long?" I asked for the third time.

Wryan sighed. "Persistent, aren't you?"

"You're not?"

She shrugged, and it was eerie, seeing for the first time,
really, myself shrug. "Not so long as your mother. About
a century, give or take a year or two."

"So I'm in love with my mother's sister?"

"You never said you were in love."

"I am, and you know it, and I'm scared." I pushed
back the chair and stood up, walking toward the window.
The thin sunlight was dimming into dusk. Diving around
the planet can play hell with your biological clocks. "I
don't think you are. You've waited so long and hoped, and
here I am."

"How do you know you're in love? And not looking for
your mother?"

"Because I found her, and she's dead." Outside, a
grossjay hopped along the raised brick curbing, looking
for something to scavenge.

"I never knew your mother, Sammis."

"But the three of us all look alike. Too much alike for
mere coincidence."

Wryan sighed. "All witches look alike."

"Then why don't all timedivers look alike?"

"Witches are timedivers, plus some different traits. Odin

Thor is probably a stronger diver than either one of us, although he couldn't navigate his way from one side of the planet to the other without help.'' She stood up and went over to the cooler.

I followed her. Witches or timedivers or both, we were always hungry.

"Not much here."

"You didn't answer my questions."

Wryan took a bite from a pearapple and chewed it slowly. The color began to return to her face almost instantly. So I took out the last one and took a bite from it, hoping for some near-instantaneous rejuvenation myself.

"I can't. I grew up in the Southpoint orphan home. My mother was the captain of a Southpoint coaster, an independent woman who did as she pleased. But she died after I was born—or so the Ladies of Mercy told me. I asked about her when I was old enough to get away from the home's walls. Some of the oldsters remembered her—with a tinge of admiration and envy. But no one could or would say what happened to her, not to her daughter, or to any fifteen-year-old girl."

"How long ago was that?"

Wryan took several more bites from the pearapple before attempting to answer. "Long enough. I could be your grandmother in some ways, but it doesn't make any difference."

I had to shake my head. "Doesn't make any difference? Compared to you, what I know wouldn't fill a thimble, and you'll still be young centuries from now."

"So will you."

There was that. I chewed some more of the pearapple, trying to digest everything. My stomach was doing better than my mind.

"Sammis." Wryan's voice was soft.

I stopped and looked at her.

"What you are is more important than what you know. Especially now, because the whole world is changing."

I thought about that. The world was changing. More and more people with the time-diving ability. Even with fewer people after the onslaught of the Frost Giants, the infrastructure of Westron was tottering because of the continuing failure of fragile high technology. "Changing or collapsing?"

"That's up to us."

"And Odin Thor. He wants to build a military dictatorship."

She looked at me, and I looked at her, and I could see the darkness behind her eyes. What scared me then was the thought that she saw the same darkness behind mine.

One way or another, there would be no more war on Query. One way or another. Even if it took the witches of Eastron and their offspring and their talents.

# LX.

I WAS WRONG about the war, because I had forgotten about the Frost Giants. They hadn't forgotten about us, and Odin Thor hadn't forgotten about them.

*EEEEEEEeeeeeeeeeeeeee* . . .

The scream of the vest-pocket nuclear device vibrated even in the undertime, even from the geographic distance I had put between the trap and myself. The location was north of Inequital, almost a wasteland, that had yet to recover from the first Frost Giant attack. Then it had been industrial.

The trap? Simple enough. Odin Thor and Weldin had rigged a fusion power plant to run at full output and linked it to a modified arc furnace of some sort, figuring that the combination of heat and energy would be enough to tempt a Frost Giant into appearing. Then they rigged the nuclear device to a thermocouple trigger. The instant the temperature began to drop, the bomb blew.

Not terribly elegant, but effective.

. . . *eeeeeeeeeeeeeeeeeeee* . . .

My head ached from the vibration and energy flashes that weren't supposed to have a physical impact in the undertime, and I was kays from the blast.

". . . noooooo . . ." The non-voice was mine, trying to close eyes that would not, could not, close in the undertime.

. . . blue flashes, like jagged edges of a mirror, cut through my head . . . an image of a small blue and blocky figure, four-armed, surrounded with warm blueness . . .

. . . a dull red plain . . . standing beside another blue-block figure . . . reassuring heat . . . flashing back and forth . . .

. . . so much heat . . . pressure . . . like knives cutting from inside . . .

. . . and more blue shards knifing their way through my head, already fading as they cut.

I time-staggered back to the divers' village, stumbling out of the undertime and losing the contents of my guts right into the sink.

Cold water helped my appearance and that of the sink.

By the time Wryan appeared, I was back to normal, if pale.

"For someone who has created so much destruction, you certainly have a nervous stomach," she observed, wrinkling her nose.

I went on cleaning up the mess, opening the window. The cold winter air was preferable to the odor.

"Staying around to experience death close up doesn't do much for me."

"I take it Odin Thor's trap was successful?"

"Too successful, I suspect." I dried my face, and folded

the towel. The wind almost lifted it off the rack. I slid the window half-closed and took the chair across from Wryan. She was pale, though not as pale as I was. "You? You felt it, too?"

"No." Her lips quirked. "You're not exactly good for my digestion. I felt you feel that thing's death."

"Oh . . ."

I stood up, feeling the unease mount within me, the sense of an avalanche overhanging. Opening the cupboard, I took out some hard crackers, tossed one to Wryan, then caught the towel as a gust of wind from the window blew it past me. After closing the window the rest of the way, I began to chew on the cracker, slowly, until I was sure that my stomach would take it.

The mental unease continued.

"All hell is breaking loose. Better warn all the divers. Shut down the power plant—ours anyway."

Wryan looked blank. I just dropped undertime and sprinted for the Bardwalls. I wanted something left to re-build with, and the one power plant, the duplicator and the parts we had stashed there would be enough.

In the undertime, I could sense the distant rush of blue, but it wasn't close . . . yet.

Wryan broke out as I was shutting down the system. The cold of the location and the time-protected walls should have been enough to insulate it from the Frost Giants. They couldn't easily get inside, nor pull the energy through the walls, I didn't think, but there was no reason to provide that temptation.

"Do you think . . . ?"

"I know. Now let's tell whoever we can reach. I'll take Odin Thor."

Wryan's eyebrows raised a notch, even as she completed the shutdown I had started. Outside the double doors, the winter whistled, throwing more snow against the rocks below and building the drifts.

The retreat was mostly complete, with glowstones on the floor and some furniture, and the workroom we had moved from the cave. But we had not used it much, partly because of the time difference. Living a quarter of the way around the planet from where you spent most of your waking hours could be more than a little disruptive. Besides, who wanted to advertise it?

The cold—and the lack of energy—might protect us . . . that and the fact that the Frost Giants didn't seem to move much out of the now, except as a group or when pushed.

I could hope.

Wryan looked at me, although her face was dim in the low light from the storm outside, now that we had shut down the power.

We left, sliding across the now.

Odin Thor was sitting in his office, Weldin sitting across from him, and two other forcers, Carlis and someone I didn't know, in the other chairs. Each had a glass—old Imperial crystal recovered from who knew where—in his hand.

"What . . ." gaped Odin Thor, as I dropped into the space between the chairs.

"Sorry to disrupt your premature celebration, Colonel, but it appears as though you have made the Frost Giants really mad. A force of them is headed this way through the undertime, and I frankly have no idea how to stop them. You might think about dispersing your troops and personnel. That way, some of them *might* survive."

"It's your doing, witch," snapped Carlis.

I looked at the idiot. "I told him not to attack the Giants. And I told him then that we didn't have any way to stop them as a force. You all agreed to this idiocy over my strong objections. Now, you'll have to live with it."

I glanced undertime, feeling that the blue rush was nearer, but unable to judge how much nearer.

The unknown forcer, a heavyset and older man, nodded, then asked, "How long before these attacks start?"

"Assuming they stay close to the now—the present time reference—I'd guess it might be a day, perhaps two, before the mass of Giants strikes Query."

"That soon?"

"I don't understand exactly how they travel the undertime, because it's hard to track unless you're right with them, but they move at an angle—that's the only way I can describe it . . ."

Odin Thor stood up, his face slightly flushed. "You have the—"

At that point, I lost it.

I slid under the now, inside his big arms, and cracked him on the jaw, then was back across the room before he could react.

"I could have killed you right there."

The room got very quiet, so quiet that the faint whine of the wind seemed like a shout.

Carlis looked at me with the look one gives a snake.

I almost smiled, but I was looking at Odin Thor. "You have blundered and blasted your way to power. And you almost saved Westron. But you couldn't wait. We gave you weapons and tools. We brought back the technology to make food. In time, we could have stopped the Giants. But you couldn't wait. I'll do my damnedest to find a way, but not because of you. And if you *ever* threaten the safety of the divers or the people again, you won't live long enough to realize what you did."

I looked at the others. "The only thing you can do is to scatter and stay away from power plants, hot areas, and large groups of people. I know it's winter, but this wasn't our idea. You can thank Odin Thor for it."

I dropped undertime and behind Odin Thor, touching the gauntlet bosses to deactivate his weapons, before moving aside and reappearing.

He glared as the gauntlets failed to trigger.

"You don't listen, do you?" I forced a smile. "Now, gentlemen, the choice is yours. Partly. The divers will tell all the women and children, and I think they'll choose survival. I hope I can find it in time."

I left, dropping back to the cottage to stoke up on food and equipment before beginning my solitary quest. Wryan was better at organizing people. I just hoped I would be as good at searching.

# LXI.

SOMETIMES THE ANSWERS are right in front of you, if you can only see what they mean. Or, perhaps it's more accurate to say that the pieces are all there, but it takes a new or different perspective to combine them to reach a solution.

Odin Thor had used one of the few remaining vest-pocket fusion devices to pot his Frost Giant. The Frost Giants, predictably, had retaliated, and what was left of Westron was generally uninhabited mountains, swamps, deserts, and whatever structures the divers had managed to warp undertime—like the unfinished tower.

Now the Giants were trying to track down individual divers, without too much success, because they were even noisier than Odin Thor in the undertime. Whether I liked it or not, we had to find something to stop them. And only massive jolts of energy, such as a fusion device or a massive particle beam, seemed to affect them.

The problem was simple enough.

We needed to destroy Frost Giants. Destroying Frost Giants took energy. The gauntlets worked fine, except they didn't handle the massive amounts of energy required. We could no longer produce those old-style energy-intensive weapons, and only a few of the fusion devices remained, far fewer than the total number of Frost Giants. Far fewer.

Not many high-tech races we could observe and steal from produced mass destruction energy weapons, or, for that matter, much in the way of any weapons at all. Those that did, like Ydris, produced weapons that were more like mobile forts.

The logic of what had to be done was simple enough. We needed to use *someone's* existing technology to apply enough energy selectively to individual Frost Giants. And whatever it was had to be light enough for a timediver to carry.

Simple and apparently impossible.

I went back to Muria. The gentle Murians weren't destructive, but they did have some interesting technology, and not all of it was obvious.

So I watched from the undertime, subjective day by subjective day, and scoured the planet from one island continent to another, from laboratories to the very small proto-factories they used. Each day, at first, I staggered back to Query, back to our retreat in the cliffs of the Bardwalls. At least there, I could look at the starkness of the cliffs and the play of the light in the canyon below. With the timewarped nature of the walls and the cold location, it apparently wasn't too attractive to the Frost Giants. Neither was the tower, still only half-completed, but who had time to build anymore?

Sometimes, Wryan wasn't there. Mostly she was, as if she knew when I would return.

"Any luck?"

"It's not a matter of luck, just perseverance," I mumbled through a full mouth.

"You've lost more weight." Her voice was gentle. "You can't keep this up for too much longer."

"Do I have a choice?" I swallowed some more of the underbaked bread, which had to have come from Sertis originally, via the duplicator. Without the duplicators, we already would have starved. All the fields were dust, along with the remaining Westron farmers.

Since Wryan didn't answer, I jammed some more bread and a hunk of unidentified cheese into my mouth and continued chewing. Then I swallowed some Quin. Drinking beer after diving can destroy your balance and then some, but I wasn't going anywhere for a while, and from Wryan's comments, I needed as many calories as my system could take, followed by as much sleep as I could get away with.

"How is it going?"

"You know. Otherwise, you wouldn't be out there day after day, killing yourself. You have to be careful. I don't want you ending up like—"

"I know." I cut off her words abruptly. Some comparisons, well meant as they may be, are too painful to hear. "What's the esteemed Colonel doing?"

"He's located another vest-pocket device, and they're baiting another trap." Her thin face was as white as mine still felt.

The off-focus glimmer of the time-warped walls went even more off-focus as I swallowed, hard. Almost, almost, I felt as though I were falling through the armaglass into a two kay long drop to the Dyel below.

Wryan nodded, slowly. "Everyone is so bitter about the destruction that they can't wait."

Pushing aside the Quin, a bottle duplicated from the late Duke of Eastron's hidden private stock, I forced another mouthful of bread and cheese into my stomach. The room settled back into semi-solidity.

I joined Wryan in the headshaking, not having anything else to add.

My legs were rubbery when I tried to stand up, and the out-of-time glimmer of the retreat's walls flashed at me.

Wryan slipped under my arm and helped guide me into our bedroom, where I ended up sprawled face down on the old-fashioned bed. The last thing I remembered was her hands kneading the tightness out of my back.

When I woke, she was gone. But a faint spiciness remained around the pillow next to mine. The sun was well into the sky, almost straight over the canyon, lighting the tumbling waters of the Dyel so far below.

Rolling onto my back, still tangled in the quilt, I closed my eyes without drifting back to sleep.

Odin Thor . . . vest-pocket devices . . . Frost Giants . . . Wryan . . .

With a sigh, I struggled upright and swung my feet onto the glowstones, another theft from the Murians, but one I was certain they would not have minded. The slight warmth in winter and slight chill in summer, and the everpresent luminescence made the retreat just a touch more special.

"Oooooo . . ." The exclamation was mine. Despite Wryan's ministrations of the night before, my shoulders still ached.

About then, the guilt hit. I'd been avoiding Odin Thor, while trying to track down a weapon, a way to drive off the Frost Giants. Wryan had to have been shielding me—again.

A hot shower helped, as did some more bread and cheese, along with a ripe chyst. Both guilt and aches subsided.

As I sat in the stool overlooking the canyon, the problem remained—how to concentrate enough energy in one spot when we couldn't even generate it. It was too bad we couldn't just toss them into a nearby sun—since there were plenty of those and they certainly had enough energy.

I ate a second chyst and then stood, heading for the sleeping room. There I began to dress, slowly.

Energy . . . Frost Giants . . . compactness . . . energy . . .

As the words drifted through my thoughts, I finished my pre-dive preparations.

This time. This time I was going to find what we needed.

# LXII.

EVEN FROM HER protected position, the woman shivered, though shivering was not physically possible, as if she could sense the absolute chill that lay only instants from her.

From where she viewed, through the dark lens of time, she could see both the flattening swirls of ambient energy flows being sucked into nothingness and less clearly, the new-formed snow cascading downward and the soft explosions of vegetation being frozen nearly instantaneously.

She concentrated and removed herself to another locale, only to find a circular gray-brown wasteland, covered with fog as the heat from the surrounding area poured back over the frozen surfaces. A wall of thunderclouds towered against the low mountains.

Again, she concentrated, this time on a plateau that had been tree-covered with a walled encampment centered upon it.

A series of pelting rains and gusty winds swept across another gray brown wasteland. In places, new gullies appeared in the waist-deep sludge of fragmented cellular matter that had been largely living days earlier, cut by the force of water and gravity. The stone walls stood stark where they had for centuries, now alone in rearing above the gentle undulations of the plateau surface. Stone and sludge. Just stone and sludge and rain.

Once more, the woman concentrated . . . and disappeared . . .

# LXIII.

Now THAT I had steeled myself to develop whatever was necessary, I stayed on Muria, continuing to concentrate on discovering something that either concentrated energy, stored large amounts of energy, or transported that energy.

As far as I could discover, in sliding from undertime locale to undertime locale around the Murian systems, they had little need for storage of massive quantities of energy. Their closet-sized fusion generators and their light, thin, and all too durable superconducting cables took care of that aspect of energy.

In the end, the fact that I could sense energy flows from the undertime led me in the right direction—to a small series of structures located directly under the south magnetic pole of Muria. At the time, I didn't know it was the south magnetic pole, but Wryan later assured me that it had to be.

The complex seemed inactive, but the spray of energy ghosting around it in the undertime indicated that at infrequent intervals massive amounts of energy had been expended.

The initial observation was easy. The eight buildings, arranged as points of an octagon, were all closed and without inhabitants. So was the central eight-sided structure, which enclosed an eight-sided platform. In the center of the platform was a shimmering circular plate half a rod across and perhaps the thickness of my thumb. Connected to the plate were sixteen of the thin superconducting cables—apparently two from each outlying building.

A quick series of dives verified that each outlying building contained an inactive fusion power plant.

The ghostly energy lines looped around the plate, then, about a handspan above the metal, disappeared.

I dropped backtime, perhaps a local decade or so, before any activity appeared, and watched as three Murians employed what might have been a forklift to place a cube covered with the shimmering insulation used for their superconducting wires on the plate. A burst of energy from all fusion systems, and the box was gone.

That meant more backtiming, since there was no way to determine where the box had been destined. Instead I forced myself back to the construction of the facility, getting hell-fired close to my personal backtime limit, in order to follow the equipment back to its point of fabrication.

There were two plates. One went somewhere in an interstellar ship. The other went to the site where I had found it. That cinched it. The Murians had a matter transmitter. But they didn't use it often at all. And its use required the output of eight fusion generators at peak load.

Still . . . I wondered about the possibilities. So I went back a touch farther and liberated a set of the plates . . . and did a few experiments of my own. They worked. I didn't know much about physics, but when you can see the energy flows certain alternatives show a possibility. Like using the direct energy from a sun instead of one fusion generator—or eight generators.

It sounds easy. It wasn't, and it took subjective weeks before I was convinced that what I had in mind would work. That's the way it is with all brilliant discoveries. They become grunt efforts. Great ideas are easy. Getting them to work is the hard part.

After figuring out the pieces for a my gadget, I had to get all the pieces home, all the time hoping that there was a home left for me to go back to. I suppose I could have checked in periodically with Wryan, but that would have taken twice as much subjective time as staying on Muria, and time was something we had little enough of in any case.

Carrying all of the equipment was a chore, requiring about three times the number of breaks and stops to get me back to our Bardwall retreat. At least the retreat, with its time-protected stone, would have survived the worst of any Frost Giant attacks.

Empty . . . and dusty—that was the way I found it. The single workroom off the minuscule kitchen showed no recent footprints.

"Wryan?" My voice echoed.

"Wryan?" Again, no answer.

"WRYAN!" *Wryan, Wryan, Wryan. . . .*

My stomach was so tight that I was shaking all over.

Had she run into the Frost Giants—or Odin Thor? Was I too late? Again?

As the questions swirled around in my head, I reached out and managed to steady myself on the long workbench. Another look through the archway told me that it was midmorning in the Bardwalls, and there was no reason Wryan would be home in mid-morning. None at all.

That reasoning didn't calm either my guts or my shaking.

*Wryan, dear, where are you?*

"Sammis . . . are you all right?" She had apparently broken out in our sleeping room. Her light steps scuffed toward the kitchen.

"Where have you been?" The words came out before I had a chance to even think about them. Or glimpse her face.

She stopped silently in the archway, and I could see the exhaustion and the strain, the lines in her face, the blackness under her eyes, the sandy hair wisps framing the high cheekbones.

"Oh, Verlyt . . ." *Wryan . . . Wryan . . .*

"Wherever I was needed." Her voice was husky, in a

way I had never heard, as if she had cried and cried. And then had to cry again.

There was so much to say, and no words for me to express those feelings.

Wryan took another step forward.

"I'm sorry . . ." It wasn't the right thing to say, but I said it anyway. "I'm sorry."

"The Woods are gone, and the Plain of Cannorra, and Camp Persnol . . ." She shook her head. "And, yes, one Frost Giant. One more Frost Giant. Two in all."

I let go of the bench to reach out to her, but the room began to spin. So I put my hand back down and concentrated on keeping my balance. Before saying anything more, I went to work unstrapping the equipment from the complex harness that wore me, rather than the other way around. I couldn't talk; so I might as well do something.

*Clunkkkk.*

Despite my best efforts, the main tube hit the work bench top harder than I had intended. That might have been because my hands were still shaking, and because the room kept trying to spin around me. The pair of plates in their insulation were all the rest that I could manage.

*Clannkkk.*

Rather than argue with my body, I sat down on the floor to finish disentangling myself from the rest of the components.

"Sammis!" Wryan didn't seem to mind the components, but her arms had trouble encircling both electronics and me, especially in the cramped space between the equipment bench and the timewarped stone wall.

"Sorry it took so long . . ."

"Some of us knew it would . . ."

Her arms stayed around me, and I could tell she was shaking, crying without tears, perhaps because she had no tears left to shed.

"I think I have what we need." What else could I say?

She held me, still without speaking, still shivering, although the workroom was warm enough for me to have begun to sweat. I scarcely smelled human, even to me, but Wryan didn't seem to mind.

"Let's get the rest of the equipment off you." Her arms squeezed me, then dropped away.

With her help, stacking the rest of what I had brought back took only a few moments longer, even if I kept having to take a deep breaths and concentrate on keeping the universe steady.

"You need something to eat." Her voice was almost back to the no-nonsense tone of Dr. Wryan Relorn.

"Yes, Doctor."

"I'd hit you for that, but you'd fall over."

She was right, unfortunately, and I had to lean on her to get into the stool by the dusty counter. I just sat there while she tossed together something on a plate.

I ate it, more concerned with raising my blood sugar and with the exhaustion in Wryan's face than the details of what I was eating.

"You have something, too."

"Too tense to eat—"

"You've lost weight you can't afford—"

"You should talk, Sammis Arloff Olon . . ."

"Just humor your returning explorer and eat."

Finally, she sat down on the stool next to me. When she got around to it, she ate every bit as much as I did.

"So you couldn't eat?" I could feel the tiredness in every bone, and suddenly my bladder was demanding relief, but the room had lost its disconcerting tendency to whirl around my head. "Don't you feel better?"

"Yes." She tilted her head at me in that elfin way.

I waited.

"Outside of the divers, there are probably less than a million people left alive."

"In Westron?" That was hard to believe, even with the Frost Giants.

"Everywhere. There must be a thousand Giants. They've sucked the ambient energy out of everyplace where there might be people."

"Hell . . ."

"We can keep ahead of them, and we've saved some of the children, those of us who can carry them undertime. But they won't leave."

"Verlyt!"

She tilted her head again, wordlessly asking for my reason. I touched her shoulder, squeezed it gently, feeling both smooth black cloth and muscle before letting go. As close as Wryan was, I could smell the spiciness of her, that brought up thoughts of holding her, and more. But she was waiting for my explanation, and some hope of a solution. I just hoped I had it.

"Maybe later," she answered my unspoken question.

"Energy," I answered. "The plates tunnel matter or energy from point to point."

Her face screwed up.

"Drop one into a sun—timewarped—and the other near a Frost Giant. Should overload them. More energy than a particle beam or a small nuclear device."

She still looked puzzled. "Do you want a thousand gateways to the sun scattered all over Query?"

"Oh. . . ." I thought for a moment. "The timewarping will only last a short time once it starts passing energy."

"That's still a lot of energy." Wryan pursed her lips. "Why do you have to do it on Query?"

"That's where—oh . . ." As usual, I was still thinking in linear terms. There really was no reason why I couldn't backtime outsystem and plant the suntunnels. Given Wryan's Laws of Time, that wouldn't undo the deaths, although it might undo some of the environmental damage, but it wouldn't require baking the planet, except for the few Giants who decided not to leave and whom we couldn't track backtime.

"Are there any energy storage devices in that assortment you brought back?"

"No. Straight duplicating job, and the duplicates work."

"Then, after you take a short nap, after you take a shower, we need to start duplicating. And hunting."

So I took a shower, and a nap, and took care of a few other things, like hanging onto Wryan, who was hanging onto me, as if we had discovered each parting could be the last.

As I fell into the depths of sleep, I wondered how and why Wryan had arrived back so quickly at the retreat. But how seemed so much less important than the fact that she had.

# LXIV.

DUPLICATING THE SUNTUNNELS was the easy part, especially since Wryan and Jerlyk and a few of the other divers had, while I was hunting, moved one fusion plant and the duplicator into a small rebuilt and time-warped stone barn in the middle of Hardle, north Westron. The Frost Giants had ignored or avoided it.

Then I had to see if the theory actually worked in the real world. I decided that a few sunpoints in the colder areas of Query wouldn't hurt, not if they were areas already destroyed by the Giants.

Finding a Frost Giant would scarcely be difficult, not with close to a thousand of them grazing Query.

Wryan watched as I linked the two heavy discs to my equipment belt—one on each side. My breath was white steam in the cold of the barn.

Jerlyk looked at the glistening metal. "Are you sure this will work?"

"No. Do you have any better ideas?"

Jerlyk shook his head.

"Then I'd better see if it does. They can't destroy much more."

Wryan's lips brushed my cheek. "Try to take care."

I shrugged. Of course I would. Whether it would be enough was another question.

First, I dropped along the black arrow that led to the sun, forcing myself against the waves of time pressure that spewed from that nuclear depth. My experiments with time-warping made the drop-off of one disc possible. I just willed it out of the undertime. Clearly I couldn't have survived if I had tried to physically place it there. Solar surfaces and innards are not forgiving, even to timedivers.

Then, I just let the time pressure throw me back to Query, looking through the blue flashes from the Giants, seeking one that was isolated.

That didn't take long, either subjectively or objectively.

A strong and jagged blue trail led me to a plateau north of Southpoint.

Not being particularly heroic, nor caring to relive another being's death again, I didn't even break the surface of the now. Instead, I willed the disc out of the now and over the Giant—and mentally sprinted toward the retreat, dropping onto the glowstones.

. . . *cracccckkk* . . .

Even though my break-out cut off the jagged blue flashes, I sat there shivering for several moments before looking for something to eat. I wasn't really hungry, but I wanted some time to pass before I re-entered the undertime.

I munched on more hard crackers and watched the wind whip snow from the Bardwall spires. After finishing two crackers, I dropped back under the now and headed back to Hardle.

My breath still came out white in the barn's air.

"Success?" asked Jerlyk.

"Probably. You go check." I wandered over to the wall map of Westron Wryan had taped to the stones. Duplicated, it had wrinkles and creases, even a red stain across the lower right corner. Red crosses surrounded with circles marked the destruction she had been able to verify. Where she had discovered the original map, who knew?

I pointed to the approximate location where I had dropped the suntunnel. "Should be right here."

Jerlyk looked from me to Wryan and back again. Wryan said nothing, just returned his glance.

"They can't touch you in the undertime. If you feel anything cold or blue, it didn't work." I added.

Jerlyk checked his gauntlets, straightened his belt and disappeared.

"The same problem?" asked Wryan. Her breath smoked in the cold, just like mine. She was wearing a heavy black fur-lined parka.

"Almost got clear this time. Went to the Bardwalls. Waited. Then I came here." I felt cold in the thin insulated jacket. So I put my hands up under the jacket, and walked toward the duplicator. "Take another set."

"You think it worked?"

"The only question is how long the links lasted. You calculated a maximum of—"

"That's enough to vitrify stone, Sammis."

"*If* your calculations were right, we ought to use them as much as possible on Query in deserted areas."

Wryan shrugged. "I suppose you're right."

"Two reasons."

"Two?"

I nodded. "First, who can track and attack the Giants?

Me? You? Jerlyk? Maybe Mellorie. And Odin Thor and a guide.''

"You forgot Kerina."

"Is she that strong?"

Wryan nodded.

"Anyway," I noted, "the second reason is a warning. We need to post the system, so to speak, to make sure that Frost Giants understand it's death to poach here."

"Are they intelligent enough—"

"I'd say so." Alien, but not without brains.

By now, I was wondering about Jerlyk. Of course, he dropped into sight as soon as I really began to worry.

He was bobbing his head enthusiastically. "It worked."

I didn't believe him so I followed up myself, probing backtime just enough to check. But he was right.

Wryan was also right. There was a section of ground a hundred rods across fused into solid rock glass.

So we went hunting, the three of us, without even telling Odin Thor.

By the end of the day, we had placed nearly a hundred suntunnels.

By the end of the ten-day, after notifying all the divers, we placed over a thousand.

We also lost four divers, including Arlean, who broke out and didn't make it back under the now before the tunnel triggered.

That left one problem—perhaps an even bigger one.

# LXV.

THE HALF-BUILT TOWER was untouched. So were the buildings around it, although they had been built by the ConFeds without time-warping the stones. They had used the duplicator, which Wryan and I had installed in the subbasement of the tower, for production of the building materials.

At the time, Odin Thor had complained about having to carry the stones and braces up the long ramp. The complaints about that hadn't resumed with the rebuilding.

A gaggle of summer lilies peered from the small flower bed planted by Jianne, one of the younger divers. Deric had insisted on flower beds around the Tower. So we had flower beds. I stopped on the steps leading to the uncompleted south portal to look out at Mount Persnol, noting the too-frequent circular patches of brown on the lower slopes, wondering how many years before the vegetation erased the scars.

From the tower, I could not see where Camp Persnol had been, nor where the ill-fated non-divers' village had been. Both were gone, just a few stone walls rising from brown dust and rock.

"Sammis?" Amenda, fragile-looking in divers' blacks, appeared at the foot of the steps.

Two ConFeds, sweating in the sunlight as they toiled on the new ConFed administration building across the open space that was planned for a square by Deric, stopped and watched. One made an obscure sign, a ward against evil. The other laughed at him and said something, drawing an imaginary weapon, waving it in our direction. They both laughed.

"Yes." I waited for Amenda, although I was really waiting for Wryan.

She looked overhead. "It's . . . impressive . . ."

I thought so, too. For all his finickiness, Deric understood something about architecture. Either that or he knew where to find good design. I didn't much care which as long as the results were good.

"The crystal lattices work . . ."

"Good." I nodded. She had taken over the library functions after Arlean had died. The lattices were a Ydrisian invention for storing information, practically indestructible and with unlimited capacity, it seemed. One lattice the size of my fist could hold all of the information that had been in the entire Far Travel Laboratory.

Unfortunately, Arlean's biggest problem was finding the knowledge to save. Most of the divers thought I was a little fanatical about my two projects—information storage and what I called the duplicator library—mint condition originals of any equipment we might need.

Already they saw the value of the second. So they just shook their heads about the first.

"What about the underground ConFed fort?"

Amenda shivered. "It takes a little getting used to, but I've located some engineering texts . . ."

"HUT. . . . two, three, four. . . . HUT . . . two, three, four. . . ."

We both watched as a squad of ConFed recruits marched by the tower. They wheeled toward the ConFed building across the field that would one day be a square.

"HUT . . . two, three, four. . . .''

The forcer marching them wore a heavy Ydrisian energy pistol—a copy of the one I had originally brought back for Odin Thor, before I had been so successful in my time-meddling.

The sight of the energy weapon on the forcer's hip sent shivers down my spine. With a duplicator . . . every ConFed could have such a weapon . . . but it was too heavy for most people to use. Except for Odin Thor's troops. The gesture of the ConFed across the square took on more significance.

"Are you all right, Sammis?"

"Sorry, just thinking."

"About what?"

"I'd be interested in that as well," added another voice, one I knew well. Wryan appeared on the step next to me.

I squeezed her hand for an instant.

"Are you going to tell us?" asked Wryan.

I shrugged. "Just thinking. One of the reasons I was so effective as a diver was because of the physical conditioning I got from the ConFeds. One of the ongoing problems of too many divers has been lack of strength."

"You want to make the divers into ConFeds?" asked Amenda.

"No. Physical conditioning wouldn't hurt. Start with the younger ones . . ."

"Sounds like another one of your projects," added Wryan.

"I have to go . . ." pleaded Amenda.

"You don't . . ."

"Really . . ."

Wryan looked at me when Amenda had hastened toward her new crystal lattice library beneath the tower. "That wasn't all you were thinking."

"You don't miss much, my lady."

"Remember that. I am your lady." She smiled and waited.

"I wouldn't have it any other way."

Her smile faded.

I sighed, enjoying the breeze, but knowing she would wait longer than I could. The ConFeds halted by the uncompleted building and broke ranks. In instants, there were a score working there, instead of a handful.

"Odin Thor is good at discipline . . ."

"So are you," noted Wryan.

"I don't like it."

"What?"

I gestured toward the ConFeds. "They look like nothing's changed, ready to use what we've provided to take over the world."

"You could stop them." Wryan's voice was even.

"Why should I have to? It's better that it never gets started. I need to talk with Odin Thor."

Wryan frowned. "He doesn't listen very well. Still." Her face was troubled, yet faintly amused.

Across the field, the building rose, even as we talked.

I squeezed her hard, then let go. "No time like the present."

"What do you have in mind?"

"Call it a smaller force, a guard of some sort, half old ConFed, half new diver. Couldn't be any more ConFeds than divers."

Wryan pursed her lips. "He won't agree."

"I have to ask." First, I added.

"I'll come."

"No. If he doesn't see me as strong enough . . ."

She nodded, almost sadly. Then she squeezed my hand.

Walking through the uncompleted central hall toward the west wing, I could almost visualize what the tower would look like centuries into the future. And it would stand, more than centuries into the future. That I knew.

"Halt."

Outside Odin Thor's closed door—he had the only finished space in the tower, I suspected—stood a sentry. Hasslek. I remembered him.

"Hasslek, do I have to turn you into. . . ." I paused.

He had one of the energy guns pointed at me. He also had a nasty smile. I didn't like either.

*Crack.* Half-sliding under the now, I disarmed him with a chop to the wrist. Then I finished the job.

*Thud.* I let his unconscious body drop face-down on the glowstones, hoping he lost a few teeth in the process and gained a little more respect for his betters.

Opening the door without knocking, I stepped inside and closed the door behind me, not bothering with the useless lock.

Odin Thor pulled his polished black boots off the desk and stood up.

"Sammis, how good to see you." The stench of false

jollity was almost nauseating. He must have seen something. He stopped. "Would you have a seat?"

I smiled as falsely as he had. "No. This won't take too long. Since when have you been issuing energy guns?"

Odin Thor looked at me, then walked toward the window. "Well, Sammis . . . it's like this . . ."

At that moment, I had the strangest feeling, as though Odin Thor and I were being watched from the undertime. I smiled, then gave the unseen figure I remembered the old Temple peace benediction.

Odin Thor, insensitive as he was, didn't even notice. He was watching the ConFed building crew. ". . . we really can't maintain the projectile weapons. And after we routed the Frost Giants, a lot of the men didn't feel really secure . . ."

I snorted. "We don't need a force like you're building."

"Oh, and how would you keep order? Or have you forgotten Llordian?" He turned from the window.

"No. That's why I want to propose something else."

He walked back to the big desk. I wondered where he had found it and how many men had worked to refinish it. "Such as?"

"How about a guard force composed half of divers and half of ConFeds? It ought to be called a guard, a civil or a temporal guard."

Odin Thor was shaking his head before I finished. "Won't work. You don't have enough divers." He smiled, again broadly and falsely. "But we could use a timedivers section in the ConFeds. You could head that up."

"I think you're missing my point. If we don't put the ConFeds and the divers together now, working side by side—"

"A lot of your divers are women . . ."

I'd thought of that. "I know. They're a great stabilizing influence, and they'll also reassure a lot of the remaining farmers and the few townies left.'' More important, in time, they'd change the whole character of the ConFeds.

"They aren't tough enough.''

"Is Wryan tough enough?''

"Yes . . . but . . .''

"Fine. I'll guarantee the divers' physical conditioning.''

Odin Thor was shaking his head violently. "It won't work. It won't.''

I waited, knowing he'd find some way to reject my suggestion. Except it wasn't a suggestion.

"Sammis.'' He was back into false jollity again. "You've done wonders in finding tools, in getting weapons, and in helping destroy the Frost Giants. And in time, the whole planet will be properly grateful to you. Right now, though, they're scared of your timedivers. They need time to accept you. Setting up a divers section of the ConFeds would be a first step toward what you want.''

It wouldn't, because Odin Thor would use us for all the dirty and hateful work, and then we'd be forever beholden to him for protection.

"I don't think so. We need a dual guard, and we need it now.''

"Sammis, let's not be hasty. We have a planet to rebuild.''

I took a deep breath, wondering how to set it up.

"Believe me, I have a lot more experience in this,'' he continued expansively.

"No.'' I smiled. "We'll do it my way. You, Wryan, and I will head up this guard.''

"Sammis . . .'' The phony heartiness disappeared, and his voice was heavy and rough. He also towered over me, even from a rod away.

Not that his size bothered me.

"There's no way I would ever agree to that. No way.''

His voice was honest and cold, and I liked that tone better than the phony jolliness.

I smiled. "But you will, Odin Thor. You will. Just think about it."

Then I dropped under the now, leaving him with a puzzled look on his face.

# LXVI.

ODIN THOR—WHY had I let the idiot who had created the mess get so far? That gesture of the ConFed had chilled me to the bone, bringing back all the old hate memories, the class distinctions . . .

But who was the idiot? Odin Thor or Sammis? I had known he would botch it up, but I had let him run the ConFeds. I had known killing the Frost Giants with nuclear weapons would fail, but I had let him use them.

Wryan, perched on a stool by the wide glass window, watched as I paced the glowstones. She sipped a beaker of citril.

"Still thinking about Odin Thor?" she asked.

I nodded.

"I let him get too far. Now . . ." I shrugged, stopping to watch the dark clouds form and reform over the needle peak of Frythia. In the twilight, they appeared even more threatening. As often as the clouds threatened the peak, assaulted it with thunder and infrequent lightning, it never changed. Neither would Odin Thor, not unless . . .

I walked to the bedroom, the glowstones warm under my bare feet, and began to pull on the blacks that had become my uniform, and by extension, I suppose, the uniform of the timedivers. Then came the black boots from Sertis, and the gauntlets, with the quick timeloop to arm them. Then a knife, a sharp one.

"Sammis? Are you sure?"

"Yes."

The tone of my voice must have indicated my intent and my resolve. Wryan shivered by the window, but her eyes remained strangely calm as she watched me complete my preparations.

I glanced again at the tip of Frythia, disappearing into the coming night, then took a deep breath and dropped under the now—

—and broke out in Odin Thor's new office, in the west wing of the tower, further around the globe that was Query, around to the site of lost Inequital, where the sun still shone.

"Sammis . . ." He was still in his fancy new ConFed uniform. He wore both the heavy energy pistol and gauntlets—a needless duplication.

But then, I had never seen him without them, not since I had given them to him.

"No. Call me Verlyt, or Hades, or fate, Odin Thor."

He wasn't slow, but I had seen his action coming and dropped sideways and undertime even before the energy sheeted off the time-protected stones behind where I had stood.

*Crack!* My stiffened hand slashed across his unprotected wrist.

"Fate, Odin Thor."

He tried to bring the gauntlets to bear again.

This time I dropped out of the undertime and slashed the other wrist. "Verlyt, Odin Thor . . ."

I slapped his cheek.

"Coward! Dancer!"

I answered his taunt with a well-placed kick that threw him onto the floor beside his enormous wooden desk.

"Why don't you just kill me?"

"Because," I answered from behind him, dropping undertime and reappearing again to finish the sentence, "you have to live to make amends."

"Coward! You can't kill me! You don't have enough nerve."

I slipped behind him, delivered another side kick hard enough to crack his ribs, and dropped away.

Another blow to the face, and I barely dropped undertime before his good arm clutched for me.

I watched for a moment from under the now, sliding with the real time as Odin Thor peered around the disordered office. One corner of his new desk smoldered where his gauntlets had burned it.

With help from my jab, he crashed into the chair, then teetered to the floor.

His own weight snapped the wrist.

". . . bastard . . ."

I watched in realtime from the corner behind him as he staggered upright, blood streaming down the back of his neck, one wrist off-angled.

"We're going to take—"

—a trip," I concluded from the opposite corner.

My knife nipped his right biceps, a little deeper than a surface cut.

A cut across his thigh, and I was gone.

". . . coward . . . stand . . . fight . . . bastard . . ."

"Fate, Odin Thor . . ."

Another slice on the left biceps.

He stood there, panting, looking from one side of the room to the other, twirling to try to surprise me if I came up behind him. I let him twist and turn, twist and turn, just hanging in the undertime, waiting.

Another slash, this time across the back of his shoulder.

The room was smoky, laden with ozone, and reeking from Odin Thor's sweat and blood, the chairs strewn around. My own forehead was damp, my sleeves streaked with blood lost in the black fabric.

". . . never take me . . ."

I had to disagree. So I planted a fist in his gut, and an open-palmed slam on his chin.

*Thud!*

After hitting the stones, trying to cushion his fall with his good left hand, he turned, and I ducked undertime.

I was less delicate, with a kick to his jaw.

He was out, sprawled on the floor. His jaw was probably broken as well.

I took off his gauntlets, his knife, and the energy pistol, then bound his wrist up as well as possible. The jaw would need more professional help.

Sitting there, I sheathed my knife, after wiping it on his uniform, and waited until he began to wake up. Then I forced us both under the now.

. . . back toward Bremarlyn, toward a house being fired, and the agony of two people . . .

. . . back toward a crossroads where an innocent girl was consumed in flames.

There I held Odin Thor, letting their agonies flow through me and into him.

. . . back to an underground camp where. . . .

*AAAAAAeeeeeeeeeeeeeeeeeeeeeeeeeeeeeeeeeeeeeeeeeeeeeeeeee-eee. . . . . . .*

*Noooooooooooooooooooooo!!!!!!!!!!!!!!!!!!!!!!!!*

*. . . Verlytttt!!! . . .*

*. . . dying . . . dying . . . dying . . .*

Red lenses slashed across my eyes—again. Needles lanced my lips, and acid etched my throat. Breathing fire, I tried to rip my guts out, spew my innards across the cold of undertime . . . trying to escape the pyramiding agony . . .

Flares flashed across my visions . . . the visions I threw to Odin Thor—

. . . a thin man slashing his own throat . . .

. . . a woman grabbing a brain-spattered projectile gun

from a dead ConFed's hand, to turn it against her own skull . . .

. . . a man with shaking hands injecting himself, biting his lips raw and trying to keep from screaming . . .

. . . a young soldier, crawling, scrabbling, leaving a pink-frothed trail on the stone behind him . . .

. . . a Captain, standing in the doorway of an underground barracks, propped against the casement, slowly bringing up the heavy riot gun while trying to keep from shaking, trying to bring the gun to bear on the men writhing on the floor . . .

The second time, or was it the third—wasn't so bad, perhaps because I knew I wouldn't die, or perhaps because I threw all the agony at Odin Thor.

Then, before that muted pain could subside, for I knew the ConFed did not feel so sharply as I did, we dropped foretime to . . .

. . . Llordian, where on a black hillside lit by torches . . . *WWWWHHHHHSSSSTTTTTTT!!!!!* The entire pile of etheline missiles burst into flames, cremating a dozen townspeople as instant torches.

Using the light of the human bonfire, and shooting from the shadows uphill, the farmers dropped three more townies, as the mob began to trot toward the farm buildings revealed near the hill crest by the flames from the road.

". . . food . . . we want . . . food . . ."

Burning flesh, reeking, and the searing agony of death by fire, again charred my soul, and again, I poured it through the undertime link to Odin Thor.

Then, I staggered forward in the undertime, to . . . *EEEEEEEeeeeeeeeeeeeeee* . . .

The scream of the vest-pocket nuclear device vibrated even in the undertime north of Inequital, from the wasteland that had yet to recover from the first Frost Giant attack.

. . . *eeeeeeeeeeeeeeeeeeee* . . .

My head ached from the vibration and energy flashes that weren't supposed to have a physical impact in the undertime—and my soul wept from the old pain and from throwing it at Odin Thor . . .

". . . noooooo . . ." The non-voice was mine, trying to close eyes that would not, could not, close in the undertime.

. . . blue flashes, like jagged edges of a mirror, cut through my head. . . . an image of a small blue and blocky figure, four-armed, surrounded with warm blueness. . . .

. . . a dull red plain . . . standing beside another blue-block figure . . . reassuring heat . . . flashing back and forth . . .

. . . so much heat . . . pressure . . . like knives cutting from inside. . . .

. . . and more blue shards knifing their way through my head, already fading as they cut.

I staggered back toward the now, wondering if I could take another jolt, knowing that Odin Thor needed one last agony. So we stopped and watched and found . . .

. . . a circular gray-brown wasteland, covered with fog as the heat from the surrounding area poured back over the frozen surfaces. A wall of thunderclouds towered against the low mountains.

. . . a plateau that had been tree-covered with a walled encampment centered upon it . . . covered with lifeless sludge, screaming with the death agonies of two hundred hapless souls . . .

. . . pelting rains and gusty winds sweeping across another gray-brown wasteland, where new gullies appeared in the waist-deep sludge of fragmented cellular matter that had been largely living days earlier, cut by the force of water and gravity. The stone walls stood stark where they had stood for centuries, now alone in rearing above the gentle undulations of the plateau surface. Stone and sludge.

Just stone and sludge and rain beating down on the echo of another hundred deaths.

With a final push, I broke out within the west wing of the tower, almost losing my balance.

I dropped Odin Thor on the floor of his office, as gently as I could manage. His eyes were open, and he was breathing, although his fancy ConFed uniform was a mass of cuts and blood.

My guts were close to turning inside out, but I just stood there and watched until his self-awareness began to return, amazed that he was insensitive enough to recover at all. Asking myself if I should have exposed him to even more, although I wasn't certain I could have taken any more myself.

His eyes blinked, then came to rest on me.

"Fate . . . Odin Thor . . ."

". . . you . . . the damned deathgod . . ."

I shook my head. "That would have been easy. I want you to live with the feelings of all those deaths. If you ever put on that ConFed uniform again . . . if you ever think about forgetting . . . if you ever . . ."

Odin Thor shuddered and dropped his eyes from the blackness he saw in mine.

". . . and much as you hate me, we work together . . . because I'll always be here . . . always . . ."

I took a ragged breath, forcing back the still-felt screams of the dying, and the searing throbbing within my head. ". . . remember . . . death is easy . . . you ever *think* about playing emperor . . . I'll leave you dying . . . forever . . ."

He didn't look at me, but he didn't have to. He knew, and I knew.

Odin Thor would recover enough without me. He could get his own help. So I dropped back undertime and across continents to where I belonged.

Wryan was waiting, not that I expected otherwise, pacing before the black expanse of the window. She was looking toward Frythia, though the time difference between the retreat and the tower at Inequital ensured that mere eyesight saw nothing except the darkness.

That was all we often ever saw—the obvious light or dark.

Her eyes widened as she stepped toward me, then stopped.

Looking down, I could see why, with the blood splattered on the back of my hands, caked on my sleeves enough to be obvious despite the blackness of the fabric.

"You . . ." Her eyes were neither upset nor accusing, just asking.

"No . . . he is somewhat . . . scored. At least one broken wrist, some cracked ribs, and probably a broken jaw. That doesn't include the severely punctured ego."

My lady nodded slowly. "Now you know, and Odin Thor knows."

I shrugged. My shoulders ached, and my skull throbbed with the still-remembered agonies I had forced through myself to our would-have-been tyrant. "I suppose so. I suppose so."

It wasn't a question of supposing. Odin Thor knew. Knew that I had held him in the palm of my hand and judged him. Knew that I could visit death—or even worse— upon him. Knew that I understood death better than death itself, something that had taken me a long time to accept. But after feeling, individually, hundreds of deaths, I knew that death was not to be feared. Dying was another question, and I could leave Odin Thor dying endlessly.

I dropped the morbid thoughts and half-smiled at the sandy-haired woman who had trusted me more than I trusted myself.

Her hands took mine, those slender and strong fingers intertwining with mine, and I understood also why she had let the decision be mine.

"There's a lot to do . . ."

She shook her head. "Tomorrow will come. You've made sure of that—"

It was my turn to disagree. "*We* made sure of that."

"Then, hadn't we better make sure of us?" Her eyes sparkled like the sky over a rainbow, and her fingers tightened around mine.

She was right, of course.